The Testing Ground

Volume 2

The Journey

Louis Evan Grivetti
Sargent Thurber Reynolds

Published by EditPros LLC
423 F Street, Suite 206
Davis, CA 95616
www.editpros.com

First edition

ISBN-10: 1-937317-27-7
ISBN-13: 978-1-937317-27-0
Library of Congress Control Number: 2015944429
Printed in the United States of America

CATALOGING INFORMATION:

Grivetti, Louis Evan, and Reynolds, Sargent Thurber

The Testing Ground: Volume 2 – The Journey
Filing categories:
- Fiction: Science Fiction - General
- Fiction: Science Fiction - Adventure
- Fiction: Action & Adventure
- Survivalist Thriller

Acknowledgments

Journey Maps (p. 439–453) by Steve Oerding, Academic Technology Services, Mediaworks, University of California, Davis

Portions of lyrics identified here appear in the present manuscript. All are either in public domain (published before 1922) or meet each of the four fair use criteria (published after 1922).

Banks of the Ohio. Date written or published, 19th century. Composer: unknown (traditional American folk song). Lyrics: unknown.

Bard of Armagh. Date written or published, c. 1697. Composer and Lyricist: Patrick Donnelly.

Beautiful Ohio. Date written or published, 1918. Composer: Robert A. Bobo King (pseudonym, Mary Earl). Lyricist: Ballard MacDonald.

Birmingham Jail (Down in the Valley). Date written or published, c. 1800. Composer: unknown (traditional American folk song). Lyrics: unknown.

Carry Me Back to Old Virginny. Date written or published, 1878. Composer and Lyricist: James Bland.

Chicken in the Bread Pan. Date and source of words unknown (traditional American square dance call/refrain).

City of New Orleans. Date written or published, 1971. Composer and Lyricist: Steve Goodman.

Do You Know What It Means to Miss New Orleans? Date written or published, 1947. Composer and Lyricist: Eddie DeLange and Louis Alter.

Down by the Riverside. Date written or published, 1902. Composer: John J. Nolan. Lyricist: John B. Toorish or John J. Nolan.

Hard Times Come Again No More. Date written or published, 1854. Composer and Lyricist: Stephen Collins Foster.

Lonesome Valley. Date written or published, unknown. Composer: unknown (traditional American Negro spiritual). Lyrics: unknown.

Lorena. Date written or published, 1856. Composer: Joseph P. Webster. Lyricist: Henry DeLafayette Webster

Minstrel Boy. Date written or published. c. 1798. Composer: unknown (traditional Irish folk song). Lyricist: Thomas Moore.

My Old True Love [*As I Walked Out One Evening Late A-drinking of Sweet Wine*]. Date written or published, 1710. Composer: Unknown (traditional English folk song). Lyricists: Gladys Helen Davis and Flossie Ellen Evans (revised 1937).

Notre Dame Fight Song. Date written or published, 1905. Composer: Michael J. Shea. Lyricist: John F. Shea. [Notre Dame copyright, 1928].

Oh! Carry Me Back to Ole Virginny [*De Floating Scow*]. Date written or published, 1847. Composer: unknown (traditional American folk song). Lyrics: unknown. Note: initial publisher F. D. Benteen, Baltimore, Maryland.

On Top of Old Smokey. Date written or published, c. 1840, Composer: unknown (traditional American folk song). Lyricist: unknown.

Tenting Tonight on the Old Camp Ground. Date written or published, 1863. Composer and Lyricist: Walter Kittredge.

The Girl I Left in Sunny Tennessee. Date written or published, 1899. Composer: Stanley Carter. Lyricist: Harry Braisted.

The Last Rose of Summer. Date written or published, 1805. Composer: Edward Bunting. Lyricist: Thomas Moore.

The Wind that Shakes the Barley. Date written or published, 1872. Composer and Lyricist: Robert Dwyer Joyce.

There Is a Tavern in the Town. Date written or published, 1883. Composer and Lyricist: unknown (traditional English folk song).

Vacant Chair. Date written or published, 1861: Composer: George Root. Lyricist: H. S. Washburn.

West Point Hymn [*Alma Mater*]. Date written or published, 1912. Composer: Friedrich Wilhelm Kuecken music and lyrics *Treueliebe* [True Love] 1827. Revised lyrics for the West Point Alma Mater written by Paul S. Reinecke c. 1912.

Wildwood Flower. Date written or published, 1860. Composer: Joseph Philbrick Webster. Lyricist: Maud Irving.

All other lyrical passages included in the present manuscript were composed by the authors.

Table of Contents

This Book,

The Testing Ground: Volume 2 – The Journey,

is a sequel to

The Testing Ground: Volume 1 – The Cave

(ISBN: 978-1-937317-21-8)

Pre-Word: Arrival and First Meeting

Voice Transcription: Theodore Ikado, Junior Quartermaster

Log Entry: 3rd work shift

Oh the tedium of tracking the radar images of wild game grazing within this beautiful valley!

I am still tired from last night's festivities where Joint Deputy Commander Louis Carpenter hosted and entertained the Gold Group members with music, dance, and drink. Have I enjoyed the assignment of tracking wild game? No. But each of our officers and crew members are required to take turns as our assignments rotate through the needs and demands of adjusting to the living conditions posed by our new land.

I watch the scanner track pivot around a central node as the view extends outward for 15 kilo-miles. Each sweep takes 45 counts, then around again and again for hours on end. Each successive loop of the greenish scanner tracker dulls my senses and lures me towards sleep as the morning progresses. Blips appearing on the screen reflect off regional large animals and denote the geographical positions of these beasts. These animal-based blips identify meat sources used by the former biped residents of our beautiful valley as we do still today.

Allison Currie, my counterpart and mate partner, has been assigned to take turns with me to track movements of these beasts. Together we log animal dispersal patterns into our daily work sheets, data that will facilitate hunting trips over the next several days. Our daily logs are filled with the identifications of these beasts, lists of their former names, terms used by the extinct bipeds that inhabited the valley before arrival of our exploration ship, *KosMa ExPlor*er. Do any of us really care what these animals originally were called? Still, I love the slabs of meat from these beasts, roasted and served at mealtime.

Some of the animals were known to the extinct bipeds as *D-R,* but no examples of these types were detected this morning as they were not grazing in their usual localities. Perhaps they were frightened by the local cat-like *Kou-Gar* predators that sometimes lurk along the forest margins? Perhaps the usual herds of *D-R* were startled by some other source of potential danger and they took refuge in the tall pine forest up-slope from the valley floor? The next sweep reveals 16 images of animals grazing together, moving westward down-slope from the forest margins towards the river meadowlands. These images I recognized as *L-K,* and joining them just off to the south there appeared the characteristic signal of a rogue male *Mo-Ose*.

These various herds of beasts, along with fish and occasional wild fowl, have served us as major meat food resources during the past four solar cycles. Animals plodding here and there across the landscape, images reflected on my scan screen – bringing boredom and lethargy to Allison and me. I stare at the screen, my thought patterns adrift. Everything seems all right, but then …

Five uncharacteristic blips of unknown and unexpected configuration suddenly appear on our scanning screen in valley sector 3-BR-9. These are not reflections from wild game. Allison and I look at each other. Nothing with these characteristics has been tabulated previously in our scanner logs. With each successive sweep of the scanner, we plot their movements as the images pause. We watch as the blips continue across the vision screen. One image appears to lead. Three follow, clustered together pushing what appeared to be a large opaque object. A fifth image follows behind, as if protecting the group. I refocus the scanner magnifier. No wild animals these! With enhanced magnification the opaque object appeared to be a two-wheeled cart identical in design as the type described and reported in Document Six retrieved previously from the stash of cave items. Such carts used by bipeds that previously inhabited our valley region were described to us by Franklin Egenda, former Ad-Miral, and captain of the *KosMa ExPlor*er, during one of his evening presentations to our crew shortly after we had landed on the orb.

These blips on our scanner screen certainly were bipeds, but not our type.

I immediately pushed the alert siren.

***

Interview Voice Transcription: Roxanne Hernandez, Senior Lieutenant

During the early morning hours Junior Lieutenant Janice Upton and I received orders from Senior Legender and Primary Security Officer Thomas Dickinson, to reconnoiter and map mountain slopes in sector 24-B-3, southeast of our settlement. We were instructed to pay special attention to relationships between exposed strata and types of vegetation growing on hillsides associated with each rock type, factors that could help in our understanding of local botany and geological relationships. On an earlier outing, Dickinson had noted that a certain variety of tree, called *Pi-Ns* by the earlier biped residents of this valley, grew in linear strips in north/south-trending directions. Other *Pi-N* varieties appeared in clusters and grew randomly along the slopes. Dickinson observed that minerals eroded from the distinctive strata types influenced and/or determined whether or not pollen, seeds, or other growth products thrived or not, based upon basic mineralogy principles.

During late morning, we were inspecting an area of considerable erosion caused by rainfall torrents that had exposed the base underling strata after the runoff had removed centimeter-inches of rich soil. I started to relay my observational information to Janice. As she recorded my descriptions into her notebook, I looked up and not 10 meter-yards away three female bipeds not of our type appeared before me.

Janice and I were startled, but we sensed no initial threat from these three. We offered cautious words and hand signs of greeting, which clearly they could not understand. We heard them speak among themselves in unintelligible sounds. Then suddenly within what seemed to be a mere moment, the three females were joined by two males also of their kind. I now became worried and sensed danger.

The five bipeds were taller than us, disheveled with long unkempt braided locks. Their arms and legs were muscular, and covered with tattoo symbols unknown to us. Their clothing was difficult to describe, a mix of items prepared from animal furs and delicately woven pieces of cloth. Both male and female bipeds carried a suite of weapons: wooden bows with quivers and metal swords of exceptional design. Short broad-blade knives similar to what we called stripper knives were secured in their waistbands.

Janice and I remained transfixed, scarcely able to move. We started to speak but were quickly surrounded and restrained by the two male bipeds. The eyes of their leader, an older female, gazed into mine and, for a moment, I sensed relief and felt no danger. Danger and uncertainty would come later.

Using hand signs, the bipeds forced us to follow in their tracks. We were marched down-slope to a location where they had stashed what best may be described as a pushcart. Both Janice and I recognized its design as the type used by former valley bipeds described and portrayed in the cave documents. We were not allowed to see the interior contents of the pushcart. Who were these bipeds? All evidence available to us from the cave documents suggested no survivors within the valley. If correct, our captors must be outlanders or outsiders. If they had been former residents of the valley, where had they ventured? How had they escaped the terrible epidemic described in the translated documents that we had uncovered in the cave? And if former residents, why did they return and what did their return signify? Did they pose danger to our settlement?

The seven of us walked north together – we beside the pushcart – not knowing what our reception would be and whether or not we would be harmed. As we neared our outpost, we paused and, in the near distance, we saw that members of our community had taken defensive positions with weapons at the ready. The danger was real. Janice and I now feared for our lives.

Looking out across the meadowlands towards our assembled settlement defenders, the female biped leader took me aside and spoke. Her language, however, was unintelligible. Still, it became clear to me from her hand gestures and finger signs that she and her group did not want a confrontation. She gazed into my eyes and continued to speak. I gestured the best I could to her trying to convey that I did not understand her words. She continued speaking. The tension I felt was terrible. I saw my friends and mates armed and ready to defend our settlement. At the end of one linguistic outburst, the older female biped paused, pointed to herself and spoke two words – words that I understood from study of the documents left behind in the cave – Reese Saunders.

I immediately grasped her right hand in mine and waved with my left hand to signal those confronting us with weapons raised. I shouted to them: Lower your weapons! Let us advance. Standing beside me is Reese Saunders. She is alive!

***

Interview Voice Transcription: Senior Captain Richard Engels

I was the first to interact with Reese Saunders after she arrived at our settlement. She and members of her group immediately were attended by Primary Security Officer Dickinson. After a quick-scan medical examination, the new arrivals were ushered into our commissary area where food and beverages were offered to the travelers. I was instructed by Joint Commanders Carpenter and Evans to meet with Saunders to record her words on my exponential linguistic recorder (ELR) for initial analysis to be fed into our axial digital translator (ADT). When all had finished their meals in the commissary, I turned to Saunders and hand-signed for her to follow me.

Together we entered the room that housed our master computer facility. My next task was to convince Saunders through hand-signing that we wanted her to speak into a voice pick-up device, using the natural tones and sounds of her language. The process would capture her words, segment and categorize the primary, secondary, and tertiary vocabulary rings that would permit production of a basic master list of the most used 1,500 words, which would allow initial mutual communication. Further analysis would permit development of drop-space and sequential configurations where additional words and vocabulary nuances subsequently could be added to the master list that ultimately would capture the full nuances of this new language.

And thus it was that Reese Saunders spoke into the voice pickup device. What she said was captured, absorbed, and transcribed digitally by the ADT unit. After about two hours of voice recording, we drew the exercise to its conclusion. I signaled for Commanders Carpenter and Evans, as well as our security officers Dickinson and Foster, to join us in the transcription room where the digital output translated Saunders' words into terms that could be viewed on screen.

We sat together, not knowing what to expect. Reese's words streamed out from the ADT. We were stunned at the richness of her language, and we were deeply touched by the translated content. Using the collateral post-transcription device, Saunders now could hear and understand our words as well. It was difficult to contain our mutual emotions as we listened to her descriptions of earlier times at what she called the Bison Camp settlement group; words of love for her deceased mate Travis; and descriptions of their trans-continental trek and return to what she called the Big Hole Valley that once was her home.

Reese Saunders had been born and raised at Bison Camp. Her mate, Travis Saunders, was a member of the last Data Survey sponsored by Montana State University. She related how an extremely deadly and contagious disease had swept through New NorthWest Configuration after the return of Travis' group from old California. Most poignant were descriptions of her children, Adam and Anna Saunders, and how she had nursed them through the dark days where all in Bison Camp had been infected by the medical virus. Words spoken reflected the sorrow and mental agony she suffered when both of her children died, and how she had taken ill with no one to assist or offer care. Saunders related that through the worst night of her illness, somehow she had been tended to by an unseen force, something almost like a guardian spirit but not of this world, a present but unseen entity that spoke, comforted, and aided her during this darkest period of her life.

Reese related how she and Travis appeared to be the sole survivors of the Epidemic within immediate and nearby regions and how they ultimately left the Big Hole Valley to seek survivors and to learn more about the Epidemic and its spread. They had traveled by river and land ultimately reaching the city of New Vicksburg, located in old Mississippi a former state now within the New Confederacy Configuration. Here they had rested and stayed, welcomed by all city residents into community membership. She related that during their land crossing through the New Confederacy Configuration, somewhere in the vicinity of Stone Mountain in old Georgia, that she had become pregnant once more. At New Vicksburg, attended by old and new friends, Reese delivered twin daughters, Laurel and Sage.

Saunders related how New Vicksburg had seen the return to prosperity, that some sectors of the local economy were based upon north/south trade along the Great River as it was called. Here, too, at New Vicksburg, the twins Laurel and Sage grew and flourished, and ultimately selected mates during their 13th solar cycle. Laurel chose Joseph Emory son of Preston Emory. Her twin sister Sage chose Adam Lange. In accord with practices at the time, the mating ceremonies lasted 10 days – much to the joy and pleasure of those attending.

Shortly after the unions of his daughters, Travis experienced a terrible accident and was incapacitated. During the following days, he languished as his health worsened. Reese, along with friends and family members, provided all aid possible to facilitate Travis' recovery, but to no avail. Speaking his last words, Travis urged Reese to make a commitment to lead their daughters and their mates on a return trek to Bison Camp, to re-settle the land if still unoccupied, and to spread the word wherever possible that survivors existed elsewhere in the continent. Reese gave her promise.

She continued …

I made my promise to Travis, and I am here today accompanied by my daughters and their mates. I bring with me three items to be returned to this land in and around Bison Camp. The first is Travis's promise ring given to me when we pledged our love for one another. I now wear this ring on my left hand. I wish it to be buried with me at the appropriate time. The second is the collection of our words – written in diary form – that document our experiences during our journey. These we have protected with our lives and have carried with us in our pushcart. May these documents become part of our overall group heritage and pave the way for better understanding of the cycles of life on our planet. The third is a small vial of ashes from Travis' funeral pyre, to scatter within his beloved Big Hole Valley. These items represent three never-ending circles: an unbroken circle of love, symbolized by my ring; an unbroken circle of written accounts from the beginning of our trek to our return to the ruins of former Bison Camp settlement group where we now meet together; the third represented by the few ashes of my departed mate, link me with him once more and with the land that we both loved dearly.

The short transcription record delivered by Reese during her discussion with me was sufficient to create the basic vocabulary exchange lists. I followed the next step in the process, which was to imbed the exchange lists into translator pins to be worn by all. These simple devices created many solar cycles previously had been components of personal equipment on all previous exploration voyages. Simple in operation: two bipeds speaking different languages – both incomprehensible to the other – activated their pins and started speaking. Voice-wave pickups translated the conversations at sound speed to the master computer (ADT) where the tones were re-booted to the translator pins in the respective language required.

This technique usually was the initial process in all recent inter-orb biped communication. The next step was for both groups to study and learn the other's language for both oral and written communication. The orb biped language spoken by Reese, her daughters, and their mates was a single-level tone, without variability in high and low pitch, thus making it easier to learn.

In the days that followed, Reese and her traveling companions learned our language quickly, as we did theirs. Within a quarter of a solar cycle, we had no further use for the communication pin devices.

***

Voice Transcription: Mavis Stronghaven, Senior Colonel, Strategic Operations Coordinator

Others present: Senior Legender and Security Officer Saranda Foster, and Senior Legender and Security Officer Thomas Dickinson.

At the suggestion of Joint Commander Carpenter, Thomas Dickinson and I approached other members of the Saunders group for interview time. Travis and Reese had traversed a large part of the continent, and had met and lived with survivors of the Ripple Event, Dark Time, and the more recent Epidemic Many survivors in these groups had formed militias or military-style protection units (MPUs), and this concerned us given our responsibilities for group security in the Big Hole Valley. After only a few interviews, we realized immediately that while all members of the Saunders group had information to share, the most valuable and complete descriptions could come only from Reese.

I was assigned to approach Reese to encourage her to dedicate significant time to share her experiences with all of us. I thought back to the way information discovered in the cave had been related during evening sessions by our earlier Commander Franklin Egenda, and how we as officers and crew members of the *KosMa ExPlorer* found the information exceedingly valuable. It was important for us to know and understand the trials and efforts that Travis and Reese had experienced, as the information revealed not only would enlighten us, but could serve as background information to protect our settlement from outside forces should the need arise in the near or distant future.

I asked Reese for her consent, which she graciously provided. In accord with our commander's wishes we were called to assembly at designated evenings in the Great Room to listen to Reese and the others. Members of the Reese group – now known collectively as The Returners, were welcomed into the hall and given seats in the first row. Our joint commanders introduced Reese once more to the assembly and invited her to the lectern where she began the first of her oral reports, presentations that would hold our attention throughout the evenings.

***

AFTERNOTE: As it was in solar cycles past when we had assembled to learn about the bipeds that inhabited the orb where we had just landed, we in the audience listened to Reese's account how she and Travis had left the Big Hole Valley, and embarked upon their journey of discovery and exploration. She captivated us through her words, drawing our attention to key places, events, and descriptions in remarkable descriptive detail.

Reese's words related to us during evening assemblies would set the stage for planning our next activities and exploration ventures facilitated by our scout ships – visiting lands beyond the confines of the Big Hole Valley – elsewhere within the continent, and perhaps even westward or eastward across the Great Ocean into regions known as Africa, Asia, and Europe.

Through these sessions with Reese Saunders, we better understood the life forms that once inhabited this planet, especially the advanced biped units that had once lived in this valley and those surviving elsewhere

CLOSE VOICE TRANSCRIPTION LOG: Mavis Stronghaven, senior colonel, strategic operations coordinator.

***

The Journey: Part 1

Chapter 1

Departure: Bison Camp to Three Forks

Pre-Note

And thus began the first presentation by Reese Saunders.

***

I understand that some here tonight may not be familiar with who I am or my story. In short I will introduce myself before relating to you what I simply call *The Journey*. I am Reese Saunders. I was birthed in the Big Hole Valley at Bison Camp settlement group almost 34 solar cycles ago. Travis Saunders my future mate was birthed two cycles earlier. We both completed childhood during the period when the Dark Time was fading.

We were always busy. Life was hard here in the valley, but for us youngsters we found joy in many of the tasks required for community survival. Travis' father was a great hunter. In fact, I first met Travis when his father took both of us along on an antelope hunt in the meadows out beyond Outpost Badger – the defensive redoubt constructed several kilo-miles south and east from our current location. His father assigned Travis and me to be his flaggers. Our task was to entice the grazing antelope beasts into an ambush. We would creep ahead and wave our long sticks with pieces of cloth attached to the end. Our motions would attract attention of the curious antelope and as we waved or flagged as we called it, the beasts would saunter unknowingly into arrow or javelin range. We never failed to return to our settlement with enough meat to last for several weeks.

Through the early solar cycles of my life, Travis and I became good friends. We attended classes together at Bison Camp School. After graduation, we both enrolled at the college located in New Bozeman, the former Montana State University. In addition to our studies, we became members of what then was called the Looper Group. These were small, organized teams of students assigned to data collection trips to record stories and histories of people who had survived the Ripple Event and Dark Time. These exploratory loops could be long or short, sometimes lasting only a few weeks, but at other times considerably longer.

Shortly after our second Short Loop journey, Travis and I were mated in a traditional ceremony. We had the approval of our parents, and they soon became grandparents to their even greater joy. Our first two children were a boy and a girl, Adam and Anna. Travis and I felt complete. We were a family and watched our children grow for several solar cycles. Then came the Epidemic.

We were living in Bozeman at the time. The children and I decided to leave town to visit Bison Camp, since Travis was away participating in a Long Loop expedition. We little understood at the time the speed and impact the Epidemic would have on all of us in the settlement. The fever and body markings came upon us suddenly with unbelievable speed and, within a week, left behind unspeakable horror. I tried my best to care for and heal our children, but I was unsuccessful and both died. I, too, became deathly ill and barely could differentiate day from night. The illness pain I suffered was nothing compared to the grief that poured out from my heart after the death of our children, Adam and Anna. All I remember of this terrible time were the daytime and nighttime visions where I sensed I was being cared for by an unknown shadow-like form that attended and nursed me from the brink of ever darkness back into the world of the living. I was the sole Bison Camp survivor of that dreadful time.

Travis ultimately returned to Bozeman from his expedition where he, too, experienced the deaths of his data collector mates. For reasons unknown, he found himself to be the sole survivor of the campus and surrounding community. Worried and alone, he quickly returned to Bison Camp to search for me and found that only the two of us were alive. Why were we saved when all the others – family, relatives, friends, acquaintances, thousands upon thousands of regional residents unknown to us – but all human – had perished? We grieved long and hard as we buried those who died during this terrible time. We laid to rest more than 300 of the Bison Camp residents in a common grave just north of the settlement.

Why were we alive? We had no answers.

During the next several months, Travis and I made several trips to Bozeman to salvage and retrieve looper team reports and data collector diaries. We piled these important documents into pushcarts and, using teams of horses, hauled them to Bison Camp. We secured the documents and equipment items in chests, and placed them for safekeeping inside a former defense redoubt just east of the settlement area. This location was the cave your crew members found upon your arrival. I learned this past month that many of the documents we had saved were translated and read to you over the course of several evenings.

You might well ask why we were compelled to salvage, transfer, and protect these materials? We did so out of a strongly felt need to preserve our history. Could it be that Travis and I were the only ones alive? Given the deaths of all the Bison Camp residents and that there were no survivors in Bozeman or any of the regions we trekked through, we could not be certain whether or not others had escaped the Epidemic and were alive elsewhere. The documents we salvaged, therefore, contained the heart and being of who we were. Among the more important documents were survivor reports: first-person interviews of those who had survived the Ripple Event and Dark Time. Their stories were lessons for us all. If others survived elsewhere, perhaps we could find them. At the least, our human stories would be preserved, hopefully, forever.

After completing document transfer and protecting the cache, Travis and I decided to leave the Big Hole Valley and trek outward to discover if human life remained elsewhere. Our outbound trek and my return took more than 16 solar cycles. Along the way, we found survivors: not millions as would have been the population prior to the Ripple Event, but thousands. These mostly were hard-working people living in communities and settlement groups slowly recovering from the Epidemic. Those 16 solar cycles included travel across the vast Flatland Configuration; passage by horseback, boat, and on foot. During our journey, we also discovered that our former continent had been invaded by others from across the

Great Sea. Along the way, I ultimately would experience great joy with the birthing of our twin daughters, Sage and Laurel. They and their mates, Adam and Joseph, are attending our meeting tonight. My joy of their birth, however, was tempered with the sorrow caused by the passing of my mate, Travis, during our residence at New Vicksburg, a settlement in the New Confederacy region. It was my promise to honor Travis's wish that the five of us embarked upon our journey to return to the Big Hole Valley and to our former settlement at Bison Camp. I have honored his wish; I and my family are with you tonight.

But enough of this background. Let me begin the story of our journey.

***

Ijano Esantu Eleman. I begin by speaking these three words to you because they have heartfelt meaningful to me tonight. They have been comforts to me and Travis in solar cycles past, and to all former residents of Bison Camp settlement group who once flourished within this beautiful valley. During the darkest days of our existence, beginning with what we called the Ripple Event and subsequently the Dark Time, all at Bison Camp would repeat these words upon greeting one another. We would speak them when we left the settlement on work details, even as we sat and held hands prior to partaking of our daily food.

Ijano Esantu Eleman – As It Was in the Beginning.

I emphasize this phrase and share it with you in the belief that you, our friends and new arrivals to this planet that once was ours alone, may better understand our distant and present history and how we have survived during recent solar cycles. I speak the words to you tonight so that you may have a better knowledge of how our cultures, while different, are similar in many ways. I share this information with you to demonstrate how we lived before the terrible events that caused the destruction of our once-great cities and settlements, and how we struggled to survive and regain our dignity.

Ijano Esantu Eleman – As It Was in the Beginning.

***

I show you this sketch of what once was called the North American Continent. Shown here is the route Travis and I followed from Bison Camp settlement group, as we trekked and passaged eastward into new lands not before visited. Identified are the geographical locations of the new configurations that formed across the landscape during the Dark Time Recovery Period: New PlyMouth, New Confederacy, TAR or Texas Across the River, Flatlands, New Deseret, New SouthWest, and New NorthWest. Each evening I will update the map with markings that designate the overland and river routes that ultimately led us to New Vicksburg, a settlement in the New Confederacy, where we remained for 15 solar cycles. Additional maps will document New Confederacy militia excursions, where action was taken to repel groups of river pirates and the nomadic wanderers that preyed upon regional settlement groups. Additional maps will document the return route from New Vicksburg to Bison Camp taken by me, my daughters, and their mates – we you call by the collective term *Returners.* Yes we are *Returners,* and yes we are proud of the name.

***

Departure

Ijano Esantu Eleman – Travis and I decided that the quickest and safest departure route out of Big Hole Valley was to follow a path once blazed long ago by General Taylor James. He was instrumental in the foundation of the first formal settlements in the valley and, long before the Ripple Event, had established a retreat for visiting tourists and survivalists. Taylor James spent weeks and months exploring the Big Hole Valley, and marked trails for easy passage both in and out of the valley. You will recall from documents retrieved from the hillside cave and already translated to you that Bison Camp became a haven, a place of security for those settled here. Those inside the valley survived the Ripple Event and developed a new community during the Dark Time.

The path for departure we chose led eastward from the valley floor upslope through the dense pine forests, then entered a zone of mixed and restricted vegetation where the higher elevation stunted growth of some species. Once through the restricted plant zone, where snow and ice sometimes lingered into the months of May and June, we reached the peak junction where we paused and camped for the evening.

When morning came, we doused our fire and trekked downslope into the Madison River Valley. The Taylor James trail led directly to the former settlement of Ennis. As we neared the valley floor, we chose to circumvent Ennis and also bypassed the smaller settlements constructed after the Ripple Event that had been erected south of the Ennis ruins.

We exited the Madison Valley upslope, taking the little-used Johnny France Trail, named after a well-known and popular regional sheriff. This decision took us up the west side of Lone Mountain, another hard climb that took us nearly six hours to master. Just east of the crest, we halted our journey and encamped below a rocky outcrop that sheltered us from the swirling winds. The crest once had been touted as a snowboarder's retreat. The rocky walls of the shelter were decorated with hundreds of letters and symbols, spray-painted during different solar cycles by young adventurers who arrived in winter to test their skills and risk their lives tackling what they called the LLM or Lone Mountain Madness. These adventurous youths, both male and female, would arrive at the eastern base of Lone Mountain – most without significant funds. The more clever ones would manage to catch a free ride on the gondola that took them to the crest. Then, they would snowboard down the snow, ice, and boulder-strewn eastern face of Lone Mountain. If successful during their descent, they finally would reach bottom at the Big Sky meadows more than six kilo-miles below. Later, we would pass several hundred stone cairns, marking locations where young snowboarders miscalculated turns or drop-offs and lost their lives in their pursuit of danger.

Travis wrote the following passage in his daily journal:

> *We have camped just along the southern ridge near the crest of Lone Mountain. Our view extends eastward down the rocky slope towards the grassland meadows and abandoned houses that once formed the thriving vacation settlement of Big Sky. Off in the distance to the southeast, I can see several log-cabin structures, one being Buck's T-Four Ranch house where countless families once vacationed and were entertained prior to the Ripple Event and Dark Times. Tomorrow we will pass through the remains of the old Big Sky settlement, then will continue south along the road once named Highway 191, a route that parallels the north-flowing Gallatin River. Our goal ultimately is to reach the geyser basins of old Yellowstone. Once within this noble landscape, we will circumvent the so-called hot-spots and avoid the herds of elk and buffalo. We then plan to exit eastward towards New Cody, a well-known settlement along the western edge of the Flatland Configuration. Will we find survivors there? Only time will tell. We know that beyond New Cody lies the vast Flatland Configuration with its multiple shattered zones and the potential dangers posed therein. We will need to be most careful*

and observant. Some have suggested that beyond the Flatland Configuration lie other groupings, as well, one called The New Confederacy and a second located in the continental northeast, named New PlyMouth. Will we locate survivors there? Only time will tell.

In our loneliness we are without others
Travel on – Travel on!

We aim for unknown lands beyond the far horizon
Travel on – Travel on!

Two as one together we face an unknown future
Travel on – Travel on!

Ijano Esantu Eleman

***

I remember Travis's words, but the reality at the time was that I did not listen well: I still mourned the deaths of our children and little cared what the future would bring to both of us. In my mourning, I felt as if I had lost a part of my soul, and the days just seemed to drift on and on and on …

***

Big Sky Region

Early morning, we left our summit shelter and started our descent – past Lone Mountain Ranch. It was here during the fateful year of 1984 (old date calculation) prior to the Ripple Event so much excitement had occurred, caused by the two mentally ill mountain men – a father and older son – who murdered and kidnapped their way into local history and legend.

We reached the Big Sky meadow, and briefly explored ruins of the long-ago destroyed settlement. Nothing remained of the former grand tourist condominiums, except cracked cement and rock foundations. Swimming pools that at one time were afternoon pleasure sites for vacationing families, now were filled with accumulated trash, wind-blown soil, and the bones of wild animals that long ago paused to drink and were poisoned by the corrupted waters. The shops at the east end of the settlement once had been filled with a myriad of tourist items – specialty T-shirts, golf-related accouterments, and examples of works by local artists. These were no more; all had been abandoned or looted.

We walked slowly and reached the junction of old Highway 191 that paralleled the Gallatin River Valley. In the near distance to the south of the Big Sky meadows was Buck's T-4.

Some time back, data collectors from Montana State University, Bozeman, had attempted to identify the original owner of the ranch called Buck's T-4. All attempts, however, had been unsuccessful as original deed documents could not be located. Further, the name Buck seemed not to be associated with one specific family, but several. In fact, it was not clear who Buck was. Even the so-called Buck's trademark – the T-4 brand – was open to debate and various interpretations. Some reported the brand recalled the debut and model year 1954 (old date calculation) of the classic automobile known as Thunderbird or T-Bird. This could not be correct, however, since those knowledgeable in 20th-century history would know that the initial Thunderbird automobiles produced by company called Ford debuted in 1955, not 1954. Others supported a more creative origin for the brand, and traced the name to a local event that had occurred nearby along the Gallatin River in 1873, when four horse thieves were captured and hung the same day. There was some evidence to suggest – as related by some early Gallatin River pioneer family members – the T-4 hanging was followed by a grand barbeque.

Whatever the origin of the Buck's T-4 name and brand, the ranch with its tourist services and saloon had survived the Ripple and Dark Time, and achieved widespread fame as a gathering place for locals and regional visitors alike.

We approached the ranch and stopped outside the once well-known dining facilities. Travis explored the exterior of the structure, and we debated whether or not to enter, thinking that the building might be booby-trapped. As Travis continued to search the building's exterior, I located an envelope nailed to the side-door kitchen entrance. I found that it contained a descriptive note with unusual content, written by a woman named Sylvia Thompson:

> *I can't believe what has happened. The rush of wind through the valley seems to have brought with it danger to all. Frank, Jessie, Ward, and the others all are in the bunkhouse seriously ill with what seems to be a flu-like outbreak. Already seventeen children, once housed up at the big house, have died; the two doctors with practices at the Big Sky settlement have not responded to our requests for aid. Are they ill, as well?*
>
> *I came to this place more than 30 solar cycles previously. I sought peace and serenity here in this glorious valley, where a river runs*

through it, where in the evenings we gathered around campfires, drinking, singing, and telling heroic tales of past exploits. Jessie would bring out his Martin tenor guitar, Ward would tune his Gibson banjo, and Frank would loosen-up the group with his harmonica riffs – and then – all together we would bellow out the words to the songs that once symbolized and characterized our youthful days at college. Once we started to sing, most of the tourists attending would join in – as they, too, recalled the songs of their youth:

In the Evening by the Moonlight;
Home on the Range;
Down in the Valley;
I've Been Working on the Railroad;
My Bonnie Lies Over the Ocean;
Darling Clementine;
And many, many others ...

Afterwards we would drift off in pairs leaving the campfire to pass pleasurable moments together among the pine trees that sheltered us from the curious eyes of others. We then would walk back slowly to the bunkhouses where we would share one last embrace and say good night.

I came to this place, Big Sky in the Gallatin River Valley, long before the Ripple Event to escape the stress of my everyday employment. Yes, I had followed my parent's desires. Yes I had graduated from a well-known and respected college. Yes I had taken employment – like all responsible graduates should – but then had become just like the thousands of organizational women sitting at desks doing the same repetitive motions each day for hours, days, months, and solar cycles on end.

I left it all and gave it up: my financial security, local friends, even payments on my expensive car. My parents were angry. The parting words from my father still echo in my ears:

You are so irresponsible; you have ruined your life ...etc.

But I left anyway. I hitchhiked alone at some relative risk to myself and well-being, but was fortunate. A kind semi-driver stopped to pick me up outside of Portland took me all the way to Missoula and, from there, it was but a hop-skip-and-a-jump down to Bozeman, then further south into the Big Sky region.

I was nearly penniless as they used to say. A penny? What a laugh. We don't use coin in these Post-Dark Time days do we? The folks at Buck's T-4 took me in, gave me my initial employment. I worked for two solar cycles as dishwasher, then I moved up to assist tending bar. About 12 solar cycles ago, during the Post-Darkness Recovery, I became a senior bartender, known for my ability to mix drinks of unusual fluid combinations, while at the same time being able to belt-out a suitable song or two directed towards the patrons. I would ask a designated patron his or her name, occupation, and region of origin, and then would create a song spur-of-the-moment as they used to say ... something like:

Georgie graduated from Graton U
As a chemist he made lots of glue
He came from Oxnard to Big Sky
To dine on fish that he will fry

CHORUS:

Drink it down Georgie
Drink it down Georgie
Quickly take a bow
Drink it down Georgie
Drink it down Georgie
Turn your glass over – reorder now!

I post this message to the door of the structure that had become my home and my life. Read my words and contemplate what it means to be wanted, desired, and to be a part of a family where we helped each other and took joy in our small and large successes. Now that is gone.

Do not grieve when you read this message. My life has been full; the joys I have experienced here in the Big Sky region have been endless. I remember the words that Jessie and I would sing:

I met my little bright-eyed doll (way down) down by the riverside,
Down by the riverside (way down) down by the riverside.
But if I have my way, maybe some sweet day,
My name and yours will be the same ...

But it was not to be. So my friends or whoever finds this note:

Search for me not high or low ...
Down by the riverside I go
To join the waters that I know
To feel the restless current flow

Sylvia Thompson

***

Along the Gallatin River

About four kilo-miles south of Buck's T-4 the valley narrowed. Here along both sides of the river were massive rock spires known as the Gallatin Gates. We paused briefly near the river's edge to enjoy the beauty of the scene, perhaps more enjoyed by Travis than I. Across the placid-flowing waters, herds of deer grazed along the forest/river-bank edge. Further south, the scene opened into lush meadowlands where our eyes caught glimpses of moose and elk.

The Gallatin River meandered through the grasslands. Throughout this area grew hundreds of low-lying berry bushes. We stripped and ate the fruits as we passed. Walking along, we had no fear of wolves or other predators as all around us as the region was filled with wild game – easy takings – so the canine and feline predators left us alone.

***

Ruins of West Yellowstone

The buildings that now characterized this once wonderful tourist town appeared run down and many had collapsed. The busy streets once filled with people now were empty of all life, save one or two packs of dogs scavenging through back alleys. The once-grand Smith and Chandler store on old Yellowstone Avenue was abandoned. This wonderful establishment once had served the souvenir and supply needs of tens of thousands of tourists passing through town on their way into Yellowstone Park. The structure, once partially rebuilt and expanded after the Ripple Event, suffered terrible economic losses during the Dark Time Recovery Period. Few tourists visited as before, and the family descendants and owners Frank and Mary were devastated. Most of the shelves that once were stockpiled with emergency equipment, sealed ration packets, and water-carrying devices mostly were empty, but other shelves remained stocked. Walking through the outlet produced an eerie sensation: all around were items that could sustain life – but there were no survivors throughout the settlement. Apparently all perished in the terrible Epidemic.

A passage from my diary:

> *Adjacent to Smith and Chandler's was a jewelry shop. In the past the owner would have trafficked in decorative pieces for men, women, and children. Exploring the shop further, I found one display case filled with bracelets of unusual design – created out of cob silver and decorated with stone-studded black widow spiders and web strands. Other items in the cases included steel-blade knives with hilts made of finely decorated deer or elk antler. Mounted on the shop walls were several dozen framed Native American sand paintings, whose origins and symbolic designs I could not interpret. Scrawled on one wall was a statement, perhaps the final message of a distraught father crying out for help:*
>
> > *Please – please anyone: if you see Martha, tell her that we can wait no longer. It is too dangerous – we must move the children to safety and cannot remain here. We will meet at the family cabin and remain there until the Epidemic has passed.*
>
> *The pain of these words echoed through my being. The few short lines perhaps written by a distraught parent caused me sadness equal to that I felt when the Epidemic took the lives of our two children. I experienced deep sorrow for this family – and for all in West Yellowstone who had lost their lives during this terrible time.*

***

Departure South

We spent the night inside what once had been the Yellowstone Historic Center. The museum's displays had not been looted. That the center basically was intact signified at least some initial survivors of the Epidemic had stood guard and protected the site from intruders. Several objects in case 47 caught my eye – two 19th-century trade items. These were ceremonial axes, once called tom-hawks or something like that as noted on the museum display card. These short-handled axes had highly decorated hafts with eagle feathers attached. Who had presented them? Who had received them? What was their use? Such questions remained unanswered.

Just behind the Historic Center were corrals filled with horses and mules. The feed storage areas had been kicked-in by the beasts themselves so they could enter and make good use of the hay and oats. We borrowed two mules and walked them back to Smith and Chandlers. We pulled saddlebags off the shelves, and began to stockpile rations and necessities. We broke into one locked room and located fire-making equipment, camp cooking utensils, and knives. We also helped ourselves to additional clothing and extra boots. We took two revolvers and two rifles in anticipation that we would be able to locate ammunition along our way east, a wish perhaps, since no ammunition could be found inside the store.

Were we thieves? In accord with our upbringing and family training, the answer was yes. However, after rethinking events as they happened, I now think not. I prefer to consider ourselves at that time as – survivors – and surviving the best way we could.

***

Trek into the Park

We approached Yellowstone Park through the west entrance, and took a route paralleling the Madison River. We passed through vast areas of lodge pole pines, then open meadows filled with wild game, especially large herds of bison. We turned south along the Firehole River, and entered the geyser basin sequences. We dodged the so-called hot-spots and picked our path carefully. Along the way, we encountered herds of buffalo, deer, and elk. Off in the distance, we saw clusters of bears foraging for food.

We approached the iconic OFI or Old Faithful Inn from the northeast, but encountered no one. It seemed that we were the only living humans throughout this whole region. In the eerie silence, we explored the lobby of this once-magnificent structure. Atop the main lobby desk next to the guest register was a small book. I opened it, and showed it to Travis. It was a diary written by James Tucker Benson, the innkeeper. He had maintained his journal for nearly two solar cycles. The last pages of the volume were telling:

> *Now I sit alone in the lobby of the OFI. There is no one else, and none for the last 25 days. I am surrounded by the mounted heads of deer, elk, bison, and the spectacular collection of antlers. This day these mountings give me no satisfaction as they once did. This great place: a building constructed by many hands, destroyed by fire, rebuilt and expanded, then again threatened by fire more than once during past solar cycles – now only an empty shell. No one has registered for any of the 327 rooms; no staff to assist guests; no*

cooks to prepare food; no vendors to sell trinkets, and no tourists to buy:

Once there was a stately inn
Close by a geyser's majestic plume
To miss it, friend, would be a sin
May I save for you a room?

You used to come each summer time
We walked, we talked we drank our wine
But now no more I see your face
No more your smile, your soft embrace.

The mountains rise, the rivers flow,
Tis sadly time for me to go.

I write these words as I sit on the veranda of the great inn looking towards its namesake. I watch as the event begins: first a small rumble of the earth announcing the start of the eruption, then the spitting of boiling hot waters upward a few meter-yards, and then the glory – the climax – where the height of the earth's ejection reaching some 56 meter-yards towards the sky. Then the softer residual pulses sputter as the heated ejection declines and quiet resumes once more – until next time.

I have experienced a timeless joy of watching the magnificent OF geyser erupt. Each time I am touched by her regularity and predictability – factors that I pride in my own personality and behavioral composition. To be the innkeeper of OFI – what an honor and responsibility. But that was then and this is now.

No visitors – no staff – the pantries filled with unused food soon to disintegrate and spoil. Yet my life goes on.

If in the future you come to the OFI, search and you may find my body on the north-side veranda, if it has not already been disassembled by roaming clusters of brown bears that frequent the garbage bins behind the inn.

Another eruption is due ... one last look and at its peak ejection – I will cause myself to be no more...

***

We spent two days and nights at the Old Faithful Inn recuperating from our trek. We awoke on the morning of the third day to a most ominous sight. The horizons to the east and south were engulfed with smoke and flame – an enormous conflagration that blocked out sunlight producing a dull amber-brown overcast. More important, however, the fires blocked the track of our planned exit from Yellowstone eastward into Wyoming and the Central Flatland Configuration. Would it be safe or even possible to continue along our original plan?

We feared the worst and it came to pass: all trails exiting the park to the southeast were blocked, so we were forced to reconsider what to do next.

We made our decision and returned north through the geyser basins and re-entered West Yellowstone. We revisited the animal stables and, in addition to the mules, we had taken originally, we also borrowed two horses.

We resumed our journey northward along Highway 191 to the junction with 287, towards Hebgen Lake. We followed the lake north along old 287, until we came to the first Madison River challenge. Here at the abandoned ferry crossing were two large flatboats. Travis and I spent a full day lashing the flatboats together. We then loaded the horses, mules, and our belongings, and began our float trip north towards Ennis.

***

Ennis and the Judge

At one time, the small town of Ennis was part of an early pioneer homestead located along the Madison River. It served as what might be called a port for travelers making their way west to the gold strike region of Alder Gulch. Both the settlements of Ennis and nearby Virginia City served the basic needs of the miners, who were extremely unruly. Both locations experienced numerous assaults, murders, and robberies. Only structural walls remained of the once-popular Bear Trap Grille – famous for grilled cheese and trout dinners. Also on Main Street were the foundation stones of another popular restaurant, the Gravel Bar and Grill – now overgrown with star thistles and a myriad of other weeds.

A settlement extension had developed to the north sometime during the middle solar cycles of the Dark Period. Travis and I rode through this area and encountered a substantial house, much larger than any in the surrounding vicinity. We dismounted to explore. On the porch of the abandoned structure, we found a set of memory books, clusters of photographs taken decades earlier – most from locations unknown to us. Inside the home was a study filled with legal volumes, thus identifying at least one of the occupants as either a judge or lawyer. Resting on an exquisite oak roll-top desk was an envelope addressed – To Whom Ever Finds this Letter – Open and Remember.

The cover signature was that of a woman legal expert, Sylvia Makry.

> *How many cases did I win during the good years in Ennis and the surrounding region before the darkness? Most, but not all. But each person I represented deserved council. Early in my career, I regularly was identified as the best regional advocate. During the post-darkness recovery, I was sought out to judge cases in Bozeman to the northeast, and Butte to the northwest. My objective was to render justice – quick justice, not the type characterized days long ago past when death sentences were assigned but criminals lived on, many times outliving the family members they harmed.*
>
> *In solar cycles long ago past, those who received death sentences commonly lived out their existence in prison cells; still incarcerated, many died of old age. In the days that preceded arrival of the Epidemic in Ennis, I heard and ruled on two cases: both were quick trials where evidence was presented, refuted, debated – with quick verdicts followed by executions. The methods of choice were determined by the victim's family and carried out down by the lake.*
>
> *My most recent court case – heard just yesterday – was unusual, challenging and made me smile:*
>
>> *Joseph Adams' dog barked and scared the neighbor's tomcat – The cat leapt from a second story window and landed upon an elderly lady walking along the alley below. The weight of the cat caused her to fall. As she fell and flailed about just before hitting the ground, her arm dislodged a brick from an unsteady pile stacked the previous day by Jamson Talbot, who had been intoxicated at the time. The act of dislodging the brick caused the unsteady pile to crumble, burying Josie, the infant child of Thomas Jenkins, who was unattended and had fallen asleep in the alley. Josie cried out in pain and terror from beneath the pile of bricks, screaming for the settlement nurse, Apsis Moran, who had been assigned to care for her. Josie's screams and pleading for extraction from beneath the pile of bricks went unheeded. Inattentive nurse Apsis had abandoned her charge albeit momentarily to fiddle-fiddle with her boyfriend Alex Boron in the basement of the*

nearby community granary and storage supply store. Had Apsis remained with Josie and if both had walked through the alley towards the community recreation area as originally planned, and had Apis and Alex not been so indelicately engaged, infant Josie would not have died.

Oh, how I love tort analysis! There is something wonderful about the intricate relationships between cause-effect, and ultimate responsibility.

The jury hearing the evidence presented concluded that Alex Boron was responsible for the death of infant Josie. The logic being: had Boron not seduced Apsis and led her astray by taking her into the community granary and storage supply store basement for their rendezvous, then Apsis would have been present, on duty with Josie, and Josie would not have died.

Ergo!

Oh happy day! I smiled at the jury's verdict, and chose not to overrule or interfere with their logic.

I reaffirmed the sentence on Apsis and ordered it carried out later in the afternoon before my scheduled 4:00 tea-time. Potential executioners with standing in my court included: Josie's father, Thomas Jenkins, and her elder brother, Jason Jenkins. I approved their request to participate and offered them their choice of execution method. Alex Boron's advocate, in turn, issued a strong dissent but was not persuasive. I reaffirmed my ruling. A simple case: no need to forward the verdict to the regional court at Butte for review and consideration.

Is it not said:

Obscurent eum tenebrae Lumine iustitiae!

[Let the darkness be illuminated by justice]

***

Travis and I marveled at the letter and debated its content long into the afternoon. Did not the letter from Judge Makry reveal diligent effort to determine the facts and offer competent consideration of the events that had transpired prior to the death of the child Josie? The content also revealed swift justice for both the defendant Boron and for the surviving members of the Jenkins family – a child had died too soon because of another's neglect.

Much to ponder: should Travis and I praise Judge Makry or not? How should we view her logic? Through which prism of justice did she view and evaluate the evidence and testimony? Who were we to say?

***

Northward Continuation

Reaching the southern outskirts of Three Forks, we polled ashore and camped on a river bar where the land offered our animals rest and feeding opportunities. After we established camp, Travis waded across to explore the upper river terrace. He returned quickly and encouraged me to accompany him to observe something special.

What he showed me was quite remarkable …

In the solar cycles prior to the Ripple and Dark Time, local farmers had tilled the upper Madison River terrace and planted wheat in the fertile fields. As time passed, the fields fell into disuse and were not re-plowed or re-seeded with different crops. On this day of our arrival and laid out before us was a shimmering field of what could be called wild wheat. But that was not the interest or attraction. Travis and I walked through the wheat field over an agate-strewn trail that once had served as a harvest road. All around us the wheat field shimmered and moved, taking on almost a life of its own. The sound all around us was piercing, an eerie high-pitched whine, almost a chirping sound produced by what appeared to be an infinite number of "hoppers."

***

From my diary:

> *Travis took off his deerskin jacket, waded into the knee-high stand of wheat and started flailing about. He called out to me – Reese – do the same; here is our dinner for tonight. We used our jackets to smash the wheat, killing or stunning hundreds of hoppers. I followed behind Travis and gathered the insects using my cloth shirt as a collection bag.*
>
> *That night we dined on two delicacies. The first was singed hoppers roasted on skewers. The second a stew of wheat and hoppers blended with wild onion cloves, juice and leaves of wild mint, and tart mustard greens.*

Recipe:

Sift the wheat kernels to remove any stones
Bring the kernels to a boil
Wash, slice, and mince the wild onions

Add 3 handfuls to the pot
Stir-in 8 handfuls of hoppers
Stir-in 2 handfuls of mustard greens
Dice and press juice from mint leaves to add flavor
Add water to fill potCook over open fire until water boils
Let cool and dig-in.

***

Three Forks

The easiest way for me to describe the settlement of Three Forks is to turn once more to the pages of my diary:

We secured our flatboats along the western shore of the Madison River, and rode into the settlement of Three Forks. We were close to the junction where the Gallatin, Jefferson, and Madison Rivers joined to form the Missouri River. I had passed through Three Forks several times on my overland trips between Bison Camp and Montana State University, Bozeman, and was familiar with the settlement.

We paused first before the once grand Sacajawea Hotel complex, a structure named in honor of the Shoshone woman who guided the early pioneers Meriwether Lewis and William Clark through this region during the early solar cycles of the 19th century.

Although Travis and I searched for two days, we found no survivors within the confines of the Three Forks settlement. Shops on the central streets had been looted; shards of glass were everywhere, grocery stores that had recovered during the Dark Time were empty of all consumables.

We rode our horses and led our pack mules along east Fir Street and reached Stevenson Park. Opposite the park, we located a house with an unlocked front door and entered. We were fortunate. We had chanced upon the home of what best might be called a survivalist family – members who had stashed quantities of water and MREs in the basement, along with ammunition and literally hundreds of batteries of different types.

We tended to our animals and let them graze upon the lush grass behind the house. We ate a filling dinner selected from among the varieties of MREs listed as: chili with beans, shredded BBQ beef, chicken with noodles, beef brisket, and beef and black beans.

***

Dream Time Visitations

It is important for me to share with you something that occurred during our first evening in Three Forks. Whatever the reason, and we could not be certain, perhaps it was caused by something we ate or drank from the reserves in the survivalist's home. Whatever the origin, we both were visited by dreams of extraordinary color and memorable content.

Our dreams had similar threads as if both dream time images occurred not by chance but were visited upon each of us by what might be identified as a supportive protective spirit.

> **Summary vision to Travis:** clarity of route after Three Forks along the Missouri River – junction of the Great River reached – overland exploratory excursions to undefined locations ravaged by war (?) – resumption of river journeys – abandonment of water transportation and overland by horseback into the New Confederacy Configuration – travels within and without the NCC – sire of twin girls – peaceful experiences among friends and family – illness followed by [awoke immediately from dream].

> **Summary vision to Reese:** gradual return of strength and vitality – visitations by spirits of unknown origin forecasting future activities – appearance of shadow peoples – touched by one known as The Minstrel and his soothing ballads – conception and birth of daughters – peaceful experiences among friends and family – images of Travis vanishing – eventful return to Bison Camp – unclear images of meeting others similar to but unlike ourselves [awoke immediately from dream].

We shared our dreams the following morning, and both of us commented on how they were vivid, with great depth of content. While many of the images were clear and logical, others remained vague, confusing, and open to different interpretations. I was stunned that in my dream I would conceive twin girls with Travis. How could this be foretold? Who was this individual, the so-called Minstrel, and why did he appear only to me and not to Travis? Were the dreams self-induced, or had they been introduced by an external force or spirit that somehow was guiding us along the path we had embarked upon?

***

After-Word

And as predicted in Travis' dream, we left Three Forks and returned to the Madison River where our flatboats had been secured. Knowing that the rapids ahead at Great Falls would block a free-float journey, we abandoned our flatboat travel plans. After spending the remainder of the morning reloading supplies onto our pack mules and horses, we began the next leg of our journey north and east upon the Missouri River.

***

Ijano Esantu Eleman.

Interlude-Conversation: 1
What If?

***

What changes and chaos the Ripple then the Epidemic left in their wakes, K'Aser. Do you ever wonder what life on this planet would be like had this never happened?

At times I ponder this, A'Tena, especially when visiting the beach. I keep concluding matters might not have ended all that differently.

Not all that differently? How can you say this?

The people on this planet were very near unleashing substantial chaos, you must admit.

For true it was not difficult to see that major wars would erupt, especially in regions of perpetual conflict and between certain cultures and religions. It seemed all about smaller conflicts simmered and erupted without end.

Such was obvious to many inhabitants of this planet but little or nothing was done to reduce the dangers. Indeed, the Ripple itself arose from one of the conflicts most inhabitants considered of minor import. But even without the possibilities of ongoing greater or lesser conflicts, matters were unsettled. High stress levels being the general rule rather than the exception pointed to the likelihood – perhaps certainty – of economic collapse in many regions. Would it not be for true, A'Tena, that social collapse would follow as an inevitable consequence of economies that failed? Could it not be argued the Ripple, as improbable as it was, merely was the outgrowth of existing trends? As for the later Epidemic that emerged from across the Great Sea inside the Han Confederacy, its effect – as pronounced it was in certain regions – would wane as the two travelers ultimately would discover. It would appear that recovery and repopulation now is ongoing elsewhere.

Yes, K'Aser, those laws of probabilities – that you often prattle on about in the not altogether vain hope of improving my understanding – these probabilities coupled with the reality of the Epidemic took the inhabitants by surprise. But, the laws – the formulas, if you will – of economics were well known before this time, were they not?

Well known, perhaps, but little understood and applied unevenly through the subsequent solar cycles. The lessons were obvious, hard lessons, but apparently never learned by the residents. The need for application of sound economic practices was apparent well before the Ripple, as the orb already was on the edge of a major collapse. Need I say again both trends and potential remedies were ignored? It is for true, A'Tena, that if remedies had been implemented, such actions also would have caused chaos and loss of lives, but not as great as those suffered during the Ripple. Would the power of the Epidemic that followed have been more pronounced or not? Who could say?

A'Tena, pondering what may or may not have happened most often is a futile exercise. But I do find myself wondering concerning one thing.

And that is?

Did Sheldon and Amy marry at the end of it all?

I don't believe it! Be serious! You wonder about some characters – what the inhabitants called actors – performing in an imaginary world. You cannot be serious, but if you are and your intent is to know the outcome of their actions? There is only one solution: go back in time and find out for yourself. You have traveled through the space/time continuum many times, so just do it!

A'Tena, to embark upon space/time travel and return to a place/time event that happened previously, requires reality. The question I continue to ponder never existed in reality.

So ... construct your own resolution.

A'Tena, that would be unsatisfactory at least to me. At least in reality we can adjust, alter, change ...

Or remove ...

Yes, remove any given reality if need be where the results of the interaction can be seen and judged.

Be that as it may, K'Aser, what is your opinion: do you think Sheldon and Amy would have married?

I doubt it. Sheldon to state the obvious was a unique individual. What have you concluded on this matter?

It is for sure, K'Aser, that Amy had set her sights on Sheldon. Our observations on this planet, in the real world as you say, indicate that when a female sets a plan in motion, the male sooner or later is reeled in, so to speak. I anticipate that wedding bells were in their future, as imaginary as that future might have been, but cannot be certain.

Reeled in? Do you mean, A'tena, like a fish on a line?

The same and human males usually don't fight much. Some don't even realize they're caught. I see Sheldon as one of these, but cannot be certain.

Chapter 2

Missouri River Passage: Three Forks to Saint Louis

Pre-Note

Three Forks was left behind us. Ahead lay the unknown. As we started our ride paralleling the Missouri River, our horses disturbed flocks of birds that took flight as we approached and passed near their nesting areas. Ducks and geese rose in great numbers from the sheltering reeds and bushes along the water's edge. Overhead, hawks circled with other predator birds, swooping down upon the rising mallards and teals making easy kills. We rode by herds of antelope, the adults standing alert for predators that might lurk nearby. We watched their calves approach the riverbank, wading first through muddy silt then outward into the gentle river eddies where the waters ran clear and cold.

We reached and passed through the abandoned settlements of Broadwater and Canyon Ferry, then approached Helena. Still no sightings of humans, only numerous groupings of large and small wild game animals, and herds of domesticated cattle, standing quietly or ambling slowly through the low brush and forest edges along the settlement peripheries. These beasts now appeared to be the only survivors occupying this vast verdant landscape.

Great Falls

We had anticipated considerable difficulty along the Missouri, and knew that our first major test would have been to circumnavigate the rapids and dams constructed during past decades. A river journey by flatboat would not have been possible. What we did not anticipate, however, was the widespread destruction of these barriers at Great Falls, and the impact upon river currents and levels.

To our astonishment there were no dams at Great Falls. Each had been destroyed by terrorists. The river now flowed gently through what once was the center of a great city. We tethered our horses and walked near the water's edge. Along the way, we encountered dozens of buildings with walls defaced by spray-painted words, hundreds of slogans and messages left by what appeared to be at least three competitive ecological terrorist groups:

> *Let the rivers flow freely: We the LRFF claim responsibility for destruction of the dams.*
>
> *Friends of Free-Flowing Rivers: We the FFFR cadre caused the bang, not the LRFFers.*
>
> *River Freedom Collective: Remember well – we the RFers destroyed these dams!*

The scribbled messages seemed strange. Why announce the destruction of such valuable river landmarks? Was destruction of the dams a useful recruitment tool to one's cause? Who would read and rejoice in such efforts? Also appearing on many walls was a common poster, a political manifesto produced by merger of two additional terrorist groups who together claimed that they had destroyed the dam structures. I copied one such message into my diary

MANIFESTO

GREEN ALLIANCE – RIVER FLOW ALLIANCE

[GA-RFA]

Preamble: We the Green Alliance and River Flow Alliance hold the following ...

Lakes, rivers, soils, and vegetation form the earth's soul ...

Humans are destroyers and enemies of the earth ...

Only earth abides ...

Call to Action: Read and Understand!

Be It Known –

Vegetation flourishes only in natural habitats ...

Humans have altered original plant distributions ...

Species out of place harm the earth.
Be It Known –
Water flows naturally from source to sea ...
Water flows through naturally formed channels ...
Barrier dams and impounded water harm the earth.
Believe – Then Act!
Destroy transplanted species: uproot plants from unnatural habitats ...
Destroy dams and river barriers created by humans ...
Bring the earth into balance!
Join: Support our demand for ...
Ecological justice ...
Redistribution of earth resources ...
Return to topographical fairness ...
Be one with nature and the earth ...
Commit to our goals ...
Reject our call at your peril ...
We are watching you!

***

Looking out at you assembled here this evening, it seems to me that some smiled as I related these words. Are your responses related to curiosity and insufficient clarity of my language, or because the GA-RFA statements appear so foolish? I would smile with you, too, but the reality was and remains that members of GA-RFA re-grouped since the Epidemic and gained considerable numbers of dedicated adherents. GA-RFA, along with other terrorist cells, re-established themselves in portions of lands we passed through on our trek east. These eco-terrorists would like nothing better than to dominate the de-populated regions of New NorthWest Configuration and re-establish their ecological agenda once more. Recall from the cave documents that there were few initial numbers of such eco-terrorist cells. Recall how one group arose in the East Bay region of old California and implemented their botanical terror tactics. Remember that most residents at the time considered the Green Alliance to be an inconsequential group and as such their initial activities were ignored. But recall, too, that by ignoring the GA agenda their membership grew in numbers and caused the destruction of the medicinal plant research fields at the University of California, Davis, an event that brought the Triplets and their mates here to the Big Hole Valley on the eve of the Ripple Event.

***

Missouri Breaks

Beyond Great Falls, we followed the south river bank and traversed several kilo-miles of shallows riding towards the badland region known as the Missouri Breaks. The river landscape initially presented a common similarity broken only by stands of cottonwood trees and small terraces that extended along both shores. But as the days passed slowly the horizon landscape began to change.

Wind and water-based erosional channels soon became the norm as we entered the Missouri Breaks region. It was here countless generations of different Native American tribes found shelter from the cold northern winds of winter. The rugged and irregular landscape seemed carved out of soft stone. Eons of wind blasts had created strange almost eerie formations of pedestal rocks that resembled ghost-like figures. Ancient narrow streams drained and seeped to the Missouri River, their channels forming twisting coulees that offered shelter from the winds. It was here we took refuge and remained during that first winter of our journey.

Our key for survival was maintaining warmth and access to fresh water. Dominant vegetation within the coulees included stands of cottonwood trees and scrub pine. Broken branches and dried cones became our campfire fuel. Irregular patches of green grasses, reeds, and horsetail rushes produced vegetation trails that we followed to sources of fresh springs dripping from water-worn caves.

One such cave provided the shelter we needed and became our winter home.

We shared the badland topography with wild game: jackrabbits, grouse, and even rattlesnakes became our food resources. On days when the temperatures warmed, Travis and I hiked upslope to the prairie flatlands where we often espied solitary deer, big horn sheep, and herds of antelope. Such hunting times were uncommon during our winter stay, but reminded me of my childhood back at Bison Camp when I accompanied Travis on antelope hunts:

> *Travis would lie low and creep towards the grazing herd then rise slowly, holding a small white flag on a long pole. The antelopes*

being curious were attracted to the movement, and one or two gradually would work in close enough for Travis's father to bag one or two by bow and arrow. Later, after Travis had reached maturity and had been initiated, he replaced his father's role in the hunt and hid in the brush taking the antelope ambush position. At these times, it was my turn to work the flag and draw in the beasts. Travis's aim always was on target.

Evenings inside our cave shelter were spent carving pieces of antler and bone, making small images of animals. I also spent evening hours writing notes in my diary and sketching daily activities. Sometimes I wove bracelets and necklaces, taking segments of horsetail rushes, pulling the units apart, and rejoining them to make circles. During most evenings, however, we just sat and enjoyed each other's company.

***

Came a time, however, when we learned we were not alone inside the breaks.

On two occasions when out gathering firewood in the early morning, I glimpsed brief movements just inside the tree-line shadow areas. On other occasions, I saw human footprints in the sandy bottom of the more remote coulee twists. I could not be certain that the tracks were recent, or that the rustling of shadows among the scrub pine and cottonwoods were from others like us. Perhaps they were Wanderers, taking shelter in the breaks. If so, we had to be on alert throughout the day and night.

One morning, I went down to the river to wash and saw still other sets of prints, not just one or two as before but sets that clearly were different. I was accustomed to the marks and spore left by animals, whether coyotes or the tracks of birds, but the prints that day were unlike the occasional marks left by bison that wandered down to the water's edge to drink. These were deep imprints left by horses. Their depth revealed to me that the horses were not wild but had been ridden. Their directional orientation was southward. Horses and riders had crossed the river and entered the southern portion of the breaks. We no longer were alone! I retreated carefully to our cave shelter to alert Travis. We armed ourselves not knowing what to expect next. When they appeared, we were apprehensive!

Riding horseback single file up the coulee path towards our cave was a group of eight men and women. Four small children on ponies rode behind the adult group. Travis and I stood at the coulee junction and raised our weapon-free arms in a traditional sign of welcome.

The group was a mix of Apsaalooke and Niitsitapi, who had left the town of Havre in north central old Montana, New NorthWest Configuration. The eight adults plus children had escaped exposure to the Epidemic. They had camped together outside Havre to celebrate the marriage of two of their members. Returning home from their weekend of joy, they found only death, destruction, and horror: all residents of Havre had perished.

The group knew not why they had been saved, only that they had been protected by Apistotoke Maxpe, the Great Spirit.

There was space in our cave shelter for all.

Together that first evening, we celebrated the gift of life.

Through the days and weeks that followed, we flourished, sharing food, taking turns gathering firewood, and helping with the children. Slowly, we changed from two independent groups of people into one. While unrelated and from different cultures, we had survived the Epidemic and now joined with each other for aid and protection.

I learned from the women the best way to calculate time on our journey. They did not to follow the old system of months of variable numbered days, but used an average women's cycle of 23 days and counted this period as one month. Grandmother Avis braided my long hair and showed me how to remove even the worst tangles. She marveled and laughed at the body hair on my legs and under my arms, since she and the other women of her clan had little such growth. Through her giggling laughter, she taught me a Niitsitapi technique how to mix mint leaves with antelope fat and where to smear it onto my body to attract Travis. I will remember forever the sparkle in her eyes as she touched my flat belly and spoke words that I longed to hear:

> *Reese, once more you will bear children, and they will honor you and Travis.*

In the evenings, we joined together – young and old – around our central fire. When the wind gusted and blew the campfire smoke into the face of one of us seated, I remembered the old adage often told at Bison Camp:

> *Do not wince – campfire smoke follows beauty, and the smoke has chosen you.*

We told tales and laughed together. Then time would come for one of us to take turns, stand and speak out the story lesson of the evening.

Travis recalled his memories of the last data collection Long Loop trek into old California, where he and his team interviewed the settlement cluster of elderly survivors of the Ripple and Dark Time.

When my first turn came, I described my life as a little girl growing up at Bison Camp, how we were schooled, our celebratory rites-of-passage, and how we flourished as a settlement during the Post-Dark Time Recovery. I shared the joy of first meeting Travis, growing together, and becoming his mate. I spoke of the sadness and pain of our children's death during the Epidemic. I also spoke of the joy of friendships recently formed by arrival of the Apistotoke and Niitsitapi.

One evening, Elder Jackson l'Infant, rose to speak. He shared words that captivated us all:

> *You can tell by my name that while I am Apistotoke, my family roots also lie across the great waters in a country once called France. My original family name was La Treckq – as best I can spell the word. Francois La Treckq sailed from France to the port of New Orleans, now located in what some call the New Confederacy Configuration. He bore an unusual nickname, Flit, because he moved from town to town just as a newly hatched mosquito flits from here to there. As a young man, Flit went up the Great River to the port of Saint Joseph, where he mated – or what they used to call married at that time – and joined a wagon trek westward. He and his mate had a child. As his travel group crossed the sacred lands of the Apistotoke, they were attacked by our warriors. Only the infant child survived the attack, and he was cared for by what you today would call my great, great, grandmother. My name, l'Infant, stems from that history. Growing up in Havre, I defended my family name almost weekly as older and stronger boys attacked me at school. My grandfather, Tourme l'Infant, taught me to ignore such taunts, and his words strengthened both my mind and body. After the Ripple Event, my family and I survived taking strength from the spirits of our ancestors. And it was this strength that guided me as leader of our combined group to seek shelter in the Breaks – and which brought us to you, Travis and Reese, who we always will remember and respect.*

***

Came the time when we were greeted by the sunshine and fair weather of early spring. The day that I dreaded had arrived for it would be the time for parting. Travis and I would continue along the southern shoreline of the Missouri River ever eastward, while the vision quest of our friends and adoptive family members would take them southwestward towards old Bozeman and ultimately into the Yellowstone region.

How strange our circle of life. We had started our trek from Bison Camp in the Big Hole Valley, rode south to Yellowstone then were forced to turn back. Now our adoptive family members would ride south into the Yellowstone, where they hoped to find peace and tranquility.

Travis shared with them our experience in the Yellowstone, where we were forced to turn back because of the great fires that had engulfed the region. The elders understood our concern, but replied that such fires were cyclical, and that by now they would have extinguished themselves, leaving behind in the ashes the potential for new growth to return. So it would be as part of the great cycle of life.

Came the morning of our departure – the word *kitatama'sino* was spoken again and again as we mounted our horses and trailed off into the distance.

We never saw each other again.

***

Further East

As the kilo-miles passed by, we saw only wild game and pondered the geographical extent of destruction caused by the plague from the west. We approached the town of Sidney, after passing through a beautiful section of grassland. Just before reaching the settlement, we camped at the junction of the Missouri and Yellowstone Rivers.

We established camp in the late afternoon. Travis scoured the nearby river terrace, and returned with driftwood and six or seven dried buffalo chips to be used as fuel. I boiled water for coffee and shaped the sheets of aluminum foil reflectors around our fire to concentrate the heat and warm the few MREs that remained from our winter meal stash.

We finished our meal and were engaged in conversation when we were startled by the sound of approaching footsteps. We reached for our weapons and stood to confront the potential danger!

Standing distant just inside the ring of light cast by our campfire was the outline form of a man. We gazed at each other for several moments then the stranger spoke:

> *Do not be afeared. I am unarmed. I wish you no harm. I will not approach your fire unless you invite me. Know that I am armed. I have with me two knives, bow with arrows, and lance but I wish you no harm. I have my food and water. I will not take yours. Again I say: I will not approach you or your fire unless you invite me.*

And so it was that the Shaman entered into our lives. After further conversation – questions posed and answered – we invited him to join us inside the ring of flickering campfire light.

The Shaman's Lakota name was Nacacijin Wanbli or Loyal Eagle. He preferred to be called Franklin. His home was Pine Ridge, in old South Dakota. He was traveling on foot northward using only the sun and evening stars for navigation. He told us his vision quest would take him far into the great northern reaches to greet White Bear, where he would become one with the bear's body and spirit. In so doing he would join his ancestors and recently departed friends and family members who died during the sickness. Entering the embrace of White Bear would relieve him of the pain and sorrow experienced with the death of so many that he knew. Later this first evening Franklin related his story:

Loyal Eagle's Journey

> *Among my people the Lakota, I am a holy man or wicasa wakan. I lived alone near the junction of White Clay and Wolf Creeks in Pine Ridge. The Epidemic started slowly, but then accelerated at an unexpected pace. I know not why I was unaffected by the disease. Throughout the neighborhood, friends and family members suddenly became ill, too ill to walk the single kilo-mile distance to the nearby former United States Public Health Service clinic.*
>
> *I helped others within the settlement, and led children and their parents to the clinic facilities. The waiting room was filled, the corridors packed with poor souls suffering from the illness. Many of those desperately ill saw little hope for cures from the U.S. Public Health Service doctor or his assistant; western medicine in the view of many of my people could not stem the severity of the symptoms. I did my best to allay the fearful minds of the ill, but one by one they*

passed on to their final destination where their souls embarked upon wanagi tacanku – the final path – where each must face judgment and selection before entry into the spirit world.

Why was I left behind to remain among so much pain and sorrow? I have no answer.

I remember walking to the south rim of the settlement, where I fasted and prayed for a vision. Returning home, I slept, awaiting hanbleceya – the dream that would set me on the correct path. As a young man, I had been initiated in the ways of chanunpa, smoking the sacred pipe to reach out to the spirit world for answers that would come to me in song. Is it not correct, my young friends, that all objects and beings have their own song? Is it not correct, my young friends, that rocks and sunset colors also sing? Even the fire we sit next to this evening has a song. Listen and you will hear it clearly.

My dream that night filled me with wakan tanka – the spiritual power of the universe. Came morning I entered into the inipi sweat lodge where I stayed for five days. Through the ceremony I was re-born to live again, my body was spiritually quartered, and I was led through the successive realms of air, earth, fire, and water. And throughout inipi, I became purified with sweet grass smoke that cleared my mind and cleansed my body.

The decision made, I began my northward waziyata, the journey of self-realization to reach the great Missouri River, and from there to continue across the waters and northward to find White Bear and eternal rest. Along the way I was protected by sunka wakan, the spirit dog who became my companion. Sunka wakan led me through the dark times when my mind faltered. I hunted wild game and shared meat with my travel companion. During early evening time, I ate blueberries, currents, and raspberries gathered along the way.

Every third day I fasted to strengthen my resolve. Herbal teas I prepared from chicory root and sage leaves. As the sun passed overhead on day 17 of my passage north, when the cast of my shadow was shortest, I reached the junction of the two rivers – it was then I saw you along the shore walking together in the late afternoon. But I waited until evening to approach you and stood outside the light from your campfire – then you invited me to join you.

Through the short time of our visit you have shared with me your stories as I have mine with you. You now are part of my family, what we at Pine Ridge call tiospaye. Travis, I look upon you now as my nephew or tonska. Reese, you have become my niece or tojan. Forever now we are linked together in word and in spirit.

The next morning we shared food and beverages. Franklin rose and reached into his amulet bag. He withdrew two tiny objects, petrified remains of ancient sea creatures. He presented one to each of us; a clockwise spiral for Travis and a counterclockwise spiral for me:

Today is a good day – leela ampaytu – and so it is once again we start our journeys – wash tay. The dawn now blesses us. We part as family members and as fellow travelers. I have given to each of you on this morning of departure and separation an object for your protection, power stones to aid you through the difficult times ahead as you make your way eastward towards the rising sun. Hold these stones in your hands; look at their pattern, feel their structure, the tight coils, the rough ridges that form an ever-expanding circle of harmony.

May the Morning Star – Weechaxk pee he huh nee – bring forth each day a new beginning and joy to your lives.

Before we part, let us link arms and speak aloud – wash tay – may goodness and safety follow each of you forever. Travis and Reese – you always will be in my heart – cante waste nape ciyuzapo.

***

Unusual Sky Lights

We continued on our Missouri River shoreline trek. Prairie landscapes flowed ever onward, basically flat with only low undulations. Numerous herds of antelope gathered here and there near the water's edge. As we progressed, the days merged together through the sameness of the surrounding vistas. When we stopped, I dismounted and took rest on the prairie grass gazing at the cloud patterns overhead thinking back to the time when I grew up in Bison Camp settlement group. I remembered the training in herbal medicine that I received from our settlement Sage Femme. It was she who taught me how to differentiate the toxic from safe plants, their respective uses, and how to dry and prepare barks, berries, leaves, and roots keeping each separate inside well-labeled containers.

Each day when dusk approached, we camped along the bank. After a brief time scouting the landscape for security, we tethered our horses and mules for the night. We attached long leads to each animal that allowed the beasts to wander nearby, graze, and exercise. Each evening we established a campfire for warmth and cooking needs. We slept under the stars looking upward into the heavens and wondering what the next days would bring.

On several nights, Travis noticed the appearance of unusual lights in the sky, quite different and distinct from the stars overhead. The lights suddenly appeared in pairs, sometime in groups of four or six. The lights were characterized by unusual brightness as they streaked across the sky from their original location in the high north reaches, then sped eastward at a sharp angle for a few slow counts. They were unusual and nothing like any sky object we had seen before.

The objects could not be meteors because they sometimes abruptly changed direction. What were these?

***

Dream Time

In the solitude of many evenings after Travis slept, I sometimes remained awake enveloped with a sense that we were not alone. At such times I would arise, take my weapon, and walk the perimeter of our camp site to check security but always returned to the fire warmth without evidence that we might be harmed. Returning to my bedroll I would continue to lie awake. In the flickering embers of our campfire, my thoughts returned to memories of my children.

I cannot describe the pain I felt during those terrible days and final hours as my children lay ill. How was it that I as a trained assistant to our Bison Camp Sage Femme, and with my knowledge of healing herbs and plants, that I could not save them? The pain of this loss remained even as Travis and I continued on our journey.

During one of my worst nights I sobbed quietly and then fell asleep. The dream I experienced that night was like no other. After I awoke just before dawn the following morning, I recorded the following thoughts and images in my journal:

> *I was alone drifting in space between two spheres: I perceived one sphere to be the real world, the second sphere a spirit world. I felt my body suspended in time, elevated and floating above the ground.*

I looked down and saw myself sleeping next to Travis where our bedrolls were laid out near the campfire. Immediately my vision shifted and reversed. I now lay upon the ground next to Travis. Looking upward, I saw myself suspended some 15 meter-yards above hovering in space looking downward at myself.

I was disconnected in body and reality.

She – unknown to me – suddenly appeared in my dream and spoke:

I am Ptesan-wi, White Buffalo Woman. I come to you Reese, Tojan of Nacacijin Wanbli. It was he, my Shaman, who you and Travis fed, helped, and offered friendship. Nacacijin Wanbli, through his prayers, asked me to visit and console you to lift the pain of your departed children from your heart.

You, Reese, Tojan of Nacacijin Wanbli, during your life will pass through four stages, as I have done. Born a maiden I transformed to black buffalo, to red-brown buffalo, to yellow buffalo, and finally to white buffalo. With my last transformation, I took my place in the clouds where now I reside until called forth to aid others like you.

You, Reese, Tojan of Nacacijin Wanbli, will pass through four stages as well. These will be the four stages of pain experienced by most women. I will assist you through these stages at the request of Nacacijin Wanbli.

You, Reese, Tojan of Nacacijin Wanbli, already have passed through three of your four stages: pain caused by your emergence into the present world; pain of childbirth; and pain of early death of your children. The fourth stage of pain you will experience later upon the death of your mate, Travis, for it is he who will precede you into the thereafter world.

You, Reese, Tojan of Nacacijin Wanbli, the pain you feel now – the third level pain – is hardest of the three. Know now, Reese, Tojan of Nacacijin Wanbli, this pain you feel will pass if you call out your children's names and speak to others of the joy each brought to you. Your pain slowly will be replaced by a sense of joy, the joy that you gave them life – even for a short time – the joy that comes from knowing that you and Travis formed their spirits – that their spirits exist in the thereafter world awaiting you. In future time, you will be greeted by your two children – they will call out to you – you will join them in the thereafter world. You, Reese, Tojan of Nacacijin Wanbli, your pain also will be relieved with the knowledge I bring to you this evening – once again you will give birth to others. You will be the mother of two girls, twins. They will be strong of body and mind. They will outlive you and carry your spirit, and lead others along paths of honor long after you have joined Travis in the thereafter spirit world.

This I tell you, Reese, Tojan of Nacacijin Wanbli.

Awaken and remember!

***

Travis extinguished our campfire the following morning. We packed our animals and resumed our journey along the Missouri River. I scarcely knew what to say and debated whether or not to tell Travis about my dream. I decided to say nothing.

As we rode off, I turned to look back at our campsite. In the distance, along the southern ridge of the nearby river terrace – head lowered and grazing on sweet grass – I saw a form. Was it an illusion, my imagination, or was it Ptesan-wi? As I watched, the image disappeared.

***

Williston

For the next days we rode eastward and approached the abandoned town of Williston. Prior to the Ripple Event and Dark Time, Williston had been the center of economic activity in this region of old North Dakota in the Flatland Configuration. The town had experienced an influx of tens of thousands of persons attracted to employment opportunities made possible by expanding underground petroleum production needs.

When the Ripple Event disaster struck both Williston, the town and the oil industry collapsed. In the months that followed Williston became the focus of terrorist attacks perpetrated by an offshoot of the GA-RFA. The eco-terrorists entered the settlement and destroyed the crude oil storage reservoirs, and dynamited the gas-flaring towers. What began as a limited attack on Williston, led to a massive fire that ultimately destroyed most buildings located along the periphery of the once-thriving settlement.

To the south, beyond the two oxbow lakes just north of the Missouri River, were several wharfs. We tethered our horses and pack animals and crossed the river to the north bank. We walked along West Broadway Avenue to explore the remains of buildings. No one was in sight.

One establishment we entered was called the Bakken Café. The interior while messy had not been looted or destroyed. That the café seemed basically intact seemed curious to us, given our observations of the rough and tumbledown appearance of most buildings along West Broadway. Menus were strewn here and there over tables, counters, and the floor. All in all, the interior status was reasonable, given what had occurred elsewhere in town during the GA-RFA attacks. Travis retrieved a menu from the floor, laughed, and showed it to me, his eyes smiling.

– BAKKEN CAFÉ –

Note – we don't serve wimps or wusses or feel-good PCers; if you feel entitled or believe that you are not receiving your fair share of food, then get your ass out of here and eat elsewhere down the street.

The Management

Drinks: *Coffin Coffee (four shots of espresso with two fingers of rum or whisky); Iced Bombshell (three varieties of tea mixed with three types of vodka served over ice – sure to please); Mountain Milk (from Ibex goats imported to Williston from New NorthWest Configuration; a sure-footed guarantee); Instant Creation (tell us what you want; if we have it, we will make it for you, if not – think again and order something else).*

Burgers: *The Freeker-Frakker; a one kilo-pound burger, just like Josie the Pole Dancer used to prepare during time-out rest periods over at the Sling-Song Saloon; The Vaso-Dialater, a two kilo-pound burger sure to evoke heart-stopping memories of times long past; The Buffalo Dump: two prairie chicken patties on either side of a slab of buffalo rump – smothered with a heap of our famous Bakken chili; NOTE: All burgers come with prairie lettuce, choice of cheese (dripping or solid), and fries (boiled, cross-cut, hammered, or extruded).*

Steaks: *Step 1: Select from antelope, buffalo, elk, moose, or flatland beef; Step 2: Name the slab you desire; Step 3: How you want it served? Raw or cooked as you desire.*

Desserts: *Chocolate Ooze: just like thick black gold, oozing directly from the well-head; Or – try our famous Dingle Berry Pie: a cacophony of colors and textures (from berries in season: blackberries, blueberries, gooseberries, and strawberries). NOTE: For a special mental treat, ask for two holly berries to be mashed up and added to the mixture! Yum, Yum, and Wow – a vision of loveliness!*

NO FIGHTING – NO GAMBLING – NO SOLICITATION!

NO IOUs – BARTER TOKENS ONLY – NO DOUBLE OR NOTHING!

***

We returned to the south shore in the early afternoon. Off to the north, east, and west the destroyed flaring towers still ejected gas that erupted into billowing flames arching high into the atmosphere. We counted more than 50 such fires. Smoke drifted westward, leaving much of the horizon covered in shimmering darkness. Off to the southeast oil draining from destroyed holding tanks poured into the Missouri River in three places, streams of dark-black crude darkening the waters. The oil just seemed to ooze and spread over the damaged retaining walls before it entered the river. The angle of evening sunshine lit the surface of the water and revealed a radiating spectrum of colors – swirling violets, blues, greens, yellows, oranges, and reds – hues that hid the toxic elements contained therein. Off to the east, we saw the glow of a massive conflagration where destroyed oil wells and tank batteries holding the Bakken formation crude had been set alight – a vision that resembled descriptions of the fiery furnace of ancient religious texts.

***

At our noontime meal Travis related his dream of last night.

You and I were back at Bison Camp hunting antelope using a stick and white flag. A small buck antelope separated itself from the herd and moved closer to me. Suddenly I heard words spoken directly to me – coming not from you, Reese, but from a jackrabbit squatting nearby. Impossible, I thought. I kept my eyes on both the antelope and the jackrabbit, and both beasts spoke – two words, repeated three times:

Travel on – Travel on – Travel on.

I was unable to move, covered by the cloak of night. It descended and enveloped me, the antelope, and the jackrabbit. After a time, the cloak was blown off by a mysterious wind – before me I saw that the two beasts had fused into one, forming the jester spirit, inxtchlt, or jackalope – swift of foot, agile, able to dodge all hunters. Atop the head of inxtchit was a set of two-prong horns emerged between two long, floppy ears. The inxtchit turned and looked directly into my eyes.

I awoke screaming.

***

Along the Outskirts of Pierre

We followed what once had been a vast lake of impounded water. We rode east along the south shore characterized by a suite of staircase terraces that revealed the height of the former lake. Next, we encountered the ruins of another great dam that once blocked this section of the Missouri River. Nothing remained intact except great blocks of concrete. Just to the south of the ruins was the settlement of Pierre.

The town had been constructed on bluffs above the Missouri River. As we rode through the streets, most of the town appeared in ruins as smoke billowed upward at several locations. We observed and avoided two individuals off in the distance who appeared to be thieves. The town basically had been abandoned. It was unclear whether or not the Epidemic had reached Pierre or whether the Ripple Event been so severe here that the settlement never recovered.

We departed southeast along the river and encountered a small group of Native Americans numbering about 30. We offered signs of peace and were invited into their encampment. The majority were Lakota with territorial origins beyond the badlands to the southwest. Travis mentioned the Shaman from Pine Ridge, Franklin, or Nacacijin Wanbli. Several of the adults recognized him and asked about our relationship. We unpacked the two amulet stones given to us by Franklin and showed them to the group elders. After a brief discussion, Travis and I were invited to join the community for a meal and sharing time – when we would be called upon to exchange information regarding our respective travels.

After a hearty meal in which we feasted on fry bread served with venison ribs and a variety of *wojapi,* composed of crushed blueberries and chokecherry berries mixed with cornstarch. Bowls of hazelnuts capped the dinner. These were passed around as snacks throughout the evening.

Travis and I were first to stand and relate information from our journey. Our hosts were most interested in our experiences between Great Falls, the winter time we spent at the Missouri Breaks, and traveling on lands leading up to and beyond Williston. We related what we had seen regarding the destruction and contamination of the Missouri waters.

One of the Lakota elders, Hanska Ohanzee or Tall Shadow, had reached Pierre after a very long trek northward out of Pine Ridge. We were especially interested in his descriptions of the southwestern portion of old South Dakota, Flatland Configuration. I copied his words into my diary:

> *I, Hanska Ohanzee, left Pine Ridge four solar cycles past. I journeyed with two friends but both died when the Epidemic struck our camp. Why I survived and did not even become ill – I cannot understand. They were my friends, we were equals. Why should two of the three of us die? Why was I left to make the vision quest alone? I have no answers.*
>
> *I reached the sacred black hills of He Sapa, and searched the ground below the great stone heads for ancestor-related information. My great grandfather told me that within the boulder field below the southern-most stone head, there was a small cave with a hidden entrance. He claimed that inside the cave were relics of our Lakota past, and other objects left by previous peoples who once occupied the lands before our Lakota arrival, these being the Chaui and Pitahawirata, as well as the Kaiewa, Sutaio, and Tsitsistas. I searched but could not find the cave opening.*
>
> *The great stone heads looked down upon me, their great eyes burrowing into my mind. They seemed to tell me that I was not welcome here and should leave. But why? Did not this land originally belong to my ancestors? Why should I be made to think that I must leave? Still, I did so.*
>
> *As a young man at Pine Ridge, I heard stories how gold had been discovered in the He Sapa – how many thousands of Whites had invaded our sacred land to search for the yellow metal. Gold meant something to the Whites – something economic. To the Lakota, gold meant the color of nature. When boys become men, or a girl becomes*

a woman, they offer flakes of gold to Nagi Tanka – our Great Spirit – and in turn receive blessings.

But the outsiders came by the thousands and more thousands and the land suffered. When I passed through their settlement of Deadwood, all I could see were the looted remains of tourist shops, saloons, or hotels – no living persons. The Epidemic had carried them all off to their individual spirit worlds.

The White Man's word, Deadwood, is interesting. As I walked alone along the streets, dead wood was everywhere; cottonwood trees had shed their branches in sorrow, pine plank sidings of various shops structures had fallen into the street. Even the sign at the entrance to the settlement – DEADWOOD – Population 1,458 – Drive Carefully – had fallen into a culvert along the wayside.

I walked eastward out of Deadwood towards Sturgis – once the August rendezvous site for motorcyclists that attracted over 400,000 persons each solar cycle. Then the Ripple Event erupted in Sturgis; no accommodations, no communications, no gasoline. There was so little food that within 10 days after the Ripple hit, only 12 people were living in the whole community. The others had died or left for destinations unknown. Up and down the streets of Sturgis thousands of unusable motorcycles were parked. At the repair shops literally hundreds of thousands of metal scrap machine parts remained.

As I left Sturgis, warning shots were fired at me – first over my head and the second shot about a meter-yard into the dirt in front of me. Leaving quickly I continued southeast towards Rapid City – a settlement that I bypassed previously – then followed old Eye 8-0. I existed on water supplies available at abandoned gasoline stations that had been converted during the Dark Time to personal travel stations, the famous PTS locations. Each of these had adjacent water wells that could meet the needs of wanderers like me.

You Whites call the next location Wall – not The Wall, just Wall. Our name for this location is Makhosica Aglagla Othunwahe – or in your language, Town alongside the Badlands. This strange site consists of an unusual general store located in the middle of the plains. I remember my mother and father taking me, my brothers, and sisters to visit. What I remember most? I remember the white and red colored peppermint candy sticks and the machines outside the store entrance that children could ride – mechanical horses and even something called an airplane. I remember, too, some talk about a movie made in the region where part was filmed nearby up on the plains plateau, where buffalo herds were kept by White ranchers ... something about Wolves of this or that (??) – I just don't remember the name of the movie. Why would White ranchers raise herds of our sacred tatankas? They continue to use the strange word, buffalo – which means nothing to me or to my family members.

All this was very long ago; different times, different places long before the sickness.

***

Random Notes

I conclude this evening's presentation with several notes from my diary written during this early portion of our journey. The selections cover different activities and observations and reveal more about who we are as *Returners:*

Travis and I constantly scanned the horizon and sky looking for weather and animal-related signs and attempting to interpret them. We marveled at the great wing-spanned eagles passing overhead, and when they circled and dived downward to capture their food – we marveled at their success, how they held fish and small earth-bound game in their talons, even striking and grasping ducks in flight.

***

On occasion, as when our supply of meat and wild fruits or vegetables became low, we sought out the earthen mounds produced by small creatures such as ants. We sifted through the detritus that formed the larger anthills and collected the cereal grains that we could cook for snacks when we were hungry. The large black ants that populated the riverbanks or high prairie terraces could be gathered, mashed, and eaten. They had a tart flavor, not unlike the red and green peppers we once cultivated in our gardens at Bison Camp settlement group. Travis avoided the larger beetles as food; I found their taste curious but interesting. At other times, we scoured the riverbank backwaters for the hopping creatures. When skinned, skewered, and roasted, they provided meat that lasted us several days. Once we encountered a pit of rattlesnakes. It had been very cold that morning. The snakes scarcely moved and could not easily strike. I remember on this day that we used our long knives and sticks to separate four of the larger rattlesnakes from the entangled mass of reptiles. We decapitated the snakes gutted, and roasted them for dinner. We dined well that night.

***

We rarely saw vultures circling overhead nearby. When sighted, however, we always rode over to inspect what had died. On several occasions we found the fresh remains of a buck, doe, or faun that only recently had been killed. Upon our approach the vultures flew off, but continued to circle overhead. If the kill was fresh, we concentrated our butchering efforts on non-spoiled parts, those without maggots. Commonly, such sites would be leg portions. As children, both Travis and I had learned to judge the relative quality of meat from animal kills encountered in the wild. We also learned which leaves from local plants native to the Big Hole Valley were cleansing, in that they imparted a sweet smell/taste during roasting to the meat from such kills. Other people we knew at Bison Camp would not touch such foods, saying that game killed by wild animals was contaminated, against the rules of this or that former god, or some other excuse. But throughout our childhood teachings, we never heard that Etowah [may its name always be blessed] commanded us to avoid such.

***

Throughout our childhood at Bison Camp, we had been trained to recognize the sounds of nature, how the calls of different animals revealed locations that facilitated their capture. We learned to differentiate how the sounds changed during different times of the day or night, how the morning calls of animals welcomed the sunrise, and evening cries and sounds settled over the land in preparation for sleep. The nature sounds we liked and treasured included:

Raindrops falling in pools along the river lulling us to sleep;

Babbling sounds of the Missouri River lapping along the shoreline;

Cries from small birds;

Whippoorwills – bringing memories of home;
Loons – plaintive cries like lost children;
Doves – lilting sounds bringing joy in the early morning;
Owls – haunting but welcome sounds at night;
Yapping and baying of coyote females calling their young;
Resounding cracks of deer or elk horns as males fought for dominance;
Croaking of small frogs at mid-day;
Humming of cicadas throughout the day;
Baying of coyotes welcoming moonrise; and
Piercing sweet sounds of unknown beasts as they mated at night.

Other sounds of nature, in contrast, put us on alert:

Wolves snarling as they circled our campfire;
Grunts and growls of large black bears disturbed as we passed by;
Screams when one animal was killed by another – followed by the sounds of silence.

***

An unexpected surprise ... Nearing Omaha and the junction with the Platte River, we came across an abandoned cache of food and personal belongings. The items had been left inside what we in the Big Hole Valley once called a Chevy-Kart. These Karts made from old automobiles once were treasured prior to the Ripple Event. The best Chevy-Karts were cut-down, leaving the front grill intact with a lockable cab where goods could be stored or transported. Such karts were hauled by a two-horse or two-mule team. The Chevy-Kart we found was filled with dried meats, and sealed boxes that contained many pounds of dried fruits, vegetables, and ground wheat and corn meal. Appended to the exterior of the kart was the following note:

Take and use –

– We are dead and have no use for the food

– Take what you need – leave some for others

– Have a good life if possible

– Treat people with respect – only if they deserve respect

– Kill those who would harm your sons or daughters

– Exalt the name of Etowah
– Respect the Earth!

***

During recent nights as I prepared for sleep, I sometimes sensed the form of a man standing (?) or lurking (?) at the edge of the campfire halo, a strange man-shape unknown to me. He wears a curious hat, something like those worn by jesters in times long past. He carries something that resembles a musical instrument, but I cannot be certain. Sometimes he appears like an ancient troubadour or traveling minstrel; other times his appearance is vague. I cannot determine whether or not my vision is real. If real, why does he always remain outside the halo of campfire light? If real, what does he want, since he does not speak? If unreal what does my vision signify? Why does this vision never appear to Travis?

***

Saint Louis and the Mississippi River

We both felt remarkable relief about reaching our mid-journey destination. We had traveled the length of the Missouri River, a difficult decision that was not our initial choice. Out of necessity, we were forced northward out of the Yellowstone basin into the small settlement of Three Forks, where the three rivers formed the headwaters of the Missouri River. Once the decision had been taken not to attempt the river by float barge, but to make the journey on horseback tracing the river course, we embarked on a personal trip of discovery.

We learned that the terrible Epidemic had not completely blanketed the Flatland Configuration. We encountered locations here and there where survivors continued to eke out their existence in their attempts to recover from this terrible event. Our faith in the overall goodness of humans, too, was bolstered through our encounters along the way. Oft times we were befriended by strangers and made welcome.

Travis and I grew closer as a couple during our Missouri River ride. The child-loss pain I suffered early on eased after Shaman Franklin lightened my burden. Wintering-over in the Missouri Breaks taught us both additional skills for self-reliance and independence. We came to realize that not only we would survive and continue onward to complete the second, third, and final legs of our journey, but that we could do so with personal and mental strength. All in all, we were made stronger as individuals and as a couple through the rigors and hardships of our journey.

We stood along a river terrace just south of the great confluence, and paused to enjoy the scene where the Missouri joined the Mississippi. At this point their waters mixed and flowed to the sea. We gazed and marveled at the breadth of the Great River, the Mississippi, but what attracted our attention immediately was the astonishing memorial arch that reached upward into the sky.

After-Word

Were we the first travelers from the New NorthWest Configuration to reach the Mississippi River? We could not be certain, but we certainly felt like explorers as in olden days. Along both the western and eastern river shores were anchored large boats that once plied the waterway up and down river – transporters filled with goods reflective of a vibrant trade between the eastern Flatland and New Confederate Configurations. We had reached the Great River; we were well and we had each other.

***

Ijano Esantu Eleman

Interlude-Conversation: 2

River Flow

***

Those GA-RFA groups made quite an impact on the landscape, did they not?

For true, A'Tena, and like such inspired people some believed their actions were for the better good, others acted out of mixed feelings, and still others destroyed the water barriers for no reason other than they liked to destroy objects.

Is the word destroy or change?

The answer to your question depends upon the perspective. Yes, such events could be changed if I so chose to do so, but I do not. To me it is easier to see positive results when change occurs rather than dwell on negatives. It is for true, A'Tena, that sometimes results have harsh impacts on the residents. I understand it is your nature to see all, however, my nature is to be judgmental.

So I have seen and experienced your nature in an unbiased way, I might add.

So, again, I chose not to intervene, adjust, or whatever else you might call such actions. Not all that came about during the Ripple and Dark Times was of my making, indeed very little. The ability of those GA-RFA fanatics to effect matters faded rapidly during the Dark Times.

So what about the here and now?

In the here and now certain rules have been restored, for example the rule of flowing water. Mountains are eroded by flowing water, sediment fills the lowlands, reservoirs behind dams fill with sediment and the once proud structures no longer function. The powers of flowing water are wondrous to see and understand. Note that flowing waters cannot and will not be controlled.

I do not fully comprehend your comments, but for here and now the flowing waters are open to facilitate travel and commerce, matters of no small significance.

To be for true, A'Tena, and another good example is salt.

Salt? What do you mean?

Trade in salt as an economic commodity moves along the flow of great central rivers. The salt flow preserves food and enhances economics of all concerned.

Once more, K'Aser, your standing aside and not becoming involved was both fitting and proper. Not all Overseers would have done so. They could learn much from you.

Not that even a few ever have sought my suggestions.

Chapter 3

Three Rivers and Overland: Saint Louis to South Bend

Pre-Note

What a remarkable morning. Early after sunrise, Travis led his horse and crested a small hill not more than 100 meter-yards in elevation. He paused at the top and shouted back to me. His words were a blend of excitement and joy. I joined him and below was a wonderful vista where the Missouri and Mississippi Rivers joined. From atop the rise, we gazed southward where off in the near distance the great arch rose among the ruins of old Saint Louis.

Continuing on, we rested our horses on the outskirts of Saint Louis at a location that once had served as a farrier/livery stable. No one was visible, and there was no evidence that the facility had been utilized for many months. The horse stalls were musty with the smell of moldy hay. Inside the livery area, we located six hay bales that tested all right without odor. We hobbled our horses, fed them, and rested. How far had we trekked and ridden during past months? We had no way to measure distances accurately. Most of the signs used previously to document kilo-miles from one location to another had been destroyed or salvaged for their metal. But for us distance did not matter: we had arrived at a key destination of our overland journey.

Saint Louis and River South

After two days of R&R we continued south through what once had been an urban jewel of architectural history. Along the western shore of the Great River were parklands that once rang with the sounds and songs of childhood play; the soft words spoken by young couples walking and speaking terms of endearment; elderly men and women seated on benches gazing out across the green expanse towards several moored river boats now silent, their great stern wheels no longer rotating. Still readable were the clapboard signs attached to the river boat super structures, advertisements for casinos, restaurants, and travel opportunities for down-river exploration.

Amid all of this there were no signs of human life. Packs of dogs roamed nearby, seemingly cautious to approach us perhaps because we were astride our horses with our pack mules behind. Perhaps it was not caution they exhibited, but the fact that they already were well fed. Throughout our ride through the city ruins, we saw no evidence of bodies.

We approached the great arch. According to our history teachers at Bison Camp, many solar cycles earlier the monument had been erected to commemorate the westward movement of pioneer families who left the eastern portion of the continent to find new homes in old California, or the region known then as Northwest Territory. This gateway arch to the new lands rose high above us as we marveled at its construction. An inscription at the base read:

The Gateway Arch – Dedicated to the people of the United States

The date given for construction was 1968 (old calculation). It was difficult to imagine how the arch had been erected, and we agreed that such a monument could not be duplicated in the present days of uncertainty and trial.

Inside the north stanchion of the arch, we found an abandoned box, obviously left behind on the ground to honor the site. Inside were votive candles dedicated to Our Lady of Guadalupe, objects to be illuminated on December 12th (old calendar system). There also were crosses, icons, and religious images; even manuscript pages covered with sacred symbols. Why would the arch attract the faithful of such different religions? Was there something about the structure rising upwards towards the heavens, as in a heart-lifting plea for protection during the Epidemic? One manuscript page inside the box attracted my attention, a hand-written piece penned by an unnamed young girl who had left behind a thoughtful and poignant message:

In my sadness I sing to you
I offer prayers to help all people

Please heal my mother, father, brothers
May the illness among us pass
Carried away like leaves that fall
Into the Great River.

In my sadness I sing to you
It is not too much to ask
Please heal my mother, father, brothers
So many have been taken
Carried away like leaves that fall
Into the Great River

Please hear my words.

Two bridges over the Great River remained, but no traffic crossed the spans. We could see tall buildings along the river's east shore, large signs visible advertising repair shops, food distribution centers, educational sites, and what probably was a carpenter's haven as the street in front of the building was filled with stacks of logs and cut timbers apparently for household construction.

As we continued southward only a few large paddle-wheel boats remained moored along the western shoreline. We would later learn from interviews with survivors of battles with the Northlanders that when the Epidemic reached St. Louis, those with trade or barter goods and persons with political connections jammed aboard the boats with their families. The rich initially escaped the Epidemic by going southward down-river to unknown destinations. Whether or not they survived could not be answered. It was hard for us to envision the chaos of those last days along the Saint Louis waterfront. May Etowah grant those who fled find quiet rest in the unknown island lands off shore within the great Southern Sea.

Several hundred solar cycles earlier, great boats such as these had traveled back and forth along this river, facilitating trade in commercial goods, especially foodstuffs, equipment, and salt. Major stops along the river included ports too numerous to list and repeat here. At the present time there appeared to be no trade at the wharfs where we stood gazing out over the empty placid waters. Storage buildings and sheds were unattended. The only evidence of other life forms were the rats scurrying here and there at our approach. They seemed to be the territorial possessors of these abandoned river stations.

Who heard it first, was it Travis or I? The sound was that of a riverboat horn. The boat appeared off in the far distance, churning northward towards Saint Louis.

There was life on the river!

We hailed the ship as it approached and, in turn, received acknowledgment of three high-pitched horn blasts. Our first assessment about St. Louis had been wrong: there indeed was trade – or at least contact between the city and points south. The river ship that approached was the *Aurora Inferus* or *Southern Light*. The captain, a young military officer dressed in a uniform that we did not recognize, did not initially welcome us aboard. Captain Forest O'Malley commanded a crew of five men and two women, also decked in military uniforms. Once ashore, he and his crew approached us cautiously, not knowing whether or not we might represent an ambush threat or possibly could be infected carriers of different diseases. As the captain later told us, we appeared hale and hearty and thus his fears lessened, and therefore we were invited to join in conversation over a shared repast of what he called "boat food" – a rather meager meal composed of various vittles that included dried fish, re-constituted dried apples, and what the captain said was Mississippi Tea – a brew of unusual and undefined flavors that most likely contained an added fermented or distilled product.

After dining, Captain O'Malley sent his crew to forage through the city ruins to collect items identified on what he called his Select List. This was a document issued prior to each trip by military headquarters at the port of old Cairo, now spelled and pronounced Kai-Row, located at the juncture of the Mississippi and Ohio Rivers. On his current northern salvage trip, the captain and his team had been instructed to locate sheets of galvanized metal roofing and kegs of carpenter's nails, especially small brads and large types that once were called 10-penny for a reason none of us recognized. Also on the list was the scribbled notation with his commanding officer's name (illegible) to collect and bag as many aluminum cans as could be found.

Captain O'Malley enquired about our previous travels and our future destinations. He seemed a bit awed that a man and woman traveling together without additional protection and support could have survived a trek from Three Forks, a location he had heard of, and then could have made their way down the Missouri River all the way to Saint Louis without being killed by animals or predatory Wanderer groups. Travis smiled at O'Malley's assertion, and simply replied – *Ijano Esantu Eleman*. I laughed when the captain did not comprehend the three words.

After ten days spent collecting the listed materials, the *Aurora Inferus* was ready for the return trip to Kai-Row. We requested passage for ourselves and for our horses and pack animals, which Captain O'Malley graciously granted. The float downriver to our destination was uneventful. We hugged the eastern shoreline as we passed by the settlement of Festus then approached the ruins of Chester. We changed river course several kilo-miles later, and moved into a mid-channel float. Continuing south, we changed course again and steered close to the western shore as we approached and passed the port of old Cape Girardeau. Next, we reached the Great River bend – mentioned during long-ago times in both song and poetry. We entered the first loop and followed the channel arc back northward, then drifted through the eastern bend and the immediate southern turn. Exiting the Great River bend as it was called, we continued on until we approached the junction with the Ohio River and the settlement once named after that grand city in far off Africa.

Kai-Row

The *Aurora Inferus* slipped past Stevenson Bayou where the Mississippi River split into two channels. We entered the narrows between the mainland and Angelo Towhead Island. Captain O'Malley steered east and then immediately northwest, as we entered the main channel of the Ohio River at the land point dominated by the ruins of old Fort Defiance. The initial meter-yards of passage up the Ohio River took us past the area known as Da'hat Kai-Row, or Lower Kai-Row. We then slowed as we neared the commercial dock area that fronted Ohio Street.

In sharp contrast with Saint Louis, the dock area lining Ohio Street was alive and bustling with human activity. Here were hundreds of survivors of the Epidemic. We gazed upon streets filled with merchants and soldiers. Numerous children played about, dodging in out, chasing each other around the horse-drawn carts and wagons moving goods up and down the street.

Captain O'Malley levered the *Aurora Inferus* into quay number 16A, where stevedores tossed up mooring lines allowing us to secure our ship. During the next six hours, crew members unloaded the salvage cargo onto pallets. These wooden carrying cases then were loaded onto carts and disappeared down Ohio Street to destinations unknown, probably for use by local carpenters, masons, and others who needed materials for building reconstruction and town improvement.

Travis assisted crew members of the *Aurora Inferus* while I stood on deck watching all these activities unfold. Docked immediately next to our ship was what appeared to be a military transport ship. I was informed that their cargo consisted of corpses, soldiers who had died at different battlefield sites in north central old Ohio. They were being transported south to Kai-Row for burial with honors at a vast cemetery north of the town opposite Union Street. Other ships docked along the waterfront bore unusual colored markings. One of the female crew members of the *Aurora Inferus* told me that use of distinctive colors was warranted so that allied shipping would not be mistaken for potential enemy transports and fired upon.

Who is the enemy, I asked?

> *Miss Reese, surely you have heard of the Northlanders and their continued quest for regional domination? Evil peoples, these Northlanders. They demand from each person and family full compliance with their economic, political, and religious views. They give only death for those who do not agree.*

What was she talking about? She continued:

> *Others in town at the several camps can tell you about the Northlanders, Miss Reese. Let me inform you regarding ship color markings.*
>
> ***Orange:*** *these are prisoner ships. Captives taken after the Battle of South Bend initially were held in stockades. Later they were transported overland and down the Ohio River to the decision point here at Kai-Row. All such prisoners ultimately will be deported. Once here, they are interrogated again and a decision is made: life or execution. If the decision is life, the prisoners have but two choices: transportation north into the cold, unhospitable lands of old French Canada, or south into the warm and humid stretches of the Southern Sea, where they may or may not find acceptance on a*

secluded survivor island – or simply remain adrift. If execution, have someone else describe this for you (not me).

White and Blue: *these are salt trading ships with regular schedules up and down the Ohio River and south along the Mississippi reaching the restored settlement of old New Orleans. At various locations along the southern coastline salt-brine pits have been worked for many solar cycles, and the salt product produced through hard labor provides wealth and income to these salt miners. We also receive shipments of salt from the mid-continental Configuration known as New Deseret. Their salt is in greatest demand for its high quality and purity.*

Brown and Green: *these are military transport ships showing regional colors of New Confederacy and Texas Across the River (TAR) Confederations. These are used to transport military goods, survival rations, and carry military units to select locations. The B&Gs as we call them are especially important these days as they patrol along the central and eastern reaches of the Ohio River.*

Red: *These colored ships easily can be seen from afar and indicate cargoes of field produce and processed foods for market distribution at ports along the Ohio and Great River.*

After her interesting account, I tended to our horses and pack animals then disembarked for a walking tour of Kai-Row. As most of the unloading already had been completed, I was accompanied by *Aurora Inferus* crew member, Private Anna Campbell, who had been birthed and raised at Kai-Row. She had not only survived the Epidemic but also had experienced the terrors caused by the Northlanders, and lived through the influx of refugees and wounded that poured into her town during military clashes.

Kai-Row was a community of modest size, laid out geographically in a north/south-east/west grid. Campbell identified the key town administrative and medical centers, the latter constructed quickly as required by the extraordinary influx of wounded. Between Elm Street and Highlander Avenue, north of 33nd street, she showed me two different sets of holding camps filled with tents, and each surrounded by barbed wire. The better of the two camps contained more than 300 individuals and families, refugees from the recent Battle of South Bend. The second camp, seeped in squalor with ponds of muddy water and latrine filth, had been erected quickly and with little care to hold Northlanders captured at the earlier battle at Paducah and the subsequent attacks on South Bend.

Campbell scowled as she spoke of the evil Northlanders who forced their ways upon good people living in what she called the Wild Zone – a geographical area east of the Mississippi River, north of the Ohio River, and bounded at the far north by the Great Five Lakes. There was no sense of "live-and-let-live" inside this Wild Zone. Northlanders with extreme views forced their way into settlement groups and demanded compliance with their ideologies – their battle cry resounded over the land, bring fear to all good and kind people. They shouted out: *A-D* – A-D time and time again – two simple letters that brought fear to most not associated with Northlander culture: *Accept or Die!* There was no room for tolerance in Northlander culture.

I asked Campbell if we might secure permission to interview several individuals, perhaps a Northlander as well as displaced refugees, or possibly a medic who had worked among the wounded soldiers. She accommodated my request.

Prisoner Detention Center – Building 5-D
Meeting with Northlander, Amos Steel

> *I speak because the section guard forced me to appear before you – I could care less about what you want. Since I am forced to, I will speak briefly. At the battle you call South Bend, my unit was covered by a great mist and we were unable to advance. We were surrounded and taken prisoner by a group of unrepentant non-believers who told us we would be transported to Kai-Row and imprisoned. They said we would be interrogated there for an unspecified period of time and then our captors would make a decision. We would have two choices: in both instances we would be removed from our lands and family roots forever. One choice would be transportation by riverboat north into unknown lands beyond the Great Five Lakes. The second, also removal from our lands and family roots forever, would be transportation by riverboat south along the Great River to the western edge of what you call the New Confederacy and what we call Land of Greatest Evil. With this choice, we would be forbidden to touch shore under penalty of death and, ultimately, we would exit into the Great Sea, where we may or may not find an island upon which to re-settle. If not, or if we were repelled by local island militias, then we would be forced to live out the remainder of our days either aboard the transport boat – or die. The choices did not make any difference to our captors or interrogators.*

Our culture and religion were demeaned by people like you. As captives, we were beaten and told that we should take our "twisted ideologies" either north or south into the unknown, that the decision depended mainly on whether each of us preferred warmth or cold. I remember the last words of the interrogator – we are glad to be rid of you and your kind!

As I listened to Amos Steel's words, I felt a sense of cold. He was unlike any person I had met previously, certainly not like any we encountered who had survived the Ripple Event and Dark Time. There was a sense of ideological superiority in his demeanor and words, something that characterized his Northlander being:

Reese: *To the outside world your culture, politics, and religion seem rigid and without variation. You force your beliefs upon others, presenting only two options – accept or death. You claim there is but one way to live, and that is life only by your Northlander credo. By your own words, you exhibit intolerance towards others and your dogma of accept or death reveals lack of compassion and a cultural-religious rigidity like no other.*

Steel: *Do not tempt me to leap over this table and strike you silly. You condemn Northlander culture, politics, and religion, but what do you and your kind have to offer as an alternative? Has your culture always fostered compassion, forgiveness, and tolerance? How many deaths were the result of wars you implemented centuries before the Ripple Event and Dark Time? Who are you standing there so aloof with your own self-importance – to accuse me and my Northlander countrymen of being evil, and without compassion and tolerance? What have you shown us in turn, when in the past you rained death down upon our wives and children wantonly? And when we attacked your settlements, how dare you thrust words at us pleading for your lives – your lives of evil. Is it not said an eye-for-an-eye? Yes, many of you we executed simply and quickly – on the spot as you like to say. Other times slow and exacting methods were chosen to demonstrate to you the seriousness of our intent. But at*

> *other times as well we spared your ilk, where some were allowed to live among us, provided that you entered into a new mind frame and adopted a new type of life – one that mirrored ours.*
> *So it is that you think you have won – that your so-called battle of South Bend is an event that you hale and proclaim as a great victory. Yes, we have lost one battle, but we have not lost the war. Time is on our side. We Northlanders ultimately will claim regional and continental victory as we spread the true word and gather followers into our fold, even if it takes more than a 1,000 solar cycles to come.*

I pondered his words and thought to myself how many more must die in the meantime through Northlander attacks and the potential expansion of their cultural and religious pontification? It seemed to me that 20th-century philosophers and culturists erred when they said peoples of the world are alike with the same needs and joys. Their statements certainly were naïve and untrue.

***

Refugee Relief Center – Building 2-A
Meeting with Northerner, Alice Martin

Campbell spoke with the building matron, and we entered the women's partition with permission. I paused for a moment still stunned after our meeting with Amos Steel. Campbell said that not all who lived within the Wild Zone north of the Ohio River were Northlanders, as the term applied only to the rigid cultists. All others living within this geographical region were referred to as Northerners.

Greeting us inside the Refugee Relief Center was Alice Martin. She was a Northerner refugee from old Chicago who, along with her family, had been forced by Northlander cultists to vacate the family residence on LaSalle Street. During the forced eviction, she was separated from her husband, Dale, and their two children by arms-bearing thugs and never seen again. Alice has weathered this terrible trauma and ultimately found shelter and safety in Kai-Row. She agreed to speak to us so that we would a better understand the Chicago political divisions and geographical territories claimed by different sects, especially during the Dark Time recovery period on the eve of the Epidemic.

During the Dark Time we suffered greatly, since our residence was on the boundary line between two competing political groups: Northlander Radicals, or NRs as they were called back then, and the Mediterranean Ethnics, or MEs, composed primarily of 2nd-, 3rd-, and 4th-generation Greek-Americans. The Northlander Radicals primarily occupied the eastern zone of old Chicago within an area bounded by the river waterways and the west shore of what we called Great Lake One, perhaps better known to outsiders by its pre-Ripple Event name, Lake Erie. The ME territory centered near the intersection of South Halsted and West Van Buren Streets. It was here that the NRs wished to expand their territorial sway. Little did we know that we residents would become pawns in their terrible territorial battle.

Prior to the days of pain and suffering that followed, I remember when the residents of old Chicago struggled during the Ripple Event and Dark Times. My family had few personal effects, and most families like ours sought to locate temporary housing. Still, in the quiet solitude of early spring evenings we sometimes gathered together in Grant Park near the Buckingham Fountain. These events, called trio gatherings, were held in the early evening and consisted of dueling musicians. My favorites were the three trumpeters: Jose Mendez, with his unique mariachi style and unusual melodic version of the plaintive solo known as the Virgin de la Macarena; Isaac Benson, my favorite Black trumpeter, entertaining us in the style of the pre-Dark Time soloist, Wynton Marsalis; and Jake "Flutter-Note" Sawyer, an exceptional musician who could fashion triplets of sound far above high C with ease and delight.

As the musicians assembled near the fountain, large crowds gathered. Those in the audience who had extra food brought cans and packages, sometimes even fresh items. As the different style melodies echoed out across the lakefront, those with food placed the items in front of the trumpeter they liked best to honor his performance. Towards the end of the concert, the audience always shouted for more, and the three musicians always replied by playing the same haunting piece with notes that struck the hearts and souls of each of us in the audience recalling memories of better times when life was good before the Ripple Event and Dark Time. It seemed as if their trio melody struck nostalgic notes that impacted us deeply, an instrumental song of survival that was uplifting and played out along the western shore of Great Lake One. As the trumpet notes rang out, we in the audience in near unison almost at once would break into song – our plaintive cries for peace and justice in old Chicago echoing across the landscape. Please – I am nearly lost in my memories: let me stop for a moment to catch my breath.

I remember a few lines from that song. As I relate the words to you, please record them in your diary and as you write look into my eyes. Doing so you will see how homesick and sorrowful I am for our once great city. I seem to recall that the name of the song played by the trumpeters was called Lake Side Serenade:

> *Remember when we walked this shore,*
> *Wind blowing lightly through your hair,*
> *We paused to view the sunset rare,*
> *City sounds we loved – no more.*
>
> *Fireflies would light our way,*
> *Along life's path together now,*
> *Two hearts as one on knee I bow,*
> *Your hand in mine this eve of May.*
>
> *Will you my love forever be,*
> *Together raise a family,*
> *Your beauty rare I'll always see,*
> *Unlock my heart, you have the key.*

Sorry, I can't go on ... reciting the lyrics is too painful.

How I hate what the Northlanders did to us, and how they destroyed our city. What I have heard recently is that with victory over their evil at the Battle of South Bend, some of the most radical elements already have been shipped northward into the distant lands of cold and ice. May they freeze and forever leave us in peace to act, speak, and worship as we please. Be gone! No more will they be permitted to force their way of life and belief system upon us. Be gone – forever!

***

Refugee Relief Center – Building 2-A
Meeting with Northerner, Michael Stanton

Building 2-A also housed living quarters for adult males. Campbell previously had identified refugees who had personal experiences with the Northlanders during the period prior to the battles at Paducah and South Bend. One of these was Michael Stanton, a trained hydrologist and survivor of the Northlander attack on his settlement group, Shawnee Forest:

Thank you for visiting our camp. As an outsider guest, I seek your help and ask that you assist in reuniting me with my wives and children. When Shawnee Forest was attacked by Northlanders, we withstood their initial and repeated advances for more than nine days. On the morning of the 10th siege day, the Northlanders broke through our defenses. A group of Northlanders separated from the main band, taking with them our wives and girl children. Elderly residents and teenage boys were herded into the communal meeting hall where they were held for three days without food or water. At the end of the third day, all hall exits and entries were blocked and the building set alight. May you, Reese, never be exposed to or hear the terrible sounds like those coming from people trapped inside.

The same morning, we adult men were led outside the settlement and paraded across the adjacent grassland. We in this group numbered more than 70 men and older boys. The Northlander squad forced each of us to dig holes that would hold the vertical execution stakes. We knew at once the horror that was to be visited upon us: we were to be impaled using the Northlander traditional execution system of Khazouk. We were tethered in a long line standing before the Khazouk stakes and the Northlanders laughed almost in unison and began their death chant – död till icketroende – louder and louder – död till icketroende!

And so it was that the tethers were removed from the first five men and two older boys in line. One by one each was roughly handled and carried quickly to the line of stakes. During the struggle each victim was lifted, their legs separated, and one by one dropped onto the stakes – their screams unbearable, rising above the Northlander death chant – död till icketroende – död till icketroende – död till icketroende! These horrible sounds echoed across the landscape.

We who were still tethered and awaiting death also screamed, as we prayed for intervention from the horrors of Khazouk.

When interviewed later none of us could explain what happened, for it was by a miracle that we were saved. As the next line of prisoners were led towards the death stakes there suddenly appeared members of the 65th unit of the 3rd New Confederacy Militia. They had crossed the Ohio River following northward on the tracks of Northlander raiders. Quickly they engaged the execution squad, launched their projectile explosives, and loosed their dogs of war. The confused Northlanders fled this place of execution, leaving us survivors behind – shaken, fearful, and in desolation. We could do nothing to alleviate the suffering of our five comrades already bearing the pain and slow death of Khazouk. No doctor or nurse could repair the impalement wounds. Out of compassion, we agreed with their wishes and executed each with dignity to eliminate their pain.

We had been torn from our settlement homes but still were not free. We were held captive by militia interrogators, wanting to be certain that our culture and religious sect was not in a secret alliance with any Northlander elements. After two days of interrogation, we were allowed to return to our settlement and enter our homes to retrieve whatever valuables might have remained. Following this, we were re-assembled and marched as a group south towards the Ohio River. Along the way, we scrounged for food each day. Although we were thirsty, we avoided ponds contaminated with sewage and/or human or animal corpses. Occasionally we snared small rodents for food.

In time we reached the river port of Metropolis, where we ultimately were loaded onto an empty troop ship heading downriver to Kai-Row. Reaching the port, we were housed, fed, and further interrogated – but treated with dignity. One Northlander spy was found among our group and forced out – it did not go well for him.

I must tell you, although the lives of most of the adult men and older boys were saved, our wives and younger children have remained captive, and we have little hope for their recovery and reuniting. Please note that I have remained in the Kai-Row refugee camp now for nine solar cycles. I have chosen to stay and work to help new refugees that have been housed here since the Battle of South Bend. I have nowhere else to go. In my heart, I remain with the hope that our wives and children are alive and safe, but the reality is that this merely may be a dream that I hold dear.

***

From Kai-Row to Paducah

In the week that followed, Travis and I bid farewell to our friends, the captain and crew of the *Aurora Inferus.* Captain O'Malley coordinated our departure up the Ohio River and arranged transport for us and our steeds aboard the *Kentucky Challenger*, a ship plying the river course with various stops to unload and transport passengers at the small river ports of Mound City, Olmsted, Joppa, Metropolis, and Brooksport before reaching the key regional center of Paducah at the junction of the Ohio and Tennessee Rivers. Please note that the name Tennessee River commonly appears on navigation and land charts in shorthand designation as 10-S-C.

Private Anna Campbell, who had been such a help facilitating our interviews at the Kai-Row prison facility and refugee relief center, had a sister who was a nurse serving at the military clinic in Paducah. Bess Campbell greeted us upon our arrival. She looked considerably older than Anna, but in reality they were birthed just two solar cycles apart. The lines etched on Miss Campbell's face foretold of inner demons and the daily pain of nursing the badly wounded soldiers from two encounters – almost 12 solar cycles apart – the battle of Paducah and the more recent hostilities at South Bend.

Nurse Campbell admired our steeds, the intricate leatherwork on our saddles, and the metal ornaments on the reins of our horses. She told us that she had seen work of similar quality on the mounts of cavalry officers serving in the New Confederacy Militia. She described her duties and the types of injuries suffered by both civilian and military combatants, and recalled that the survival rates of the wounded rose or declined sharply whether or not medical supplies could be located. She said that the wise women or sage femmes from nearby settlement groups assisted, and used their knowledge of medicinal plants and infusion preparations to relieve pain and suffering. Sometimes they applied different types of honey to seal wounds, a technique that often limited infections.

Bess expanded upon her descriptions of hospital care during the battle of Paducah.

> *The attending physicians and nurses treated a broad range of arrow wounds and saber cuts; especially vicious were injuries received through mass archery launches and close hand-to-hand encounters. We observed something horrible for the first time, as Northlanders ordered selected children and elderly women beyond*

child-bearing solar cycles to rush our lines using human wave tactics. Northlanders who survived the battle told our interrogators that the children and elderly women were volunteers – that they accepted their role as a cultural duty and social responsibility. Their explosive suicide vests were filled with nails, screws, and fecal pellets – the latter ingredient added to assure lethal infections if any of our defenders long the periphery of the blasts received only what seemed at the time to be minor wounds. Most of the injuries we treated were cuts from lances, dirks, and occasional massive contusions caused by hammer or mace. Our wounded languished through their pain. We had no facilities for blood transfusions, which would have been common support methods prior to the Ripple Event. Survival rates varied considerably, based upon availability of medicines, generally between 5-15 percent depending upon wound type. As we in the nursing cadre used to say:

The smell of battle knows no name –

To friend – to foe – death smells the same.

Travis expressed interest in learning more about the history of Paducah, especially the early cross-river raids by Northlanders during the Dark Time Recovery Period. After learning of his interest, Bess walked us to the home of Michael Simmons, a respected Memory Guild member who had left his settlement group to take up residence in Paducah on Norton Street just west of the Owens Island dock area.

Mr. Simmons met us on the veranda of his home that overlooked the Ohio River. The scene was placid, quiet, and inviting in the late afternoon gloaming. He served us tall glasses of an iced sun-fermented beverage, a specialty that he had brewed just that noontime. We clinked our glasses and together sipped his specialty drink. I sensed that mine tasted as if something stronger had been added, perhaps to augment or accentuate the flavor.

Simmons leaned back in his rocking chair, gazed out over the Ohio River and spoke… "So you want to know about the Northlanders? An evil group they!"

As you may know, Travis and Reese, the beautiful Ohio always has been a geographical line – an artery for trade and exploration, a passage for military adventurers, and boundary between the old

North and old South. Still today these dark flowing waters continue to protect us from Northlander evil.

Not long ago, only 15 solar cycles past, probing groups of Northlanders thought that if they crossed the Ohio River they would have a rapid advance southward through the flat agricultural lands and settlement groups that characterized our region, a passage that when successful, would allow their forces to sweep east towards their goal of old Nashville. It turned out there were five initial probes where Northlanders crossed the Ohio, all of these ventures took place several kilo-miles west of Paducah, and each was thwarted. Then came time when a more directed probe was launched. The Northlander's plan was to bypass settlement groups located near Mayfield, Murray, and Paris, and establish a military redoubt and arms cache near Camden, before crossing the Tennessee River at New Johnsonville. There, they would await the arrival of the main Northlander Militia, and together would wage a coordinated attack on old Nashville from the west.

Our scouts probing the hinterland near Mayfield learned of the Northlanders' plan after we captured several of their people. We encouraged them in different ways to tell all – something that you needn't include in the notes you are taking, Miss Reese! With strong additional encouragement, we learned how they planned to signal their support troops massed along the northern banks of the Ohio River as to the precise day and timing of the river crossing.

As you would have known if you were from this area, all this took place during the cold of winter months when the Ohio River had frozen, a timing that in the minds of the Northlanders was optimal for their initial forays and their main invasion. But we were ready. The Northlanders planned their river crossing within a concentrated zone between the ports of Joppa and Metropolis. With our advanced knowledge, we massed our fighters and militias behind berms on the south side of the Ohio, north of Ogden Landing and Anderson Roads, where we had stockpiled explosive packages that could be catapulted onto the ice.

Onward they came! The explosions shattered the ice, sending the advancing Northlanders to their death in the cold swirling Ohio waters. Northlander troops on the north shore ceased their advance and retreated into their Wild Zone. Approximately 35 or so Northlanders escaped drowning and slithered onto our Kentucky shore. These misfits and killers easily were captured and escorted under heavy guard down river to Kai-Row, where they were interrogated, ultimately placed aboard a prison ship, and sent south into oblivion beyond the mouth of the Great River.

This early defeat did not sit well with the Northlanders. Once again they attacked us. Let me think for a moment, this would have been about six solar cycles prior to onset of the Epidemic. This second attack was the worst ever in our region. I remember the events well. It was springtime and the ragweed pollen swirled in the air causing sneezing fits among some of our little ones and older folks as well. We in the vicinity of Paducah were caught off guard – as the saying goes – as the Northlanders initially overran our settlement. The Northlanders swept across the Ohio River in barges and landed to the west and east of Paducah proper. As it turned out, a group of border protectors and New Confederacy military units had encamped in this region along Highway 24, between Redland and Hendron. As justice would have it, the Northlanders met our troops in a desperate battle, one that ultimately determined the survival of our culture, history, and way of life.

News of the battle spread widely throughout the nearby settlement groups south and west of Paducah, and many marched north to join in repelling the Northlanders. Especially important to our defense and ultimate success was the participation of many Northerners who previously had fled Northlander persecution, and had found safety and comfort among our people. After our victory, the bodies of Northlanders killed at the Battle of Paducah were left to rot where they fell. This decision was made by the victorious combatants and meant to serve as a blunt warning for all to see. Many weapons were collected from the battlefield, but various others we left behind, scattered here and there. Perhaps you would like to visit the site if you have time? I believe there also is a battle report in the Paducah historical library, composed by one of the border protectors. I think his name was Oren Denevan. If I recall correctly, he mentions several innovative military techniques used during the defense of Paducah, one being the hurling of beehives at the advancing

Northlander invaders, another one was use of attack dogs that on command would lunge forward into the fray to attack the legs and bellies of the enemy. I also seem to remember that Denevan wrote something about the use of homing pigeons carrying encrypted messages on the legs of these delicate creatures. The messages contained information vital to defenders at our outposts.

If you like, I can escort the three of you to the primary battlefield site, as it lies not far from where we now are resting and relaxing with good company, drinking our sun-kissed beverages in the peace and quiet of our beloved homeland. Bess, remind me: was there not a song about the Ohio River that all of us used to sing during our younger years? Perhaps you remember?

Beautiful Ohio, in dreams again I see
Visions of what used to be.

***

We left Michael Simmons's shelter porch, and together walked the short distance to the central location that took the brunt of battle long ago when the Northlanders attempted to absorb this northern outpost of the New Confederacy Configuration.

The scene over the battlefield was peaceful, in sharp contrast to the five-day period when the best youth and adults of the New Confederacy fought and repelled the invaders who had crossed the Ohio River. The battlefield was readily apparent. Strewn across the slight undulating landscape were paper containers that once held field rations and pieces of metal of unknown origin, perhaps from exploding canisters? Still recognizable weapons lay abandoned on the ground: items used in hand-to-hand combat, among them, brass knuckles, dirks, hammers, even awls and screwdrivers. Also areas of scattered bones – bleached white by the sun.

Travis and I walked slowly over the sacred ground. At one location, he looked down and pointed towards two objects. One was a saber or long sword used for slashing, while nearby was a second bladed weapon partially covered by dense vegetation. Travis picked up the saber. I pushed back the soil and vegetation and brushed away the earth. What appeared was the hilt of a short sword used in hand-to-hand combat of a type used for many centuries. Travis recognized both bladed weapons as characteristic of border protector units – weapons of fallen soldiers who had joined in the defense of Paducah. We held both swords in our hands, and honored the sacrifice of the border protector soldier who always would be remembered.

Two swords we hold
The long and the short
Symbols of honor and status
Always with us.

***

From Paducah to Sin-Sin-Natty (old Cincinnati) and on to South Bend

We thanked Michael Simmons and Bess Campbell for their assistance and warm hospitality. Two days later, we embarked with our trek animals on a third riverboat, the *Covington Belle*, that made twice-monthly trips along the Ohio River between the eastern ports of old Cincinnati now called Sin-Sin-Natty and the western terminus at Kai-Row. It took us four boat travel days to reach our eastern destination. Aboard ship, we mingled with other passengers, mainly young military officers and their mates being transferred to different duty stations along the southern borders of the Wild Zone, north of the Ohio River.

As we put into ports on both the north and south sides of the Ohio River, it was obvious that the New Confederacy military had established temporary fortifications and arsenals at key river crossing points to minimize the threat of Northlander cultists re-grouping and resuming their fanatical southward invasion. After Paducah, we passed the small port of Galonda, then we cruised under the bridge at Cave-in-Rock, where the river channel turned north towards Mt. Vernon, Henderson, and ultimately to Evansville. We learned that Evansville had been the target of several serious cross-border raids with Southerners and Northlanders crossing at different times, and the once-proud town lay mostly in ruins.

Beyond Evansville, the river wound south and east. We experienced a brief stop at Owensboro, where a contingent of troops disembarked to relieve the local garrison. The *Covington Belle* did not stop at Rockport, Grandview, Troy, Tell City, or Cloverport, as there were no signals from passengers to disembark. We approached Leavenworth in late afternoon and spent the night moored at the facility adjacent to 1st Street. We departed early morning, and reached Louisville in late morning. To our surprise, the *Covington Belle* was greeted by a welcoming group of musicians and explosions, Militia troops standing at attention along the quay saluted one of the passengers as he disembarked. The focus of their attention was Captain Louis Quinn, a hometown favorite and hero at the Battle of Paducah who, after nine solar cycles of rehabilitation, once again was able to walk. He was greeted with great fanfare by family members, as the administrative council at Louisville welcomed him home. If Travis and I previously had known of his exploits, we would have interviewed Captain Quinn in depth during our upriver journey. We had missed a remarkable opportunity.

Beyond Louisville, we bypassed small settlement groups located near Westport, Milton, Brooksburg, and Ghent before once again turning north towards Hamilton, Aurora, and Lawrenceburg. By dawn of the fourth day, we could see the spires of old Cincinnati, with its sister-cities Covington and Newport along the river's south bank.

Cincinnati – in olden times – once was declared to be the Queen City of the West. That was when the old state of Ohio had served as the western boundary, beyond which were the endless flatlands trending ever onward into what then was mostly uncharted territory. We passed under two of the former five bridges that once crossed the Ohio River that linked the former states of old Ohio and old Kentucky. Only two bridges remained intact. We thanked the captain of the *Covington Belle* as we moored at Newport and disembarked.

We rested our horses and pack animals at Johnson's stable, just off Riverboat Row on East 2nd Street, Newport. We remained ashore on the south side of the river, using our time to interview locals whether or not it would be safe and/or advisable to cross over into old Ohio and pass through the ruins of Sin-Sin-Natty, as the once proud city now was called. We learned that the Northlander defeat at the Battle of South Bend had made possible the re-opening of vast areas of the Wild Zone, a condition that allowed travel north through the region to be resumed. But we also were cautioned to remain alert for the ever-present gangs of Northerners – not associated with the Northlanders – who even with defeat of the Northlanders remained disgruntled and sometimes accosted travelers.

We rode west along the river shore to Covington, then crossed the old suspension bridge that linked this southern suburb with the riverfront area of once-proud Cincinnati. A memorial erected not far from the northern side of the suspension bridge related the information that Cincinnati had been named for a Roman politician – Lucinus Quinctius Cincinnatus –

who through strength of character, military prowess, and political skills, had saved Rome. After assuring governmental and social stability in Rome, Lucinus retired voluntarily from power and returned to his farm to resume the pastoral life that he always craved. That a national military leader would give up power was hard to believe, given our past and current times of economic and social crisis. Lucinus was a politician who was honest, one who relinquished power because it was the right thing to do. Impossible to believe these days.North of Sin-Sin-Natty, we reached the outskirts of Dayton where we visited the former Wright Patterson Air Force Museum. The base facilities and museum all were in ruins. The buildings had been vandalized, displays shattered, and materials salvaged by raiders. Travis and I never before had seen anything flying through the air except birds, whether the sparrows of the field or the giant cranes almost as tall as a man. The elders at Bison Camp had told us about such machines during our schooling many solar cycles past, but the reality was that most of us as students doubted the assertion that such heavy machines, the so-called aero-planes, actually could fly. The museum was filled with pictures of these once-great service aircrafts. As to the once-proud collection of aircraft formerly on the ground nearby, nothing was left; all had been disassembled and pieces of aluminum, other fine metals, Plexiglas, and the tens of thousands of kilo-miles of copper cable and electrical wiring had been stripped and removed during the Dark Time.

A message scrawled on one of the museum walls read:

B-53 Noble once, now in ruins,

B-52 Feared once, now ignored,

B-52 We flew together, you and I

Each way too old, so many thought,

We did our jobs, now all forgotten,

The Ripple did that.

We had no idea what the words meant.

After the Dayton and Wright-Pat disappointment, we re-grouped and angled northwest along route 35 that took us into old Indiana towards the city of Muncie. We crossed the White River, where we paused and rested for two days on the grassy commons of the once-thriving campus known as Ball State University. While our horses grazed, we explored several of the buildings of this once-elaborate campus, known in earlier solar cycles for the excellent training of culinary specialists and dietitians, and for a formable co-educational sports program. The beautiful houses that once graced the area just west of campus now mostly were in ruins. Travis said that these homes reminded him of a basic housing cluster just north of the University of California, Davis, campus that he once had visited during one of his early treks.Leaving Muncie, we hopscotched along east-west/north-south trending county roads until we reached the ruins of Kokomo and old Highway 31. From there going north, we bypassed the ethnic enclaves of Peru, Mexico, and Rochester, and approached Plymouth. Here we were challenged for the first time by New Confederacy Militia, who had occupied the settlement after the Battle of South Bend.

We were interviewed extensively by Lieutenant Colonel Maxwell Rodgers and his subordinates, Staff Sergeants William Jennings and Norris Beaverton. We showed them letters of support we had secured at Kai-Row and Paducah that requested consideration for our visit to South Bend. With our documents in order, we were approved to enter the occupied zone. After victory over the Northlanders at the Battle of South Bend, a no-entry cordon had been established around the community with a primary entry checkpoint located at the gate to Gulivoire Park military compound. Lieutenant Colonel Rodgers asked if we would like accompaniment for protection as we visited South Bend and the battlefield site – just in case, he said.

In case of what, we asked?

He offered us just a smile in return. In keeping with what we presumed to be militia protocol, we told him we would be pleased to accept his offer. William Jennings was assigned to accompany us. As events would turn out, we would be grateful for his companionship and observational skills.

After-Word

Our journey had taken us up the Ohio River and overland to reach our destination, South Bend. Along the way, we were greeted warmly and with hospitality by many who had suffered dearly during the Ripple Event, Dark Time, Epidemic, and the more recent Northlander invasions. Despite suffering – in some instances experiencing pain too difficult to contemplate – there emerged from these survivors a sense of purpose, and commitment to help relatives, friends, and neighbors. The spirit that characterized these survivors mirrored that of our own families back in the New NorthWest Configuration, before arrival of the recent Epidemic that had taken so many lives. What would we learn as we visited the battlefield site of South Bend? What lessons would their valor and spirit tell us?

***

Ijano Esantu Eleman

Interlude-Conversation: 3
Bombers

***

K'Aser, Reese especially was much taken by the pilot's ode to this aircraft. Not that there was much left, mind you. This could only have been stronger had she actually seen one in the air. They were most impressive, as I recall.

They impressed both friend and foe, for true, A'Tena.

Still they and other bombers – they were called that weren't they – were not enough to defeat the forces of evil.

Deflect, yes but The Ripple left the end game – defeat – unresolved. And this could have gone either way as matters were developing. Even so, the B-52s were impressive. Quite the sight to see when making a "delivery," but my favorite bomber – yes, such aircraft were noted thusly – was the B-36 Peacemaker. There is – or was – one at Wright-Patterson, along with the B-52 and many, many other aircraft. All now are little more than piles of scrap surrounding what's left of their engine or engines, and even these have been stripped bare.

"Peacemaker" – a strange name for a weapon, let alone a warrior, if you ask me.

Those who flew them saw them both ways. The name did fit. There were no major conflicts while B-36s were in the front lines. Potential enemies feared what it might be able to do, its friends what it might not be able to do. In this way, the B-36 was indeed a Peacemaker.

Sadly, there were not more such weapons. Were these Peacemakers also impressive in the bargain?

Yes, but in a way different than that you intend. They were not the B-52s you know of. No they were not sleek either in the air or on the ground. There have been those who, from time to time, prove beetles can't fly, and many thought the same of a B-36 when seeing it on the ground. Ah, but wait, the engines have been fired up the behemoth now is moving making its lumbering way down the runway with six turnin' and four burnin' – as they said at the time – amongst much rumbling and clatter. What's this – it is off the ground! Oh, so slow, but airborne! Large aircraft seem to move slower than they are, but in this case the illusion mirrored reality.

Impressive nonetheless?

Not in the way you may intend, A'Tena. But, ah, be back when near the right airbase and experience the slow rumbling – almost vibrating – approach of B-36s practicing sensor evasion (radar it was called) and see – after a seemingly overlong period – these monsters in the air ambling on their way. Then you'd be impressed for true and sure.

Perhaps I'll do that. Might you wish to join me?

Indeed, yes, A'Tena.

The Journey: Part 2

Chapter 4

South Bend: Battlefield Landscapes and Memories

Pre-Note

How did it begin – this cult of Northlanders? Not all immigrants entered old America with visions filled with anger, revolution, and conquest to force upon residents of their new land. The great flatlands of old America once were filled with hard workers who sought freedom from oppression and opportunities. The original Northlander cultists came not from a single overseas land, but from many states in Africa, Asia, and Europe, countries usually with military dictators and religious leaders that touted superiority of their belief systems to followers, sermons of hate for the land that took them in and provided refuge. How bizarre in logic: why would such individuals incite their followers to disrupt the political-economic system that had offered a safe haven, or attack residents who disagreed with their views and preachings?

After crossing the Great Ocean these disruptive immigrants found their way westward, many settling in what then was the heartland of the new continent. Decades before the Ripple Event some found support and home in two great city complexes: Chicago-Evanston (C-E) and Detroit-Dearborn (D-D). Here the employment opportunities were many for those who sought work. But many of the new arrivals chose lives of sitting-and-waiting, as if financial promise and wealth somehow would drop from the sky. The streets of their new country were not lined with gold, but golden opportunities were widely available to those who worked hard. It was among these sitters-and-waiters that the teachings and dogmas of the Northlanders took root and flourished.

Rise of the Northlanders and Early Military Decisions

Prior to the Ripple Event and Dark Time, a relatively quiet and unobtrusive group of gang leaders arose within the immigrant communities located in Chicago-Evanston and Detroit-Dearborn. These firebrands, speakers with honey tongues, proclaimed what they called the rule of Limited Good. Through their writings and sermons, they touted the belief that there was only so much so-called good to go around in any community or environmental setting. If someone had amassed more goods or wealth than another, it was not because of hard work, dedication to education, and self-motivation, it had to be that those with more goods and wealth, somehow had stolen it from others. It was because these wealthy persons had denied others their rightful educational and employment opportunities and, as a result, remained poor. At every opportunity the leaders chanted similar mantras:

TAKE IT – TAKE IT
You deserve better;
Why be a debtor;
Get what you deserve;
Don't lose your nerve ...
TAKE IT – TAKE IT
When others have more than you?
You deserve better, what will you do?
Why should others have everything?
Take what you want, live like a king ...
TAKE IT – TAKE IT
It don't matter what others say;
You deserve better, so do it today;
Take from the Haves, they won't resist;
Show them your muscle, your iron fist ...
TAKE IT – TAKE IT
[Other verses were crafted as well.]

Within these shallow-thinking groups, there emerged a variety of sects, some slightly more liberal in their thought and organization. Other sects, however, were extremely intolerant and ultra-conservative. These groups demanded unwavering alliance and adherence to specific dogmas and behaviors, where deviation led to expulsion and often death by execution. Because of these cultural differences, many individuals who expressed tolerance towards others elected to leave their homes and emigrate. Leaving C-E and D-D for safety reasons, they formed long lines of migrating individuals and families who left the urban areas to seek new homes in the surrounding hinterlands. Some found acceptance along the way. The majority of those who left, however, died of either thirst or hunger before sanctuary could be located.

Due to this mass exodus, the once-great urban centers of Chicago-Evanston and Detroit-Dearborn became havens for intolerant extremists holding the concept that only their cultural behaviors and views were correct. Little by little, the firebrands espousing these views rose in prominence and expected allegiance from all like-minded urban residents. The concept – conversion or death – expanded further and dominated their thinking, public proclamations, and documents.

Prior to the Ripple Event and Dark Time, the metropolitan areas of Chicago-Evanston and Detroit-Dearborn regularly experienced terrible civic unrest, with near weekly sequences of rioting and destruction of urban centers. Stores serving local customers regularly were looted and burned. Local and regional police forces seemed unable or were unwilling to contain or halt the cyclical pattern of violence and vandalism.

There came a time when due to such urban unrest, administrative officials and police at both metropolitan complexes met independently with community members to make plans for a week of cultural outreach. The meeting objectives at both C-E and D-D were to help the poor, seek out and aid those in need, and bring together the divergent cultures and ethnicities of their great cities. A second objective was to re-establish the celebration of Thanksgiving as the most important American national holiday, and to incorporate the diverse communities into supporting a new era of urban harmony.

But then on that fateful Thanksgiving morning, the Ripple Event happened.

The Northlander cultists initially were only one of many groups on the fringe of general acceptable thinking and social behavior at the time. With the onset of the Ripple Event, Northlander leaders acted quickly to consolidate their power and territory. Their extreme elements forced thousands to decide on the spot: join or die. Faith groups were caught off guard by such demands. Within five days of the Ripple onset, the great city complexes of C-E and D-D were wracked by even worse civil strife. Thousands of residents attempting to leave the cities were ambushed and their belongings stolen; others remained behind to accept their fate.

Residents that converted were brought into the Northlander fold; those who did not were executed. Some religious groups, especially those with a military component, escaped the Northlander consolidation of power. Some fled west and found refuge along the banks of Rock River; others established settlement groups within the Pecatonica Wetlands. Still others chose a southern destination, crossed the Little Calumet River and headed towards the southern suburbs of C-E near Thorn Creek and the Kankakee River, where they were welcomed by settlement groups adjacent to Aroma Park. At these locations, the refugees thought that they would be beyond the influence zone of the Northlanders. They were correct, but only for a short time.

The Northlanders pushed south and west out of Chicago-Evanston, establishing their own settlement groups. These Northlander settlements multiplied southward and westward, joined administratively in thought and behavior like the links of a chain. A toxic chain indeed they were. And from these Northlander outposts, the tentacles of evil continued to spread as more ambitious plans were developed. Decisions ultimately were made to attack and spread Northlander beliefs into the heartland of North America – into the lands south of the Ohio River, and west of the Mississippi.

There came a time when the Northlander leadership of Chicago-Evanston and Detroit-Dearborn met at Belle Isle to plan and coordinate their ambitious dreams of expansion. Notes taken at this meeting unfortunately have been destroyed, but transcripts of interviews conducted later reveal that agreement was reached to form a Northlander military alliance known as – Arrows of the Faithful (AoF). The alliance symbol consisted of two crossed arrows upon a shield. Above the shield was a single star that symbolized the oneness and unity of their view to the exclusion of all others. Decisions were reached regarding texts and symbols to be used on recruitment posters and advertising banners. Steps were taken to produce large quantities of such materials to help in Northlander recruitment as their militias advanced outward from C-E and D-D to expand and consolidate their lands. Signs bearing Northlander slogans appeared almost overnight .

Now is the time: take from the rich – join us;
Now is the time: take your fair share – join us;
Now is the time: if you want to eat – join us;
Now is the time: if you want the good life – join us;
Now is the time: adopt our beliefs or die – join us.

The second day of the Belle Isle meeting, a mutual decision was reached to attack the important food-production center midway between the two urban centers of C-E and D-D. The community of South Bend was at the heart of this region, a thorn that had resisted conversion to Northlander thinking, an area of tolerance and freedom that needed to be obliterated.

The settlement of South Bend suffered terribly during the Ripple Event, but had maintained its basic cultural integrity and community diversity. Since South Bend was midway between C-E and D-D, the Northlander leadership agreed that their militias should be combined for a merged frontal attack on South Bend. The Northlander leaders discussed only one outcome: victory. The rewards of victory would be shared equally. All attending the Belle Isle meeting perceived that South Bend would fall within a half day or at the most a full day after initial military contact. All that was needed was to select the date to amass the two militias – the exact date was to be determined by Northlander astrologers.

Jason Asmith, leader of the C-E Northlanders, suggested that the attack should commence on the eve or day when the South Benders celebrated the winter solstice, Christmas, or the New Solar Cycle. Abril Hollingsworth, geographical councilor to Ash-Ton Barvin, leader of the D-D Northlanders, interrupted Asmith and rose to speak:

Don't be stupid! The Winter Solstice, the festivals of Christmas, and New Solar Cycle are in winter. Why do you think it appropriate that we attack in the midst of ice and snow? Yes the Saint Joseph River at South Bend is frozen at this time, but did we not learn from past forays across the frozen Ohio River when we attacked Paducah, that such winter river crossings led to disaster? The best opportunity for attack and military success will be when the South Benders are least alert. This would be during their celebration of the Spring Equinox, when most of their adult residents will be in states of intoxication and revelry (may such actions never infect us). They will be lax after heavy drinking, and the timing also allows for the most sunlight hours for success of our troops. To attack during winter clearly is stupid.

Documents captured later reveal that Hollingsworth's counter idea and insolent words caused a considerable stir in the room, and led to his expulsion from the inner core of the D-D Northlanders and ultimate execution. Northlander Chairmen Asmith and Barvin ultimately agreed on a date to attack South Bend. Orders were issued to commanders: develop a combined pincer campaign where C-E militia assemble and attack South Bend from the west while the D-D Northlander militias approach and attack from the north.

South Bend on the Eve of Northlander Attack

The regional militias at South Bend and nearby settlement groups sensed the political military changes in Northlander thinking and regional behavior. Almost daily they were subjected to Northlander probes and incursions, testing defender alert responses.

The community of South Bend had survived the Ripple Event and had emerged through the Dark Time with most of their settlement intact. South Bend was well watered by the Saint Joseph River. Protected farmlands to the west, south, and east produced sufficient food supplies. During the Dark Time Recovery Period, the campus grounds and buildings of Notre Dame University had become a haven where Northerners who rejected Northlander dogma could find tolerance and community acceptance. No longer was Notre Dame University the venue of one faith but had opened its doors to protect community and regional diversity.

Settlement groups to the west of South Bend adjacent to the North and South Chain lakes presented security difficulties for local Militias. Community members then were relocated and welcomed onto the Notre Dame campus where several residential structures were opened for family occupation, especially Carroll and Cavanaugh Halls.

Militias associated with settlement groups to the south also were alerted to move their families into other university residence halls. The militiamen and women then established defensive positions north of the Saint Joseph River in a west-to-east line, anchored on the west by the South Eddy Street Bridge and on the east by the riverfront berms of Battell Park. This defensive line presented the militia members with the opportunity to supplement troops in either direction, depending upon location of the initial Northlander attack. By anchoring their defensive line at the South Eddy Street Bridge, attackers coming from the west could be forced into an easily defended narrows. An initial attack from the east similarly could be thwarted.

Scouts sent out by various South Bend militia reported that the most probable attack direction by Northlander forces marching south from Detroit-Dearborn, would be to the northeast. Accordingly, decisions were made to evacuate settlement groups east of old Edwardsburg that had arisen adjacent to the shores of the Seven Lakes region. The defenders perceived that through careful troop disposition, the Northlander advance could be funneled towards the lakes, where passage southwest into South Bend could be thwarted.

The defending militias, each with prominent battle-tested leaders, met in the rotunda of the Notre Dame University administration building. Only one name was put forth to unite and lead the regional militias and volunteers as commander for the defense of South Bend, Charles Singleton. Documents discovered after the Battle of South Bend reported that at this meeting Singleton accepted his appointment as commander. It is written that he initially spoke in generalities, but then dramatically changed tone rallying those attending with specific and moving words:

> *Comrades: we know not what tomorrow or the next days may bring.Reports by our reconnaissance members reveal Northlander stirrings . Two groups have massed – one moving eastward the other southwesterly. When might we see their battle banners, hear their obscene chants? Time will tell.*
>
> *Comrades: we are ready to receive them – South Bend will be defended. The attackers will be defeated because we stand united. They will be defeated because of our dedication to protect our families and ways of life. Our dedication to personal choice and family values Northlanders do not understand. They cannot take our way of life from us, and they will not. Know this. There will come a day when they will arrive at the boundaries of our homes. As we await them on this battle eve. When silence fills the air. When heartbeats quicken. When fears and doubts are raised.*
>
> *Comrades remember: we stand together to defend our freedom! Fidem iustitiamque! Onóir agus ceartais! Honor and justice!*

According to several reports, immediately after Singleton spoke these stirring words, a raven flew into the rotunda through the open door and came to rest upon the commander's shoulder – an omen that foretold of events to come

***

Battle of South Bend Told Through Observations and Documents

With visitation permits in hand, Staff Sargent William Jennings led Travis and me to the initial checkpoint. We passed through and began our inspection tour of the key battlefield sites. Early in our walk, we were joined by two others, both retired non-military, Sexton Aniel Jefferson and Historian Francis Perkins. They took us to the steps of a rather nondescript building that Perkins called the Dedication Room. Inside were displays of Defender battle banners and postings of personal letters of faith and prayers for protection against the Northlanders.

Reading these documents, we learned that the Defenders were both men and women, young and old, of different ethnicities, and religious practices. It was clear how each played different and valuable parts in defending the community of South Bend and the campus of Notre Dame University. As we stood before the displays, taking it all in, historian Perkins identified his specific tasks during the days that followed the Northlander attack and defeat:

> *I was a member of the 10th Northern Kentucky Militia. Our role was to defend the rampart sections. After victory, my assigned task was to bury the Defenders who had fallen, and to do so with honor. Yes it is true that the dead no longer care, but it also is correct that the living need to remember the names and faces of those who fought and gave their lives for honor and justice. Atop the chest of each fallen Defender, it was my responsibility to attach a unity symbol, a token embossed with the image of a shamrock and four letters, N-D and S-B, recalling our campus and community. Over each grave I repeated these words:*
>
> *Opus tuum en pace –*
>
> *Rest in peace your work is done –*
> *Requiem aeternam dona ei terram tu servasti –*
> *Rest in peace you saved our land –*
> *Filiola et filius in pace –*
> *Rest in peace dear daughter/son –*
> *Opus tuum en pace –*
> *Rest in peace your work is done –*
> *Opus tuum en pace.*

> *I present to you, Travis and Reese, your personal unity tokens. It is my wish and that of Sexton Jefferson that you will remember what occurred here at South Bend, and always keep us in your hearts.*

ND ND ND ND

SB SB SB SB

Raven Banners

Sexton Aniel Jefferson drew our attention to several Defender banners carried during the Battle of South Bend. It seemed curious to Travis and me that ravens would have played an important part of Defender military culture. Jefferson commented on our question:

> *In many ancient and modern societies, ravens are known as harbingers of evil and dark magic. But in the far-off distant Celtic days during periods of the ancient kings of Eire, ravens were held in high esteem and deemed to be messengers associated with the prophet goddess Morrigan. It was a raven that perched on the shoulder of our Commander Singleton and issued the initial cry – geewan – a tone that alerted us that the Northlanders would arrive soon and that we must be alert and on guard. I remember that the prophetic raven had flown into the rotunda area from the north door entrance, and that it circled west before landing and connecting with our commander's shoulder. Older Defenders present also told me that the specific direction of this raven's flight foretold the need to be alert that events to come would change our lives forever. I remember just after the raven landed on the commander's shoulder, it cried out a second time with three sharp sounds – cras-cras-cras. We knew from our early school education in Latin that this call meant – tomorrow.*
>
> *As we continue our walk across campus, we will stop at the site where the decisive moments of the Battle of South Bend occurred. You will see where Commander Singleton's grave is located, and the spot where he fell and uttered his last words. Even today ravens circle this site each morning and late afternoon – as if to pay him respect.*

Sexton Jefferson unlocked a cabinet along the north wall of the Dedication Room. He withdrew five documents and motioned for us to join him in the center of the room where he displayed the papers on an oak table. He held up each and then spoke:

What I wish to show you are five of our most precious relics related to the Battle of South Bend. The authors of the documents are unknown, only that the words were penned during lulls in the fighting, or shortly after the conclusion of hostilities. The documents are referenced by the initial words in their titles: Plague; A Terror From the North Came Upon Us; Confrontation; Fog of War; and Aftermath. They are written in different hands. The paper base of each is crinkled, dirty, and in some instances smeared with blood. Let us review them one by one.

Travis and I were transfixed as Jefferson held and read from the documents. As we listened to his summaries, the unknown author's words seemed to leap off the pages into our minds and hearts.

Plague

The plague came upon us driving all before it. The plague advances towards us – the Northlanders driving all others before them, forcing those who have not accepted their radical views to flee towards South Bend. They accumulate outside our settlement. They are a locust-like swarm of desperation. They tell us that others who have not accepted Northlander behavior and culture have been executed. On and on – ever onward – comes the plague towards our settlement. Then soon the Northlanders will arrive. We hear off in the distance sounds of their battle drums, the syncopated rhythms resounding over the nearby flatlands reach our ears. The noise of evil is approaching. They are close. The sounds of evil ring louder, ever louder. Soon it will be decided: will the Northlander plague be repulsed, or will we Defenders be visiting Tech Duinn our otherworld home of the dead? We have been told to expect initial skirmishes of unbelievable fury. And so it will be. So it is we await the morning sunrise; we will know our fate soon enough.

***

Terror from the North Came Upon Us

The terror from the north came upon us. From the beginning of the Dark Times collective groups of passive and aggressive peoples dwelt north of the Ohio River. The aggressive ones separated themselves and took the title Northlanders. The passives, known collectively as Northerners, were forced into conversion or fled in advance of Northlander raids. There was no middle thought where tolerance and mutual understanding prevailed. The Northlanders attacked as part of their determination to convert all to their belief systems. Soon their small raids and incursions increased in intensity and violence. Northlander raids were sudden, with little to no advance warning. Their raids were characterized by forms of violence that numbed the souls of thoughtful men and women. We living to the south turned the river bank into as much of a barrier as we could, and we launched retaliatory expeditions northward from time to time. Our militias, the border raiders from western lands, even troops from New Confederacy came to our assistance, but we could not contain the Northlanders or pacify the region. Their hit-and-run tactics expanded: attack – retreat – attack – retreat. Such events produced a regional stalemate. As casualties rose, there was no peace throughout the region, each side winning here, losing there, but always with the Ohio River flowing between us.

Within the heartland of Northlander territory there existed a geographical region where forced conversions were rejected, a broad land of undulating flatlands crossed by rivers and lakes with numerous settlement groups. This was our land – South Bend – and we stood midway between the polar Northlander capitols of Chicago-Evanston and Detroit-Dearborn. And it was we cried out:

> *A terror from the north will come among us –*
> *Ad me ab aquilone et veniet in nobis*
> *Protect us from the wrath of the Northlanders –*
> *Nos ab hoste protégé Northlanders ira.*

Confrontation

Confrontation came upon us. The western force of Northlanders massed along the Saint Joseph River. Their attack line extended from Highland Cemetery south along the grassy berms of Woodlawn and Keller Park. The Northlanders had prepared in advance for river crossing. They carried with them equipment to facilitate spanning the river. Their attack focus was directed towards the east bank grassy meadows of St. Mary's College. Their objective, once their main divisions had crossed the river and established their presence in the vicinity of August Drive, was to thrust eastward into the heart of the Notre Dame campus where the Defender militias were concentrated.

Defender troops facing the Northlanders directly across the Saint Joseph River retreated as planned. The Northlanders took our maneuver as a reflection of our fear and rushed across the river on makeshift rafts. When they reached the east shore, the Northlanders rushed forward to engage us, not knowing that on both their southern and eastern flanks, other Defenders had crossed the previous night and secluded themselves amid the riverside ruins. As the Northlanders advanced east of the river, our Defender militias closed on the Northlander flanks. The invaders now were trapped between our militia arrow hurlers and lancers – both front and back – and the enemy lay open to our combined assault. We continued firing into their confused mass. We whittled their numbers down until only 35 remained alive. They were disarmed and surrendered to us.

The Northlanders had underestimated the military savvy of our Defender militias. In a bold move Commander Charles split his forces into three units. The main force was assigned to defend a line between the two lakes with barricades erected across Saint Mary's Road. This directive would force the Northlanders into a narrow, less easily defended position. As a second tactic, we tricked the Northlanders by appearing to meet them in the vicinity of Madeleva Avenue, where we quickly withdrew to the southeast. At the time of our withdrawal, two of our militia groups crossed the Saint Joseph River – one to the south near the ruins of the once proud Memorial Hospital – the other crossing to the north of Pinhook Lake. Both militias then moved south and north, respectively, and charged back across the river. The main defending van through its disguised retreat between the two lakes, pulled the Northlanders eastward and into the trap: there could be no Northlander retreat, as escape routes to the west were sealed by the combined armies of our settlement group Defender's units. A classic double envelopment.

Fog of War

The fog of war came upon us. Confusion reigned on the battlefield; missed messages, misinterpreted signals, recommendations and plans not followed, troop movement to the left when repositioning to the right was required. Was it not once said in the long distant past that for want of a horseshoe nail a war was lost? What factors trip the tide of battle in one direction or another? Does logic always prevail on the battlefield of life?

And it was that the Battle of South Bend took place on the campus of Notre Dame University. The attacks and confrontations occurred for seven days. Deadly hand-to-hand combat favored neither side as casualties mounted. On the morning of the seventh day, after five continuous hours of intense battle, a weather inversion produced a fog that covered most of the battlefield – a dense mist that took the combatants by surprise, perhaps caused by the rapidity of the changing weather pattern.

The southern attack wing of the Northlanders continued to advance as the weather worsened. Within minutes, the battlefield was covered by a dense fog of eerie origin. Northlanders and Defenders alike could not see the other and, while the combatants faced each other, conflict suddenly ceased. The fog of war deepened as the Defenders stood their ground opposite the Northlanders. Suddenly the unexpected happened: the Northlanders began to lay down their arms and started retreating west and south. During the Northlander retreat, the dense fog lifted. Being now without arms and surrounded by Defenders, many were taken prisoner.

Northlander prisoners interviewed by our Defenders claimed that a voice was heard emanating from the fog. A voice of unknown origin had hailed them in various languages with the following words: Lay down your arms, retreat, and you will be victorious.

And so they did.

But how could troops involved in battle in which abilities and weaponry appeared to be evenly matched retreat and claim victory?

How could rational soldiers in the midst of battle discard their arms and expect to be victorious?

Several prisoners interviewed by Defender militias related that the words emanating from the fog were comprehended only by the Northlander militiamen, not by their commanders who continued to urge them to continue fighting. No Defender interviewed after the Battle of South Bend or in the solar cycles to come, ever stated that they heard any voice emanating from the fog. One prisoner related in a sworn document that at least two Northlander commanders were slain by their own men, after being urged to do so by the voice emanating from the dense fog.

How can this be interpreted? The events that tipped the scales and assured South Bend victory defy logical analysis.

With the Northlanders in full retreat, the immediate the Battle of South Bend was over.

It was reported by numerous Defender militia members that as the Northlanders retreated, the noise of their field boots resounded and produced a sound that called the ravens. And it was that flocks of ravens rose from their quiet resting places on the campus of Notre Dame University and the central portions of South Bend. This mass of birds swooped out over and across the battlefield. It was reported that the raven's shrill harsh caws continued for several minutes, screeches that seemed to echo and proclaim Defender victory.

***

Aftermath

Although hand-to-hand combat has finished, the mind continues to see images of spilled blood and the carnage of battle. Even when arrows are returned to their quivers, when swords are re-sheathed, when clubs and maces, dirks and knives, and lances and spears no longer are held – the aftermath of battle continues in our minds.

There came upon the wind an initial raven's caw, like a catalyst, a sound that aroused many black-feathered watchers to take flight. There came the caw of the second bird, then four more, then eight, then sixteen. The bird sounds echoed across the green fields of South Bend, not as a call to battle, but as a plea for peace.

Early the next day came the dawn of freedom. But there remained decisions of what to do with the Northlander prisoners. The captives were chained together and marched inside the ruins of the old stadium on campus. On the infield of this once great athletic venue the militia guards listened to impassioned pleas for all prisoners to be executed. Most of the cries were unified: the Northlanders had executed thousands of other Northerners and militia prisoners – they should receive the same justice. The crowd became ever more noisy and unsettled. Then it was that a young militia fighter rose out of the ranks to address the crowd. He called for silence and spoke:

> *We the Defenders of South Bend on this day of deliverance defeated the Northlander invaders, the plague responsible for*

so much pain, destruction, and loss of life. There are among us those who would urge compassion and understanding, that the actions of the invaders were the result of training and brain-washing by their leaders, and as such they should not be responsible for their actions. They also would make the argument that the Northlanders would not have invaded our lands and slain our civilians and warriors had it not been for the training and mind washing imposed by their leadership. Such naïve pleas for Northlander lives must be rejected: we are who we are and must take responsibility for our own actions. Perhaps there are among the Northlander prisoners in this venue some individuals who could be rehabilitated and the evil instilled in their minds washed away – like bathing in the waters of the Saint Joseph River. Citizens and comrades, we should reject this naïve argument: too many good people have suffered for too long at the hands of these irresponsible invaders who claimed that only their way of life should be allowed, who urged the convert-or-die dogma. They are not repentant: they all should be executed.

The crowd roared: hear, hear – hear, hear!

Another Defender demanded attention and spoke:

My family suffered under Northlander injustice. My father and mother were murdered; my sisters .... But I say this. Just as the ancient Romans implemented decimation verdicts, where every 10th individual was executed, I propose here today that we as victors in the Battle of South Bend implement our own justice – the octamation. Each prisoner will be numbered and lots drawn – the first seven numbers will be executed cleanly and swiftly in contrast to the brutal techniques used on my mother and father. Each eighth name drawn will be given two choices: execution or to live in exile. If the choice is execution, their deaths will be swift. If the choice is to live in exile, they will remain prisoners and transported to Kai-Row and from there to one of two destinations – depending upon transport facilities and weather. One destination will be the cold lands north of the Great Five Lakes, the other will be a hot-humid prison on an abandoned island in the Great Southern Sea. Life or death, but on our terms. I have completed the count: on this day and inside this stadium there

> *are 192 Northlander prisoners. Implementation of the octamation would result in 21 prisoners being given the choice – the remainder will be drowned in the Saint Joseph River.*

The crowd roared: hear, hear – hear, hear!

Sexton Aniel Jefferson smiled as he related this information. He informed us that of the 21 Northlander prisoners taken at the Battle of South Bend, 18 chose life and exile, while three were unrepentant and executed along with the others. The so-called "give-upers" or "lifers" were trekked southwest under heavy guard to Kai-Row, where they were interned in the regional Northlander prison camps. Over time, additional Northlander prisoners were housed at Kai-Row. Eventually, about half of these were forced to march northward along the east side of Great Lake Erie and ultimately towards the ruins of Mackinaw City. There, the guards and prisoners crossed into the former French zone boundary at Sault St. Marie, and from there the prisoners disappeared into the cold unknown. The other half was escorted onto a prison ship for downriver transport past the ruins of old New Orleans. Such prison ships passed through the Great River delta into the Great Southern Sea to an unnamed and uncharted isle, where they presumably passed the remainder of their lives sweltering in hot insect-infested quarters.

***

Jefferson related that three days after battle, Defender groups were seen wandering about, speaking with one another, recalling events of the past days when the Northlanders attacked and ultimately were defeated. Men and women, old and young came together, initially in groups of two or three, then coalescing as others joined – bands of bloodied, dirty, tired Defenders of varied origins and cultural backgrounds. They made their way slowly to the central administration building capped with its golden dome. The Defenders entered into the rotunda beneath the dome, and gathered silently to remember their fallen comrades. It mattered not this day one's religious preference, the Defenders were united one and all: Catholic, Orthodox, and Protestant; Hindu, Jew, and Sikh; those who had lost their faith as a result of the Ripple Event and Dark Time – Free-Thinkers, Agnostics and Atheists. Each different, each free to practice their cultures, politics, and faiths as they themselves determined. Many Defenders had died for the right to be alone or to be able to gather in groups, to speak without fear of interference of others, to speak out different opinions, and to write and create art as each saw fit. Victory at the Battle of South Bend reflected a new day, a new dawn for the Northern peoples, now released from the fear of Northlander domination.

Sexton Jefferson reported that within the rotunda the voices of the assembled began to echo and rise, first one, then a second and a third, then all joined in reciting the well-known words. As tears flowed, the Defenders knelt to honor their fallen comrades:

Cheer, cheer for old Notre Dame
Wake up the echoes cheering her name

Swordsman Michael Pendergast, former student of Latin and ancient history, stood and moved to the center of the group. He raised his hand, a gesture for silence and he spoke:

I speak out these words in memory of my parents and sisters, slain by the Northlanders:

Esto animo Veteris Notre
Suscitate struxisset ciens eius nomine
Mittere nubes animo alto
Tonitruum decutito de caelo
Etsi magnum aut parvum dissiden
Old Notre feret omnia
Dum fido filii are marchin
Accepta ad Uictoriae castra communiuere.

Next, moving to the center of the rotunda floor was Erin Mackelvee, who in turn spoke the words in a time-honored way that reflected her Irish-American heritage and that of other Irish-American militia fighters:

Hail clocha sneachta do Sean Notre Dame
Wake suas an macallaí cheering a hainm
Seol an volley clocha ar ard
Croith síos an toirneach ón spéir
Cad cé na odds a bheith mór nó beag
Beidh Sean Notre Dame bua thar gach
Cé go bhfuil a cuid mhac dílis máirseáil
Ar aghaidh chuig bua.

Jefferson recalled a moment that followed as if on cue all stood and recited another version, the poem by Archer Annalise Jakawski, written and shared with the troops on the eve of battle as the Defenders prepared to face the

Northlander onslaught. Jefferson said that he remembered how her words had encouraged and guided him and others through that fearful night on the eve of battle, words that lifted him and others out of the darkness of fear and despair into the new light and dawn of freedom:

Cheer, cheer Northlanders be gone
Come greet the new day, come greet the dawn
Raise up your voices shout out we won
Northlanders vanquished now on the run
Many Defenders have answered the call
Gathered at Notre Dame early in fall
Now our loyal sons and daughters march
Onward to Victory...

He recalled that archer Annalise Cohen had survived the Battle of South Bend and was among the Defenders in the rotunda area. She had experienced serious arm and leg wounds that needed tending, but in her own words later she told us:

I needed to be here – to honor my friends and companions.

Jefferson continued … Was it Jackson Gomez, or perhaps another – I can't remember – who espied Annalise among the crowd inside rotunda area. He ushered her to the center where we, her comrades in arms, recalled the battle slogans of our various militia regiments – slogans that we shouted out before battle to taunt the Northlanders:

Molon labe ... Molon labe ... Molon labe
Bring it ... Bring it ... Bring it!
You ain't got game ... You ain't got game ... You ain't got game
We will piss on your graves!

***

Jefferson told us that in the first five solar cycles following the Battle of South Bend, the campus had become a pilgrimage site where Northerners now freed from fear and enslavement could visit and pay homage at the site where so many brave men and women fought for freedom. Within ten solar cycles after the victory, the present commemorative museum was opened for the display of battlefield memorabilia and objects of reverence. He showed us additional documents in the room, items that revealed a unique Defender vocabulary used to describe Northlander individuals, groups, and behaviors. Among the more curious and interesting were the following:

***Chickens** (noun): Applied to Northlanders who exhorted and urged their troops forward, but always stationed themselves in the rear lines where they remained, never engaging in combat. As our Defender militias turned the tide of battle, the Northlander chickens were the first to flee. They abandoned their troops and screamed for their lives when captured. It always was a great joy when we surround and isolated a chicken – how we taunted and teased them – watched them squirm and plead for their lives. We soon tired of such activities, however, and then we stripped off their britches and branded the letters CSB on their asses. No need to translate the letters, right? We then sent them pants-less back along the trails leading to Chicago-Evanston or to Detroit-Dearborn – which, of course, they could never reach. Along the way, these branded chickens would be captured and cooked by members of communities they previously had ravished.*

***Dragonflies** (noun): Applied to tethered prisoners forced to march in lines ahead of the main body of Northlander troops. Like their namesakes, they stood still (almost hovering), until prodded forward, then rushed quickly ahead several meter-yards, then stopped – before being prodded forward once again. Sadly, most such dragonfly lines of prisoners fell beneath our descending flights of arrows.*

***Dung Beetles** (noun): Applied to modified or cut-down old German-origin automobiles with interiors filled with animal and human excrement used to fertilize urban gardens. These wheeled units were pulled by mules or horses.*

***Fireflies** (noun): Applied to advance scouts sent out by Northlander leaders to search for weaknesses in our militia defensive lines. From the safety of our trenches, we could see these fireflies darting here and there, hovering and looping about just like their namesakes. How many of such firefly lights did we extinguish? Too many to count.*

***Head Lice** (noun): Applied to the collective Northlander leadership;*

***Trotters** (noun): Applied to Northlander prisoners who, after drinking water of uncertain quality, experienced acute digestive reactions that necessitated quick trips to the prison camp latrines.*

***Turtles** (noun): Applied to groveling-crawling Northlander militiamen who thought themselves secure if they covered their* *bodies with armor. They stood out from the average Northlander soldier, with their barbute helmets; gorget throat protectors; cuirass-protected chest pieces; arm gauntlets; and leg-protective greaves. How these turtles slogged about thinking themselves safe from our arrows and lances, that we could do them no battlefield harm. In reality, we found the turtles to be among the most timid and poorest fighters of all the Northlanders. And like the turtles they emulated, once they stumbled on the uneven battlefield, it was difficult for them to again rise. If our troops approached a fallen turtle, oh how it would squirm and flail about. We hated the turtles intensely, because they fought without honor. How we laughed as they clinked and clanked aimlessly upon the ground – just before a well-placed sword or lance thrust ended our amusement.*

Another document displayed in the House of Honor was written by an unknown but highly educated chronicler. Sexton Aniel Jefferson and Historian Francis Perkins commented that based upon style and word choices the assumption could be made that the author was an immigrant of ethnic heritage from the southern Balkan region, most likely Sarakatsani or Vlach. The original rhymed quatrains have been lost and only the rough English and Latin translations have remained.

The overall style of the unrhymed lines, however, lent an important historical aura to the text. Parker related that there was evidence that the words were sung on special occasions, where militia members gathered in subsequent solar cycles to visit with old comrades in arms. These military reunions commonly lasted for several days and, during the evenings assemblies, there were campfire celebrations. As the embers swirled and warped skyward – one or more veterans of the Battle of South Bend rose and repeated portions of the lines transcribed here

Canto 1. *Across our furrowed lands with crops,*
Northlanders marched upon our gates,
Demanded entry and faith conversion.
We of Notre Dame withstood,
Denied Northlanders entry to our home,
Go now in peace we urged them leave,
Back to their northern city home.
Depart now we urged their army leave,
Leave us in peace our faith to keep,

Our words ignored as through deaf ears,
Northlanders they signaled – attack!

Canto 2. *Charles Singleton led our troops,*
Against the Northlander hoard,
Six days the battle raged on high,
Six days we fought the Northlanders well.
Charles Singleton martyred on day seven,
Brave he led the vanguard archers,
An arrow straight brought instant death,
His troops surged forward against the hoard.
Young Andrew led the swordsmen onward,
Behind the Northlanders western camp,
Encircled all were trapped inside,
Young Andrew took Northlander surrender.

Canto 3. *Peace then came to South Bend land,*
We of Notre Dame withstood,
Northlander prisoners given choice,
Live in peace – or – disappear,
Upon the bloody fields of battle,
Swords now lying on the earth,
Reminders of the lives and loss,
Victorious we but at what cost,
Walk upon this field of battle,
Listen to the sounds of wind,
Last words of the dying,
Now words of the living.

Canto 4. *What have we learned by standing here*
Amid the bones of yesterday,
That good men who strive for peace,
Must defend their land in battle,
It is not enough to promise peace,
Peace must be defended,
Lives put to the test,
If true peace is to last,
Battle of South Bend River,
Defense of Notre Dame.

***

Inside the Room of Honor were many different items written by veterans and civilians at various times: on the eve of battle – left behind for survivors to read – if the battle won. Some of these appeared to have been penned quickly, once victory had been assured. Examining these relics, it was clear to us that the Defenders represented different groups from settlements and that they had come from far and wide to support South Bend in their time of need – peoples with ethnic ties to Africa, Asia, and Europe; Native Americans; peoples of different heritage all gathered at South Bend to stand fast against a common foe.

Sexton Jefferson guided us through the collection. Of special interest to us were banners, collected from the field of battle and prominently displayed. These banners were prepared from cloth of different sources and embellished by words dear to different militia regiments:

The character of man is his fate
We make war that we may live in peace
Death to the Northlanders
The Guard dies but does not surrender.

Posted behind glass on the east wall were the handwritten pages of two songs, written by veterans at an unknown time after hostilities had ended:

Song of the Teenage Archers (author unknown)

Send up the loud cheer hear now our cry
Break out the whiskey bottles of rye
Send young Frankie out for gin
Don't let a sober archer in
We never staggered we never fell
We killed those bastards sent them to hell
Look our fearless leader lies
Stone drunk on the barroom floor

Hear-hear-hear ... [loudly shout out]
Pour more beer ... [loudly shout out]
We are the Archers ... [loudly shout out]
We have no peer ... [loudly shout out]

Bartender barmaid give us more beer
Pour from your barrels bringing good cheer
Fill our glasses up to the top
Keep the beer flowing do not stop

Our glasses stand empty fill them again
Stand up and sing our victory refrain
Raise your voices join us in song
For we are the victors strong

Hear-hear-hear ... [loudly shout out]
Pour more beer ... [loudly shout out]
We are the Archers ... [loudly shout out]
We have no peer ... [loudly shout out]

Sexton Jefferson told us that the first two verses and the shouts were followed by four lines, repeated over and over with ever growing sadness:

We the Archers sing and drink until tears of pain stop flowing
We the Archers think of comrades dear who died in battle
We the Archers honor those who fell beside Saint Joseph's river
We the Archers sing and drink until tears of pain stop flowing

On the opposite wall beneath a glorious stained glass window, a second manuscript was posted under protective glass. The inscription provided a title and dedication, but no mention as to the author, only that he (or she) had been a member of the South Bend Lancer militia.

Song of the Lancers (to honor the memory our Captain James Smyth)

Etowah great spirit of the void
Whose vision commands our restless orb
Unto our home Northlanders came
Through endless time we endured pain
Across St. Joseph's River now
We await their crossing, our heads we bow
Etowah we cry out to Thee
Protect us in peril, give us victory.

Their deadly arrows arching high
Overhead we watched them fly
Now hand to hand, short sword and mace
Our lances thrusting face to face
Dear Captain Smyth on horse astride
A wound he took far deep inside
His last words I remember well
Fight on young Lancers, send them to hell.

Etowah deemed our battle won
We stood together father, son
A quiet swept across the land
Trumpets sounded near at hand
Upon the wind their plaintive tones
Swept o'r the green grass strewn with bones
All for what – I shouted loud
Dear Captain Smyth – my head I bowed.

What have I learned by standing here
Midst bodies cold, dead friends so dear
I learned we must defend our land
From every evil roaming band
And on this day Lancers stood tall
Recalling names of friends who fell
And on the breeze we heard the cry
A raven's caw screeched a sad good-by.

Inside the museum was another inscription left by a combatant clearly of Irish heritage. The words, spoke not of the Battle of South Bend, but to a much earlier conflict well before the Ripple Event and Dark Time. The words inscribed were dedicated to Irish volunteers who rebelled against the harshness imposed by occupiers of their sacred homeland. As Travis and I gazed into the case holding the document, the words touched us deeply as we read the two verses, words originally penned by an ancient one named Thomas Moore, to commemorate the lads who took up arms and repelled attackers during the battle of Oulart Hill in the far away Irish County of Wexford.

But who could it have been that copied and left behind this poignant message of valor and dedication to what is right? And who in this terrible age of territorial battles based upon cultural and faith differences, could recall the words at this difficult time, write them down, then leave behind such a dedication to the victors of the Battle of South Bend:

The minstrel boy to the war is gone,
In the ranks of death ye may find him;
His father's sword he hath girded on,
With his wild harp slung along behind him.

***

Sexton Jefferson and Historian Perkins drew our attention to what they considered the most important item in the museum, one guarded carefully by alternating watchmen and watchwomen. The document had been composed and signed by Commander Charles Singleton himself, and ultimately became known as the *Demand Notice*:

To you the Northlanders who would attack us we demand:

The right to live freely
The right to live in honor
The right to live without fear and intimidation
The right to live as we choose
The right to live in an atmosphere of tolerance and self-respect
The right to live without demands forced upon us
We the brothers and sisters of South Bend – these rights we demand
We the brothers and sisters of South Bend – stand united against you
We the brothers and sisters of South Bend –will defend these rights to the death.

Charles Singleton

***

Other displays inside the building, but separate from the Room of Honor, were items of a sinister nature, also for visitor viewing, lest through the passage of time visitors forget the events leading up to the Battle of South Bend. Behind protective glass were examples of Northlander recruitment pamphlets; diagrams for suicide vest construction; manuals describing hit-and-run tactics; suggestions how to intimidate gatherings of free-thinking Northerners. Historian Perkins unlocked a cabinet that held a vast collection of documents related to Northlander actions and deeds, items considered too gruesome for general display but nevertheless maintained as important relics for future scholars to inspect. There were sketches and descriptions of: torture and mass executions; forced labor camps; starvation of captive children; military training of new Northlander recruits; and examples – too many to count – of ill-treatment of the poor, homeless, and helpless.

Exiting the building, Jefferson and Perkins led us along several well-landscaped paths to view the bronze and stone monuments that had been placed at key locations to commemorate the Battle of South Bend. They explained that each of the memorials were prepared in three languages: Gaelic – to recall the Irish heritage at South Bend; the second in Latin – to honor the memory of educators executed by Northlander extremists; and the third in English, the language common to all the Defenders, residents, and volunteers from afar, who fought and defended freedom.

Near the ruins of a building that once had served as a field hospital for the badly wounded was the first monument placed by members of the 4th Militia Volunteers from Elkhart settlement group along the eastern stretch of Saint Joseph's River.

CUIMHNIGH AN TITE

Sa lá de fada ó shin an baird penned uair a scéalta dána
Conas i bhfianaise na gníomhais olc Honor reigned agus chas an taoide
Línte ainmneacha agus gníomhais cuimhne , feats gan choinne de valor
Ar fud na cnoic agus Dales áit a raibh fir maith i gcoinne an namhaid

BVM MEMORARE RESURGENTI

In diebus antiquis bardos semel praesaepibus eorum fabulas audet
Quo pacto auertisse regnavit honos malis
Lines his nominum et facta recordatus insperatis probitate fortissimi
Trans colles, et ubi bonum lum viri steterunt se in hostem

REMEMBER THE FALLEN

In days of long ago the Bards once penned their stories bold
How in the face of evil deeds honor reigned and turned the tide
Lines of names and deeds remembered, unexpected feats of valor
Across these hills and dales where good men stood against the foe

***

Just outside the former administrative building was a second monument that recalled the valor of militia troops from settlement groups nearby: Granter, Osceola, and La Paz, who stood their ground before the advancing hoard of Northlanders …

On this place beneath our golden dome we took a stand,
Repelled those who came to conquer our minds and land,
One hundred 58 were we
Who fought the foes, turned them away

***

Travis and I were led to a commemorative garden filled with lilies and marigolds – gold and white colors symbolic of life and death. Here was the cemetery of the fallen, eternal resting place of the 37 known and unknown militiamen and militiawomen who gave their lives for freedom at the Battle of South Bend:

Here on this place recall names of the fallen,
Names of those who died to save this sacred land,
Read aloud the names of each,

We who survive,
Remember well the sacrifice of the 37.

***

After-Word

What have we learned by standing here – amid these graves from yesteryear?

Travis and I sat together on the grass of the campus commons area just west of Washington Hall. We spoke of what we had seen and heard this day during our discussions with Sexton Aniel Jefferson and Historian Francis Perkins. Our tour of the battlefield sites with the recently placed memorial stone and the discussions that revealed the personal and tragic sides of the needless battle that took place here at South Bend. The anger and self-rightness of the Northlanders should not have been directed towards others who rejected their strict, unwavering cultural attitudes: convert or die should not have been the words pouring from their mouths.

What we learned this day was that not every human thinks the same, and that people are not all alike. Mercy and justice are not universal attributes or characteristics. Through the documents we viewed in the House of Honor, it was obvious that pain can be felt by all – whether friend or enemy, but for some like the Northlanders, the pain that they inflicted on countless Northern peoples was unnecessary and evil.

We learned that education of children is critical, that knowledge or lack thereof can be fatal. The behaviors and actions of the Northlanders did not start suddenly, but were born in the minds of individuals many solar cycles earlier, decades long before the Ripple Event. Behaviors that foretold the expansion of Northlander ideology were well known, but tolerated through the solar cycles by naïve others who elected to ignore such practices in the belief that live-and-let-live was a smoother, softer way to approach differences rather than to confront and stop inappropriate actions when initially manifested.

It cannot be that the Northlanders or the Defenders of South Bend were born good or evil. Both characteristics exist within each person. Through education, parenting, environmental and cultural opportunities – or lack thereof – the evil twin rises while its good counterpart recedes. And into the mix of every person comes opportunities for power, whether at the family, community, local, or wider level. Power can be noble when balanced with compassion and tolerance, but power shifts to incompetence and evil when charismatic leaders twist cultural and faith practices. And thus it was that the Defenders at the Battle of South Bend stood against a flood of others whose aim was to bring chaos, corruption, and danger to their communities.

We learned, too, that what earlier had been called the Wild Zone, that poorly described area of anarchy, danger, and death, nearly had been tamed and now was referred to as the Heartland Configuration (HC). The stable boundaries of the HC were the Mississippi River to the west; the Five Lakes and New Canada border to the north. Two poorly defined buffer zones (BZ) had been established to the east and south. The eastern buffer zone spilled back and forth between eastern Pennsylvania and western New York. Regarding the southern buffer zone, the Ohio River no longer was the boundary, as New Confederacy troops currently occupied a demilitarized zone from the river north to an east-west line of key observation posts, extending from Springfield old Illinois east through old Indianapolis, Dayton, and Columbus in old Ohio, then eastward to Wheeling old Pennsylvania along the eastern margin. The military commanders we spoke to believed that occupation south of this line may be necessary for 15-20 solar cycles until all cells subscribing to Northlander ideology were ferreted out and eliminated.

We saw evidence that throughout South Bend the surviving residents slowly had reconstructed their homes and businesses. Travis and I spent several weeks assisting builders and sharing meals with local families. Discussions always included poignant messages how the Northlanders had taken advantage of what once was the American Constitution and Bill of Rights; had found nooks and crannies in the law that favored expansion of their ideologies; and especially how Northlanders had taken advantage of the kindness of others.

Thus it was the Battle of South Bend that changed human actions and behaviors throughout the Heartland Configuration. Settlement groups both north and south of the truce line would need to develop and maintain strong military units able to repel any Northlander cells that remained – like the Minute Men of old – such volunteers would serve their settlement groups well.

And throughout our meetings with the Defenders who had survived, we heard three phrases repeated time and time again:

Forgive and forget – not
Trust but verify
Love us or leave us

***

Travis and I prepared to resume our trek eastward towards the Great Ocean. Our return journey from South Bend to the Ohio River would take us along a track through the settlements of Muncie, Dayton, and ultimately through the city whose slang name brought a smile to both of us whenever it was mentioned – Sin-Sin-Natty. Ours would be a long but interesting ride on horseback and, when we reached the Ohio River, we would board another vessel with fond memories of South Bend.

As we prepared our mounts and pack animals to leave, Sexton Aniel Jefferson visited us to share a last good-by:

Jackson: *Travis and Reese, you always will be welcome among us. You have seen and experienced much during your visit to our community, South Bend.*

Travis: *Truth be told, Sexton Jefferson, almost too much to fathom; heartbreak balanced with valor and the elation of victory. Thank you, too, for clarifying the difference between Rock Knee and Knute Rockne. I had thought originally that Rock Knee was an injury some men received when they played the old game of football. Now I understand!*

Jackson: *Travis and Reese, just yesterday one of the groundskeepers found a capsule buried beneath one of the trees at the center of the star-shape path just south of Morissey Hall. Inside was a tattered piece of paper that I thought you might enjoy reading before you depart. You may consider the context humorous, but the words are reflective of our Defender spirit:*

Dear Alice:
We lived to see another day
How we made those bastards pay
Battle buddy you did your share
You smiled at me, upon my dare
You chased that chicken up a tree
We laughed together watched him pee
We launched our arrows down he fell
Hard onto earth then straight to hell
Alice Trent I love you,
Your Battle Buddy
Alex McPherson
XXX-OOO-XXX

***

Ijano Esantu Eleman

Interlude-Conversation: 4
Battle of South Bend

***

It was vital for the Northlanders to meet sound defeat at the Battle of South Bend, was it not, K'Aser?

Vital and even more so, A'Tena. The Northlanders could not be let loose to behave as they want. For the Northlanders to be victorious would have been yet another evil to befall the inhabitants of – what was it called – old U.S.A. I tried means subtle and not so subtle to bring the Northlanders into better ways, more peaceful outlooks, but all my attempts were rebuffed. This being the case and with the battlefield being drowned in more and yet more blood, I intervened – and you must understand by now this is far from my preferred ways.

Very far, K'Aser, but the crisis point had to be addressed. So it was you brought the fog?

And the voice, A'Tena, but only to the Northlanders.

That voice, a most clever ploy! Then all ended as well as could be hoped given the situation. Sadly we seem never to be able to prevent wanton bloodshed.

Or at times stop warring sides even a little. Etowah, blessed be his name, be thanked for the power of my intervention this time at the Battle of South Bend.

Doubly thanked and blessed but do you think the ravens – good touch though they were – were perhaps a bit overdone?

The ravens? They were not of my doing, A'Tena. I cannot say they were unnecessary. At times I wonder if we ourselves are but units, pawns in another's testing.

I have pondered this myself, K'Aser, and have concluded it is best not to dwell on such matters.

I find it difficult to contend that outlook, A'Tena. Let us be thankful the Battle of South Bend is long over. Etowah be praised.

Chapter 5

Kanawha Passage: Point Pleasant to the Falls

Pre-Note

We left South Bend with fond memories of Sexton Jefferson and Historian Perkins. We would long recall their kindness and the many hours spent together where they revealed the strength and valor of the Defenders and how defeat had been heaped onto the Northlanders.

Our return to the Ohio River was uneventful. Once again we passed through settlements rebuilding from the damage and destruction caused by the Northlander raiders. Muncie and the campus of Ball State once more were rising from the ashes of despair and pain brought upon the residents by the Epidemic. Then we passed through Dayton and on into old Cincinnati with the streets of this once queen city of the West still labeled as Sin-Sin-Natty.

We crossed the Ohio River to Covington and negotiated passage to Point Pleasant some 25 kilo-miles southeast. Labor and commerce divisions of recent solar cycles designated that certain riverboat companies could traffic only between Kai-Row-Covington/Newport while a second group of riverboats was restricted for use between the two Points – Point Pleasant, Ohio (PPO) – and Point Pleasant, West Virginia (PPWV). This agreement necessitated the development of a thriving river-taxi business between Covington and Point Pleasant, Ohio.

After lengthy negotiations, we and our animals were accepted aboard river taxi *Covington #7,* a rustic converted barge large enough to carry

15 passengers, along with horses and pack animals. The trip upriver from Covington to PPO took a little less than five hours, and we arrived about noon. Once docked and unloaded, we walked our horses and pack animals along the riverfront. We traded for supplies using some of the metal ingots that we salvaged with permission at South Bend. The trade value for these small iron ingots was such that we would be able to remain independent from other passengers as we traveled upriver.

Between the Two Points

Several choices were available for our upriver transportation to PPWV. We selected a curious-looking double-decker vessel christened *Ohio Express*, captained by retired militia officer Major Bruce Willcocks. The ample deck space of the *Ohio Express* was sectioned into double births and storage facilities for about 75 passengers. Aft were livestock feeding and watering facilities where horses and mules could be curried and well-tended. Stable Master Marvin Rice informed us that at each port where we put in to take on more passengers and supplies, there would be ample time to disembark and exercise our animals.

And so we began the next portion of our journey.

Point Pleasant to Portsmouth

We left Point Pleasant and passed by the ruins of Moscow, a small settlement founded by French immigrants, veterans of Napoleon's Russian campaign long ago past time on the far side of the world. Then followed in sequence the shoreline settlements of Chilo, Augusta, and Ripley. Each small riverbank community appeared depopulated and reduced to ruins by Northlander sorties and the Epidemic. We then passed Manchester and Vanceburg.

As the hours passed, we wandered the deck of the *Ohio Express* and mingled with passengers. Some remained isolated and turned their backs to us as we approached. Others were more forthcoming; some merely smiled while others welcomed us with different greetings, such as *hollo, halloo, howdy, how-goes-it, greetings y'all,* and other terms we had not heard before.

We started conversations with those who seemed pleasant. We exchanged experiences of the Ripple Event, Dark Time, and the more recent Epidemic. We heard stories of their families, backgrounds, and travel destinations. The tone and content of some conversations were sad, sometimes uplifting, and still other times funny even droll. Together we listened intently as they related their stories. I copied their words into my diary:

> **Barney Appleberry,** auto shop detailer – *You ask what I do? I have to laugh! I once had a shop in a small town outside of Dayton. But as you can see these days, there are no cars anymore, just parts of once-beautiful automobiles now cobbled into what are now call wonder carts. Do you have these out west too? Travis and Reese, you may be too young to remember the smooth lines and fins of classic automobiles like the 1956 Bel Air Convertible – ohhhh – or the shape and form of the grill mounted on the front of a 1982 Oldsmobile Cutlass. Customers would ask me to detail and decorate the hood of their car – perhaps a painting of a mythological hero or a scene of forest and lake sunsets on the side panels; and whatever on the back of the trunk. My artwork blended with the geometric intersecting lines of these cars. I was the best detailer in all of central old Ohio, known for my fine work and attention to customer's needs. Then one day the Northlanders appeared on the scene. The morning the bastards arrived, they executed two of my best workers. I survived only because I provided them with a false conversion statement. Can something really be a lie if it saves your life? Well my false statement gave me about 10 days to plan an escape. When I took off southward, I had to be careful to avoid Eye-75 and Highway 42 because the Northlanders had roadblocks on both just outside of Lebanon. To avoid them, I took off cross-country through Goshen then down to Owensville, where I had a cousin who put me up for a couple of days. We parted and I headed south again through Batavia, then Amelia, and ultimately reached the Ohio River near New Richmond. You may not believe it, but I swam across the Ohio and found safety and sanctuary with a New Confederacy Militia team encamped just outside of Carthage. They asked me if I knew cars – because they needed a supply of wonder carts to carry weapons and supplies. I told them that I was their man. You ask what is the rest of the story? Well here I am headed up river towards the other Point Pleasant. I hear there are opportunities there for hard workers like myself. What do you think?*

***

Two large signs along shore signaled our approach to the tiny hamlet of Friendship. One of the passengers, William Bidanski, told us that

Friendship was his birthplace. During the early solar cycles of the Dark Time Recovery Period he and his family moved south across the river where they were accepted and found work. During his later teen solar cycles William helped rebuild the riverfront northern New Confederacy hamlets of St. Paul and Firebrick:

> **William Bidanski,** carpenter – *All communities need carpenters, right? Who else built shelters for family units during the Ripple and Dark Time? I found out quickly as a kid and then as a young adult that nearly any survivor could pound nails as well as me, and that others could hew and trim timbers, and erect walls and roofs just as well. I soon realized that I had nothing special to offer, and that my existence ultimately would be challenged. So I had to take on something different in order to survive. What I developed no one else had conceived before – a way to combine carpentry working skills with recreation. It was I who invented the Carpentry Games, and these became my baby and the games really caught on. The concept basically was this: teams of males and females would vie against one another in contests and events, such as the hammer throw, where bottles or cans were stacked into pyramid piles, then knocked down by contestants throwing ballpeen hammers. The best idea of all, however, was the compression-powered nail gun survival course event, where participants competed against one another by negotiating a twisting/turning route, evading pop-up Northlander images. Those running the maize with their nail gun weapons got extra points if they hit the heads and groins of the images. Some fun, right? Sometimes the maize paths crossed at key intersections so the participants had to be careful not to fire and hit one another. The participant who completed the course quickest with the least number of nail wounds was declared the winner. Other events I developed for the Carpentry Games included hurling the 4 x 6, something similar to the caber of the ancient Scots. Others included the hubcap throw for distance and sawing the log – with one hand. Over many solar cycles different New Confederacy militias competed at the Carpentry Games held in the open fields just south of Firebrick. This way I got to know many of the troopers and their commanders. When the call came to repel the Northlanders who were advancing on South Bend, I lined up with the 38th mobile Kentucky Militia regiment. I was part of the joint militia southern force that turned the tide. I*

recall with great joy the Northlander retreat. I remember, too, the fog that enveloped the battlefield, and that the scene was eerie. Some of the men I fought with said that the Northlanders retreated because voices in the fog told them to lay down their arms. I don't believe such nonsense. Voices from the fog? Come 'on now, let's get real, right? The Northlanders retreated because we were whipping their indelicate asses. What do you think? In about an hour, we will reach Portsmouth. I'm getting off and heading back to Friendship to participate in the reconstruction of my birth home to honor the memory of my mother, father, and sisters.

***

Portsmouth to Ashland

We put into shore at Portsmouth along Riverfront Park, opposite the ruins of Shawnee State University. First Mate Ellwood Greenstreet told us we would be loading passengers and supplies for about six hours and, if we wanted to disembark with our horses, we might find it enjoyable to ride through portions of town where reconstruction was taking place.

The once-proud steel plant with open-hearth furnaces stood vacant and in ruins. The exteriors of four or five buildings in the historic portion of lower Portsmouth were being rebuilt, a sign of community pride and recovery. The location that appealed most to us, however, was the prehistoric mound complex near the confluence of the Scioto and Ohio Rivers.

On our return back to the *Ohio Express,* we passed through Riverside Park and encountered a singer of songs, a street minstrel of sorts with two instruments, one a simple four-string tenor guitar, and the other something called a dulcimer. The minstrel's hair was disheveled, and he had wild piercing eyes, similar to the type I sometimes encountered during strange dreams when my sleep was fitful. He fixed his gaze upon me and asked if we might be interested in a performance, otherwise he would resume resting. We had nothing for which to barter, and so told him. He paused at our words and then stood and once more fixed me with his eyes, and said, "Here's to you, lass, remember well, do not forget, I will not tell the others." I had no idea what he meant. And then he began his song…

I asked my love to take a walk
To take a walk, just a little way
Down beside where the waters flow
Down by the banks, of the Ohio.

Then only say that you'll be mine
And in no other arms entwine
Down beside, where the waters flow
Down by the banks of the Ohio.

He stopped and again fixed me with his eyes, and once more spoke directly to me:

I will not sing to you the last verses of my ballad
Your time will come but it will not be soon
Another that you love will precede you.

Then he turned and walked away. Travis and I thought all this very strange, indeed.

As we re-boarded, Stable Master Marvin Rice helped us re-berth our animals. Then gangplanks were drawn aboard and, after two short boat whistles, we resumed our Ohio River journey.

On past New Boston, Wheelersburg, Lloyd and Greenup; then Wurtland, Worthington, Ironton, and on towards Ashland.

Elaine Ferrell, dance instructor – *I've seen it all: Square dancing, hip-hop, waltz, ballet, foxtrot, minuet, quickstep, salsa, clog, Irish, Greek, and even Albanian. I could train anybody to dance, from the youngest to oldest, from the coordinated to the – well you know; male and female, single or group sessions. I was a dance instructor, the best. And then the worst times came with the arrival of the Northlanders forcing me and my mate to flee south into the hinterlands. We joined a roving gang in order to survive. I no longer taught dance, but watched others take part. My favorite was what we called the bullet dance. When we caught a thief or another gang member, we fired rounds at his or her feet making them dance – just like in the old cowboy movies. Then the ammunition ran out and we had no more bullet dances. No one really likes to dance much anymore. The Epidemic seemed to have taken the heart and spirit out of folks. How I long for those good old days. I really liked hip-hop, but now my knees and balance are shot, and I can't repeat the moves that yielded me the championship trophies that I once stashed in my bedroom. Those trophies I left behind when we fled south. Bad mistake: I could have melted them down into metal exchange ingots. But who knew at the time we would need such items for barter? Now no one cares* *about dancing, and the children these days never learned to waltz or foxtrot, and don't even know what the words mean. Do you?*

***

William [Sweet Willy] O'Keefe, casino dealer – *I dealt Blackjack at the Red Star Casino in Columbus, old Ohio. Once money vanished, my job followed. I left Columbus and headed south towards Chillicothe. I was really slick at handling cards, a real sharpie, so I set up a street-side table near the intersection of East 4th Street and Douglass Avenue over in east Chillicothe. I entertained passing survivors with card tricks six hours a day, weekends included. During an average stint on the street, at least during spring and summer, I earned about a gallon of water and perhaps a quarter of a loaf of bread. But all such winnings vanished during fall and winter, when the violent cold winds blew through Chillicothe freezing everything in sight – including me. So how would a street performer card dealer respond to such adversity? I needed an alternative line of work, so I focused on developing a product that I could use for barter, a product that I convinced others that they needed to survive. What I developed was an alternative food supplement that would cut the consumer's appetite and ward off or minimize seasonal cold or flu symptoms. This product was easy to develop, as all the ingredients were available at vacant lots and city landscape areas. I prepared this elixir myself from dried creepy-crawly angleworms, and flavored it with an extract of red and black ants which when blended together gave the powder a tart tangy flavor. When hawking my product, I told passersby that it would add vim and vigor to all who consumed it, and what do you know? I succeeded beyond my wildest dreams and ultimately became well-known locally. In this way, I exchanged my appetite-reduction product for enough food to keep me in calories over the next two solar cycles, and didn't have to do card tricks anymore. Yes, I survived the Northlanders and the Epidemic, and would like to believe that the ingredients in my product protected me somehow. And something else is curious: how could it be that so many people died during the Epidemic, but that I and the primary customers of my product – those who used a little every day – survived? I'm no doctor, but there must have been something protective in that worm and ant powder. What do you think?*

***

Ashland to Crown City

Shortly after passing Worthington and Hanging Rock, we reached Ashland on the south bank in old Kentucky of the New Confederacy. While most maps listed the site as Ashland, some cartographers continued to use the original name of the settlement, Poage's Landing. Ashland was once a prominent producer of steel but the Ripple, Dark Time, and Epidemic reduced the workforce to fewer than 200, so production was abandoned. We disembarked and rode through the nearly deserted streets of this once-grand city. We could sense despair all about. I had to ask myself, why did the *Ohio Express* put into Ashland? The answer revealed itself once we rode east along Front Street and then turned south on 20th street into the Central Park area. The reason now was clear. Small clusters of families were situated in the park, crafting and assembling military weapons using copper, bronze, iron, and steel pieces gleaned by children and young adults. These hand-produced weapon items could be bartered for food and various beverages, and formed a lucrative business up and down the Ohio River.

We re-boarded the *Ohio Express* and continued past South Point, Ceredo, and Burlington; then Huntington, Proctorville, and Lesage towards Crown City.

***

> **Maria Jones,** housekeeper – *Some say that simple tasks reap the greatest rewards. Before the Ripple Event, I provided a neat and tidy home for my family members, for my husband, three children, pet dog, two cats, and three cockatiels. I was content with my life. I poured my love and hopes into building and nurturing our family, and I stressed the importance of education and self-responsibility to my children. Then came the Ripple Event and Dark Time when food was short. Others in the neighborhood starved, but we did not. When I was a child, my great grandmother taught me how to prepare porridge and bread from acorns – those terribly bitter nuts that grace the branches of the stately oaks that grow across the length and breadth of our nearby valley and foothills. My friends rejected such products, but I went about collecting acorns. Leaching the tannins from the nuts and grinding the flour was time-consuming but provided my family with sufficient food so that we survived. These simple nuts, and the tasks taught to me by my great grandmother, saved the lives of my children.*

***

Dwayne Thompson, tenets of life chaplain – *I am not really happy speaking with you but since you have been kind to me, I shall indulge you. Ask your questions, and I will respond. I was called to the ministry when just a teenager, it was like I heard an actual voice urging me to accept, a responsibility to assist others. My family was not religious so I was not raised within a specific denomination, cult, or sect. In fact, had I been a member of what might be called a standard faith. My actions and thoughts would have called for my excommunication, since I rejected the concept of being bound to specific dogmas. You might say that I came to my specific calling as a deist – believing in a supreme being – but not of a specific earth-bound group. I learned the tenets of Buddhism, Christianity, Islam, Judaism, and other once global religions. I participated in vision quests and walkabouts, taking part in different Native American, African, and Australian spiritualistic programs. I fit not into any of these. Then came the dream wherein a voice spoke to me with a precise message. I took the dream words to heart, continued my studies, and ultimately formed my religious practice around what I called the Seven Tenets of Life or the 7ToLs – a list of behaviors revealed to me in that long ago dream conveyed by a universal guiding force, behaviors universal expected of all humans:*

Aid the weak and helpless;
Treat women and men equally;
Appreciate differences;
Reject behaviors that degrade or harm others;
Welcome each newborn to the family hearth;
Respect and honor your mating partner;
Celebrate those who help you through life's passages.

I preached the 7ToLs on street corners and on the grassy quadrangles of many once-great universities. I was ridiculed by students and faculty members, but I continued because of my firm belief and dedication to the 7ToLs. I did not elevate one faith above another in my presentations. I sought the core goodness of each. I raged against intolerance and bigotry as both evils continued to grow and expand across the sweep of our once-great nation. Then came the Ripple Event, Dark Time, and the Epidemic. It was as if all living on earth were being tested – but being tested for what? I had no answer. I saw no future in my work. Now I am aboard this ship heading eastward towards the rising sun – not knowing what each day will bring. I am confident, though, that better times are coming but I do not know how, when, or where. It is getting too painful to speak more about this. Let me leave you with the following words that continue to haunt me:

Oh why have we been abandoned?
Why does evil flow across the verdant fields?
Oh why have we been abandoned?

Oh why have we been abandoned?
What purpose lies ahead?
Oh why have we been abandoned?

Oh why have we been abandoned?
We cannot see the future?
Oh why have we been abandoned?

***

Crown City to Gallipolis

The small settlement of Crown City loomed on the northwest river shore. The central portion of the hamlet was a square, bounded on four sides by Galia, Vine, Walnut, and Williams streets and bisected by Crown and Charles streets. Once a relatively small settlement, the Wayne National Forest and nearby Wildlife Area west of Crown City provided lumber and wild game both in high demand up and down the Ohio River. The Green Bottom Wildlife Area across the Ohio River to the southeast served as a secondary source of animal protein. Here at Crown City, the residents erected facilities for deer and elk reproductive activities. Once these had proved effective and economically profitable during the Dark Time Recovery Period, then buffalo also were introduced and raised in herds like cattle.

Travis and I rode around the central square of Crown City, dismounted, and observed the meat production line where the game animals were killed and where the meat was sun-dried using energy and heat from solar collection panels. The dried portions were wrapped and packed in reed/wicker baskets, then transported by wonder cart to the dock at the east end of Main and Mill streets.

After we returned to the *Ohio Express,* we watched the loading of the meat-filled baskets that finished in the late afternoon. We ate dinner with several passengers as we passed by Glenwood, Ashton, and Apple Grove: we were due to reach the port of Gallipolis in the morning.

Tanisha Oliver, crossing guard – *I was a volunteer crossing guard on Jensen Road that ran north/south in front of Pickens Elementary School in my hometown. I will not tell you the name of my community because my memories still remain painful, and I cannot return to that settlement because of a problem I don't want to discuss. I served my community well for 27 solar cycles and then came the Ripple and Dark Time – school was out. During my service, I saved the lives of seven children and was instrumental in working with the local police to apprehend those drivers who ignored the posted speed limits near the school, who on occasion bashed through the crosswalk where I was standing. By my quick reactions, I thrust the children aside before the speeding cars could strike them. For my actions, I received three commendations, and the school children knew me by my first name, Tanisha. Today no one calls me Tanisha or Tani. During the last several solar cycles, I am seen only as an old woman taking up space and eating food that should go to younger others. No one remembers my efforts and how I saved young lives. I keep my anger inside, at least for now, but I have a plan the next time I am disrespected, a plan that will deal with those who disrespect me. That is enough for now: leave me alone!*

***

Jason Bui, barber – *Not much use for barbers these days. I was told once that decades ago, long before I was born, there were people called Hippies who let their hair grow long. But if you look carefully at the people today, especially since the Northlander raids and the Epidemic, almost everybody has long hair. If you look carefully you can distinguish different cultural groups and their affiliations by the shape of their haircut and the trim of their beards. Not many men are clean-shaven these days; even old women with faint mustaches cause me to smile, since I know that I could serve them well. But that is another story. And these days who cares about shaving arms and legs? While I am sometimes called shorty, or made fun of because of my stature, those who taunt me should beware since I keep my straight razor in my back pocket – just in case. You want to see it?*

***

Gallipolis to Point Pleasant

As expected, the *Ohio Express* slowed as we approached port at Gallipolis. We knew from speaking with Major Bruce Willcocks, our ship's captain, that Point Pleasant was just a few kilo-miles north from disembarkation point. The reason for stopping at Gallipolis was both medical and economic. Point Pleasant, West Virginia, commanded the confluence of the Ohio and Kanawha rivers. The New Confederacy Militias stationed at PPWV demanded medical checks of all passengers attempting passage east along the Kanawha River to stem the possibility that the Epidemic might spread further. While the main impact of the Epidemic had passed the militia force, checking health of all prospective passengers remained in place. The economic reason for disembarking at Gallipolis was because the Ohio River ships had been forbidden to proceed eastward along the Kanawha River, due to competitive restrictions that excluded all Ohio River ships in favor of West Virginia transporters.

This regional dispute between the more unsettled lands to the west and the New Confederacy did not result in armed conflict, but stirred the anger among managers of the Ohio River boat companies operating between Covington and Point Pleasant, old West Virginia. How could it be that ship owners with the objective of improving commerce and trade, up both the Ohio and Kanawha Rivers, could not agree? Their inability to compromise forced implementation of restrictive rules upon hard-working shippers and passengers. It seems that old politics of favoritism had returned to this region.

Travis and I thanked Major Willcocks and Stable Master Rice for their kind help and assistance. We off-loaded our animals and rode into Gallipolis, a community originally founded by the French. In the center of the city park was a commemorative stele with the inscription:

Nous prenons cette terre pour Notre localité où nous vivrons toujours [*We take this land for our settlement where we will live always*]

The words were not prophetic, as the only French person we encountered riding through town was the owner of a recently renovated bakery that, according to the sign, once was known as Shari's Berries. The new manager, it seems, was a distant cousin of the original Shari LeCont, who was visiting Gallipolis at the time of the Ripple Event. The current manager Francoise Bouganie was most pleasant and suggested that if we had time, we should ride up the east side of Chickamauga Creek since the view of the river valley from that elevation was spectacular.

We were in no hurry, so we took Bouganie's advice. Riding upslope among the scattered pines and occasional oak we came to a stream junction. The main contribution to Chickamauga Creek entered from the west, while a smaller unnamed stream joined from the north. At the center of the "Y" confluence, Travis spotted something unusual, partially hidden by broken tree limbs and leaves. We brushed the detritus away and found a flat stone upon which were carved words that appeared to be French:

Cette terre qui était autrefois nôtre nous réclamons
aujourd'hui au nom de la Nouvelle-France.

I copied the text into my diary with the intention of having them translated at a later date. I could not identify the complete message, but was certain that it had to do with something about the land where we stood with our horses and pack mules, and something about New France. The full translation would have to wait.

Point Pleasant to Winfield

We returned down-slope to the shoreline and resumed our trek north towards Point Pleasant. The primary bridge across the Ohio River connecting Gallipolis with Henderson and Point Pleasant West Virginia had been destroyed during the Dark Time and had not been rebuilt. We were assisted across the river by Jenkin's Ferry, which put us ashore with our animals at the docks below the green zone, known as Point-Between-Two-Waters or *Tu-Endie-Wei*. Just to the east were moorings for the Kanawha River transport boats.

We negotiated our fares with one of the local brokers and were accepted aboard the *Coal Miner's Daughter,* captained by Mildred Smyth. According to local legend, Smyth earned her right to captain a Kanawha River transport by her superior test scores and considerable knowledge of the river course, how it changed between spring and winter, potential dangerous sand banks, water level fluctuations, and overall knowledge of channel depth. Captain Smyth's stable master was Cassius Mayweather. He had won his militia and cavalry stripes long ago, pursuing bandits in the desert lands of the SouthWest Configuration. He took charge of our horses and pack mules. We were in good hands.

Leaving Point Pleasant and starting up the Kanawha River, we passed by Leon, Arbuckle, Grimms Landing, Buffalo, Frazier's Bottom, and Midway on our way to Winfield. Aboard the *Coal Miner's Daughter* there was the usual group of passengers, some friendly and gregarious, others sitting or standing off by themselves. Like our experience on the *Ohio Express,* Travis and I engaged a number of them in conversation as we shared information about our respective lives.

Alice Cummings, grocery checker – *Once long past before the Ripple Event, my mother's life was hard. Every day she labored at our local grocery store: scan and bag, scan and bag. Once there was rhythm to her task. She would scan the customer's item quickly, then slam it inside a cloth, paper, or plastic bag. Scan and bag, scan and bag. She would say, "Here you are sir/madam, may my assistant here help you to your transport vehicle?" That was long ago. No more scanning and bagging groceries these days. But there was something about her words – scanning and bagging – that continued to stay with me. Since the Ripple Event, Dark Time, and the past Epidemic, I have continued to practice my art of scanning and bagging in a different way. Instead of scanning those funny-looking stripe lines on food packages as my mother did, I scan the landscape for large animals that could serve as food for my family unit. Once I see potential dinner on the horizon, I practice my stealth approach and bag the game animal using my 125 kilo-pound bow with arrows tipped with hardened silver. I love to hear the sound my arrows make when loosed – ssssffffitttt – the game animal never hears it, but I do. Oh, that wonderful sound. And I have good aim too. Once my arrows are loosed, they travel at high speed towards the game animal's chest. Quickly I re-aim and ssssffffitttt, another arrow is loosed. The game animal staggers, stumbles, and falls. Scan and bag – same words, different outcomes. I'm really good at what I do. What else do you want to know?*

Isaac Ford, auditor – *Numbers in balance, columns of data all correct to the nth detail. But life now is unbalanced, making no sense. North has become south, joy has become sorrow, we have become dead in life. Nothing balances except in my dreams or nightmares, where I stand atop a tall building looking out over the ledge down upon the destruction of my city. I balance to and fro debating whether or not to lean forward to my death, or to lean backward and join once more the living. What am I to do these days? So much has been lost. I survived the Ripple, Dark Time, even attacks by the Northlanders, and this last horror, the Epidemic. What can anyone say?*

Money once was my goal: then money became useless. During the Ripple Event and Dark Time, I broke in and entered any house, any store. I took anything I wanted. But at other times upon entry, I just looked about and left everything intact. I have slept on actual piles of money, but those green rectangles serving as my mattress had become worthless. I had become a cash millionaire – and when inflation came – a cash billionaire. Then my money became useless. Today, I have nothing; my family is gone, my wife and children perished. In my dreams I teeter on the precipice, rocking to and fro. What direction will I choose? Let me think more upon this. Just to let you know, I have no current occupation and live from hand-to-mouth. Why, you ask, am I taking this trip up the Kanawha River? Why am I here? Perhaps to begin again. I don't really know. I'm getting off at Winfield. I plan to hike deep into the Blue Ridge where I can lead a frugal life existing on wild nuts and berries. Will I emerge on the other side with my body and soul cleansed? Will I find what I am searching for? Who knows?

***

Winfield to South Charleston

We approached Winfield in late afternoon and put into the south bank at the 2nd street docks near the head of Ferry Street. Across the Kanawha River to the west was the Red House district, named long ago for the color of the soil here used by masons to make bricks. No intact homes or businesses were visible, as the hamlet had been attacked several times by Northlander incursions.

Winfield was our first opportunity on the Kanawha to disembark with our horses, and we received permission from Captain Smyth. She cautioned us, however, that the *Coal Miner's Daughter* would leave 30 minutes after the ships' siren announced eminent departure. Riding through Winfield, we encountered not more than 30 or 40 residents up and about tending to business. Most appeared lean and gaunt with thinly drawn faces and sad expressions. There appeared to be a food depot located at the Winfield Middle School off Sabre Street, but the doors were locked and we could not enter. Upon hearing our ship's siren, we rode quickly back and re-boarded the *Coal Miner's Daughter*.

We next passed by small communities of Hometown, Plymouth, and Black Betsy. Captain Smyth informed us that the unusual name stemmed from two possible sources: a Black woman named Betsy who reportedly sold local coal miners alcoholic beverages called moonshine. Alternatively, Black Betsy was the name given to the product that she sold.

We then passed Raymond City, Poca, and Scary. The origin of the name Poca for the settlement was lost with the mists of time. Nevertheless, the name offered bright humor to its residents, since the local school athletic teams were nicknamed the *Poca Dots*. In a similar and amusing light, the school sports teams at the settlement of Scary were called *The Hatchets* – said to date back to a skirmish during the long ago American Civil War battle fought here. Scary indeed!

We moved on past the settlement of Nitro, towards our port destination of South Charleston.

***

> **Deborah Cooley,** court translator – *My talents once were in high demand in the local and regional courtrooms of Bloomington, old Indiana. Few court translators had my breadth of skills and talents. My biological father, who raised me until I was seven solar cycles old, spoke Arabic, an Egyptian dialect. My mother was Hispanic-American, born in old Arizona, and relocated to Bloomington with her family. So it was that Arabic, English, and Spanish became my languages. I graduated from the University of Indiana at Bloomington with my undergraduate degree in linguistics. I immediately found employment with the firm of Jenkins, Jones, and Knight, where I was a legal assistant reviewing Arabic and Spanish documents for our trial lawyers. This task, however, became too boring for me, so I enrolled in the Avery Simmons Professional School and entered their court translator certification program. My most interesting case was the trial of Frankie "Fingers" Bonner, who dipped his wick – as they say – into the financial pockets of local crime boss, Deacon Duncan. It turned out that Bonner embezzled some 13 million in gold bullion. So much for all of that, which I am sure doesn't interest you.*
>
> *With the onset of the Ripple Event and Dark Time, there was no need for court translators. Justice was swift and, as they say, draconian, if you know what that word means. I lost my job and struggled through two solar cycles but eventually wound up here in the New*

Confederacy, where I took on short-term jobs at various locales along the Kanawha River. Today, no one seems to care about the nuances of language and understanding the law. In fact, I now believe there is no law except that of the jungle – swift verdicts followed by even quicker executions. You ask, what did I learn from all of this? Well, college education is a good thing so long as peace and harmony exist. But college education isn't worth a whack if you don't know how to survive after economic and political collapse. I would have been better able to survive the Ripple Event and Dark Time if I had previous training how to hunt wild game and how to identify edible wild plants. Take this as a given truth – from a one-time court translator.

***

Louis Evans, fast-food cook – *I was a really good cook. I could flip burgers two at a time and make 20 kinds of different omelets. My fried chicken was tender and tasty beyond belief. Nowadays it is impossible to be a fast-food cook – slow-food cook, yes, but fast food cook, no. I honed my present skills making one-pot dishes over small campfires deep in the secluded alleys of my former home city, Cincinnati, a place that people today joke about. Now I cook for myself. I keep a set of kitchen knives and cleavers in my belt for easy access if and when – more when than if – food-grabbers appear and threaten me. The only way to keep those indigents at bay is to toss them peelings from the potatoes I have stolen, or hurl over to them scraps of celery stalks. The struggle for food during the Ripple Event and Dark Time was terrible. And now, even after the Epidemic, I must be careful and constantly on guard. I continue to see food-grabbers fighting over my discarded scraps. Whenever I cook, I keep one hand on the skillet and the other on my stainless steel meat cleaver.*

***

South Charleston to Prat

Due to river traffic restrictions that prohibited boats of our type from tying up at old Charleston, we docked at South Charleston. The decision as explained by Captain Smyth was part political and part for health reasons, especially lingering fear that the Epidemic still had not abated and politicians wanted to limit city access.

We disembarked with our horses and ambled through South Charleston, drawn to the singular formation of a relic Native American mound called the Criel, a site located along MacCorkle Avenue, between Oakes and Seventh Avenues. We had first observed the structure while standing at the rail of our boat. We were told the mound was constructed by a culture referred to as the Adena. Modern steps cut into the side of the mound enabled visitors to climb to the top. We tethered our horses and did so. Atop the structure, we pondered who would have built the structure and whether or not it served as burial or some other purpose.

Rejoining the *Coal Miner's Daughter*, we passed by the hamlets of Malden, Rand, Marmet, Belle, Diamond, Dickson, Chelyan, Shrewsbury, Glasgow, Hansford, and on to our destination, the small community of Pratt.

***

Christine Hanley, historian – *Those who know and understand history keep track of time. But how many do so today or even care? Do most people know and understand their past, how the present came to be? Do most people know the twists and turns, the events that brought each of us to any precise moment in time? Most of our children these days care not for history. They say, "We are in the now, not the past." They ask, "Who cares about events leading up to anything?" They say, "What is, is, and cannot be changed, so why worry and ponder the past?" They say, "History is the realm of you old one," meaning anybody over the age of 30 solar cycles. They ask, "Why are you bothering me with all of this old stuff?" They say, "If you want to teach, then do so, but teach us how to make weapons so we can defend against the Northlanders." They ask me to teach them how to improve their ability to track animals and thieves. They want to leave the study of history to those assigned to the Memory Guild. They say, "Let the old ones in the MG debate what the results would have been if this or that had happened instead of other sets of this and that." One student said recently, "Leave me alone! Can't you see that I have a deer in my sights? If you keep bothering me, I will miss the shot and not be able to bring food to our family table, Gitawayyouhistorian!" What do you think, Travis and Reese? Was it the same with the young children and teens at your Settlement Group? I think you called it Bison Camp, right? Is it not said – if you do not know history, you are doomed to repeat it? The young* *children and teens today have heard this phrase time and time again. But the words have not become a part of their being, of their minds and hearts. I fear for the future. Travis and Reese, I fear that the Dark Times once again will descend. Yes the Northlanders were defeated at the Battle of South Bend, but only a few of my students know of the defender's victory. And if they do, they do not understand the significance of the victory. Even adults traveling with us today on the Coal Miner's Daughter have told me, "Well that was that – now we can relax." Who was it that once said, "Vigilance is the workhorse of freedom?" I don't remember – I must be getting old.*

***

Caesar Martinez, gardener – *Long ago I came to this country to seek a better life. I followed the coyote's route and avoided capture, incarceration, and deportation. Through the solar cycles I flourished. I earned in one month what it would have taken me 10 solar cycles in my homeland. And then came what you call the Ripple and Dark Time, and what some of us with southern roots beyond the other Great River call the Tiempo Oscuro. But others of us with the same heritage but stronger work ethic call the Tiempo Oscuro by a different term, the Oportunidad!*

During and after the disaster of those past days, we worked hard and rebuilt our communities through opportunities presented. They now call me Mr. Martinez, La Mejor Gardiner. And I tend my garden and weed carefully, removing some plants, adding others, until my garden developed into a giant collective based upon hard work. And with hard work and good results, I have provided for my family and expanded until now more than 2,500 additional families of hard workers comprise my company. Truly, I came to a land of opportunity and I am proud to be a citizen of this country. I am traveling aboard the Coal Miner's Daughter to seek additional opportunities. What will I find, and will the opportunities be presented? Only time – and hard work – will tell.

***

Pratt

Captain Smyth asked us to stand by. After tending to landing duties, she spoke with us about the village just opposite. Pratt had been one of the major coal mining operations in the region and now was the reason the *Coal Miner's Daughter* made regular stops. The main coal-producing seams were discovered in the late 1880s near what still is called Paint Creek. Smyth related that during a period of union and company upheavals, there arose a dominant woman named Mary "Mother" Jones, who fought for worker's rights. She, the so-called grandmother of all labor agitators, was known for her words:

Pray for the dead, and fight like hell for the living!

Captain Smyth told us that Mother Jones had four children, but all had died. What she related next touched us deeply:

Mother Jones and I are linked in spirit. My great great grandfather fought alongside her for miner's rights here at Pratt. I always have considered Mother Jones to be my alternative grandmother. In my dreams I was, in fact, the Coal Miner's Daughter. So now you know why I always stop my vessel at Pratt. Look about. There is little to see. If you go ashore, you can visit the location where Mother Jones was imprisoned during the coal strike of her era. If you want, I would be pleased to walk with you to visit the site. The house is gone; only the foundation remains, but the site remains important in my heart.

Together we disembarked. We crossed Paint Creek using a rickety wooden bridge that needed serious tending, and found ourselves on Center Street. A few paces later, we encountered a sign identifying the location as *Former Boarding House of Mrs. Carney and Former Prison of Mother Jones*. The house was no more. Tradition, however, was to pay due respect. Captain Smyth drew our attention to a small pile of smooth round stones near the walkway and told us:

Pick up one – spit on the ground three times – then lob your stone into the central foundation area for good luck. In this way, we honor the memory of Mother Jones.

***

We re-boarded and resumed our journey, passing by Handley, Montgomery, Smithers, Boomer, Alloy, Deep Water, and Charlton Heights towards our final destination Kanawha Falls.

Lily Carpenter, hairdresser – *As the young would say to me, lady you're really old. And I in turn reply to them, kid you're really* *young. My grandmother told me that before the Ripple Event and Dark Time, townies would come into her hairdressing shop to get prettied-up. Strip the color, twist the strands, slice and shave the sides, apply the glop, and let it set. She would receive payment and the client would leave her shop and go off strutting down the street. Then men started to request her services: slick side patches combed back, waves, curls, whooping across the crown, ducktails, buzz cuts, a greaser look. Then, when all the crap happened, the only thing anybody wanted was a head shave so they wouldn't collect lice and other bugs that sometimes hopped here and there when hair grew long. But that was long ago.*

When I work these days and evenings, I sit the client down, lather up my homemade lye soap (scented with wild mint leaves), and do the best I can to shave their heads. The usual deal at least during the recent solar cycles is to charge clients this way: each is measured by the number of nicks and cuts I make. Four accidental cuts or less, I get two loaves of bread. But if I nick or cut the customer more than four times, I must give them compensation of a small jar of my special moonshine. I try my best to be careful. My customers challenge me by wiggling in the chair in their attempt to win the liquor. Through the solar cycles, I have found it best to shave the heads of my clients after they have become drunk and already passed out. I see that you are laughing. Good thing these days to laugh, don't you think? I hop on and off boats like the Coal Miner's Daughter going up and down stream. I hope to cough up more business. Travis, you look like you need a shave – how about it?

Brandon Jones, advertising executive – *I was really good. My sample slogans from times long ago past put me out in front of all competitors: eat when you can, you won't have another chance. Save water, save your life. Death to the slothful. These three were but a few of the slogans used with my advertising campaigns. Well, perhaps, not campaigns, since only my sister and I worked together, and for about five solar cycles we had no clients. I tried to interest different settlement groups in my slogans to encourage work and group cohesion. I developed phrases like: All for One – One for All. Well, you are right, I did not actually create those words and, yes, I took them out of some book one of my teachers gave me to read* *about three stupid French soldiers, or something like that. I did find success with another phrase I developed: Do Unto Others As You Would Have Them Do Unto You. What do you mean that this isn't an original phrase? It certainly came from my hard-working mind. Why are you challenging me, Travis? I never heard those words before and they just came to me, so lighten up – as they once used to say. I tried to influence several settlement groups into using phrases such as: Kill the Bastards and Chop Off their you-know-what. But these efforts were rejected. When limited trade returned during the Recovery Period, and metal ingots of various sizes and weights were used for commerce, I came up with the phrase: Buy Low – Sell High, but that didn't catch on either. Then my sister quit, and I was left to fend for myself. Advertising was out of the question, so I took up brewing alcoholic beverages and trading specified quantities of moonshine for different types of food. I should have done that in the first place, and I wouldn't have had so much trouble in life. By the way, can you lend me a couple of copper ingots? I'll pay you back on your next trip upriver.*

***

Charlton Heights and Falls of the Kanawha

Our visit to the small hamlet of Pratt had been emotional. We re-boarded and continued southeast towards Charlton Heights. In the late afternoon and early evening, we met with two other fellow travelers and sat down to speak with them.

***

Jasper Zimmerman, landscape architect – *Formal gardens and tree-lined driveways, coupled with variegated blossoms of azaleas and rhododendrons. What joy I once had implementing such beautiful vistas throughout the fine suburbs of my hometown. But with no water to spare and imposed water rationing came the death of all the plants that were special to me. I watched the leaves of my plants wither and fall. I despaired as blossom petals turned dark and shrank into unidentifiable pieces. What once was a visual silent cacophony of color became merely landscape shades of brown and ochre, akin to the desert patterns that I remembered from my childhood playing within the western stretches of the Mojave Desert.*

Because of my professional training, I once knew the potential uses of more than 350 plants, and how they complemented each other by leaf shape, color, and shade requirements. Now no one cares. My skills no longer are needed, except for requests at Sunset Parties where my concoctions of numbing but painless combinations of toxic species send consumers into deep, dreamy sleep to awaken on the other side far from the horrors experienced today. I spent five solar cycles at the university for my degree. I spent 1,500 hours working to fulfill the requirements for my professional certification, and then came the Ripple Event. The practice I now follow could not have foreseen. Yes, I am an architect – and a good one in high demand – but an architect of sweet death. The plants I now grow in my garden, and those I irrigate carefully with my salvaged bath and toilet bowl water, are for a different aesthetic, not the aesthetic of beautiful color, but for the aesthetic of death.

***

Mary James, artist – *Before the Ripple Event, Dark Time, and all that has happened since, I painted portraits of the living. During the recent Epidemic, most of my family died. Now I paint only images of the deceased. I sometimes imagine that I am going mad, especially when I paint faces of children slain by Northlanders or the images of mothers and fathers who perished in the recent Epidemic. Is it not said:*

> *Alas Babylon – Alas, alas, that great city Babylon, that mighty city! For in one hour thy judgment has come. What work do I do now you ask? Why am I voyaging along this Great River? I am returning home to our family abode in old Pennsylvania, where I will seek peace and salvation among good people who have survived this veil of tears. It is there, my friends, that I will not have to worry about the Northlanders. Sorry, I cannot go on.*

***

Our upriver journey ended at Charlton Heights several kilo-miles from the Falls of the Kanawha. Water depth east and north along the Kanawha channel did not permit boats of our type to continue. We had our terminus: this was the end of our river travel.

***

After-Word

We disembarked at Charlton Heights, and offered fond adieus to Captain Smyth and Stable Master Mayweather. We led our animals down Riverside Drive and up onto the remains of old Highway 60. Off in the distance to the north mist rose from the river, indicating the location of Kanawha Falls, the feature that blocked further boat transportation and represented the formal beginning of the Kanawha River.

We rode slowly north and crossed the bridge at Kanawha Falls. We camped for the evening and rested. The next portion of our journey would be overland and would begin at dawn along Highway 16. Together, we looked forward to the challenges ahead.

***

Ijano Esantu Eleman

Interlude-Conversation: 5

Nouveau France

***

Ah, K'Aser, I could not help but notice the French – in this case from Nouveau France – are back at it on the western side of the Great Sea and with the help of off-worlders.

Oh, you noticed that, did you?

Yes, after all I am a qualified Observer.

That you are. Little or nothing eludes your scrutiny, I myself have seen.

Anyway they are back and making trouble, if you ask me. People to the west of the Great River and those trapped to the east are concerned, to say the very least. And now there is a barrier developing in the far west.

A'Tena it is of interest how two small parts of this orb can cause so much consternation for so long, is it not?

And long it has been for true and sure, K'Aser.

All the way back to when these places were one country. One country, claimed by two kings. Then there was much trouble, but for the current and recent here and now these places act more like squabbling siblings rather than arch enemies. Why, give them a common enemy and they become the best of allies. Or at least they have. Offworlders have stirred the pot here, making serious bloodshed quite likely. This I will not have.

Well, just what do you intend to do about it?

Fret not, A'Tena. One can make no guarantees the people here have free will, after all is said and done. You shall see the Overseer will act when and where appropriate. For a start, this meddling batch of spacers will find themselves where their prime concerns will be locating and then returning to their home world. In this they will succeed and learn a hard lesson in the process – I guarantee. But it is not yet the time for this lesson. As for Nouveau France d'outre-mer, part of it will remain. There was a certain engaging aspect to it, don't you think?

Nowadays there is surely a market for furs yet again.

Indeed and this demand shall be met along with many others. Commerce will soon return to the Great River and along the eastern coast, but again not quite yet.

What of other regions?

I see no reason they won't remain pretty much the same as they are now.

The Big Hole Valley, as well?

Yes, A'Tena, the valley will always endure. How could we – I – allow otherwise? Earthers and Spacers will live together, gradually melding into one culture, one people.

Ah, but wait, might some trouble be ahead for our favorite place as part of the testing?

Perhaps – we shall see, we shall see.

Chapter 6

West Virginia Hills: Kanawha Falls to Rimel

Pre-Note

Our journeys along the three rivers ended just short of Kanawha Falls. From west to east, we had traversed the course of the wide Missouri River. Upon reaching St. Louis, we put aboard a riverboat for the short float down the Mississippi River to Kai-Row, where once again we traveled with our animals up the Ohio and Kanawha rivers. Along the way, we experienced hospitality and group friendships. We also viewed landscapes ravaged by continued solar cycles of hostility and battles between the aggressive Northlanders and various other populations who wanted only to live in peace and harmony.

The defeat of the Northlander Militias at the Battle of South Bend set the stage for potential cultural revival and renewal in which regional residents could be left in peace once again to reinstitute their selected ways of life. Now they could reform new settlement groups and live their lives to the fullest. This was a grand opportunity, one that both Travis and I wished for future generations. But would it become so?

The Epidemic that eliminated almost all human life in our homeland, the NorthWest Configuration, had spread its tentacles eastward across the Flatlands and into regions where we traveled. What we encountered along the way, however, was an enigma: how was it that some communities were obliterated by the illness, while others experienced numerous deaths but about half the population survived, and still others barely were touched? We saw and understood no reasons for such discrepancies. It was as if an unseen force directed and determined who lived and who perished. But on what bases were the decisions of life and death being made? Why were some communities favored for life and continuity over others? During one phase of our journey, we encountered two settlement groups less than 10 kilo-miles apart: one seemingly was protected, while the other was eliminated by the Epidemic. What was the explanation for such a pattern? Was launch of the Epidemic and its spread eastward some sort of test or action by an unseen cosmic force? Might we find answers as we continued our journey?

***

Overland Trek

We continued our journey heading overland through a lush green landscape. Our general guides were the pavement and road shoulders of old Highway 16, called the Midland Trail by some. In the late morning we reached the former enclave of Chimney Corner. Nothing was left except ruined homes and shops, after Northlanders attacked this tiny settlement several solar cycles past. At the highway fork, we branched off and followed old Highway 60 to the Hawks Nest Park, where we watered our horses and pack animals near the community shelter. Midway up the steep slope overlooking Hawk Lake was a sign that directed visitors to a location called Lover's Leap – a place, presumably named for the suicides of young folks who jumped into the dark waters below after being ordered not to wed. Sad stories, indeed.

Just north of Hawks Nest, along Highway 60 we entered the community of Anstad and established camp nearby for the night. We had traveled only 12 kilo-miles from Kanawha Falls, but realized that our horses and pack animals had not yet accustomed themselves to the rough disintegrating chunks of old highway pavement. We and our animals benefited from the short distance and early relaxation.

Anstad also had suffered from Northlander incursions, but was undergoing rebuilding efforts. Travis and I walked up Maple Street to the intersection with Hamilton Avenue, where we were greeted by a resident named Karl Browne who offered us what he called restful refreshments. Karl was a veteran who had served in the Regional Militia. His unit, formed of volunteers from Anstad, had been defeated at the Brownsville skirmish, a site north of Kanawha Falls. The Northlanders did not execute Browne and the others of the militia immediately, but marched them cross-country through the hills and hollows to Mammoth, where the invaders had established a prison camp.

We asked Karl about his experiences at the Northlander prison camp:

> *Worst thing about being a Northlander prisoner was learning about the work of a special Northlander execution unit known throughout the battle-torn lands as the Coin-Flippers. These horrible individuals would confront a prisoner and say these simple but horrible words:*
>
> > *Life and death are just different sides of the same coin.*
> > *You are born, you live, and then you die – so nothing's new.*
>
> *We were assembled and brought forth to the prison camp commandant, who just stood and laughed. The Coin Flippers lined us up into groups of 16 men and women. Why 16? We never were told, but the lines always were eight men and eight women. And then the coin flipping started. These evil ones – how even this day I wish all of them a horrible death – would face one of the prisoners and say: call it – heads or tails? If a prisoner was new to the camp, they initially saw this demand as some sort of game, and the new person would respond. But once the coin calling commenced, the horror of it all became apparent. If the prisoner in line refused to say heads or tails, he or she was executed on the spot. If the prisoner complied: heads meant life, tails meant death. You make a wrong call, and you were done for. And so this way the Coin Flippers went up the lines of 16 prisoners, and slowly the number of prisoners was whittled-down as you might say. And with each flip of the coin, the Northlanders laughed making belly-busting sounds that to this day I cannot forget. But what I have just said was not the worst. The Coin Flippers sometimes found among the prisoners two sisters or two brothers and forced one to flip the coin, where a wrong call caused the death of their beloved kin. If the prisoner refused, then both sisters and brothers were executed on the spot. It was horrible to watch. The madness of these Northlanders will stay in my mind forever throughout each of my waking hours and in my dreamland slumbers. How could these people have been so cruel? It was pure luck that I survived my incarceration at Mammoth. Others who were better soldiers than I, others smarter than I, others with more loved ones at home than I – they perished due to the Northlander evil, while I did not. I know not why and though I survived. The pain I hold inside,*

not knowing why, never leaves me. When Mammoth prison camp was relieved and taken by the combined attack of two different militia units, I was one of the very few who survived the initial roundup of more than 870 prisoners. I owe everything to my community. While I was a prisoner, the residents of Anstad protected my family members during this terrible page of history. Please, stay a day or two with us. There is much to see that is beautiful in and around our settlement.

***

Karl Browne was correct. Just outside of Anstad was a most unusual site called Mystery Hole. Visitors could not believe their eyes. Gravity seemed to be undefined and even water appeared to flow uphill. Brown told us that since the Epidemic, few travelers passed through Anstad or even know about the Mystery Hole. What was it about this place that caused such spatial and logical confusion? To use his words, it was due to the numerous boogers, haints, and witchens roaming their homes nearby in the forest of despair that surrounded Mystery Hole. He said that old-timers living nearby who tried to relocate to another house a distance away, frequently became ill. Browne ended his explanation with the phrase:

I'm not afeared – I'm not afeared – I'm not afeared.

We had made a good friend with Karl Browne, resident of Anstad. His stories and descriptions we long would remember.

***

Leaving Anstad, we passed nearby or through settlements at Victor and Hico. We continued along the path traced by Highway 60 and reached Rainelle. The only prominent feature there was the ruins of an old lumber company. Then we reached Charmco, at the junction of Meadow River and Laurel Creek, and elected to camp, since it was unlikely that we could reach our next destination, Rupert, before darkness fell.

The next day greeted us with a light layer of mist. It was unusually cold for spring, but by the time the noonday sun reached its zenith, we were engulfed by the oppressive heat and humidity that normally typified summers in this region. We passed nearby Hines, a tiny community where the upland waters of Mill Creek emptied into the Meadow River. By midafternoon we had reached Rupert.

Rupert was the most substantial community we had encountered after leaving Kanawha Falls. As we rode into town, we saw fewer than ten persons going about their business. We asked directions and learned that the street names, Pocahontas and Raleigh, memorialized two old-time people back so long ago that no one could remember why. We asked about camping and were directed to a trail north out of Rupert called Big Mountain Road. It was said that we couldn't miss it, since there was a large number 6 on several signs showing the way. This route 6 wiggled along Church Street then into a high-forested region crisscrossed by what the Rupert locals called *hollers,* if we heard the word and pronunciation correctly. Two Rupertese that spoke with us mentioned we would find clear water and feed grass for our animals if we traipsed up Big Mountain Road all the way to Mill Creek. There, near the high ridge crossing, we would find old-timer Avery Perkins, who would introduce himself and tell us more about local geography and cultural traditions.

***

Riding north, we continued on for the best of two hours, and then established our camp on a sandbar east of Justin's Hollow along the banks of Mill Creek. In the golden light of the late afternoon, we sat by our campfire and listened to the lilting and haunting sounds of dulcimers and fiddles echoing across the green wildflower-laced hills. The soft bubbling and gurgling sounds of the nearby creek mingled with the tones of hill music. Words of plaintive songs filled the evening air. There came to our ears the sweet soprano voices of young girls as they sang the old tunes whose words told of endless love and personal sadness, verses penned in far earlier times but befitting present difficulties. The sound of music flowed and touched our hearts. Travis and I embraced: oh peaceful rest in a troubled world

You've got to walk that lonesome valley
You've got to walk it by yourself
No one here can walk it for you
You've got to walk it by yourself.

And another …

For the leaves they will wither
And the roots they will die
And your true love will leave you
And you'll never know why.

And another …

He told me he loved me and promised to love
Through ill and misfortune, all others above
Another has won him, oh misery to tell
He left me in silence no words of farewell.

And another …

Down in the valley, the valley so low
Hang your head over, hear the wind blow
Roses love sunshine, violets love dew
Angels in heaven, know I love you.

***

Early the next morning we broke camp, loaded our mules, and continued north along Mill Creek. We rode the narrow trail through the steep slopes of the glen, past log-constructed buildings covered by galvanized metal roofs stained green with moss. The tall trees cast long shadows over the trail and, in many cases, the branches interwove across the path nearly obliterating the sunlight. At the head of the glen was a rustic log cabin. Looking up we saw an elderly gentleman, Avery Perkins, who would be our contact. He rose from his porch rocker gave us a hoot-and-a-holler and waved us forward. We tethered our horses and pack mules and climbed the steps to his home at his invitation

Perkins spoke to us using words with an accent previously unknown to us. He said that the sounds of our arrival had echoed the purpose of our visit, that it had been a long time since he had the pleasure of welcoming outlanders to his family abode.

Please, take a bench, rest a spot. I kin gather libations and eats to share.

Our host returned with glasses filled with beverages of an unusual amber hue.

Take drink and my welcome as I pass the glasses to you. This is not the black drink of which you may have heard, but it is akin, prepared from leaves of spring sumac, the safe variety. I have sweetened it with a dab of honey from my hives. We in the hollers must be careful here in the glen as the stinger beasties that make our honey are attracted by color, and they know not the poisons therein that some plants produce for protection. Springtime brings the blossoms of rhododendrons, which we call wild rhodies. Honey from wild rhodies burns the mouth, makes you puke, gives you the trots, and turns your eyes dark. The blindness usually is temporary, but sometimes not. The other wonder plant that we must be careful when we speak to the bees is laurel-of-the-mountain – a wonderful reddish pink flower that the bees love. Now if you make a mistake, dears, and eat honey from pollen that the bees have gathered from laurel-of-the-mountain, be already for the puke and gut pains. What a banger slap that is, one you will never forget: the skin tingles like an electric shock, although there hasn't been electricity in this holler for many solar cycles. If you sweeten your drink with honey from laurel-of-the-mountains, you also get the staggers and whirlies where you spin about like on a weekend moonshine jag. Now, now, don't be afeared. I can assure y'all that the honey from my hives is as pure as any winged little beasties can produce. So drink up! Really, don't worry.

Travis and I truly enjoyed our beverages and conversation with Perkins. We related to him that the people we spoke to in Rupert told us that he was a tried-and-true weather predictor, with keen skills learned as a child from his great grandfather.

That is to be true, young folks. My great grandfather telled me that he had learnt his weather skills from his own great grandfather. So I sit before you and say sure as shootin' I am indeed a member of one dag-gon long line of weathermen. Amen brother and sister.

We continued and asked: can you share with us what you look for when making your predictions? Are there signs in the sky? Do you consider the color and shape of plants or perhaps the behavior of animals? Do the omens come to you during the dawn or twilight hours?

Oh-me-oh-my, you ask too many squirrelish questions, folks, but I long to recite 'em to you, so rite these down into your book and I will axplain.

Touch a rusty nail – sure to bring hail: *We carpenters – you known me as one – are a happy lot, working summers when it's hot, we forge our nails, we tell tall tales, with hammer and saw, our hands turn raw. If we touch a rusty nail, our ruddy faces sure turn pale, and soon there comes a stormy gale, and from the clouds comes pelting hail – and so it is. Really.*

Snow in July – someone will die: *It snowed the day Aunt Josie died. I had trekked over hill and dale to be with my cousins, Franklin and Amy. Along the way the sun turned grey, dark clouds swirled overhead, black omens of the dead, and I knew that I would arrive too late, tardiness would be my fate, not to say good-by – and so it was.*

Other weather signs I learnt through my own experiences, per example these:

Mid-day heat – rest your feet: *That's always a good excuse to give to the missus for not taking out the trash every other day, or doin' too many chores about the house. You understand I pre-zoom?*

When lightening sounds – loose the hounds: *Oh my, this is a good one. Chained up in the storehouse above my cabin, I keep Bob and Ray, my two hunting dogs. If I whistle – they reply – hear them now? L'me tell you, Bob and Ray just love a good solid rainstorm where the thunder echoes down through and across the hollers. With the first clap, they start baying but get especially noisy after each lightning strike as the thunder rolls down the valley out across the creek bottom all the way to Rupert. Rain or not, I love to trek along with Bob and Ray. I loose the hounds and let them run; they always scare up some beastie that we bring back home to cook. When the missis was alive, we would eat out on this porch rain or shine – and toss a bone or two to Bob and Ray to keep them happy. Oh, those were good old days. I miss her very much, but I still have my hounds, and an occasional outlander visitor like yourselves stopping by now and then.*

Hot nights – mosquito bites: *This should be obvious since mosquitos don't like the cold of winter or the pounding rain of spring.*

Frog croaks at noon – rain comes soon: *I used to think that frogs only croaked in the late afternoon gloaming or during early evening. About 15 solar cycles back, before the Epidemic, the creek below our house changed course after a landslide, and opened up a broad place where waters flowed gently. I remember discovering this place shortly afterwards and marveling at the number of tadpoles flitting about in the clear water. When these to frogs became, their color was unusual; they did not have the regular green, black, and red hues. These orange-like flitters soon became tame froggies, and* *the grandkids could catch them easily. We called these froggies the fearless ones. The first time I heard them croak at noontime, I gave little notice, but was surprised since it rained immediately afterwards. As time passed, it happened a-gin and a-gin, so I became certain that the little croakers could foretell rain – and sure enough they did so.*

***

Avery Perkins continued:

Sometimes outlanders pass through our hollers on their way to and from their outside life. Unlike you, Travis and Reese, most do not take time to sit with us hill folk, or take time to listen to the wind, or watch the shadows creep across the meadow down by the creeks. You respect us, and I appreciate your visit. It has been difficult here in Justin's Holler, but we have food and water, and neighbors that call and stop by. We never had telephones or televisions, even before the Ripple Event – so what did we miss? What we didn't know, we couldn't miss. We had friends, and we helped each other as need be.

About five solar cycles past, many of the local deer and raccoons left for greener pastures, as they say, but some returned this past season. I remember one of my great grandchildren Ossford Mobel, son of my granddaughter Erin Perkins. He used to say: Great granddad, if it rained cats and dogs at least we could eat. How we all smiled and laughed. I often think on Ossford. The Epidemic took him from us. He is buried down by the creek, near the path where you rode up to our cabin. God bless Ossford – he died too soon.

You want sum'or hill-folk learnin'? Take these quaints and put'em in your book:A blue flame fire will not burn
When a hound bays count the days
When a cat cries – someone dies
Baby's spit – cures sister's fit
A woman's kiss brings bliss.

You axe me about my hill ax-cent and punct-u-ations. Yur questions make me wan'a laugh. Travis, say the followin' six times, faster and faster each time. Then we'll see who has the right ax-cent and punct-u-ation. Try this first one, then I give you others for a followin'.

Outsiders I heered you arrive, but I weren't a bit afeared.

You'all make me want to laugh, you sound so funny, but mine is a friendship laugh. You did it six times: at the beginnin' I could scarce understand your sound. But then as you went afaster and afaster, your words became clarity to my ear. Here's s'more language lessens fur ya:

We are plain spoken here
Come sit a spell and stay abit with us
We et so much I reckon we're plum out of vittles
Five young'uns live here
The haints may come back to bother us
We aint agin' the law but we respect truth not politics
Old Sally crazy is, she be touched in the head
Don't chew your cabbage twice
Your word don't mean diddley squat
Haven't seen hide nor hair of him
Why's you so messy: was you bairn in a barn?

***

How could we ever thank Avery Perkins for the wonderful afternoon, sitting on his porch drinking something we knew not its origin, and listening to phrases and tones of early local origin. He went to his storehouse and brought Bob and Ray down the mountain path to greet us. Two great hound dogs, their wet noses sniffing us, liquid brown eyes checking us out, and their drooping ears listening for Avery's whistle. Good-by Bob and Ray, may you have many more solar cycles to romp and hunt through the nearby hollers.

Prior to our departure, Perkins provided us with several jars of his special spring sumac beverage, the one sweetened with safe honey. We thanked him for his kind hospitality. Retracing our route, we slowly trekked downhill and paused at the grave marker we had missed earlier in the day. We dismounted and collected bunches of wildflowers and laid them on Ossford's grave to commemorate the memory of a little boy born of parents with proud traditions – taken too soon by an Epidemic that Travis and I knew and had experienced all too well.

***

We paused for a short rest before leaving Rupert, then continued along Highway 60 and rode through Crawley, Alta, and Richland before reaching

Lewisburg. We now were traveling through the midst of Greenbrier Valley, once home of the Shawnee tribe led by Chief Hokoleskwa. Lewisburg originally was a fort and trading center established along Lewis Spring. The Limestone Mountains off to the east were sources for the famed mineral springs that once made Lewisburg famous. Today, the town was in the midst of recovery. We spent the night camped in a vacant lot at the corner of North Lee Street and Silo Lane, near the burned-out ruins of the once-flourishing West Virginia School of Osteopathic Medicine.

While cooking up our dinner vittles, we were approached by an elderly lady who enquired about our purpose. We spoke frankly about our quest to seek out other survivors of the Epidemic and our ultimate plan to return to Bison Camp, our home of origin. When I mentioned Bison Camp, he looked startled and asked me a most unexpected question:

> *Have you ever heard of three sisters who were healers and knew all sorts of edible wild plants, girls from the NorthWest Configuration named Cishqhale, Sapha, and Yuhushi with family name Stone?*

Well, of course, I replied:

> *Sapha was my mother!*

The woman's name was Teresa Morgan. She related that some folks living within the Greenbrier Valley thought these three girls, triplets, were the most famous and renown plant specialists west of the Great River but wondered herself if they only were imaginary names. How curious! She knew that the three girls – Cishqhale, Sapha, and Yuhushi – had been associated during a period of their life with a settlement group in old Montana called Bison Camp. I could scarcely believe it! The fame of the Stone triplets had spread well beyond the narrow confines of the Big Hole Valley, and we had just met a woman several thousand kilo-miles east of our home who knew of our homeland and settlement group.

Morgan was a local sage femme from Lewisburg and long had been a student of traditional culture and healing methods. Throughout the evening she related local sayings and traditions that characterized the hill people living in the Greenbrier Valley region, and shared with us a wide variety of do's and don'ts:

Listen carefully to feathered hooters
Use only a rusty knife to skin a cat
Watched pots never boil
Decorate beehives with white ribbons
Grasshoppers caught on Friday bring good luck
Olden ones sing songs of love before they die
A flock of crows will bring disaster within three days
Never piss into a campfire
Never rock an empty cradle
Never rock a cradle with your right foot
Never begin a journey on a Friday
Never kill a cricket on Sunday
Never gaze into a mirror after midnight
When hunting, the eldest virgin daughter shoots her arrow first

And others

A man child singing before breakfast goes hungry at night
A woman child singing before noon will be cheerful all day
A boy child singing at dinner will wet his bed at night
A girl child who stares into a campfire will wet her bed at night

And a most interesting caution

When children sit on tombstones, their privates are activated too soon.

***

Throughout the cycles, both before and after the Epidemic, Teresa had continued to work with different cultural groups within Lewisburg, especially one group known as the granny women. She related to us examples in which several of these women could forecast certain future events. For example, some of these older women could meet with a pregger – the local term for a pregnant woman – and identify the exact day when she would be delivered. Others were adept in predicting the gender of the bairns, or newborns, as the term was used within the valley. These women commonly brewed what they called affection potions, and many Lewisburg marriages were the result of their efforts. Teresa related that one of the granny women she worked with claimed the ability to cross creeks without getting wet, but this seemed to be more of a boast than an actual skill.

Teresa suggested that since we would be traveling north out of Lewisburg along the Seneca Trail or old Highway 219, when we reached the community of Renick, we might veer off into the eastern mountain areas for additional talks with a local named Louie Ramsey, who could teach us more about what local hill folk call salvation beverages – alcohol-related religious rituals practiced at the local Church of the Good Drink.

***

We left Lewisburg the following morning and passed through Maxwelton and Frankford before reaching Renick. This small community was dominated by the ruins of two Christian churches, built during the old times. During the Epidemic peak, both had been destroyed accidently by fire. The main part of Renick fronted the Greenbrier River. We tethered our horses and pack mules on Axtell Avenue, and asked advice of several residents lounging about in the early afternoon sun. Receiving directions, we crossed the Greenbrier and made our way towards the settlement of Auto, following an amorphous sequence of trails and hollers that extended through Snodgrass Run. We were amused by the local word "run," which we initially assumed meant to walk fast or escape. Local usage meant a small stream or creek flowing out of the hills down through the hollers.

We found Louie Ramsey working in his barn. He told us that for a reasonable barter, he would be willing to show us about and make introductions to folks living at the hollers in the Auto region. We offered him two copper ingots, which he received with a broad grin and kind words, and agreed to take time off work to assist us.

***

Over the course of the afternoon, Louie gathered his team of young men and boys responsible for preparing salvation beverages for religious service use.

> *You may call it moonshine – we call our production salvation beverages. So done because a nip twice a day soothes the memories of the bad times that each here experienced. Yes, you are correct that in times long gone, we were chased and sought after by those who would revenue the products of our labor. Some deal that: we did the work, and all they wanted was money to support some government agency way out yonder over in DC. Why should we pay them, when we did all the work and they did squat? Some cat and mouse game*

it was between us and them; we knew the hollers – they didn't – and we could lead them here and there and all around – what we called a romp and hunt – until they got lost and spun just like little Joey's toy top. True be it that there sometimes were encounters where shots were fired, but mostly we missed on purpose, since we didn't want to deprive their wives and children of husbands. Our long barrel rifles, handed down from olden times, were accurate – man alive they were accurate, and still are, but we no longer have bullets and powder. These feds just thought we were poor shooters who couldn't aim because we had drunk too much of our salvation beverages. Truth be told, Travis, I used to be able to shoot out the eyes of a door mouse critter at 100 yards – as we called the distance back then. So if I could do that, then those who chased us lived because we let them. Now no one cares; no taxes; no feds; no ammunition. Just good times brewing our salvation beverages. Here have another nip.

We asked more questions of Louie: What about the Church of the Good Drink?

Oh that? Here, take another nip! You, too, Reese!

Up in these hollers there used to be quite different faith groups, but the long-ago Ripple Event and the recent Epidemic caused a humongous decline in church membership. Folks here in the Auto region gathered together and merged our denominations. The faith healers among us continue to practice; we all participate in services where the laying of hands takes place. During certain evenings when we pass around the good juice, our specially prepared salvation beverages, some of our members speak in tongues.

In addition, about one weekend meeting every month we bring out the snakes, you know, the rattlers. Handling the snakes is like a confession for the soul. First we form two lines; those who want to participate and those who are unsettled or just want to watch for one reason or another. We never ask why a member selects their line. The participants each take three nips from the common salvation beverage bowl. Pastor Allison then hands the first participant in line a rattler – I mean a real rattler – no fake snake here – all puffed up and shaking its tail making the noise of evil. The recipient takes hold of the snake then shouts out:

I am not afeared, I am not afeared
My mind is right , my body pure

Do not tempt me evil one
Begone, begone, begon

Then the first participant passes the rattler on to the next in line, who holds the snake tightly and shouts the same words. This person then passes the snake on to the next, and so on and so forth until each participant has fondled the rattler. Each has been exposed to lethal danger but has conquered fear and survived. Only two times in all my memory did I witness a rattler turn on and strike a participant. In both instances to my memory, the bitten one had committed a grievous act the previous month, something that the snakes had sensed. The next ceremony will take place in about two weeks. If you like and have the time, we will invite you to participate – either as a snake handler or as an observer. The choice would be yours.

I asked Louie what he meant when he said that some members of the Church of the Good Drink spoke in tongues.

As the service progresses, usually after the rattlers are reput into their cages, Pastor Allison calls for additional rounds of libations. My team and I are responsible for making certain that we have enough of the good stuff. As glasses of our salvation beverage are passed from row to row, even the youngins who survived the Epidemic will take a nip now and then. Some of the oldsters stand, fill the aisles and walk to the front where Pastor Allison always puts our church relics, images of this and that. He next invites the members to pass by the table and pick up and hold one of the relics. Then it happens – not to all holding the relics – but to some. Those feeling the spirit start to shout and cry out words not of our kind and era. An aide to Pastor Allison, the Rucker lad, regularly writes the spoken words down as he hears them. I remember some of the shout-outs as well, for example:

Le do thoil a chosaint dom le do thoil a chosaint dom
A bheith imithe Elsa fhágáil linn go deo

I have no idea what the shouted words mean, only that once said, the shouters then fall to the church floor and begin wreathing and flailing about like little tykes throwing anger fits. Pastor Allison then reaches out and puts his right hand upon the brow of each of the flailing, and sure as sunrise after feeling his touch they sit up and look about as if nothing has happened. We in the audience then cry out in unison: Hail to Pastor Allison. Hail to the Church of the Good Drink.Have another sip?

As we left the Church of the Good Drink we noticed an extensive cemetery adjacent to the structure. As we passed by the stone markers Louie saddened almost immediately and told us that located here were the graves of more than 25 children who had died during the Epidemic. Each grave was decorated with fresh-growing iris and metal cans into which visitors could insert messages of grief and thereby communicate with the deceased children. We walked randomly among the rows sensing the deep sorrow that the small community of Auto had experienced during the terrible time when no one – medical doctor or traditional healer – could cure the ill that swept through the region. In my own heart, I knew what each of the parents had suffered. I had experienced their pain, as well.

Louie and his kinsmen were engaging and friendly to us outsiders. We asked about a campsite and they recommended Justin's Holler northeast of Auto, a glen fed by the coal-black waters of the Haelan Taehhen Run that originated far up mountain, a feeder that flowed through Auto that eventually reached the Greenbrier River. We took his advice and after several hours of trekking we reached the site. Both of us were curious why Louie would recommend this location as the tiny slow-flowing creek emerged from a combined seepage both above and below exposed seams of bituminous coal deposits. The waters of Haelan Taehhen Run were ill-smelling and dark-colored. As we set up camp, Travis observed wild game tracks near the creek flow indicating that the waters regularly were drunk by animals. This also meant that while dirty and bad smelling, the waters possibly were safe to drink.

The trail crossing the Run was laced with footprints of past visitors. Off to one side were several stone structures that resembled altars. Several unusual terracotta statues were placed adjacent to the altars; these were unusual in design and clearly stylized images of women. Strewn about each here and there were pieces of broken glass, smooth pebbles, and dozens of buttons from different types of clothing. The Haelan Taehhen Run appeared to be a location where residents at Auto or from nearby mountain glens made pilgrimages and gathered beside the dark waters seeking prophecies and answers to questions. To me the site looked like pilgrims had gathered here for many solar cycles, perhaps even for centuries past.

We established camp for the evening on a narrow sandbar where the waters of Haelan Taehhen Run broadened slightly. Tired from the day's trek, we both fell asleep quickly. During the night I awakened and walked to the water's edge. I collapsed in tears remembering our children's faces and how the Epidemic had brought about their needless deaths. All these memories seemed to have been triggered by our walk earlier through the cemetery. I knelt on the grass near the water listening to the noises from the slow-flowing waters and the humming insects. It was there that perhaps I fell asleep again, but could not be sure – then – standing before me was a human form. Was I dreaming or was my vision reality? If a dream, it was the most vivid ever experienced.

He was dressed as a minstrel, a singer of songs. His appearance was like images from the long-ago Middle Ages, curious in dress, something like the jesters I had learned about as a child. He carried a musical instrument, perhaps a lute, but I couldn't be sure. He resembled an ancient troubadour, a traveler, a minstrel, a singer of songs. Who was he?

I sensed no danger or harm from him. His smile reached out to me as he chanted his sing-song message:

EARTH and AIR – FIRE and WATER
In days long gone I sang my song
Words and sounds crafted with care
Gaze upon me Saunders Reese
Explore the creases of my soul
Come close reach out, do not fear me
In the darkness touch my hand
Stand before me arms upraised
Listen well to my song.

EARTH and AIR – FIRE and WATER
Breath of life and touch of death
Anadl einioes a chyffwrdd o farwolaeth
Full the circle ever will be
Llawn y cylch fydd byth fod yn
Prepare the place of yew wood fire
Paratoi'r man ywen tân coed
Full the circle ever will be
Llawn y cylch fydd byth fod yn

I stood and approached him, and he the minstrel, the singer of the song, took my hand. We walked together towards the near bank of Haelan Taehhen Run. Before us was a wall of fire that engulfed the nearby grass, bushes, and stately yew trees. The minstrel, the singer of the song released my hand, turned and spoke to me:

Step into the flaming arc
Camu i mewn i'r arc fflamio
Full the circle ever will be
Llawn y cylch fydd byth fod yn

Do not fear you will not burn
Nid ydynt yn ofni na fyddwch yn llosgi
Full the circle ever will be
Llawn y cylch fydd byth fod yn

Yew wood flames will ease your pain
Bydd fflamau pren ywen leddfu eich poen
Full the circle ever will be
Llawn y cylch fydd byth fod yn

Daughters two will come in time
Merched dau yn dod mewn amser
Full the circle ever will be
Llawn y cylch fydd byth fod yn

Touch of death and breath of life
Cyffwrdd o farwolaeth ac anadl einioes
Full the circle ever will be
Llawn y cylch fydd byth fod yn

Was this dreamtime or reality? The minstrel reached out again, took my hand, and together we stepped into the yew wood flames. All around the light shimmered, engulfing of us both with an ethereal light. As we stood amidst the flames, I felt no pain. Flames enveloped my clothing but the cloth did not burn. How could this be? Was this dreamtime or reality? The minstrel told me to repeat his words:

EARTH and AIR – FIRE and WATER
Full the circle ever will be
Touch of death the breath of life
Full the circle ever will be

Full the circle ever will be
No more my eyes reflecting pain
Full the circle ever will be

Full the circle ever will be
Grief no more will slow my step
Full the circle ever will be

Full the circle ever will be
Touch of death the breath of life
Full the circle ever will be

After I had completed speaking his words, I suddenly found myself standing alone. The riverbank that once seemed ablaze was lush and green. No fire had engulfed the area; branches of the yew trees were broad-leafed and colorful. No ashes covered the ground. There was no evidence of a fire. Was my experience real or but a dream?

***

Dawn broke through the canopy of branches that arched over the sandbar where we had camped. I expected that Travis would awaken and find me absent. As it was Travis quickly ran to the water's edge where he found me resting. Overnight the flowing waters of Haelan Taehhen Run had changed color from coal black to the crystal clarity of window glass. I greeted my mate with open arms. We held each other tightly and together we expressed our love and desire for each other. We undressed and both bathed in the healing waters of Haelan Taehhen Run. It was as if the waters had washed over my soul, cleansed my mind, and bore away all my past fearful memories of the Epidemic. A great shade had been removed from my heart.

***

We returned downslope and offered thanks to Louie Ramsey. We parted good friends. His suggestion of camping along Haelan Tahhen Run always would be remembered for the dreamtime or real-time events that took place within this secluded site of ancient pilgrimage.

Continuing on we reached the community of Renick and followed north along Highway 219, passing the small communities of Modoc and Droop which, these days, appeared to be unoccupied. The Droop Mountain Battle site was off to the west, and a settlement called Spice nestled in a forested area nearby. We paused at Spice to water and graze our animals and took time to inspect the monuments.

We trekked past Hillsboro, Mill Point, and Buckeye. In the late afternoon we approached Marlinton and crossed to the southeast bank near the confluence of

Greenbrier River and Knapp Creek. We trekked along Knapp Creek paralleling old Highway 39 towards Huntersville. As darkness was approaching, we established camp south of Knapp Creek near Stillhouse Run.

Early morning saw us continuing east along Highway 39 towards Huntersville, once a rendezvous site for early explorers and trappers where they traded pelts for food supplies. Three small boys along the road waved and shouted *helloooo.* They pleaded with us to stop and inspect the goods they had for trade. The items laid out on quilts spread over the grass were protection amulets woven from freshly cut wheat and crafted into geometrical designs. We would learn later in the day that these attractive amulets called corn dollies were part of local traditions that included special rites to assure fertility of regional grain fields.

We broke our journey and camped just north of Rimel, along Laurel Creek not far from Ryder Gap. We had neared the boundary between the two Virginias. Our arrival also coincided with the Ryder Gap fertility festival. We were invited by the locals to attend the celebration and to observe and participate as we wished. Our local guides were mates Laurel Pence and Jacob Astor who described several wheat-related traditions dated to the most ancient past but still were preserved in this region.

Jacob: **Seed Wetting***: Before each planting season, seed grain set aside from the previous harvest is collected and brought to one of the central farm sheds where it is placed into shallow buckets – the number equal to the number of wheat fields in the area. Infants born the previous month are carried by their mothers into the shed and held over the grain-filled pots and encouraged to make water. The wet seeds are mixed by a young girl using her right hand. She then shares handfuls of the wet seeds with all attending. These seeds are considered especially fertile and are carried reverently to the geometric center of each family's grain field and tamped into the ground. The eldest son then walks through the field broadcasting other grains of wheat to establish the planting.*

Laurel: **White and Red.** *After the field has been fully planted, it is our tradition that boys and girls who have just become men and women then play a significant part in a ritual to assure a bountiful crop of wheat. Four boys* *who have recently become men, evidenced by expulsion of their white seed during sleep, are required to stand at the north, south, east, and west corners of the grain field. Four girls, who recently have become women, as evidenced by their red monthlies, each join one of the four boys. Together they hold hands and chant the ancient words that guarantee field crop fertility and growth of the planted grain – words they continue to chant but do not understand:*

Dod allan caeau ffrwythlon
Fel yn y blynyddoedd diwethaf
Bendithia y grawn
Efallai y bydd y cynhaeaf yn hael

Once the chant is completed at each area wheat field, regional residents gather at a central farm for a feast that lasts from evening long into the early morning.

Jacob: **Last Stand.** *When the fields ripen, we harvest each plot together as a community; after one is finished, we visit the next until all are harvested. A mature woman, still able to bear children, accompanied by four children not over five solar cycles in age, is selected to enter each grain field. She takes a sickle of hammered iron and at each of the four corners of the field slices a handful of ripe wheat, giving one to each of the children accompanying her. They exit the field taking care to protect the wheat strands against any mischief or theft attempts. They store the strands inside the great barn and stand guard, forming a barrier to protect the gathered collections.*

The harvest then begins. Harvesters enter each field from the four directions and progress inward towards the center, reaping and bundling sheaves that are removed by others. Animalia – as we call them – already inside the enclosure sensing the harvester's advance retreat towards the center. As the harvesters make progress, wheat stems in these center field portions begin to rustle and quake due to the rapid movements of the animalia attempting to escape. The harvesters approach closer and closer to the center – the central grain now is afoot

with movement of the scurrying animalia. This center grain area has become the last stand.
The eldest grandfather among the harvesters raises his hand to halt the cutting: before them the animalia attempt to find safety within the last stand of wheat but cannot. The harvests rush into the last stand, slicing everything with their scythes and sickles thereby producing an animalia blood sacrifice to the ancient harvest deities. Rabbits, squirrels, and other varmints slain during the last stand are collected and buried in a single grave along the west edge of the field. Doing so assures continued abundant harvest yields in subsequent solar cycles.

Laurel: **Corn dollies.** *The bundles of wheat protected by the mature women and their assistants have been guarded all afternoon until the conclusion of the last stand rites. Afterwards, the community grandmothers gather at the great barn to select the seasonal symbolic formations and weavings of the grain into corn dollies. Community members still use the ancient word for grain – corn – to honor the past. It is believed that the corn dollies keep haunts from bringing mischief and evil to any household that displays one or more of the annual geometric grain amulets. Each grandmother prepares her corn dollies differently, some chanting olden words of protection, others humming ancient tunes that originated across the Great Sea. What emerges from the collective effort are dozens of beautiful, intricate patterns, each designed to ward off the haunts and boogies that roam the hollers and glens after dark. The patterns can be circles, triangles, diamonds, spinning wheels, hearts, even twisting spiral staircase designs. The patterns reflect family histories, traditions that at one time could be traced back in time to ancient days across the Great Sea to the region of clan origin. But while the beauty of the woven stalks of wheat remain, knowledge of the symbols and geographical origins of the tradition mostly have disappeared into the mists of time.*

Jacob: **The Wickerman.** *At the conclusion of the regional harvest, after each wheat field had been scythed and gleaned, we hold the Wickerman celebration. Work on Wickerman construction must begin exactly 31 days before the initial swipe of the harvest sickle in the first grain field. Local residents of all ages begin collecting straight and curved branches to be used to create and stabilize the statue form. Children throughout the region take time in the afternoons after schooling to collect small thin willow branches. These are cut to different lengths and used to create the mesh exterior of Wickerman. The body of the emerging effigy usually will rise 10 meter-yards and stand on firm, stout legs with arms usually bent at the elbow with hands and fingers pointing upward towards the sky. The purpose of the hollow interior of the effigy has changed through the centuries. In the ancient times when the ritual was celebrated across the Great Sea the interior served as a holding cell for a man or woman convicted of being a haunt. Then later in more progressive times the holding cell has contained a male calf or she goat.*

After all harvesting has been concluded local residents gather around Wickerman, singing and dancing until the chimes of midnight are heard. When the 12th chime rings out, the lad and lass selected as the harvest royalty receive torches and use them to light the dried straw surrounding Wickerman's legs. All attending stand in awe as the flames engulf the torso and animal sacrifices contained in the belly holding area. When all is ablaze, the chanting and singing continue until the fire extinguishes itself and only ashes remain. After the fiery death of Wickerman, all attending walk around the ash pile three times. During each round a sample of ash is taken by those attending. The first sample is for tasting – to become one with Wickerman. The second sample is for ornamentation – ash is used to prepare lines that are streaked or smeared across the forehead and upper chest of each attending. The third sample is

> *for saving, remnants to be brought home and placed inside the family medicine chest in a special clay jar. If an illness should strike the family during the subsequent solar cycle, a portion of Wickerman's ashes is mixed with cow's or goat's milk and used medicinally. Sorry to say and with regret that this traditional remedy did not protect against or cure the recent Epidemic.*

***

On the morrow, we participated in the harvesting and observed the last stand cuttings. In the afternoon, Laurel and Jacob invited us to go with them to watch the grandmothers weave wheat stems into characteristic intricate designs. Walking back from the great barn to our campsite, we passed the wheat field that belonged to the Avebury family. Standing guard along the east side was the Wickerman effigy. We looked at each other and asked ourselves: were we in such a hurry to complete the eastern leg of our trek towards DC that we could not stay at Rider Gap to watch the conclusion of the regional harvest festival? We might never see such a sight again, so we chose to remain.

The residents of Ryder Gap had proved to be most hospitable. We shared some of our MREs and in return received plates and bowls of home-cooked vittles, prepared with special hill country patience and care. As we lingered and mixed with community members, we were taught the designs of local quilt patterns: how the images resembled bear paws, stars, honeycombs, sunbursts, even chains. We were invited to attend a quilting bee and watched young and old women – some with nimble digits, others arthritic – carefully cut, baste, and sew, working love and affection into the quilts that ultimately would grace their homes and in time become family heirlooms.

In the evenings, we met with other residents and sat on porches overlooking the blue ridges off in the distance. We heard the haunting melodies of dulcimers echoing across the glades from glen to glen, the music from single tone strummers calling up forest spirits. Together with our new friends we drank our fill of salvation beverages and spoke long into the night of things past, present, and all offered hopes for the future.

Another evening of exchanges revealed local beliefs in predictive behaviors, and gave us a better understanding of how the community viewed nature spirits, and how local sayings protected life and health during the constant battle between good and evil. Among the traditional sayings we heard were:

When visiting another's home always step over the threshold with the right foot.

A broom laid over a threshold prevents haunts and witches from entering.

Empty bottles hung from roof beams and garden trees will drive away haunts.

When a girl becomes a woman and her first red spot appears do the following:

Fold her beneath cloth, place it inside the family woman's box
Assemble family members, neighbors, and friends
Form a protective ring and surround the new woman
Circle dance around her three times chanting together
From child to woman she has become
A warrior woman she has become
A proud mother she will become
Welcome [sing out her name] to the hearth and home

And another …

When frying mushrooms, take a silver dollar [a very old type of money once used long before the Ripple Event], toss it into the skillet where the stems and caps are browning:

If the silver dollar tarnishes, mushrooms are poisonous
If the silver dollar remains bright, mushrooms are safe to eat

***

On the appointed afternoon, Jacob and Laurel came to our camp to guide us. Their garb this day was unusual; more lace and more color. Jacob's beard was trimmed, and Laurel boasted three sets of satin ribbons – red, white, and blue – that once belonged to her great grandmother. We walked together down the lane and joined groups of others. Together we approached the Avebury farmland and mingled with the assembling throng. Ahead of us loomed the Wickerman effigy.

Came an announcement: we attending were invited to touch Wickerman's legs, and most in the audience complied. We noticed that when people placed their hands on the lower branches and plant stems that comprised Wickerman's legs, many spoke the following words: *Wickerman guíimid fómhar maith an bhliain seo chugainn*

We asked Jacob and Laurel what the words meant, but they remained silent.

We mingled around Wickerman, offering greetings and sharing stories into the early evening. As darkness approached, we sensed a change in the behavior and speaking tone of those attending. Anticipation was sweeping over the crowd and growing in intensity. At the appointed time an elderly man emerged, approached the effigy, then turned to face the assembly and spoke:

With flint against steel a spark emerges
The spark will light the fómhar tóirse
Come forth young Amaethon and Ceridwen
Come forth young Grannus and Rosmerta
Take each your torch and set afire our sacrifice!

The four figures identified by the elder emerged from the shadows. Each was dressed in what appeared to be ancient hill garb. Each also carried a torch. After what appeared to be a silent signal, each torch was laid against the feet of Wickerman.

We watched in awe as the flames shot upward from the lower legs into Wickerman's torso, outward and upward unto its arms and out to its hands, ultimately consuming the head and facial characteristics. Wickerman was ablaze; the flames illuminated the skyline. Chanting from the crowd grew in intensity with each passing moment. We watched intently, our minds set adrift in time, wondering about the ancient days and how humans or animals once identified for sacrifice were secreted inside Wickerman, bound for sacrifice and death inside the torso of the burning effigy.

In time, Wickerman collapsed into a pile of smoking ashes. Torches were lit and posted at the four cardinal points. These served to light the way for the next portion of the ceremony. Travis and I joined the others, and together we circled the effigy ash pile. Like others attending, we collected samples of the ash. We paused to taste a portion then took turns smearing some of the acrid powder across our brows and upper chests. In so doing, we were as one with this community. It would be difficult to leave good friends behind.

***

After-Word

The hills, glens, and runs of old West Virginia was home to good people proud of their heritage. Travis and I found the hill people to be generous to others, especially to outsiders, and willing to share their customs, language, and traditions. How many evenings or noontime gatherings we spent with their young and old, guests at meals of fried chicken, vinegary spinach salats garnished with sliced hard-boiled eggs, followed by after-dinner fruit cobbler and nips from local salvation beverages.

Friendship gifts were many and heaped upon us; so many that we had to repack our mules to make space with special care for the items given to us out of kindness. We treasured the protective amulets we received from children and aged grandmothers: blue bead necklaces to ward off haunts; wonderful geometric corn dollies to protect us on our journey; even a spent cartridge shell from an ancient battle offered to Travis by a veteran of the Northlander incursions – the brass casing engraved with the words:

One Less Northlander.

What we learned most during our overland West Virginia trek was that hope for a better future had not died – hope for brighter futures for their children, hope for less troubled times, and especially the wish to live free without interference of those who would force their military, political, or religious views upon others. The hill people of old West Virginia could trace their family roots back several hundred solar cycles to the first pioneers of the region, men and women who braved the previously untraveled forest woodlands and trekked westward out of the eastern coastal settlements, brave men and women who pushed into the unknown in their search for freedom and independence. The price was high, but worth defending.

Tomorrow we will leave one Virginia and cross into the second. Will the residents in the hills and hollers of East Virginia be similar or different than their western neighbors? Will we find that the residents of East Virginia have maintained the practices of their historical roots, or will they reflect the encroachment and management by the political and economic beings that controlled the DC region? The answers will come soon enough.

***

Ijano Esantu Eleman

Interlude-Conversation: 6
Hill Folk

***

A'Tena, no matter what changes come at them, the hill folks continue on preserving more than some would guess of the language and customs of the olden times.

No wonder Travis and Reese found them interesting as well as more than a bit puzzling.

Could you blame them?

Not at all, not at all. And I'd say they are more than a bit puzzling these folk as well as the hills and hollows they inhabit are often quite mysterious.

The troubadour was proof of that, A'Tena, more than ample proof.

Agreed and I find the regional dialect intriguing.

Like – Miss, do ye ken where be The Place?

Why jus' a hoot 'n' holler over yonder, handsome stranger.

Might you wish to join me there for a social beverage, young miss?

I'll take a rain check on that, but you do the dialect well, K'Aser.

We both know more than a dialect has been preserved in the hills of the backcountry. Rituals near beyond reckoning are practiced there yet. Some go back to almost to the beginnings – the beginnings of agriculture in many cases.

Way, way back indeed. Some even to the days when the first concern was a grain crop sufficient for brewing sacred drinks or just plain beer. Thankfully, blood sacrifices have been set aside. Remember the horrible screams of the wicker men in ages past? Screams of virgin youths being honored as sacrifices were by far the worst; those of criminals not quite as disturbing to me.

True, but how often did the community find a criminal whenever they needed one? I fail to understand why innocent blood, let alone any blood, was required.

But sacrifices are now long past, save for an occasional animal or two, which can be disquieting enough if you want my opinion.

Both want it and respect it, as always, A'Tena. All in all, the hill folk are preserving much that should be saved, passed on to others.

Chapter 7

East Virginia Passage: Rimel to Washington DC

Pre-Note

The mountains and woods surrounding Rimel were beautiful at dawn. We were drawn to the people of West Virginia, their culture and activities, their use of language similar yet so different than ours. The next leg of our journey would take us into the northwestern sawtooth region bordering West and East Virginia where creeks and runs flow different directions and the forest coverings appear as gigantic green cloths draped over a massive dinner table where we will be guests to new groups of people.

Overland Trek

We readied ourselves to depart. The border separating the two Virginias was barely a kilo-mile east of Rimel and marked by a broken-down wooden sign. Words on the sign were curious as the text consisted of two very different letter styles; in long ago time one might have been called Old English, while the other reflected more of a dot-and-dash script typical of computer messages popular prior to the Ripple Event. Highway 39 blew past Blowing Springs, which was not bubbling at the time. At Mountain Grove we connected with Big Back Creek. Signs informed us that this section of highway sometimes was called Mountain Valley Road. We found the passage indeed mountainous and tiring to ourselves, and to our horses and pack mules.

About midday we reached Warm Springs and rested near the intersection with Highway 220. Just west of the intersection was a small church and cemetery. Travis and I walked over where we met Jessica Winters, who welcomed us and inquired about our journey. She told us that at one time she had been a day care worker at the Warm Springs community center, but because the Epidemic took the lives of so many children the center had reduced need for her services:

> **Jessica Winters,** unemployed daycare worker – *These days I do the same work as long ago past, but no longer receive food and drink. We are poor here in Warm Springs; I live on leftovers and table scraps. I also must care for three orphan children who remain in my charge. Their daddies enlisted in the Virginia Militia and didn't return from their expedition against the Northlanders. Where are their mommies, you ask? Two of the mothers of these children died during the Epidemic while the third became distraught and abandoned her child to eke out the best he could. I found the lad a'wanderin alone one morning and took him in. These are good kids, eight, nine, and eleven solar cycles in age, respectively. I do my best to teach them passages from what we used to call the Good Book. I showed them how to read and write, but since I'm not an educated woman I can't teach them history and such. Still, through it all we have bonded together like a real family and because of my efforts I have some support from the other five families living here in Warm Springs. About three solar cycles past two other town children who were older and also orphans were caught stealing food from Jackson James's silo. They were just hungry kids but they were nabbed, and forced out of our community. Jackson and his brothers chased them down old Highway 39 towards Bath Alum but they escaped. It's possible the children found homes or shelter there. But who knows. These are really hard times. Wish'in you'all speedwell and go with safety. If you can help us out with some food, we would be greatly obliged.*

We took Highway 220 north out of Warm Springs and reached a set of deserted buildings at Chimney Run. No one was nearby so we crossed the roiling waters of Muddy Run, aiming towards Singleton. Late in the day, we reached the crossing of Jackson River where we camped for the night. The region seemed deserted. There were no sounds of songs or music rolling down the hollers, only evening noises of good-luck crickets and frogs croaking near the riverbank.

The settlement of Singleton lay west of the Jackson River near Givens Run. We crossed the river and bypassed Pitt Hollow, then trekked overland to the northeast and reached the settlement of Bolar at the confluence of Bolar and Little Valley Runs. We were just at the edge of what the locals called The Opening Up – or the south entrance to the Shenandoah Valley. We were welcomed at Bolar and invited to stay-a-bit and partake of the Black Drink.

We were handed tin cups each that contained a nice-smelling beverage, dark in color. Our host at Bolar, Ralph Carpenter and his mate, Ada, explained how it was made and why the locals served the drink to guests:

> *Long ago past times the peoples of this area of Virginia and all the way south and east into the mountains and plains clear down into old Georgia, used to decorate their tribal homes with sprigs – what you call branches – of the red-berry plant with the spiny leaves. We know this plant today by the name holly. Of course it is a beautiful plant, and our early pioneer ancestors used to commemorate the celebrations of Christ-Mass, Winter Solstice, and the New Solar cycle. Well somehow the people learned to brew a beverage of the green-most leaves on the tips of the sprigs – never the berries though, since these cause your death sure as shootin'. Taste it Travis – it'll give you a bit of a kick. We always serve it to visitors and guests. It links us with the past and offers insights into the future. Drink up and you'll see what I'm speaking about.*

Both Travis and I sipped our Black Drink along with Ralph and Ada. What I noticed was a slowly creeping sensation, a sense of lightness, pleasant, no head-spinning or whirlies like those we drank at the Church of the Good Drink when we experienced salvation beverages for the first time. The Black Drink slurred my speech a bit, but only a little. Then slowly over me came a dramatic change in vision. I looked across the porch where Travis and our hosts were seated: each of their bodies seemed surrounded by beautiful, bright multi-colored shimmering arcs of light. Floyd observed me and smiled, saying that the light was a local gift to visitors but that the images would pass in a few minutes. As he said the effect vanished shortly and caused me to wonder just what was in the Black Drink.

> *The early peoples in this part of the country were of different tribes. Together they built great mounds using earth and logs. When the star patterns in the heavens were aligned during what we call the*

solstice times, they would brew up their Black Drink – much more powerful than our current recipe. The native men would form a large circle then chant, and dance. Early pioneers and later college-type professors and the like studied the Black Drink and tried to figure out what caused the colored halos of light to form around people and animals – but not around trees and rocks. I don't think they ever discovered why but, what the hey, who cares? A little drink now and then. Body rainbows now and then can't be all bad, right? We enjoyed our visit with Ralph and Ada, and they showed us where to camp over by Bolar Run. The next day turned out to be a major regional celebration. Our visit had coincided with the summer equinox and the pyre festival that the locals called the ceiliuradh an tsamhraidh. Peoples from the small settlements up and down the hollers to the north, south, east, and west of Bolar gathered on the central green at the conjunction of Little Valley and Bolar Runs. We arrived at midday. Already people from the region were milling about exchanging greetings. A huge pile of logs and tinder had been brought down to the green, fuel that would be ignited to form the central component of the celebration.

At sunset a siren alerted all that the ceremonies would soon begin.

Bolar Pyre Celebration

Two elderly residents, a man and a woman (unnamed), were given the honor of igniting the woodpile. As the flames took hold and billowed upward, the crowd murmured in anticipation. Children and young adults of less than 20 solar cycles sat apart from the others in a designated location south of the pyre.

Groups of adults participating in the ceremony approached the pyre and formed four separate rings. The first ring, known as *Servants of Terra,* was closest to the fire and consisted only of elderly men. Their responsibility was to keep the fire stoked. The next ring outward was composed of elderly women, known as the *Servants of Aeris*. Both the first and second rings began to chant in a language that we could not understand. As the chant continued, two separate groups of youngsters approached the pyre. Married women between the ages of 20 and 40 solar cycles known as *Servants of Ignis* linked hands to form the third ring, while an equal number of men the same age known as *Servants of Aqua* formed the fourth ring.

Five drummers stood off to the side of the blazing pyre distant from the swaying and chanting participants. After receiving a silent hand motion from the pyre master, the senior percussionist struck his ritual drum twice. What followed was a syncopated sequence that signaled the start of the ceremony. After the second drum beat, the elderly male *Servants of Terra* clasped hands as their bodies swayed and moved clockwise around the blazing pyre. When the *Servants of Terra* had completed two rounds, a further drum note signaled the female *Servants of Aeris* to begin the rotation of their ring in a counter clockwise movement, keeping pace and rhythm with their opposite counterparts.

The ritual drum was struck again. This signal echoing across the assembly area as members of the third and fourth rings, the young married female *Servants of Ignis* and male *Servants of Aqua* began their part of the ceremony. Both the men and women reached inside their garments and withdrew what appeared to be multi-colored hoods, decorated with reflective glass beads and metal strips. The *Servants of Ignis* and *Servants of Aqua* reached across and exchanged hoods then tied and secured them over the head and face of the person opposite as the rotations resumed.

Movement of the rings increased with intensity as participants in each line resumed chanting. Louder and louder the words echoed and enveloped the assembly. Each pair of rings – the elderly and the young – danced in alternate directions. Feet stomping and arms swinging to the drum beats – faster then slower - then a change of direction – as the percussion instruments emitted sounds of increasing intensity. The rings of dancers produced swirling images framed by smoke from the pyre as firelight reflected from the dancer's hoods, casting shafts of flickering color over the assembly.

The drummers were joined by fife players who, upon receiving another hand sign from the pyre master, emitted shrill tones from their instruments, a signal that the rotations should stop. After a pause, the drumming resumed as the *Servants of Ignis* and *Servants of Aqua* changed rotational directions once again Then followed 12 rotations in alternating changes of direction: each change symbolic of a different month of the annual solar cycle. The swirling rotations continued for approximately 30 minutes. The raging fire, the shrill sounds of the fifes and pounding drums, coupled with the spinning rotation of the hooded human moving in rings chanting and swaying to and fro – all were mesmerizing.

A final drum beat resounded, and the rotations stopped.

The hooded participants in outer rings three and four reached out to grasp the hands of the person directly opposite. The hooded pairs were led away to a special structure called the *teach cuplala,* where they received instructions from the female pyre leader. Her commands were clear: the hoods concealing the participant's identity could not be removed while inside the *teach cuplala,* and that no words may be exchanged by the pyre partners. Instructions also included ceremonial phrases regarding the need to honor, respect, and protect the community of Bolar. With their hoods intact and no words spoken to the other, *Servants of Ignis* and *Servants of Aqua* entered the *teach cupola* and mated.

After a time the *Servants of Ignis* left the *teach cuplala* through the north door, the *Servants of Aqua* from the south exit. In this way no one knew their mate. Once outside, participants re-clustered by gender, removed their hoods, and rejoined the others on the green to participate further in the pyre celebration. Revelry, dancing, and singing lasted long into the night.

Children conceived during the pyre celebration and *teach cuplala* were given the designation *Naoi mi Leanbh* – Nine Month Child – a title of honor and respect. Children thus conceived and born were nurtured, raised, and educated collectively by all adult residents of Bolar.

***

Leaving Bolar settlement, we followed Bolar Run upstream along Highway 607 and crested the rise near the headwaters of Big Valley Run. We followed this slow-moving watercourse down to Dry Branch, a route that paralleled the 607 into Mustoe, where we camped for the evening.

The region between Bolar and Mustoe seemed devoid of human habitation. We saw cabins aplenty but all appeared unoccupied. Several times we saw deer off in the distance grazing by the runs or stepping elegantly along the forested edges of the hollers. We wondered about predator animals, whether wolves or humans, and remained alert throughout the day. We kept our swords at hand both day and night.

We reached Monterey and crossed Highway 250 then headed north towards Harper, a small community along the south branch of the Potomac River. Here we rejoined Highway 220 and paralleled West Strait Creek then crossed Wooden Run near Thorny Bottom. Through a quirk of geography and odd regional planning, we exited East Virginia and re-entered West Virginia once more. Only the early land surveyors could explain why.

Harper was a tiny community rising from the flat-bottom lands west of the Potomac River at the confluence with East Dry Run. No inhabitants could be seen. We watered our horses and mules, and pushed on towards Cave, then Hammer Run, Oak Grove, and on into Franklin.

Songs of the South

We were welcomed by townspeople as we rode down the main street of Franklin. The small community, made even smaller after the terrible Epidemic, was attempting to rise from the ashes. The residents were hosting a song competition for their teenagers. We paused to watch and listen.

A group of three girls and three boys stood together on a platform singing without accompaniment. Their song choices linked images of the two Virginias, both east and west, and by watching and listening it didn't seem to matter that a geographical boundary continued to exist between the former two states. Their lilting voices reached out over the small crowd who listened silently, many with tears flowing down their cheeks.

> *No place on earth do I love more sincerely*
> *Than old Virginny, the place where I was born.*

And

> *But now I'm old and feeble*
> *And my bones are terrible sore*
> *Then carry me back to ole Virginny*
> *To my old Virginny shore.*

Their third selection took those listening far back into time of the great conflagration between the states. They had chosen the one song that touched and moved both northern and southern combatants:

> *The years creep slowly by, Lorena*
> *Snow is on the grass again*
> *The sun's low down the sky, Lorena*
> *The frost gleams where the flowers have been*
> *But the heart throbs on as warmly now*
> *As when the summer days were nigh*
> *Oh! the sun can never dip so low*
> *A-down affection's cloudless sky.*

We were approached by an elderly woman who wore a hat with an unusual insignia. She wished to remain nameless. We inquired and she told us that we must be ignorant not to know what she called the stars-and-bars. This was the first we had heard of the term and told her so. She asked us to sit awhile and palaver, and she would instruct us. After she did so, I asked about her past and how she had survived the Ripple Event: Young lady, I see you have a book where you are taking notes. I look at you and see myself 50 or more solar cycles past. Once I was a journalist. But then came upon us the events that you know about. How can a person be a journalist without a publisher and machines to print the word? As a journalist, I also kept a diary like you. Given the state of local and regional affairs at the time, I thought that my daily recording of observations and events would allow me to keep my occupational title. Prior to the Ripple Event, I worked for the Evening Standard, published out of Fairfax. In our newsroom we had electronic feeds from all over the world coming up on different dedicated computers (i.e., West Africa insurrection; Middle East bombings; rioting in Southern Peru). But none of us could have predicted the state of events that followed the Ripple, and how we were plunged into real darkness – not the allegorical/political darkness that used to hover over DC and adjoining regions like a smelly, damp fog. When all the computer screens and electrical appliances went dark, I had no job and no income. If you don't have income then you don't have food. And then you get hungry. Well, that posed ethical and moral problems. All the local stores were looted, and those neighborhoods in Fairfax with community gardens were raided and destroyed by bands of "know-nothings," who trampled the emerging seedlings underfoot during their daily rampages.

As a journalist, I selected themes for investigative coverage. I long had been known for my exposés of political corruption and instances at local courts where justice failed. Do good – as they say – and you will reap rewards. Truth or platitudes? You choose. But why was there any need to cover local injustices any more, since crime and ill-will against neighbors had become the norm rather than the exception. Was there any value in documenting the events during the Ripple and early solar cycles of the Dark Time? If so, who would read my accounts? I wondered whether or not journalism and the publication of newspapers and newsmagazines would ultimately resume? Well the answer now is clear after some 50 solar cycles since the Ripple Event.

How did I survive the Dark Time, you ask? Was the pen as they say, mightier than the sword? I see from your facial expressions that you have absolutely no idea what I am talking about. You probably were born and raised at a wonderful settlement group and educated in the important ways how to survive. But young people, there is more to life than just surviving. What about culture, history, and memories? What about the ability to remember the events important in life. What about hope for a brighter future?

Buy me a salvation beverage, and I'll read your future from my tarot cards.

Truth be, Travis and I had no idea what she meant by tarot cards.

***

We continued along Highway 220, and completed a long push through Ruddle, Landes, and Pansy to the outskirts of Petersburg. When Travis and I were schooled at Bison Camp, we were taught the basics of the Great War between the North and South. One of the key battles had taken place at a town called Petersburg, where Northerners besieged the city and attempted to enter by tunneling and detonating a mine beneath the ramparts. The explosion caused the formation of a huge crater, and the Northerners rushed through the crater towards the hole in the Petersburg ramparts in anticipation of a quick route. But the earth inside the crater was soft and the crater walls steep. Charging through the soft earth, the Unionites became entrapped and many hundreds died – picked off one by one – easy quarry for Confederate sharpshooters.

The Petersburg West Virginia we trekked through was 200 hundred kilo-miles to the northwest of the Petersburg battlefield site in East Virginia. Two towns with the same name: one in West and one in East Virginia. Confusing to those not familiar with local and regional history.We crossed the south branch of the Potomac River and entered Petersburg. We rode up Shobe Street and, near the intersection with Early Avenue, we encountered a carpenter sitting and enjoying his lunch. He eye-grabbed us and extended an invitation to sit down and join him. His name was Frank Quinn, and from him we learned about the long ago battle of Petersburg in

East Virginia. His great great grandfather, also named Frank Quinn, was a drummer boy with the Unionites at the time of the siege but had escaped being trapped in the crater. He and four other drummer boys were captured and sent to a prison camp for the rest of the war, until their release by the orders of a General named Robert E. Ligh – or something like that. It turns out that upon release, his great great great grandfather returned north and settled somewhere up near the Great Lakes.

The son of that Frank Quinn – my great grandfather Virgil Quinn – left the northern climes and traveled south into West Virginia, where he relocated to our little settlement of Petersburg. This newly adopted son of Petersburg elected to settle down and raise a family with his wife, Mable. Then there was my grandfather Virgil Quinn, we called him Virgil Two, then my father Virgil Quinn became Virgil Three. When I was born, my parents named me Frank in honor of my great great grandfather. When I was little, my father related many times the tale of the Petersburg siege to anyone who would listen. I heard it all my life and expect that every soul in town heard it from him 20 or more times. But my father told the story with such emotion and vigor that we always paused to listen once he started his epic story. Think on it: that little drummer boy of so long ago was my great great grandfather, and he was only 15 solar cycles old when he went to war. What terrible events he experienced at the battle of Petersburg and during his time in the prison camp suffering as they did? After that war and the reconstruction that followed, their fate seems to be mirrored by ours, having to reconstruct our towns and lives after the Ripple Event, Dark Time, and now after the Epidemic. I often think of that little drummer boy and the life he led – perhaps not so different than mine.

***

We pushed on to Taylor and reached Moorefield where we camped.

Moorefield was bustling. All along the streets were signs of reconstruction; new facades over older establishments, new buildings erected on once-vacant lots. But as usual, there was no electricity. As the sun set out came the lamplighters but what fuel was being used? We paused to speak with one of the elderly laborers. Turns out he had one of the more interesting background stories to relate:

***Mark Turner,** carpenter – You see me these days as a carpenter, but that originally was not my trade. My original skills were with electricity. I could wire anything and make it glow, hummmm, or purrrr. The only currents I handle now these days grow and can be picked in the wild lands north or east of us, red and tasty when ripe. No more volts and jolts these days, right? Then the grid went black and suddenly I was out of a job. I survived by barter and by my wits. Using local materials that I scrounged from nearly everywhere, I manufactured simple batteries and linked them up to small motors that could do some jobs that were needed. This skill saved my life and got me accepted into the settlement group located just outside of Moorefield, along the south branch of the Potomac River.*

The settlement group administrators designed a plan to secure river water for crop irrigation and thought that small electrical pumps might work. I countered that this would be a poor use of battery-powered equipment, since the batteries would soon fail. I argued for simple siphons and water-lifting devices that were hand propelled and explained that these would work much better. I immediately was clamped into the stockade for insubordination. Not long thereafter, our settlement group was raided by some military-style outfit wandering the shattered zones. They interrogated me, and recognized that I had a range of potential skills they could use. They forced me into a workhouse to manufacture explosive packages that could be detonated by a battery-operated switch. I don't know how many of these devices I created for those wackos. All I know is that these activities kept me in food, water, and clothing. When our workhouse was liberated, I and the others were led outside, lined up, and allowed to speak a few words about our rescue into a battery-operated recorder, some strange artifact leftover from the Pre-Ripple Event times. I still have that piece of equipment and what they call a tape of that meeting, but you can't hear it now since batteries are so rare and valuable that they seldom are used for casual entertainment without a special permit – and I don't have one. As for those battery-operated explosive packages that I built while in the workhouse, I have no idea what became of them. There were about 20 or 30 of us manufacturing these devices. Once we were liberated and set free, if you will, we were urged to be on our way and to return home. I seem to remember that a couple of co-laborers in the workhouse had homes far north of the Ohio River, but I don't know where.

***

After leaving Moorefield, we followed Highway 48 east to Bean Settlement, Needmore, and Baker. There the route number changed for some reason to Highway 259. We entered McCauley, located along the banks of Lost River and reached Wardensville late in the afternoon. At the intersection of Oak Street and Willow Lane, we were greeted by three elderly men, longtime residents of Wardensville. We introduced ourselves and broke open one of our MREs that we shared. After our meal one smiled and said – Who are y'all? After hearing his words, we replied – Just a'traveling folks mov'in on. They slapped their thighs and laughed. We were three men and two travelers sitting on a porch, survivors of the bad times and looking and wishing for a brighter future. One of the three named Lionel did not offer his last name. He spoke first:

Lionel: *Folks in town call the three of us Manny, Moe, and Jack. We can't figure out why except that we work hard and have lots of energy. Must be linked to some old phrase handed down from hill folk or city dwellers. In any case, these ain't our real names: I'm Lionel, he's Thomas, and he's Forest. Sit awhile and we'll pass the time chewing the fat, watching the fireflies, and smacking 'sketers.*

Travis: *Were all of you born and raised in Wardensville?*

Lionel: *Heck no. I was born to act on the Great White Way, that part of old New York where actors dreamed of strutting their stuff. I was a big hit in my high school plays and wanted to attend acting school in New York. Then came the Ripple Event and all that changed. I remember an actor with the name something like Towknee Curt Is. He stared in some movie film named Smart a Cuss or something like that. I expect you never saw a film or movie, Travis, since you were born after the Ripple – but this guy Towknee was a singer of songs back in really ancient Roman-like times, and he participated in some slave revolt led by this guy Smart a Cuss. His singing voice no longer attracted large crowds so although he was wimpish and not muscular, he took up arms to fight-*

off those invading his settlement. So I was something like him. I never got an acting job, so I made my way out of New York escaping danger here and there, and wound up in, of all places, here at Wardensville. Not a great place for actors and even if so, I was too old to tread-the-boards, as they once said back in old New York. Here, I found peace and friendship at last, and I wouldn't want to live anywhere else.

Thomas: *I arrived here barely escaping death many times and found acceptance in the Wardensville region. You won't believe it, perhaps because I'm now fat with a potbelly, but I once made my living as a bouncer in a bar outside of Arlington. The place was called the Dog's Breakfast. Hell 'of a name, right? Well most nights the patrons were polite and placid, until about 11:30, and then things would enliven and my services often would be needed. Bouncing somebody – man or woman – out of Dog's Breakfast required tact, good upper body strength, and muscular arms. At one time, I had all three, but Forest sitting here next to me would probably say that I am more rude and outspoken than tactful. Well what'd you know. One day, I think it was a Thanksgiving or at least some time in late November, we woke up and nothing worked: no electricity, no access to money, no nothing. The owner of Dog's Breakfast hadn't paid me for two weeks, so I strong-armed him and took my salary out of the cash drawer and became a fleeing crook with a handful of bills, mostly fives, tens, and twenties. And, guess what? This stuff we used to call money was useless after about five days, so I had robbed my boss for nothing. Not good behavior for a kind kid once raised by my long-ago church-going grandmothers.*

So out of Arlington I moved; first to the south towards Richmond, which was aflame with rioters, then I backtracked and headed northwest and ultimately located in a settlement group outside of Wardensville that would accept me. It seems that they needed someone to teach the young'un's physical fitness. I showed them how to keep in shape for hunting treks out along the Cacapon River or excursions south of the settlement down in the Anderson Ridge area. I did this for many solar cycles through the Dark Time and into the Recovery Period. I lost my true love, Jackie, during the Epidemic – bless her heart – and then I just went to pot, as they say. But Lionel and Forest, my buddies here, pulled me through my sorrow and now although I'm now fat and out of shape, I can still pull my weight on construction jobs in and around Wardensville.

Forest: *Like Lionel and Thomas, I too arrived in Wardensville as an outsider. Back in Harper's Ferry where I grew up, I was lucky and had a job just out of high school. Hard to believe, but I once got paid by the former City Council of Harper's Ferry to coach Little League baseball and softball. Back before the Ripple Event, life was simple. I coached little boys and girls how to catch, throw, bat, and run to first base. I remember the games when parents watched, smiled, and cheered. I remember when it didn't matter which side won the game, only that all the boys or girls had an enjoyable time and learned sportsmanship and respect. Then came the Ripple Event and everything that followed. Oh, how behaviors have changed since those earlier times.*

Even today you don't see small boys and girls smiling and participating in sports. They have been toughened by the difficult times their parents and neighbors experienced. If you walk today or tomorrow through Wardensville, you seldom will see a child smile; they rarely express joy in their conversations. They are hardened to the realities of life experienced by the Epidemic and from the stories told to them by their parents about survival.

Did I fail as a coach? Those little boys and girls – now not so little today as they each are adult men and women – sometimes band together in groups taking from others in order to survive. Instead of practicing their sport-related activities to improve, they practice the law of the jungle – where is the sportsmanship in that? I've never been back to Harper's Ferry and wouldn't want to visit; everything has changed. Wardensville is my home.

***

We took Highway 55 out of Wardensville to the east and crossed the border once more into East Virginia where the highway number changed to 48. After Wheatfield and Lebanon Church, the road led south to the junction with Highway 81. After crossing Cedar Creek, we approached Middletown. We camped west of the settlement along the banks of Meadow Brook.

Not far from our campsite, we encountered a disheveled older man walking along the stream bank. He did a double take, looking at us to evaluate whether or not we posed him any harm. Travis raised his right arm in a peace gesture, and the old man seemed relieved.

I cannot tell you my name or my previous occupation. I cannot say – at the risk of my freedom and life. What I can tell you – since you asked about me and survival during the Ripple Event and Dark Time – I have seen both good and evil. My family and I have risen to the heights, and have fallen into the absolute depths of hell. I was in DC at the time of the nuclear attack. I was not one of those who had a safe hole where my family and I could take shelter. When it happened I was working with friends over at Georgetown, west and slightly north of the initial neutron bomb blast. Our family apartment was downtown on 10th Street, Northwest near Ford's Theatre. My wife and three children were obliterated by the blast, but the structure of our house remained intact. And there I was safe – not knowing initially about my family. There I was in Georgetown having lunch and discussing some project that never would be completed and my family was gone, forever.

I, along with thousands of others, was stopped by the authorities from returning to our homes in the city. We knew what was meant by a neutron bomb – all life destroyed but buildings and structures remaining intact. But each of the thousands still wanted to know about their families. No chance, and we were denied entrance into the civic center and forced to turn back.

How I fled the city and survived was through pure luck. I trekked overland along Highway 66 and ultimately made it to a settlement group outside of Middletown. I was accepted because of my training and education. Don't ask what these were, since I still cannot tell you my previous occupation and the types of skills that guaranteed my safety. Through my former professional connections, a task made harder due to the Ripple Event and Dark Time, I and the others learned that the selective nuking of DC produced two groups of survivors, called the Ins and the Outs that characterized the DC landscape. In fact, these were the Pols who, after two solar cycles, popped out of their underground safe holes like newly sprouted seeds. The Outs were those who survived the blasts without benefit of reinforced shelter, and who were forced to contend with health, safety, and survival issues. My former colleagues – now do not guess or ask me whether or not my former colleagues were politicians or lobbyists – I cannot and will not tell you. What I can say is that there are many stories circulating even today how the Outs found the Pols and dealt with them. The easiest way to say this is to relate what one of my friends had observed. She saw 15 Pols rounded up and sent to holding pens across the Potomac River near the former site known as Pentagon City. What happened to these specific Pols and to the countless others that popped up two solar cycles after the neutron bomb blasts – as you know there were three blasts – you will need to find this out for yourself.

***

We left Middletown early morning, and we followed Highway 66 to Front Royal where we camped out along the banks of the Shenandoah River. That evening I wrote the following passage in my journal:

At times I sense the shape of a man at the edge of the campfire halo, a strange unknown male with a curious hat, something like those worn by jesters in times long past. Why does the vision never appear to Travis? In my dream – or in reality – my attention is drawn to his right hand that bears a red letter G with musical notations/lines that looks like a G-clef sign. Who is this image? Could it be that he is not a troubadour? Could his image be that of one of the memory guild singers that I recall from my childhood, traveling musicians who visited different settlement groups to entertain and to recite histories and events of the Pre-Ripple Event time? Perhaps if the visions continue I will know more about him and why I am haunted by these images.

***

After Front Royal, we continued southwest through Linden and Markham then reached Marshall. Although only a relatively short distance from Front Royal, we both were tired and also needed to rest our horses and pack mules. We set up camp a little southeast of Bowman's Pond, a man-made small lake caused by the dam across Piney Branch Stream. The pond campsite area was suitable with ample graze for our animals. A stone monument nearby commemorated the capture of a DC Pol, who had fled west during the Dark Time and attempted to secret himself into the life and culture of the locals. How he was captured and what happened was told in a text carved into the monument:

Here lie the body parts of disgraced Pol Alvin Spencer Stone
Captured and executed by the free citizens of Marshall
May the evil that he wrought slacken with time
May the harm he visited on local families never be forgotten
May the treachery and shame of his name forever be remembered
Alvin Spencer Stone supported the nuclear blasts on DC
Alvin Spencer Stone did so for personal gain
Alvin Spencer Stone: lie forever in the Hell you created, you bastard!

I scarcely could believe these words. Who was this elected politician, Alvin Spencer Stone? How could it be that an American politician could have organized and fostered a deal that resulted in the deaths of hundreds of thousands of DC residents and the destruction of our once-proud capitol?

***

On past Broad Run and Gainesville. In the late afternoon, we approached the Manassas National Battlefield Park where we established our camp near the stone bridge crossing Bull Run. Battalion markers and trenches once covered with the gore of battle were this afternoon overlain by the green green grass of home – home and final resting place to the more than 2,000 killed or missing due to economic and political differences that could not be resolved. The landscape was peaceful now, but at one time in the distant past carnage, destruction, and death had unfolded here among these gentle rolling fields.

Many of the former bronze monuments that honored the dead had been ransacked by metal-seekers during the Dark Time, scavengers who collected different types of metals to be melted into barter ingots. Still, many words on the stone bases of the former monuments could be read, listing names that Travis and I never had been taught during our schooling at Bison Camp. The rectangular base of a monument dedicated to an officer named Thomas Jonathan Jackson could be seen.

At twilight, we walked from our campsite next to Stone Bridge to the cemeteries shared by soldiers on both sides. We paused time and time again to read inscriptions and ponder the events that had taken place so many solar cycles past. How could it be that such a place of peace and beauty in the late afternoon sun could have been a location of conflict and horror during those troubled earlier days? Time stood still as we walked among the headstones listening to the sounds of crickets and hoppers' whirrrrs and clickkkks as they emitted their evening sounds of life. I turned to Travis and looked at his eyes; together we stared out across the battlefield – our minds deep in thought.

What have we learned by standing here
Midst gravestones fading year by year
Beneath this ground we hear the sound
Men crying out deep underground.

A single word a shouted plea
I hear them calling out to me
Was their sacrifice in vain
Men gave their lives, what was the gain.

Both dead and living want to know
Why give your life for naught to show
Then on the breeze I heard their cry
Two thousand voices shouting WHY?

A battle done two thousand dead
No more to smile to love or wed
And with the dawn another day
To shoulder arms and march away.

In the near distance atop Henry Hill, we paused to listen to a group of schoolchildren singing. Their teacher had brought them to Manassas to walk among the monuments and gravesites so to better understand the past history of this geographical region. We watched as the teacher's assistant unpacked his homemade guitar, then gave each child a piece of paper with song words. He gathered the children's attention and together they began to sing, their pristine, clear voices flowing across the battlefield into our minds and hearts:

We're tenting tonight on the old camp ground,
Give us a song to cheer
Our weary hearts, a song of home
And friends we love so dear.

Many are the hearts that are weary tonight,
Wishing for the war to cease;
Many are the hearts looking for the right
To see the dawn of peace.

And another:

We shall meet but we shall miss him.
There will be one vacant chair.
We shall linger to caress him,
While we breathe our ev'ning prayer.

We retired to our campsite, and checked our horses and pack mules. Travis and I sat around the campfire reflecting on our journey. Only a few cycles earlier we had visited South Bend and celebrated the defeat of the Northlanders. The residents of South Bend had persevered and eliminated – at least for the time being – actions by the intolerant and aggressive Northlanders. Would peace eventually come to the region bounded by the Ohio and Mississippi rivers? The promise and hope were there, but in time would the cancers of intolerance and hatred of those who were different, and the quick dismissal and anger raised by alternative ideas return once more to infect the residents?

We pondered long into the night what we had seen this day at the Manassas battlefield. We had not been taught the north-south differences that led to these hostilities. Our training had focused on survival and self-reliance. We certainly needed to know more about this great and vast confederation, so different than ours in the NorthWest. At our Bison Camp school the term confederacy simply meant a confederation of states, an alliance, a league, an association of people or groups with similar attitudes towards culture, economics, and religion. We had little to no idea that the term confederacy had a much older, perhaps darker context. But was this darkness only in the eye of the beholder, or was it real? What about the present time? On our journey through the northern portions of the New Confederacy, we encountered no slaves, no separation of races, no offensive or distinctive markings at the entrances of buildings suggesting intolerance. We saw no evidence of hooded men or women burning buildings or executing others who were different. The only hooded men or women we had seen during our trek were the pyre celebrants at Bolar. The hoods that concealed their faces were not evil but sensual, and these hoods at Bolar united a community through the gift of children and assured that all residents worked together for the protection and safety of their young.

***

Before leaving Manassas battlefield, Travis and I took another walk through the site. What we had not noticed yesterday was that at certain locations, objects had been left at gravesites and memorials to commemorate the deceased and missing-in-action. We now observed more than one tin can that inside contained poignant messages to the deceased. Other items left included flowers, most commonly hibiscus. Still other mementos decorating the graves touched us deeply; drawings left by school children, their personal sketches of the monuments and cemeteries. Their drawings commonly were accompanied by simple phrases:

No more war
Friends are better than enemies
Love – love – love
Can't we be friends?

What else could children write? Wonderful naïve words from the mouths of babes. Could they really contemplate the events that took place here long ago?

I think not.

***

We remained on Highway 66 and soon reached Centreville. Fairfax, our destination this day, was only 15 kilo-miles from Manassas. When we arrived, Fairfax was in the midst of an Irish and Celtic festival, commemorating survival and optimism for the future. We established our camp along Accotink Creek. Walking into town, we met a wonder cart driver who stopped and offered us a ride – but for the right amount of barter metal or other materials. We negotiated and agreed upon a single half stick of premium copper and a small tube of zinc oxide.

Our wonder cart driver was Gordon Haversmith, but he preferred to be called Gordy. The tales he related as we toured Fairfax caused us to smile and laugh out loud – something that we hadn't done in a long time:

Gordon Haversmith, *driver – I used to drive some of the better known Pols at DC to secret rendezvous – what we used to call Tryst and Shout meetings. This was back before the Ripple Event and Dark Time. I had a hansom cab business at that time – if you know what that was? Do you? Com'on – a hansom cab is a fancy horse and buggy deal. Well, if I remember right, back in those days there was a really cool singer who danced and pranced as he sang. His name was something like Fat Chessman – but that can't be right. Could his name have been Fact Checker? That can't be right either, but if I remember correctly his name sounded like something you might call a well-fed grocery clerk back in the olden days. In any case, back to the Tryst and Shout meetings.*

There was this one old Pol way back before the events of the past 50 solar cycles. I would drive him in my hansom cab to the clubs over near DuPont Circle, places with names something like the In and Out Club. Another one I remember was the Moan and Groan, and right next door was the No Clap Bar, with its unusual advertising sign showing a single hand clapping. Those who danced the night away called these establishments ISGEFs, which stood for IN STANT GRAD E FICATION. All this was great and good, and I was riding high, as you might say, but it all soon ended.

We less-famous folks had less than 30 minutes warning before the nukes went off. Most of the Pols on the inside knew it was coming much earlier and dived into had their safe holes. You look puzzled, Travis, let me explain. Safe holes were protective shelters within reinforced basements or pits excavated in backyards. I remember debates as to how much food should be stockpiled in these safe holes, the correct number of bottles of water and what kinds of booze and how much. There were constant debates, however, about who got to stay in these safe holes. Only family? What about friends and neighbors? The Pols who had the best safe holes just bolted shut the double blast doors that protected them and didn't respond to the pleas of outsiders to be admitted. Not enough food to go around was the common reason the Pols gave for non-admission: they protected themselves and didn't let others inside. It didn't matter which of the five political parties a Pol belonged to; they still had to stash supplies of their meds and whatever other types of pills or botanicals they craved and needed. For most of 2 ½ solar cycles, the Pols stayed in their safe holes, but then came a day where it seemed as if some sort of universal signal had been sent out alerting the Pols that it was all right to emerge. And out they came, looking pale and wan; the fat ones had become thin. We learned later that most of those Pols died in their so-called protective bunkers. Tough!

So the DC area became divided into two groups having nothing to do with elections: the Outs and the Ins. We outsiders who never had the advantage of a safe hole learned through trial and error which sections of DC could be navigated without fear of radiation poisoning. The nuked areas basically were restricted to three interlocking ovals with a core area that extended from the Capitol building down the Mall to the Lincoln Memorial. Radiation diminished to tolerable levels about 10 solar cycles later. We learned through trial and error how to navigate through the blast destruction. The Ins who had just emerged from their safe holes wandered about here and there. Not knowing anything about radiation, they searched aimlessly through the ruins for their old offices. What did they want to recover – old photos, memo books, gifts from lobbyists or the Lobs as we called them? Who knows? We Outs banded together and searched too – but we searched for any old Pol or In who was wandering about here and there. And when we found one – guess what – I don't have to tell you – right?

After the bombs detonated and the rest of the world went to hell, there was no use continuing as a hansom cab driver. The horses remained useful for transportation here and there but bicycles, once considered the bane of upscale DCers suddenly emerged as valuable modes of transportation. Especially fashionable were the three-wheeled varieties that could be modified to carry loads. I tried my hand at the bicycle pedi-cab business and built one myself. That's where you take a bicycle and modify it with a semi-closed rear carrying device that could transport people. But this wasn't such a good economic idea, since money didn't work anymore and a pedi-cab travel-barter system for use in and about the DC area posed lots of problems: how much should I charge to peddle some ex-Lob from central DC over to Georgetown or up or down river – say all the way to Mount Vernon? How many ingots of copper vs. bronze vs. bottles of water vs. vegetable seed packets would it take? You needed an additional sidecar attached to your pedi-cab just to stash the barter items. But if you operated on the street, you just advertised yourself to thieves who roamed about looking for easy marks. So I quit that job and signed up with the GET-PLAYD group and found myself working a pedi-cab west of the Potomac, transporting folks from one of their establishments to another. The GET-PLAYD group offered incentives for hard-working peddlers, so as time passed I had amassed a reasonable amount of barter items. I traded up for a horse-drawn wonder cart. And the rest is history as they say.

You ask about my work history? Before my GET-PLAYD employment I worked for COTC – Carriages of the Capital – driving fares around the capital, then over to the tidal basin and the Jefferson Memorial, then to the Lincoln Memorial and back. I knew the history of the people, the good stuff both real and made up. Now I shuttle patrons back and forth between Fairfax and Arlington – between the special GET-PLAYD establishments. Most of my current patrons are old time Lobs, plying between the feminine and masculine clubs.

The GET-PLAYD establishment in Arlington primarily serves male patrons with hostess ladies of different ages and educational backgrounds, sure to be an evening filled with enjoyment, right? We know the roped off areas in DC that are off limits due to drifting radioactivity and are trained to identify and evaluate all varieties of barter goods – as they say – from aluminum ingots to zirconium gems. Our ladies know all the ups and downs of the trade, so to speak, and how to be a polite hostess, replying to all questions with sincerity and knowledge.

In contrast, the GET-PLAYD establishment in Fairfax primarily serves female patrons, and we are known for our male companions and escorts of different ages and athletic shapes from super lean to chunky. The masculine line dances serve the feminine patrons as a preview, and provides each prospective patron the opportunity to see first-hand the shapes and sizes desired for evening companionships. Like their female counterparts in Arlington, the male escorts know the safe, risky, and dangerous locations throughout the nearby DC geographical regions and have the savvy to identify and evaluate barter goods – as they say – from agate jewelry to zinc ingots. Our men know all the ups and downs of the trade and how to be a polite host, replying to all questions with sincerity and knowledge.

Our motto: Get the Pleasure You Deserve.

What do you think, Travis and Reese, would you like to check out the Fairfax GET-PLAYED establishment or return to your campground?

Travis started to laugh. His laugh was so infectious that I, too, began to smirk and laugh. Gordy soon followed with a raspy chuckle:

Look folks, glad to have been of service. Thanks for the copper ingot and the tube of zinc oxide. Enjoy your stay in Fairfax. Be careful crossing the Potomac. Just follow directions on the yellow radiation markers, and you will be all right.

***

The next day we entered Arlington. We camped along the western bank of the Potomac River, opposite Theodore Roosevelt Island near the edge of the National Cemetery. We had reached the outskirts of DC, one of our primary eastern destinations. We had trekked more than 2,000 kilo-miles, and had seen and experienced much. Ahead of us across the river lay the once-proud capitol of the former United States of America.

After-Word

Once more I felt that spring was in the air – our journey since leaving Bison Camp had been strenuous. We passed through each of the seasons, sometimes for the better, sometimes for the worse. Soon once again all will be green and fresh, and we will experience the ever-changing cycle of life: the spring of joy and rebirth, the summer of heat and anger, and the fall and winter of cold and regret. I do not welcome the hot muggy days that soon will be upon us where we now are – so unlike those back home, as if we really had a home where we could return. But then winters have been mild for most of our journey. If nothing else, Travis and I now are well familiar with both the good and the bad.

Travis left our campsite to go hunting along the banks of the Potomac. He may have luck and bring back a rabbit or squirrel for our dinner. We have become accustomed to the bounty of the waters, woods, and fields we have traversed, never once going hungry. Hunger has not been our problem. Loneliness has been our bane from time to time, especially for me. But we now know and understand the locations where other good people live. And I know there will be even more places east of the NorthWestern Confederacy, whether north towards New PlyMouth or south deep within the New Confederation where survivors of the Epidemic slowly are recovering.

Tomorrow morning we will cross the Potomac River and explore DC, and from there we will trek onward into the unknown for new discoveries.

***

Ijano Esantu Eleman

Interlude-Conversation: 7
Voices

***

Reese seemed most disturbed by the lingering voices around and about the Manassas battlefield, did she not?

No question of it, A'Tena, she is the sensitive one of their pair and if she didn't hear voices at this location, where else could she?

Bull Run, Manassas. First or second, take your pick, both were bloody. Each left many asking why. This word we hear at many places in many tongues, yet we are unable to respond to calm the voices. Luckily they fade with time.

They fade, A'Tena, but they remain here and there, here and now as well as past, and often in the pairs we've come to know all too well.

All too well – so many ancient texts in Greek and Latin, Latin and Phoenician, Latin and take your pick of languages – the Romans were surely here, there, and everywhere back then.

Well, how about – French and German again in several places at many times; German and Russian across great swathes of Europe and Near Asia; Chinese and Japanese, and on and on?

K'Aser, you've omitted English but then, why not? We're not through getting messages in this language, I fear.

Thanks be to Etowah [may his name be praised] battles recently have become both rare and limited.

And less bloody, thanks to you, K'Aser.

When my patience has been tried or at those times the deaths would be more horrendous than usual, yes, I've directed outcomes as with the Northlanders at the Battle of South Bend. For such I make no apologies.

And well you shouldn't. If only we could answer the voices. Answers being – greed and stupidity. Greed for power, for resources or for the so-called Lebensraum as prattled about by the Germans; no matter 'tis still greed and if not greed 'tis stupidity pure and simple. No matter how noble a cause might be in defense of hearth and home, the root cause was one or both – choose one or both, the results are always the same.

A'Tena, you see things clearly for true.

At times more clearly than you might imagine, K'Aser.

Chapter 8
Washington DC to the Border: Tracing the Barrier

Pre-Note

Early morning dawn brought notes of a lone bugler paying respects to former soldiers buried at Arlington cemetery. We rode past a large memorial dedicated to United States Marines. Of this monument, only the base remained. The bronze portions had been desecrated and demolished by metal-grabbers searching for materials to melt into barter ingots.

We met our DC guide, former Sergeant Gregory Foster. He approached us on horseback. Gregory was from a military family and joined the local Virginia Militia when his unit was formed during the Dark Time. His knowledge of the DC blast and his maps of the safe venues within the former once-great city would prove highly valuable.

Together we crossed what was known as the TR Bridge, named after one of the early Presidents of the former United States.

DC

The western-most portion of the extensive mall was essentially radiation free. Gregory suggested that we tether our animals nearby where they could graze in safety. He provided us with radiation badges that would indicate when we entered danger zones and how much time we could spend in each. The edge of the irradiated areas began near the Lincoln Memorial and adjacent Vietnam Veterans Memorial located nearby. Our badges indicated that we would have a maximum of one hour to explore both sites before exiting the unsafe zone.

The Lincoln Memorial lay in ruins. The once-proud marble structure had been demolished by blast pressure. We walked counterclockwise around the broken slabs of white stone, attempting to visualize what the monument would have looked like during times long ago past. We faced the ruins and paused – rising above the mass of crushed stone was what appeared to be the broken head of former President Abraham Lincoln. At the feet of his demolished statue were fragments of what likely was a stone wall that previously bore words, perhaps commemorating the life of the president or perhaps important portions of a speech that he had delivered. We could not tell which. Nevertheless, I copied the letters into my diary:

//score and //ven years
//our fath/rs brought for
//on this conti///t a new
//ived in lib//ty, and dedi
//ted to the pro///ition tha
//all m// are created equ//

We asked Gregory if he knew the origin of the words and their meaning. He replied only that the broken text must represent something the president had once said for which he had become well known.

To the northeast of the Lincoln Monument was an unusual v-shaped slit set within the ground. This monument was black-stone lined with steps leading down into the earth. As we descended, we touched the wall that bore the names of thousands of men and women. Gregory told us that this memorial was established to honor military members who had died fighting a long-ago war in a country called Viet Nam in faraway Asia. He said that soldiers in his militia remembered stories from their fathers and grandfathers that the place was known most commonly as Nam at the time of the war.

At the base of the wall was a flat area, lined with white bricks. As we drew near, we saw that various objects had been left where the bricks touched the black wall. Included were bunches of flowers, stuffed animals, and offerings of candles and little red sticks that Gregory thought were called *jazz* or something like that, he wasn't sure. Gregory said that these sticks were lighted by some visitors to honor the memory of the deceased. The most unusual objects left next to the wall, however, were what appeared to be military medals. One was a bronze-colored star and the other a heart-shaped medal with a gold border with a central image that appeared to be the head of an old man set within what looked to be purple glass.

Off to one side next to the wall were two aluminum canisters. The tins had caps that concealed objects inside. I asked Gregory if it was permitted to open one to see the contents. He agreed and I removed the lid and withdrew a paper with hand printed words. The text touched my heart:

Once in a faraway land we were soldiers
Helping our allies their fight to be free
An enemy strong had marched down from the north
We were brothers united against this vast hoard.

Time after time the invaders pushed southward
Storming our trenches we held them at bay
Time after time we repelled their aggression
Onward they charged us again and again.

Battle sounds echoed the cries of the wounded
Hand to hand combat again and again
Cries of the wounded then terrible silence
Blood of our brothers poured over the ground.

Of in the distance the sound of a whistle
Calling retreat the invaders withdrew
We had prevailed our positions were strongest
Allies well trained could now stand as one.

Once more again the aggressors marched southward
Once former allies no longer could stand
Land that we bled for surrendered in sorrow
Lives of my comrades were given in vain.

Land we had fought for the enemy conquered
Came years of talking a peace treaty signed
What of our comrades who died in the battles
Now only names on a wall etched in stone.

Matthew: 1st Sergeant, 17th Battalion, Delta Squad
Mark: Corporal, 3rd Battalion, Baker Squad
Luke: Lieutenant, 5th Battalion, 4th Platoon
John: Captain, 2nd Battalion, 1st Platoon.

War reasons faded with time ever passing
Presidents claimed our past enemies-friends
Sounds of the far distant battles forgotten
Enemy-friends a time turned upside down.

Enemy-friends the term spoken by many
We who remembered were brushed off aside
Dwell not today on those long ago battles
Enemy-friends the new catchword today.

A gala one evening to share food and dine
Toasting the future new friendships all smiles
Sitting together to toast happy greetings
My face a mask that revealed not my pain.

The banquet concluded I walked out alone
Darkness consumed me with deeply felt pain
I walked towards the wall to be with them again
Faces of comrades and friends drew me near.

The wall pulled me closer I felt them so near
Andrew and Basil – Cameron and Drew
Edward and Frank – George and Harry
Isaac and James – Karl and Leroy.

A thousand more names ...
A thousand more faces ...
A thousand more memories ...
A thousand more tears.

What draws me close to this wall of the fallen
Why do I come here again and again
Touching their names etched so deep in the marble
I see their faces their smiles and their pain.

Dead are my comrades who fought once for freedom
What did they die for – what was the gain
Lost in confusion the reasons for conflict
Who crafted this new word – enemy-friends?

The wall reaches out to me one word resounds
Across the green hills and the near valleys wide
One word resounding again never changing
Why – Oh Why? Oh Why? Oh Why?

I shared the words with Travis. We scarcely could conceal our emotions. Gregory told us that many such items and documents are left beside the wall. At one time in the long-ago past they were collected. He did not know whether or not this practice continued and, if so, where the objects might be stored. I placed the paper back inside the canister, sealed and left it at the base of the wall. This location was the only place that made senseTravis asked Gregory if he knew about the war in Viet Nam. He replied that it was a subject not taught at his school. He knew of a place called Viet Nam, only because one of his teachers taught world geography. Travis and I, too, had received no instruction about this war in our classes at Bison Camp. We could only ponder why not.

***

Stretching eastward from the Lincoln and Viet Nam Memorials, the national mall lay open. Gregory alerted us that we could not walk or ride its length, due to dangerous radiation levels. He listed a number of key buildings that remained empty and devoid of all human life – but still home, however, to certain varieties of insects. The off-limit structures included several Smithsonian buildings and one called the White House was located off the mall to the north, and the national Capitol building at the end of the mall with its dazzling cupola crowned by the Statue of Freedom. Gregory said that the contents of these buildings were basically intact, but that it would take up to 45 or 50 solar cycles for the radiation to diminish to levels that the contents could be revisited.

Travis and I had not before heard of the Smithsonian and wondered about the contents therein. Gregory looked puzzled and said that our education must be deficient, since all persons living in the United States prior to the Ripple Event would have known of the Smithsonian. Gregory's chastisement of our Bison Camp education did not sit well with Travis, who countered that survival was the most important educational element taught us, the ability to locate and secure food and potable water meant that life would continue. Yes, history and culture were important unifiers that brought survivors together, but items of historical interest to some individuals or to some settlement groups might not carry the same level of survival value as others. Gregory was not put off by Travis's retort but asked instead:

> *Travis, have you ever seen or contemplated what the first airplane looked like? An airplane was the first object to fly through the air*

and carry humans from one place to another. Have you ever seen or contemplated the importance of rockets – you must know what these are, of course – and how one president ordered the nation to work towards landing on the moon – you know what that is, of course – and how rockets launched the space capsule that actually landed on the moon. At the Smithsonian in solar cycles to come after the radiation decreases, there will be available for inspection an actual rock from the moon, returned to earth by one of the U.S. astronauts – you know what an astronaut is, of course?

By now both Gregory and Travis were smiling at each other, shaking their heads respectfully and accepting the concept that not all education has been or should be the same.

Gregory continued:

The building known as the White House once was the living quarters of the president of the United States. The building known as the National Archives – also within the blast zone – contained the most important documents related to the early and recent history of our once-great nation. Perhaps the most important ones being the Declaration of Independence and the Constitution, with its initial Amendments that later Americans called the Bill of Rites – or something like that. These were the documents that the Pols used to administer our country – mostly good ideas, if I may say so, but sometimes used by so-called lawyers and those we called Lobs, who wiggled or weaseled the demands of one group or another around this or that for their own self-gratification and to meet their perceived entitlements.

One of the more interesting sections of the National Archives, however, was the 4th floor where visitors could look up documents related to their ancestors. My father and grandfather used this collection many times and found that our family had arrived in North America and initially settled in the state once-called Rhode Island after arriving from Irish lands that once were a part of Old England. After the radiation declines, perhaps children that you may elect to have may return to DC and search the documents for your ancestors and the backgrounds of those who were the pioneer settlers and founders of Bison Camp settlement group.

Travis asked Gregory about the DC zoo.

The National Zoological Park was outside the blast zone, but radiation clouds blew northward, and the animals all were impacted. Because of the radiation no keepers – even volunteers – were allowed inside to tend to the animals. The beasts and birds could not be released, as they would pose hazards to the human population that survived, so they were left alone.

You mean left to starve?

Well, yes, you could call it that. But what else could be done? Some DC residents suggested that the animals could become a source of meat to help stave off hunger. But that suggestion made no sense, since the animals had been irradiated. So the issue was dropped.

What happened next?

Obviously, the beasts and birds died in their cages amid complaints and protests of the SPCA-types, but what could we do? If you visit the DC Zoological Park today, which you can't because of the radiation, you would find only bones picked clean by predator birds that originally survived the blast and dined on the zoo banquet fare. These scavengers then died, as well, due to the radiation. Too bad: that's life, right?

***

We returned to our tethered horses and pack mules. Gregory examined our guest radiation badges, and informed us that our ionizing rating would permit us to remain within the base-neutralizing zone for another 10 hours. He asked our destination, which was to leave DC via Highway 29 towards Silver Spring where we proposed to camp for the evening. Gregory said that Silver Spring was well outside the base-neutralizing zone, and that we would expect to pass through a checkpoint about one kilo-mile south of Silver Spring where we would submit our badges for evaluation and collection. We thanked Gregory for his kind assistance and tour of the safe zones within the heart of DC.

***

We angled north out of the Lincoln Memorial area on Highway 29 and quickly passed the Zoological Park, since we could not pause for a look inside. As predicted by Gregory, we were met along the road by a rad-monitor who checked our readings. After we received a safe clearance evaluation, she collected our badges. We asked about campground possibilities and were referred to a location within Nolte Park.

***

Our way out of DC to the north led us past Fairland, then across the Patuxent River Bridge into Maple Lawn. We rested at noontime for several hours before continuing. We crossed Highway 32, bypassed Columbia, then trekked east cross country towards the communities of Elkridge where we camped for the night along the banks of the Patapsco River. Also camping nearby was a solitary man who we invited over to our campfire later that evening. His name was Paul Johnson. He was the son of a former DC architect.

My father assisted with the design of two of the most beautiful buildings in DC, the NAG or National Art Gallery and the GGB, the Governmental Geodesic Building where most of the Lobs were provided offices. Both buildings were ravished during the Ripple Event and finally destroyed during the Dark Time. My father told me that when the darkness descended, the residents of DC were not interested in art, as they associated paintings and sculpture with the Pols. So what did they do? They rioted and set fire to the NAG. Now I don't say that their actions were right, but one would be hard pressed in early days to have found any DC resident visiting the NAG just to see paintings and other contents when what they really wanted was food and water. Both buildings were destroyed by mobs that didn't care about so-called aesthetics or what the Pols and Lobs called artistic masterpieces. Their aesthetic was to survive: a masterpiece to them was a smooth barrel pistol.

I was born after the blast. All through my childhood I never entered DC and have not done so even these days. I only have heard about the buildings and monuments from my father and teachers. During the terrible time of the Ripple Event, my father rescued me and we trekked north to be out of the DC chaos. We were accepted at a settlement group just outside of Silver Spring. So it was that I grew up with all this madness. As the son of an architect, I was taught construction techniques by my settlement group teachers. My assigned tasks were to assist carpenters and bricklayers. Today I do odd jobs here and there. If you would like me to tend your horses and pack mules so you could walk about and explore Silver Spring, I wouldn't charge you much.

***

We departed Elkridge via Lansdowne and Cherry Hill, then approached Oriole Land.

Baltimore

This once-proud city had suffered terribly. Militia members stopped and questioned us as to our destination. Since we wanted to spend little time here in what now was called Oriole Land, we were told that visitors could camp along Waterview Avenue adjacent to the Patapasco River. The riverside park where we were assigned was guarded by Maryland Militia to preserve security. In our section of the park, there were about 15 other tent structures, some with families but mostly individuals camping. We soon would learn the importance of knowing one's neighbors. Nearby our tent was one occupied by Harold Simpson, a most interesting individual.

My father was a bank teller at the First Eastern Bank of Baltimore. Tellers, as you might or might not know, did not relate stories, but dispensed bills – money you remember what that was, right? He would say how the customers would smile, finger that green stuff, pocket it or jam the paper into their wallets or purses then walk out strutting like roosters on New Solar Cycle's Eve. I was born into poverty during the Dark Time after my father lost employment. We struggled mightily. We ate wild plants and discarded food scraps, but we survived. When I was in my late teens, my father took me aside and told me a secret: banks just didn't dispense money. Inside banks were special rooms called vaults where customers paid high fees to rent locked metal boxes to store their stuff. He reckoned that most of these boxes contained valuables. He didn't know if the vault at his former bank already had been looted or not, but wondered if I and my friends might be interested in checking out the situation.

So one night five of us led by my father broke into the First Eastern, and guess what? There was a vault but getting inside was another issue. Turns out that my father knew some set of numbers – something called a combination. He twitched the numbers on the vault lock dial back and forth for a time and then, like magic, the door opened. Wow! Inside were two dried, mummified bodies on the floor. It looked like a guard had caught a thief red-handed, as they used to say, but they had shot each other and the vault door had been slammed shut. Why no one else had entered during the following solar cycles – who knows? Perhaps all the others who knew the combo had died during the Ripple Event. In any case, we had hammers and crowbars and pried open several of boxes, and guess what? Out popped silver and gold bars, and mounds of sparkly gem jewelry. But, most of all, there was lots of paper stuff printed with nice designs, something called stock certificates. These meant nothing to us, so we tossed everything onto the floor since they were worthless. Some people had stashed guns inside their boxes. We even found strange objects like false teeth and packages of Nibs – some sort of licorice candy from long-ago past times. I couldn't resist and opened one box: hard and dry after many solar cycles. We dragged a ton of stuff out of that bank, especially the silver coin collections we encountered. These we could melt and make into fancy barter tokens. Every time I think about what we did, I have to smile. Now who in the hell would be so stupid as to store licorice candy inside a bank vault box instead of gold or jewels? Not everybody is sane, right? For a while we lived high-on-the-pig as we used to say, but then things just happened and little by little our treasures decreased down to nothing. So here I am today – back deep in the woods, so to speak, but as you can see there are no woods in Baltimore/Oriole Land – only hoods. I still remember the flavor of those old Nibs candies.

***

Our militia guard told us that we could leave our pack mules at our campsite if we wanted to ride up Kloman Street towards Ridgleys Cove and get a better view of Oriole Land. No one would steal from our belongings, he would see to it. We thought this would be an interesting excursion, but little did we know what would happen.

As we approached the harbor, our horses became skittish. Travis fell, injuring his left leg and suffering a deep gash. We dismounted just under the remains of old Eye 95 and sought assistance. Nearby there was a squatters' camp under the freeway ruins also guarded by militia members. Several of the campers seeing our plight came to assist.

One of those who helped was an elderly woman named Joan Knight. Back in Bison Camp we would have called Joan a sage femme, but here she was known as a PCW or personal care worker. She slit open Travis' lower pants leg to view the wound, which was bleeding profusely. She staunched the bleeding with a tourniquet then, after the flow had stopped, she removed a clove of garlic and a potato from her carpetbag. The potato was covered with green mold. She washed the deep gash with water of uncertain origin, then licked and spit into the wound. Next she rubbed the crushed garlic clove into the wound and took a small spatula and scraped the green potato mold onto the gash. She sealed the wound with a spoonful of honey, then covered the gash with a poultice prepared from what she said were Black Widow spider webs.

Her instructions were clear: Travis needed to rest for several days before continuing our ride. If we wanted to move our campsite to join them under the old freeway system, we would be welcome. Travis and I agreed. I asked one of the militia guards to escort me back to our tent area to collect our off-loadings and to un-tether our pack mules. Later that evening after we had re-gathered, all of us dined together, each contributing something to the pot. Joan called this dish stone stew, which really didn't have a pebble or rock base just a strange mix of different vegetables. After dinner she related something about her background and how she and the others had banded together after the Ripple.

> *As a personal care worker in Baltimore, I once had a specialization in EC or elder care. I spent much of my recent adult life caring for the elderly. Now in the twilight of my life I have no one specifically to care for me, but I have instead the friends that you see around me. The hardest part of being an elder care worker was watching my clients drift slowly into nothingness. It is true that most who survived the Ripple Event and Dark Time were youthful and vigorous; they had to be. But as time progressed through the Recovery Period to where we now are today, the minds of some of the once-youthful hard workers faltered and drifted into forgetfulness. Remember, I was but a mere child at the time of the Ripple. My father protected me and my brother after the passing of our mother. The survival skills he taught both of us saved our lives many times when we were forced to live on the streets of Baltimore, scrounging from place to place. We avoided the problems of the east side Baltimore gangs by remaining under-the-radar, as we used to say. I have no idea what that meant but whenever I said it my father smiled. I had no formal schooling*

as we were rejected by each settlement group we approached. Then my father died and I wandered alone as a young girl over the countryside always alert to danger and avoiding most.

When I was in my early teens, if I remember correctly since I don't know the solar cycle when I was born, a wonderful older woman took me in as her apprentice. From her I learned the hot and the cold, the wet and the dry, and the balance of life vs. the unbalance of illness. She taught me to treat illness using the signature of opposites and how to make my own medicines. I learned how to stop bleeding and how to treat wounds; studied the importance of juniper leaves and berries; and mastered a special way to heat water using sunlight reflected off of aluminum foil.

So it was that I became a PCW like my mentor. When she died, I assumed her practice. Day-to-day wounds I can treat well, but the patients who come to me barely knowing their own names or where they lived, these are challenging cases as I have no medicine or skills to treat memory loss. The mentally able persons who bring their loved ones to me for help – I can do little that will ease their worry and pain. Then come the decision times when caretakers of these aged, mental innocents ask for an end-of-life solution. They seek me out using soft words: is there a medicine for deep endless sleep? Of course there are many but is it right to provide such elixirs to caretakers of the elderly? Too many times I have been forced to ponder what to do. Such requests have become more and more frequent and too painful for me. I am thinking about abandoning my practice. But for now, I pass my days under the freeway, down by the sea, resting on blankets with my friends – this is where I will be – perhaps for the rest of my life.

***

We spent four days with Joan Knight and her friends. Each had tales to tell, and we shared ours as well. Day by day Travis' wound began to heal. Twice Joan lanced it to relieve fluid buildup. Each time she rebound his leg using her famous Black Widow spider web poultice.

You will have a deep scar, Travis, and possibly a limp.

But you are a strong man and should do well.

***

We exited Baltimore along a route parallel to Eye 95. The pace we traveled necessitated camping three nights before reaching Philadelphia. After Baltimore, we passed through or drew near to Rosedale, Rossville, and Nottingham. We crossed Big Gunpowder Fall River into Clayton where we camped. The next day we rode through Havre de Grace and crossed the Susquehanna River, then on to Childs, Elk Mills and across the Christiana River into Wilmington where we camped. Leaving Wilmington we passed through or near Pennyhill, Carrcroft, and Ardencroft, followed by Boothwyn, Linwood, Chester, Eddystone, crossed Darby Creek into Tinicum Township, then across the Delaware River for an early morning ride into Philadelphia. This route can be followed on old maps, and I also must say that most of the communities we passed through, or around, were severely damaged with few residents visible.

***

Philadelphia

We learned about Philadelphia during our schooling at Bison Camp, something about a building called Independence Hall and a broken bell. One of the residents at Bison Camp, I don't remember who, said that Philadelphia meant the city-of-brotherly-love. Being teenagers at the time, we laughed because we weren't sure what brotherly-love was, but guessed that if it was all right for the whole city then it was all right for us.

In contrast to Baltimore or Oriole Land we observed no military guards as we rode through the near-abandoned city. Old Eye 95 led us straight north along the west bank of the Delaware River. We established our riverside camp at Spruce Street Park. We tethered our pack mules and set out to look for the monuments we had learned about many solar cycles previously: west on Spruce Street, then north on South 5th. A region bounded by Chestnut and Walnut streets included a large central park, at one time well cared for, but not so in these difficult days. At the north end of the park was Independence Hall. Behind Independence Hall and across Chestnut Street to the north was a second grassy area. A team of militia members had assembled here. Their purpose, so they said, was to guard what the sign said was the Liberty Bell. To Travis and me, the bell looked just like a thousand other bells, and even this one was cracked. We really did not know why it was being protected, so we dismounted and approached one of the guards and inquired.

Young people, you ask me the question why we are guarding this bell? I will tell you since it is clear to me that your education is deficient.

So once again we were being belittled by persons even younger than ourselves and told that our education had been deficient, since it did not include references to governmental beginnings of the former United States. We were shown words on the bell:

Proclaim LIBERTY throughout all the land unto all the inhabitants thereof.

Travis murmured something under his breath that sounded like "Well that was then and this is now." The militia officer, some five or six solar cycles younger than Travis, told us, "Sorry traveler: move along." So much for the concept of brotherly-love in Philadelphia.

Riding west on Ranstead Street, we were surprised to see several shops open with patrons seated and drinking beverages. We stopped outside one of these so-called watering-holes where an unusual sign was posted in the window:

Long ago it was said: Eat, drink, and be merry, for tomorrow we die
Some still say today: Eat, drink, and make Mary so tomorrow we'll have children
But we say: Eat and drink your Bloody Mary here – only two copper ingots.

Who could pass up such an opportunity? We entered and, once inside, ordered and were served by a fair-haired Philadelphian maid. We struck up conversations with a man drinking at an adjacent table, a former bodyguard, named Bruce Leland:

Once I protected the rich and famous; now the rich and famous are no more. They are just like the rest of us – struggling to survive in these dark and unsettled times. Now here in Philly I guard only my own body, since my family and mate have perished. These days I take special precautions to protect me, and sometimes steal food and water in order to survive. I will be compassionate to others but only if they pose no threat to me. Last week I was wounded during an encounter. Through the years I survived and have dealt harshly with those who attacked me. My dog, Killer, now resting under my chair, is my companion. He seeks only my friendship; he hunts for food and sometimes secures items for both of us. Will he die first, or will I? It doesn't matter. Both he and I are able to protect against others who might attack us. Where is the peace and calm that once characterized our town and region? All vanished. But truly, was there ever peace and calm, or were these concepts mere illusions? Welcome to Philly, Travis and Reese; please don't pet Killer.

We enjoyed sitting with Bruce. Killer looked up at us with dark eyes and a wide yawn. Two coppers for a Bloody Mary seemed cheap. We ordered another round and spotted one for Bruce, as well. When it had become apparent that a second round of drinks was coming to our table, a woman slid up into a chair next to Bruce and introduced herself.

I'm a regular here, I guess. The drinks are cheap and the conversations lively. I'm Alexis Essex. Welcome to Philly. You asked Bruce about surviving during past days and now? Back then, during the latter period of the Dark Time, I was a research laboratory assistant and worked over at the medical school. We weren't doing any actual research any more during the DT. We just kept the labs clean in case things improved. When others fled during the DT, I hunkered down in one lab with an animal facility and barred the door: lots of water and lots of mice and rats. Not exactly up-scale food, but when hunger called, one or two small rodent snacks really hit the spot and dulled my stomach pains. I see smiles on your faces, why? I survived, didn't I? Oh well, do you want to hear any more about the laboratory rats? Ok. I'll continue on.

Back in those days there were different types: the NODs or non-obese diabetic mice with lots of fur that would scurry here and there inside their cages; the hairless INs, the so-called Immuno-deficient Nude types, once valuable for organ transplantation studies but of little value during the Dark Time or even today. Among the larger varieties were Wistars, Sprague Dawleys, Long-Evans, and Zuckers. But my favorites were the Kawasakis. My job was to keep them fed and their water bottles filled. When I approached their cages, they squeaked and squirmed about, their red eyes flashing in the afternoon daylight. I didn't eat their tails, but some of my friends later told me they did. When the animal feed pellets were finished, that was about three solar cycles later, I left the hospital laboratory and joined others scrounging on the street. I made out all right. Even today, I can find some work that keeps me in copper ingots – enough for a little food and a drink or two here at my favorite watering hole.

***

Riding back to our camp along the Delaware River, we passed wall after wall covered with unusual graffiti. In addition to the writing there were hundreds of sheets of paper pasted or taped to the wall. We halted to inspect several examples and one specifically caught our attention, and I copied the words into my diary:

> *Early in my career, I was an insurance agent or IA, and sold life and home policies. I joined the million dollar club the first solar cycles I started working for Ace Insurance. Each solar cycle that followed I exceled and met the requirements of my profession – honesty, integrity, and customer assistance. Came the Ripple and the crash – like thousands of other IAs – I became SOL as we used to say. We all were out of work and could not easily care for our families, or in my case, since I was single – I had to make choices.*
>
> *Regarding honesty: I stole for my food and water. I am not proud of my actions, but I remained alive.*
>
> *Regarding integrity: I cheated friends out of their daily necessities, and took from them what could have saved their lives.*
>
> *Regarding customer assistance: I organized a group of like-thinking former IAs, and we sought out the families that we once had assisted with their long-term needs. We knew our former customers well, and where they lived. Our group would strike at night and take what we called our fair share – leaving behind devastation and chaos.*
>
> *I write this note to confess my crimes, and the evil that I perpetuated on hundreds of innocents, victims of my immoral behavior. As I now lie dying of wounds received during a robbery I committed last eveningtide, I confess my deeds and seek forgiveness. I expect, however, that forgiveness will not be forthcoming. I can only plead that someone will append my note to the sinners wall, and that other who pass by will read my words as a cautionary tale. I am so sorry for the life I have led. I seek your understanding and forgiveness ... please!*
>
> *Jackson "Action" Jackson.*

It seemed to us that the concept of a sinner's wall would have been conceived after the demise of the major religions during the Dark Time. What was this continual struggle within each human – the struggle between good and evil? How and why is it that the poles of human behavior shifted in accord with environmental and cultural changes?

What did Jackson mean by SOL?

***

We exited Philadelphia and continued our trek parallel with Eye 95. The pace we traveled necessitated an additional three camping nights before reaching Perth Amboy and crossing into Staten Island, New York. Along the way, we passed Andalusia, Croydon, crossed Neshaminy Creek, bypassed Newportville and Hilmeville, well to the east of Levittown, then Fairless Hills. At the intersection with Highway 1, we took the route that branched off to the east towards Trenton. We camped out at Sesame Place, not far from the once-famous amusement park that we had heard about as children. Leaving the park grounds, we passed through Fallsington, Morisville, and then crossed the Delaware River into Trenton, where we camped.

Travis and I had heard about the Delaware River crossing that preceded success at the battle of Trenton during the early period of the American Revolution. We and our animals crossed by boat, just as the Revolutionaries had done so long time passing. Leaving Trenton, we continued east cross country towards Hamilton Township and rejoined Eye 95. This adjusted route now led us northeast towards East Windsor, Applegarth, Cranbury Township, Monroe Township off to the east, and into Helmetta, where we camped. The next morning, we rode towards East Brunswick, crossed the Raritan River, and reached Metuchen. From there we took Highway 440 into Perth Amboy. We rode along New Brunswick Avenue to the intersection with Washington Street, and then continued east until we reached the water known as the Arthur Kill. We ambled south to Bayview Park, just opposite Staten Island and camped. The next morning, we crossed from old New Jersey to Staten Island, one of the boroughs of New York City

Staten Island and Jersey City

We were accommodated by a pleasant ferryman plying the waters between the Jersey and New York shores. Reaching Staten Island, we rode south to Hyland Boulevard, then branched off and rode along Ebbets Street towards Miller Field, then joined up with the coastal road leading into South Beach. Across the water to the east was Brooklyn. Before us were ruins of the once-stately Verrazano Bridge, foolishly and stupidly destroyed by a dedicated gang of know-nothings who believed all connections between Staten Island and the Brooklyn should be eliminated.

We ambled through West Brighton towards the north shore and took another ferry across the narrows into the Bayonne region of New Jersey. We traced Highway 440 north towards Greenville, then angled east to what the locals called the Upper Bay region. Standing alone, magnificent, and undamaged we could see the Statue of Liberty and just beyond Ellis Island, where according to our history lessons at Bison Camp, tens of thousands of immigrants had passed through before being admitted into what many perceived to be the promised land.

This portion of our ride had been long but enjoyable. Along the way we continued to meet interesting persons, some productive and established, others drifters, still others suffering from different forms of mental illness, as might be expected during these difficult and trying days.

> **Eugene Franklin,** fireman – *So many fires; so many buildings, once beautiful and crafted by wonderful architects, smoldered and smothered in ash and burnt structural elements if not for me. Few professional firemen remain these days. No water pressure anymore, so we form bucket brigades as in ancient times. And then we have to choose almost daily: douse flames with water – or preserve water for drinking and survival needs. Apartment fires are the worst, where the embers tossed into the clouds drift down and land on potential fuel sources and spring forth again with willowy flames that dance and swirl bringing destruction all about. Such fires we can't fight: we are rendered helpless. According to my grandfather, in olden days there were vehicles called fire trucks, some with ladders that could be extended high up to rescue people in the upper stories of their apartments. Today we cannot do this. We arrive at a fire and evaluate: we can deal with small structures and the ground floors of others, but not buildings with many floors. It is a hard job: I look into the flames and see the faces of demons smiling and laughing back at me, taunting me to join them in the inferno. In a terrible way I am attracted to these siren songs but have resisted until now. What will tomorrow bring: shall I preserve my life or will I embrace the flames and dance into my eternity?*

***

Gino DeMarko, kennel owner – *How I have loved and continue to love animals: cats, dogs, birds, even lizards and snakes that serve as household pets. Our family pet business collapsed during the Ripple Event many solar cycles before I was born. I was not raised as a child with many pets. I remember seeing packs of vicious dogs roaming the streets when I was just a lad of about four or five solar cycles old. But these dogs are unseen these days, killed off for two reasons: the danger they posed, and for the meat on their bones. Whenever I find a lost or stray animal, I try to protect it from those who would carnivorize their essence. Why eat meat? Many animals eat only plant foods and survive, so why not us as well? In days long ago others like me were called vegans – no meat or dairy products for food. I thought it was wrong to kill animals for meat and to take milk from cows, goats, and sheep that otherwise would be used to feed their young. Eating cheese, milk, or yogurt was akin to stealing food from calves and lambs. During the Dark Times, my mother and father posted guards outside our kennels to dissuade roving gangs from stealing our hosted animals. After the passing of my parents and sisters during the Epidemic, I have continued their work. I would rather shoot some angry gang member than one of my baby animals.*

***

Rudolph Franklin, former apartment manager – *Really? You must be kidding. What have I contributed to society? Well if you say it that way, in your view probably nothing. Yes, I am really old and cranky these days, but in solar cycles past before the Ripple and Dark Time, I managed different apartments both here on Staten Island and in Jersey City. The people living in the apartments that I managed were treated well – providing they paid their rent – you know about rent, right? If there was a problem, something broke or didn't work well, I fixed it quickly and without complaint. As the building AM, I provided calm and a home where fear did not reside. That was until the Ripple and Dark Time, when the mobs came and I defended my apartment complex. I was beaten many times. The police couldn't help. There were too many problems, and my complaints for assistance in guarding my building went unheeded. I distributed firearms to those residents not already packing heat – as they used to say – and then the ammunition ran out. Bigger and tougher thugs* *raided us, murdered about half the residents, and I could do nothing to prevent the carnage. So I lost my building, my resident friends, and my livelihood. How did I survive? Better I not tell you.*

***

Toby Clearwater, dishwasher – *I used to get spending money and meals when I washed dishes at a small family-run restaurant in Jersey City, down on Morris Street near the intersection with Warren. I worked ten hours a day with my hands in the soap and water, spraying food residues with my steam line, then popping everything into the sanitizer for thirty slow counts. Then I did my RSS tasks – remove, sort, and stash. How many times I burned my hands right through my gloves when I removed the hot porcelain plates and metal cups from the sanitizer? Too many times to count. But that was then. Who cares now whether or not the food plates in the rehabilitation center for poor folks have been washed or have been licked clean by a hungry transient or the transient's semi-wild dog. Washing dishes is a luxury and wastes water – so who cares? Sometimes a person is lucky to get any type of food served on any type of plate, washed or not. Sanitation? Don't make me laugh. That's just a word from the past.*

***

Traveling east of Jersey City proper, towards the Hudson River, we entered the community of Hoboken. Arriving at Maxwell Place Park, we had our first glimpse of the problem almost impossible to fathom – something called the Barrier.

The Barrier

We stood on the Jersey side of the Hudson River gazing east into lower Manhattan. Something strange was happening. Boats in the channel that originated from the Jersey shore could not complete the short trip east to Manhattan, and apparently were stopped by an invisible force in mid-river. Similarly, as we watched the boats leaving Manhattan none were able to cross to the Jersey shore. Something that could not be seen or easily identified impeded all boat traffic across the Hudson River

We rode north along the Jersey shore and noticed a dramatic change in the New York landscape. Manhattan Island was opposite. Beginning at the southern tip of the island at Battery Park northward through Tribeca,

Greenwich Village, Hell's Kitchen, all the way to Washington Heights and beyond, there were no visible signs in English. All were in French. How could this be? It was as if Manhattan Island had been occupied by foreigners: English was the language of America, not French. How could this be?

We stopped along the Hoboken eastern docks and hailed a militia officer. We asked him about what we had observed. He was willing to speak with us but would not identify himself:

> **[Anonymous Militia Officer]** – *Since you and your mate have trekked eastward across the continent from your homeland west of the Flatlands, you most likely have not heard of regional political developments that occurred here during the Epidemic and shortly after. Once the outbreak began, foreign ships began arriving from across the Great Sea. All these new arrivals were French flag-flying vessels. While most of us easterners were tending to our ill family members and not paying attention to what was happening, these French ships off-loaded thousands of troops, who stormed ashore along the coast of the Confederation that used to be called New PlyMouth.*
>
> *The invasion started up north along the shores of the old state of Maine. Then the French troops slowly worked their way south through New Hampshire and Vermont, and established footholds along coastal Massachusetts. These foreigners ultimately vanquished the Massachusetts Militia, then continued through Rhode Island and Connecticut into our state. There are unconfirmed reports that the French want even more land, and that they have sent some of their crack troops through the mountains of the Blue Ridge region reclaiming lands that once were theirs long-ago passing. But for this I cannot be certain.*
>
> *When the Epidemic abated, common sense returned to us in New York. We joined forces with militias from Pennsylvania and New Jersey, and pushed the French back across the Hudson River, but we could not dislodge them further. They still remain settled in that region of old New Plymouth. The border between us and them is the Hudson River. This is not a hot zone, for it seems that the French now are content with the lands they occupy and are not pushing for more – at least for now.*

You ask why we have allowed them to keep the Hudson River as a border. We didn't just allow them to do anything. They brought to our continent a form of technology that we still cannot fathom or counter at this time. During one of the battle lulls, they erected what you have described – some sort of invisible barrier down through the middle of the Hudson River. Whatever it is and how it works to prevent cross-river traffic, we haven't any clue. This barrier extends from where we now stand all the way north to the border with Canada. As you well know, Travis and Reese, that geographical area that once was Canada now is under French control, and residents are now French-speaking and under French administration. This is a vast area under their control that stretches westward from insular Canada on the east, all the way across land to the western Great Sea.

This barrier is impossible to understand. It is invisible. The barrier makes no sound; it does not alert people of its presence. It just IS. If touched by a person there is no pain. The barrier cannot be passed, either from below or above. It just IS. All we know is that the barrier is not formed of metal. We have no idea how to remove it. If we could, we would attack and push the French back into the sea and send them on their way. What else can I say? It is something that cannot be removed by any technology that we know.

***

The next morning found us in Union City, then on to North Bergen, Fort Lee, and into Englewood Cliffs. We paralleled the Palisades State Parkway towards Alpine, and crossed from New Jersey into former New York State, west of the Hudson River, and camped at Tappan. The next morning we marveled at the huge Tappan Zee Bridge that once facilitated commerce. A monitor at the west bridge entrance turned us back as The Barrier ran north/south through the middle of the bridge. Then to Nyack, through New City and Congers towards Haverstraw, and then into Stony Point. We took the river route around Bear Mountain State Park, past Iona Island, to Fort Montgomery. Less than four kilo-miles distant to the north along the skyline were the magnificent buildings of the former United States Military Academy at West Point.

West Point

The southern entrance to the West Point campus was heavily guarded. We sought permission from an armed militia member who inquired about our trip and destinations. We were asked to tether our animals and wait outside the gate for further instructions. An officer soon appeared. He questioned us about our purpose and asked specifically about the route we previously had taken along the Missouri, Mississippi, and Ohio Rivers. We were escorted to Jefferson Hall for detailed questioning by the campus intelligence officer. All this seemed a bit curious to us, but we complied willingly.

Major Ingrham Pleasenton invited us into his office where we were served beverages and wheat cakes. He asked specifically about what we had seen along our previous route, especially whether or not we had any contact with French travelers or had seen evidence of their presence. We replied that while in West Virginia, after passing through Point Pleasant, we visited the community of Moscow, founded by French settlers in the early 19th century, and another named Gallipolis where a Frenchman had re-established a bakery. We also mentioned that along Chickamauga Creek outside of Gallipolis we had seen a flat stone onto which were carved French words. Travis looked into his diary for the notation and provided it to Major Pleasenton:

> *Cette terre qui était autrefois nôtre nous réclamons*
> *aujourd'hui au nom de la Nouvelle-France*

Neither Travis nor I knew the French language well and only thought the passage curious, something about New France. Major Pleasenton, however, seemed alarmed. He enquired further:

> *Did you see the presence of any French people along the stretch of the Mississippi when you traveled from Saint Louis south to Kai-Row?*

We replied we had not. Major Pleasenton then relayed to us his concern:

> *My worries I cannot detail here for you. What I can say is this. During your travels you have seen The Barrier running through the midst of the Hudson River, an invisible line that prohibits our passage from west to east into portions of old New York state. What we know at this point is that The Barrier was installed – if that can be the correct word – shortly after the Epidemic, and the two parts of our state since have become separated and isolated. Whether this separation originally was a product of medical concern to keep the virus from spreading, or if it was installed as a military structure,*

we cannot be certain at this stage. Our militia engineers have studied The Barrier to the extent possible. They confirm that it only runs north-south, bisecting the Hudson River. Our geographical and technical scouts think that the barrier is linked and associated in some way with north-south lines of longitude. This is why we have sent militia troops north to work with local settlement group defenders to protect the headwaters of the Mississippi in northern Minnesota. We cannot allow the French to install the barrier there; otherwise all continental lands east of the Mississippi would fall under their control. Regarding this new technology, it seems to work – at least for now – only along lines of longitude. Why? We have no idea. Our immediate concern is that the French could re-orientate the technology so it also will work along selected east-west lines of latitude, or possibly along saltwater-trending longitude lines, as well. Our scouts and field representatives report that the French are pushing west across Canada to locate the headwaters of the Mississippi. As I said, if they cannot be repelled, then a new north-south barrier could be implemented in the near future that would bring all lands east of the Mississippi River under French control. We also know from recent reports that the French already are attempting to establish a base and settlement along the north shore of the great Lake Michigan which, as you know, trends north-south. We have no recent notice, however, that a north-south barrier has been inserted here by the French intruders.

This information, while enlightening, was shocking. And if Major Pleasenton had shared these details with us, two travelers from the NorthWest Configuration, what others had remained unspoken, not divulged? Travis asked the major:

This barrier technology seems to be unlike anything known or understood today or even before the Ripple Event. What do you suspect about its origins?

Major Pleasenton replied with even more shocking words:

Your question is at the core of the problem. As hard as it is to believe, our engineers at West Point are certain that the French received this technology from an unknown source. Was it from another country in Europe or Asia that had survived the Ripple? Could it have been from an extraterrestrial force? We cannot be certain at this point in time that the people we see east of The Barrier actually are French. None of our West Point Militia members have made contact with any. Is it even possible that those we see east of The Barrier could be bipeds created to look like humans, with the capacity to speak French so as to sow seeds of confusion regarding the origin of the technology and their origin as well? All we know is that The Barrier and these French-speakers just appeared. One day our work and campus activities were progressing as usual and expected – the next day the Hudson River could not be crossed and all communications from both directions had been severed. The signs that appeared on the riverbank opposite us were in French. The people looked like us, but we could not communicate. The same day I sent out scout riders to alert the New York militias, west of the Hudson all the way north to Champlain on the Great Chazy River near the Canadian border. I believe we are entering even more difficult times.

The major asked us, if we would be willing to take on a task to be keen observers and record detailed observations of the barrier in our diaries, since we planned to trek north to the border. He also asked if we would carry a few messages upriver to Ticonderoga, where we would check in with the local militia already on alert. We, of course, agreed.

In the evening, we were invited by Major Pleasenton and his staff to be guests at dinner. The food was simple but adequate, a reasonable meal of cereals, vegetables, with small portions of beef jerky. All this was washed down with several varieties of beverages that we could not identify. At the conclusion of the meal, we were asked by the chaplain to stand as the militia members repeated these poignant words:

And when our work is done,
Our course on earth is run,
May it be said, "well done,"
Be thou at peace.

Ever may that line of gray,
Increase from day to day,
Live, serve, and die, we pray,
West Point, for thee.

Afterwards, we were invited onto the balcony to overlook the campus grounds. Darkness shrouded the central area where in times long past uniformed groups of young men and women paraded in formation. These men and women, the pride of old America, were the best and brightest. They evidenced honor in the classroom, in military obligations to their country, and later in life. These graduates of West Point were linked to each other through past solar cycles and united by concepts of corps and color:

The long gray line of us stretches, thro' the years of a century told

***

Our good-byes said, we left West Point and resumed our riverbank route. We passed through Walden, then on to Clintondale where we camped. We reached New Palz, Rosendale, Kingston, and on to Saugerties for another night spent along the Hudson. We passaged through Catskill, then Leeds, Climax, into Nannacroix, New Baltimore, and Ravena where we camped. We skirted Castle-on-Hudson and Glenmont, then managed the short ride into Albany where we camped along the river among the trees and green of Corning City Preserve.

Albany

Once the capitol of old New York State, Albany now was a mix of once-beautiful buildings and hovels. Off to the west of our campsite was a most curious structure, one still seemingly intact from Pre-Ripple times. Visually, it appeared to be a gigantic egg. Travis and I ventured over to inspect and received more than just a visual introduction to the site.

Parading up and down the beautiful walkways near the egg, an elderly woman walked up to us and initiated conversation. Her smile was infectious. The lines on her face told of a taxing and difficult life. She asked only that we call her Darla:

> *Curious-looking eh? I remember when musicians from all over hell and back came to Albany for the chance to play at the Egg venue. Those were great times, since the concerts brought in lots of very rich men who were connoisseurs of the arts and of other things. Nowadays men still seek my information services. I like to spend more time talking about the past than the present. I get paid now for my services in food, bottles of water, and ingots of different types of metal and semi-precious stones, but I must say there are not many diamonds available these days. Still, when I lay back – figuratively speaking of course – I think about the past. It is difficult for me to imagine how it was that I adopted my former profession. There I was*

in my last solar cycles of graduate school, my Ph.D. almost in hand and then came the Ripple Event. I can't say that my research focus on West African folklore traditions and their influence on English folk songs prepared me for events during and after the Ripple Event. My campus community erupted into anarchy and chaos, so there went my studies. But, as they say, set-backs just present different opportunities. I saw too many adult men and women die needlessly due to lack of food and/or water. They died because they thought they had nothing to give in exchange for these commodities. Wrong! They possessed something that we all had at the time that could be exchanged. I decided to survive and did so. I chose my clients carefully, thinking in advance how to approach each to maximize my return for minimal favors. I worked solo, never part of a group and never with a coordinator to whom many of my FFs or feminine friends gave 30-50 percent of the food and water received as gifts from clients. And when the Ripple passed and we entered the Dark Times, I had become proficient in my trade and became well known for providing for my client's needs. I even marketed my system for success using the acronym BEST, meaning best ever soothing treatments, and it wasn't long before I became a well-known and respected teacher. Today, you ask? Although I am old and my step is slow, I consider myself a success because I survived the Ripple and Dark Time when millions did not. Can I interest you in a menu of potential opportunities?

***

Returning to our campground, we passed along Pine Street and stopped for drinks. Sitting next to us was a native of Albany, a former contractor and builder of high-rise apartments and offices. He volunteered to share information with us:

My name is Addison Ringle. Once I raised roof timbers up to the sky, raised walls that encompassed vast areas of space, laid the foundations for buildings tall. Once I was paid well, but that was long ago. Now the words ring out, "Buddy can you spare some food or a copper ingot?" Several months ago in this fine city, Albany, I watched as a gang of 12 youths circled about and trapped a stray cat. The cat looked like it hadn't eaten for two months, all ribs showing, tail dragging, and patches of hair missing. As the gang of boys and girls tightened their ring around the feline, the cat snarled and hissed in a pitiful manner, striking out with its paws, raking the air to keep at bay the one girl who had crept closest. But alas, she grabbed it. Then the cat was snatched from her hands by a taller, stronger boy. The 11 others then surrounded him and offered threatening gestures. So the boy then relented and together they prepared a meal for all – the 12 hungry children. Do you believe what I just told you? If so, you are not a genius. Of course the taller, stronger boy took the cat and ran off to later devour it alone, leaving the remainder of the gang to argue and fight among themselves, and seek other food. The Albany I once knew is long gone, and hasn't been for a very long time. Good old All-Ban-Nee; home of the former Gov – but not since a long time passing.

***

The next leg of our journey north, we took trails though or around a myriad of settlements, including Menads, Watervliet, Green Island, Cohoes, Waterford, Milwood, Mechanicville, Stillwater, and into Bemis Heights where we camped at Saratoga National Park. The next leg followed the Hudson, past Schuylerville, Northumberland, and Bacon Hill, where we trekked cross country along the river towards Glenn Falls.

There was no Hudson River barrier at Glens Falls. At this location, the Hudson River flowed west to east with the out-waters from Great Sacandaga Lake. The region between Glens Falls north to Lake George, a distance of approximately10 kilo-miles, was heavily fortified by New York Militia, as this represented an east-west gap in The Barrier.

We camped and grazed our horses and mules, and immediately were approached by a squad of saber-armed militia members, wanting to know our business and destination. We provided them with the safe-passage document given to us by Major Pleasenton at West Point, whereupon we were escorted to a protected campsite. That evening we learned that there had been French probes across this region between Lake George and Glens Falls, but each had been repulsed. It seemed that in time, however, more serious involvement would occur.

The next morning, we were provided protective escort out of Glens Falls up to Lake George. Once there, we could see French language signs eastward across the lake at Pilot Knot and Huletts Landing. We paused to rest our horses at a spot between Silver Bay and Hague, along the west bank of Lake George. Moving on, we reached the community and historic Fort Ticonderoga where we camped for the evening.

We resumed our trek north towards the border. We exited Ticonderoga and passed through or around Crown Point, Port Henry, West Port, and Wadhams where we camped. We then went through Whallonsburg, Essex, Willsboro, and Keeseville, and took a short ride east to Port Kent where we camped. The next day, we paralleled Lake Champlain from Port Kent to Plattsburgh, then on to Point Au Roche Park near Ingraham where we camped, before making the short ride into Champlain along the Great Chazy River.

Champlain and the Border

Just outside Champlain to the south were squads of border guards. We showed our pass to the militia officer in charge and were allowed to proceed to the border. The border-crossing structures that once served both countries prior to the Ripple Event were no more. All their metal had been gleaned to make barter ingots. What existed now essentially was a no-man's zone, a wasteland where militias of both sides of the border were encamped, awaiting word on what to do next. It had taken nearly one month to ride from DC north to the border. We never could have predicted what the experience would have been like.

On our return from the border to Champlain, we asked permission to speak with the commanding officer. We quickly were ushered into the office of Captain Grace Heizenger. After an exchange of pleasantries, Travis presented Captain Heizenger with the sealed folder of information from Major Pleasenton and two wrapped gifts. She thanked us and asked an orderly to bring beverages. She opened the folder in our presence, read the contents, frowned, and then turned to ask us to repeat the information we related to Major Pleasenton regarding the French presence in West Virginia.

Travis did so, and I added that in my view the single Frenchman that we had identified and now running the bakery was relatively elderly and would not have been an advance scout probing for defensive weaknesses along the West Virginia mountain chain. We also shared our observations of what could be called the *Open Zone* – the land area between Glens Falls and Lake George – where no barrier exists separating portions of old New York State.

Captain Heizenger asked if we knew the location of Lake Itasca in up-state Minnesota. Neither of us replied in the positive and pondered the reason for her question, until we realized that the lake might be the headwaters of the Mississippi River.

We were asked to relate the next phase of our transcontinental journey. I replied that after reaching Champlain, our objective was to learn more about this geographical region and return to DC via Syracuse, Bingham, and Scranton, then on through Harrisburg and ultimately back to Front Royal and into DC.

Captain Heizenger paused and captured both our gazes:

> *We in the New York Militia have a potential emergency, and if you would be willing to assist us, your aid greatly would be appreciated. It is a request I do not make lightly. If you choose to assist us, you will not be rewarded with extra metal ingots. The only reward you will receive would be grateful thanks from our soldiers, who may soon have to face the eastern invaders. So please listen and ponder your response.*
>
> *Would you, Travis and Reese, be willing to forego your planned journey to Syracuse south and east to Font Royal into DC and instead make a rapid, direct trip south to DC to relay three messages as quickly as possible to our militia commander in Arlington? This will mean riding 45 or more kilo-miles per day. You would need to leave your pack mules here at Champlain. We will inventory your goods, and I will order full replacement and an additional 10 percent more food supplies. I will also replace your mules once you reach DC. If during the quick trek southward to DC one or both of your horses cannot continue, they will be replaced from our militia stock along the way. If all goes well, I will issue special orders for additional grain and forage for your horses when you reach Arlington.*
>
> *The option is yours: I request your assistance to carry these messages to DC.*
>
> *Will you assist?*

***

After-Word

What started as our personal journeys of discovery, to seek resolution after the death of our children and to interview others who had survived the Ripple Event, Dark Time, and Epidemic, had taken on an additional objective.

During the next days, we were briefed on the general state of affairs in northern old New York. We did not inquire about the content of messages we promised to deliver, and learned only the names and locations of the recipients. It was clear to us that Captain Heizenger, her staff, and militia members thought the French were going to launch an invasion of western New York, either through *The Barrier* or across the flat undulating Open Zone. We assumed the messages were related to preparations, reinforcements, and supplies. We kept our promise not to press further for information.

Good-byes and safe journeys were spoken as we left Champlain for DC. The return south was hard riding, but our horses completed the journey without fault. About 450 kilo-miles and nine days later, we reached our destination and delivered the messages.

***

Ijano Esantu Eleman

Interlude-Conversation: 8
Overlooking DC

***

How sad. Those forlorn creatures in the midst of this devastation. Why do you suppose they are here?

This is little more than one place among many they have visited and will yet visit during their search for others. A place they will soon leave. They can little know the vitality and import that were once this city's. Once the capitol of a great nation, this place in this time is not much more than a wasteland.

A wasteland for true, K'Aser. Any of the shattered zones at their worst would offer more to travelers.

Would, have, and did, A'Tena. But the wars – as limited in scope and impact as they were by the Ripple – brought down DC for such is what many called this place.

Way, way down. But why?

This, in spite of what you see around us here and now, was once the capitol of what was perhaps the most prosperous and powerful nation this planet had known.

Perhaps the most powerful and prosperous, but ...?

Many would say for true in place of perhaps. Yes, and therein lay the seeds of its destruction. Prosperity and power brought complacency in their wake. With survival and comfort of little or no concern, trivial matters assumed an importance beyond that which was warranted, often way beyond. Indeed, it was here and in the nation DC ruled that the madness began. Began and grew, blotting out sanity as it did until toward the end what was called political correctness – a form of madness.

Even so, how could that explain what we see now?

The nation was hated, even despised, by many for this reason or that while others were jealous of its prosperity. Many contrived to bring it down at the first opportunity. And so they did – DC was struck by not one but several attacks, assaults from many regions, from within as well as without. It did not survive the onslaught, nor could it have. Yes, the nation –

The United States as I recall ...

Yes, and in the end it was little more than a target, neither feared nor respected as it once had been. And, A'Tena, more than a little pride went before this fall. And the corruption and arrogance attendant with the power. Those here – the politicians and bureaucrats – came to consider themselves above and beyond the reach of their countrymen, let alone the peoples of other nations.

As well as many who lived here. As in all too many cities there were some who saw themselves as above the law, as being justified for any actions they might take from murder to looting. How sad it all was.

What we now view here would be considered justice by many – even more than a few of those the city ruled. And that, while sad, is for true.

So now all is gone.

Like Athens and Rome long ago.

More complete than Athens and faster than Rome, if you ask me.

A for true assessment, but take note of the huge obelisk standing in spite of all; this remains to honor the good that arose from this place and more than a little did before the times of corruption.

The Journey: Part 3

Chapter 9

Overland Journey: Through the New Confederacy

Pre-Note

After our return to DC from our northern trek, we camped out at Arlington for several days where we rested and grazed our horses and pack mules. It was apparent to us there were serious problems within the region once called the New PlyMouth Configuration. A significant portion of the continent north of the Ohio River had been occupied by the New Confederacy whose leaders stationed militia troops as far north as the western portion of old New York State. Further, lands east of the Hudson River and the great north-south chain of lakes that bordered northeastern old New York and old Vermont now were occupied by French forces.

What life was like and what issues and problems characterized the lands east of The Barrier remained unknown for now. We were not privy to the content of the messages that we delivered to the regional East Virginia Militia generals at DC, but imagined that defensive preparations were being made to repel any French expansion west of the north/south line.

DC to Mount Vernon

We departed DC and made our way south towards Mount Vernon, a spectacular location along the Virginia-Maryland boundary of the Potomac River. We applied for and were granted permission to camp in the grassy plain north of former President George Washington's residence. The East

Virginia Militia guarded the entrance. Display cases inside the home held Washington's ceremonial dress sword manufactured from steel and plated with silver and gold. The saber that Travis wore throughout the day for protection was simple in style and more useful as an offensive and protective weapon. Perhaps the most interesting item available for inspection was a set of George Washington's false teeth. The great general's dentures were displayed inside a protective glass case. The set had been prepared by a clever craftsman using teeth of cows, horses, and pieces of elephant ivory, anchored into a metallic base composed of brass, lead, and silver. Travis and I both smiled and grinned: at least we had most of our teeth.

Mount Vernon to Richmond

We continued south towards Richmond and crossed the Potomac River. We followed Highway 301 through Waldorf to Newburg, then re-crossed the Potomac and headed west towards Dahlgren. We resumed our journey south along Highway 301 through the settlements of King George, Port Royal, Lorne, then on to Chamberlayne, Dunbarton, and into Richmond where we camped near the James River, not far from the western banks of Shields Lake in William Byrd Park. We were far from downtown Richmond as we had been advised to avoid that location. This once-grand state capitol now was a dangerous place filled with gangs bent upon anarchy with only limited protection offered by hard-working police and militia members.

Taking their advice, we "hunkered-down" – as they say – at WB Park and planned to spend only one evening before moving on towards Williamsburg, the capitol of New Confederacy. Early evening bonfires lined the east side of Shields Lake, attracting street people to the site for warmth and companionship. We introduced ourselves to several persons, but most chose not to acknowledge us or open up with conversation. Two, however, offered their names and interesting stories.

> **Charles (Chuck) Newman,** bus driver – *Two solar cycles before the Ripple Event, I was hired as a bus driver by the city of Richmond. I was really proud. I had saved money – remember what that was? I enrolled in Triple Diamond Bus Drivers School, located out towards the edge of town near East Highland Park. I was one of the school's best students and completed my driving course with distinction. I excelled in what then was called the PT or park test. This is where the examiner sets up two buses in parallel with a middle slot of only*

12 inches to spare on either side – you remember inches, right? The challenge was to back in and park your test bus inside that slot without touching the sides of the other two. Of 75 candidates, only two passed this difficult test. I was one. I was the best.

Then came the Ripple Event and you guessed it, no buses. So in order to survive I became a thief. I did fairly well, too, in this new occupation but then the activities were too soft for me. So I asked my long-time buddy, Frankie DiJorno, if I could join his group of hit men. He liked my aggressive style and all together I must have popped 16 or 17 idiots that were eating into his street deal profits. You are looking at me strangely – being a hit man didn't matter to me, as I wasn't religious or anything like that. I just needed a job. Soon Frankie's gang took over Richmond and had the full run of business opportunities. There no longer was a need for a team of hit men, so I was un-juiced and told to go my way. Look, Frankie could have had each of us in his hit gang popped, but that wouldn't have been in Frankie's character. He was loyal to his friends; he was the best. So I was out on the street without much hope, until one day I saw a sign that attracted me:

You want to get the barter items and the street tent you deserve?
Run for office and get elected.
Kick the Ins out.
Run – run – run for office

Boy that was a hoot so I designed my own political platform. Actually I stole my campaign slogan from something that I had once heard on the radio – remember those? – before the Ripple Event:

Get what you deserve, and get it now!

Well, I was elected and became a politician. I was gifted so many barter tokens supporting this or that cause that I really didn't have to work hard, and I was able to retire just before the last solar cycle. These William Byrd Park fireside chats are great and allow me to maintain connections with the people of Richmond who once elected me. Now, I've told you my story, so how about offering me two aluminum barter items, and I'll guarantee you safe protection throughout your stay in Richmond. When you decide to leave, your safe passage out of town will be guaranteed. What do you think? Are we in agreement?

Dora Swift, dietitian – *I'm so hungry these days. Should people be advised to eat items from the basic 4, or is it the basic 7 or 17? It's been long time since I even cared. What I want is food; I want it now! I was trained in different systems of dietary balance: eat this – eat that – don't eat this – don't eat that. Dietary balance these days is a luxury. Once I was a well-trained dietitian and knew everything about protein, fat, carbs, minerals and vitamins – all with nice diagrams how to balance the diets of my clients. But how can I balance even my own diet these days when all I find on the street are moldy leftover corn cobs and on the very rare occasions when something falls into my lap that I didn't expect. Like just last week I found a box of chocolate in one of the ruined houses where I was staying. The chocolate was old and stale, but still chocolate. Yum! You know there are thousands and thousands of houses in Richmond where the occupants have died or never will return. So my friends and I check out 4-5 of these abandoned homes a day looking for something to eat, something that will halt our constant belly pain.*

Last week we entered one house and found an aquarium equipped with a non-electrical self-feeder system constructed during the Dark Time. Still alive and swimming about were lots of tiny goldfish – not much larger than the goldfish crackers my grandmother used to share with me during family visits before the Ripple Event. We had a feast!

So your eyes seem to ask me: what is a good diet? Very simple: one that satisfies hunger – at least for three or four hours. When I was very small and there were television programs – did you ever hear about television? I remember all those advertisements about good food and bad food; organic and natural food; with or without this or that – all meaningless these days, of course. All I want now is something to ease hunger. Oh, how I have these food-related cravings and memories. Oh, how I long for a plate of pulled pork at Old Joe's Bar-B-Q down on Busy Street near Courthouse Road. But then I awaken from my dream and remember that Old Joe's Bar-B-Q was destroyed by urban rioters during the Ripple Event. Jeeze those stupid bastards burned Joe's place to the ground. All that food lost. What happened to Old Joe? Who knows? Oh, how I miss his pulled pork!

***

Richmond to Williamsburg

Leaving Richmond we paralleled Highway 60 and bypassed Sandston, then through Mountcastle, Providence Forge, the small hamlet of Toano. We rode through Norge, Lightfoot, and Ewell, and then into Williamsburg. What a glorious place this ancient settlement is with wonderful buildings from the past. Williamsburg now was the capitol of the New Confederacy. We rode through well-kept streets past what the sign said was the Governor's Palace with its steeple and two high chimneys. Off to the west of the GP was a series of rooms where foods once were prepared. One of the smaller rooms was filled with unusual equipment whose purposes we could not understand. Resting upon wonderful old oak tables were large flat stones and numerous cylindrical items that looked like the rolling pins bakers used back at our home in Bison Camp. But these were all made of stone. Certainly they were used to grind something, but what? Off to one side of the room were empty jute and hemp bags. On these were written names like Aruba, Curacao, and Trinidad – all foreign and unknown to us. Could they represent locations where products were shipped to Williamsburg during earlier times? If so, what did they contain, and why were they important here at Williamsburg? One broken sign on the workbench said Theobroma cacao – we had no idea what these two words meant. Strewn over the tabletops and floor were small nuts, some shelled and others with shells intact. Travis tasted one: it was extremely bitter. We had no idea what this room was used for.

The local East Virginia Militia stood guard protecting the Governor's Palace from looters. We approached and asked for assistance. One of the privates, Cory Murchison, was assigned to escort us through the grounds and adjacent buildings. While we were inspecting several of the storage barns, we disturbed a local resident, Samuel Meese, who had been sleeping inside:

> **Samuel Meese,** re-enactor – *I am an , man as you can see, but early in my life I was what they called at Williamsburg, a re-enactor. Back some 10 solar cycles before the Ripple Event and the collapse of everything, I dressed in clothing characteristic of old Williamsburg five days a week and six during the peak summer tourist seasons. At that time my work focus included the design, layout, planting, and managing of the Williamsburg vegetable gardens. I studied hundreds of old books that described early Williamsburg and knew*

by heart the names and look of the 79 fruits, grains, herbs and spices, legumes, and vegetables grown during what used to be called the 17th through early 19th centuries. I knew how to rotate species for best returns and soil protection, how certain plants such as beans and peas added nitrogen to the ground and replaced that taken up by the grains and vegetables. The early Native Americans would take sharp sticks, poke holes in the earth, and drop in dead fish and grains of corn along with beans. The corn would sprout and the beans, after emerging, would use the cornstalks as support poles. In between the rows they planted squash, so the broad leaves retarded evaporation and minimized watering requirements. These early cultivators had a true balanced system, one that we copied here in our Williamsburg gardens. As a re-enactor, I would stand at the edge of my colonial-era garden and answer questions from tourists. When the questions finished, I would tend to my plants: weed and prune as necessary. When the Williamsburg gardens were ready for harvesting, we would band together teams to collect the ripe foods and transport them in wicker baskets to several on-site kitchens for use in mealtime preparations. Other re-enactors and I used to spend what little leisure time we had learning more about the early periods of Williamsburg history. We even had contests among each other, and once I won a kilo-pound of strawberries for the best botanical joke. Would you like to hear it?

> *She was out in the garden harvesting spices and thought she had collected a handful of oregano ... but she only had thyme on her hands. Don't ya git it?*

***

Camping on the grounds of old Williamsburg, we found ourselves sitting near our evening campfire adjacent to an itinerant tinker who lived inside and worked out of a highly decorated covered horse-drawn cart. After an exchange of pleasantries, we invited him to join us and share our evening meal. The tinker was Michael Flannigan. He was of Irish heritage with deep family roots in the hills of East Virginia. He survived these days by examining and collecting trash and discards of different settlement groups he visited. With skill and artistic abilities, he restored broken objects and cloth remnants and, in the process, created new and useful goods that he bartered with others for his subsistence.

Michael also was a fiddler and entertained us that first evening with several traditional ballads penned by long-ago Irish poets telling of ancient times in the far away home of his distant ancestors:

Although I have travelled this wide world all over
Yet Erin's my home and a parent to me
Then Oh! Let the ground that my old bones shall cover
Be cut from the soil that is trod by the free.

And another …

So soon may I follow when friendships decay
And from love's shining circle the gems drop away
When true hearts lie withered and fond one's are flown
Oh who would inhabit this bleak world alone?And another ...

I sat within a valley green sat there with my true love
And my fond heart strove to choose between the old love and the new
The old for her, the new that made me think on Ireland dearly
While soft the wind blew down the glade and shook the golden barley.

But what entranced as we sat and listened to Michael were the stories he spun and how easily he created images of real events in our minds. He shared tales of the faraway land of Eire, where kings and queens once ruled justly and before modern times when politicians lied and sowed seeds of distrust. He related tales of fairies, goblins, and hoots in the night; how the calls of animals foretold future events. He spoke tales of chance and good fortune, of missteps and danger. Our favorites, though, were his words that described wee small men and tall giants, girls and women with flaxen hair, and heroic boys and men who gave their lives to protect their families. All tales and more spun around the campfire long into the night.

The following morning, Michael the tinker hitched up his horse and prepared to leave. Travis and I approached him with a suggestion: would he consider joining us on our trek south? Since the three of us were headed southeast towards the Great Sea and then down the coast into Georgia, might we embark upon this venture together for good company?

And so it was that Michael the tinker joined us.

And through many of the days and nights that followed, we entertained each other with conversation and good friendship. The tinker remained with us throughout the southern distance until we would bid him fare-thee-well at Charleston, whereupon he would continue south into the coastal sandy lands of the Floridas, while we would turn westward across the New Confederacy towards the Mississippi River. But this was yet to come.

***

Williamsburg to Norfolk

Departing Williamsburg, we passed through Jamestown where damaged hulks of three great ships once had been anchored: *Discovery, Godspeed*, and *Susan Constant*. Half-destroyed signs informed us that these ships were replicas, modern recreations of the originals that once carried English colonists to Virginia nearly 450 solar cycles past. Continuing on and not far from Jamestown, less than a morning's ride, we looked out upon the great plain at Yorktown where memorials on the undulating grassy green told of the last battle between English soldiers and New World American revolutionaries. It was here at Yorktown where soldiers of that once-great island nation surrendered and a new country with an original 13 states took root and flourished – until the Ripple Event.

We rode into Portsmouth and crossed the harbor into Norfolk, once a beautiful city on Chesapeake Bay. The buildings and houses along the periphery had been destroyed by fire and lay in ruins. The central portion of the town, however, seemed intact and we camped along the waterfront within Town Point Park. There we met Lois Perkins, a local survivor of the Dark Time who put us at ease with a fine welcome.

***

After dinner Lois invited us to join members of the remnant Norfolk community at what she called Baker's Barn, a community shelter erected a short distance from our campsite. As we approached the facility, we could hear fiddlers flaying and banjos strumming to music dissimilar to that which Travis and I had heard and experienced crossing the Blue Ridge region of western old Virginia. Once inside we were greeted with warm hospitality and offered jars of *clear-water shine,* as our hosts called the beverage.

Not all attending the festivities, however, were so friendly. One elderly man who did not give his name approached us and asked:

> *Be ye folks revenuers? Yes be ye? Well, ah can't quite tell you fer sure but we avoidin' them. They be not trusted. So at the very least, we axe any strangers that join us in our festives what would be their*

origins and we be keepin' our eyes open jus' in case.We had no idea who and what he meant by the term revenuers, but assumed they probably were regional politicos or possibly what we used to call "grabber-gangs," intent on collecting money from local folks to pay for programs that never were implemented. We thought it best to just smile at the elderly man's questions and statements. We bid him good-by and found ourselves deep inside the barn in a tiered area lined with benches. We were welcomed to sit and converse with those around us. We shared some details of our travels and plans for the next passages of our journey south along the coastline of the Great Ocean. We spoke with many attending. These people, survivors of the Ripple Event, were proud of their past and worked hard to recover and plan for their future. These were decent folks – taking time out this evening for recreation and entertainment.

The music came to a halt. A man emerged from the crowd and spoke: there would be three sets of competitions – reelers, cloggers, and steppers. After each performed, the audience would vote by clapping and whistling for the group in each category they perceived best and who had displayed the most intricate dance moves. All was ready: the fast fiddlers and the banjo strummers took their places and the dancing began.

First to appear on stage were the reelers. These were genuine Virginians dressed in historic olden-looking clothing, the men with leather boots and buckskin vests and women in long dresses with colorful bonnets. They took to the center of the wooden platform as the fiddlers started up their mesmerizing tune.

Holy cow – what was this dance?

Two lines of men and women slowly moved forward and back, turning, arms extended, then quickly moving forward again. Then they performed something called a do-si-do where men and women rushed towards each other brushing shoulders, moving around each other but not turning, then repeating again and again, until at last the couples joined hands and slid down the middle of the two parallel lines and took their place at the end. The next couple repeated the steps and the reel continued again, and again until all seemingly were exhausted. All during this time the couples offered hoots and hollers in time with the fiddle music, something we never before had experienced during our travels from Bison Camp.

Next were the cloggers, dancing either as individuals or in groups. These were young adults and children dressed simply, their sockless-feet shod with wooden shoes. They gathered together on the low hardwood platform. When the fiddlers started the dance tune, the sounds of syncopated clacking filled the air. We watched in awed amusement and pleasure as the dancers clicked, pounded, and stomped. Their shoes produced rhythms unlike any Travis and I had heard previously. At the end of their performance, all of the cloggers took to the platform at the same time. The collective noise their shoes made echoed throughout the hall. It was wonderful and exciting. At first their steps produced almost the same rhythmic patterns, and then the majority of dancers would recede and one, two, or three would move to the front where each displayed their unique steps and talents. Shouts from the audience seemed to encourage the cloggers to perform even more difficult steps. How hard these dancers worked: they alternated heel twists and turns, coupled with toe-tapping and flat-footed stomping patterns that were easy on the eye and wonderful to the ear.

After the cloggers finished, the steppers took their place on the platform. These were older teens and young adults who performed to the sounds of fiddles and bagpipes. Their style of dance was unlike the first two groups, and certainly unlike any dancing style we knew back in Bison Camp. The steppers kept their upper body stiff, their arms pointed downward pressed against the side of their bodies. They made no body movement of any kind above the waist, except for their facial smiles and grins. The feet of the steppers responded quickly to the music and produced a near blur of motion as the dancers competed against one another, demonstrating a variety of leaps, clicks, and spins. When individual steppers had performed and revealed their talents, all on stage regrouped for a finale called the *céili* where they formed into lines of different numbers – two then four, then eight and sixteen – each line seemingly in competition with the other during the evening *feis* or festival.

It was very hard for the audience and especially Travis and me to judge and rank the winning dancers. Michael, however, was more familiar with the steps and dance music, and helped us make our decisions. As it turned out, our rankings matched those of the assembled crowd. At the conclusion of the dance competition, all attending were invited to the east end of the barn where we were treated to libations of different types and qualities. But that was not the end of the evening. This pause for refreshment was just an intermission. What followed were individual recitations also to be performed on stage with prizes to be awarded.

One of the more interesting recitations offered this evening was by a young schoolteacher from one of the nearby settlement groups. She introduced herself and her piece by saying how hard it was these days to teach proper English spelling to children as her students had difficulties with homonyms. Travis, Michael, and I looked at each other. We had no idea what the word homonym meant, so we listened intently to the teacher. Next to her on stage were two young men, a fiddler and a second holding what looked to be a flat drum with a name that I couldn't catch but was pronounced something like *bore-awn.* The three walked to the center of the platform. The schoolteacher held in her hands a simple folder that contained large sheets of paper. We in the audience were puzzled and grew still as we awaited an explanation. After a pause she smiled and held up the first sheet with clear printing that read:

Learn your words and spell them right

She immediately turned and spun around so that all seated or standing inside the barn could see what she had written. The fiddler and drummer started to play, and together the three shouted out:

Dumb twiddle rum dumb sing at night

The fiddler and drummer began to stomp as they began to play in earnest. Audience members clapped and cheered as the young teacher held up different sheets, which were the heart of her presentation. Each sign was followed by fiddling, drumming, and the trio shouting. Slowly at first and then more quickly, the audience began to join in as well:

Eight green frogs I ate last night
Dumb twiddle rum dumb my pants fit tight.

Poor bald baby boy bawled all day
Dumb twiddle rum dumb rollin' in the hay.

Little tiny flea please flee from me
Dumb twiddle rum dumb across the sea.

The careless knight slept throughout the night
Dumb twiddle rum dumb ready for a fight.

Wake up son time to greet the sun
Dumb twiddle rum dumb having fun.

After chanting these five verses, the schoolteacher continued. We audience members were laughing and rolling in stitches. The more we laughed, the more animated she became, holding up additional cards with curious spellings:

Study these words and learn them well
Dumb twiddle rum dumb time will tell.

Ant/aunt, blew/blue, foul/fowl, hair/hare
Dumb twiddle rum dumb something rare.

Died/dyed, earn/urn, loan/lone, mail/male
Dumb twiddle rum dumb don't turn pale.

Not/knot, one/won, pair/pare, red/read
Dumb twiddle rum dumb rub your head.

She held up one last sign to massive applause:

Study these words and spell them right
Dumb twiddle rum dumb learn to write.

The three performers on the platform bowed again, and again. An enormous uproar of shouts and clapping erupted from the crowd, certain signals that the schoolteacher had won the recitation contest. And what did she win? A bouquet of freshly picked flowers, two aluminum barter tokens, and a ham hock smothered with red beans and rice.

What an evening; good fellowship, great entertainment, new acquaintances, and an enjoyable English lesson tossed in to boot. Oh, how we savored the wonderful smell of that dish of ham, beans, and rice. But we weren't offered a bite.

***

Norfolk to Kill Devil Hills

We trekked south of Norfolk past the settlement of Chesapeake, along the remains of Highway 168 through Moyock and Maple. Just to the south of Maple, we followed Highway 158 into Barco and down the spine of the peninsula that guarded the approach to Albemarle Sound. Travis and I originally thought that the best southern route would be westward along Highways 159 and 17 through Elizabeth City, then there would be a relatively straight shot south to Wilmington. Michael, our travel companion, suggested that once we reached Barco we might take a southerly side trip and head down the peninsula. He thought we might enjoy exploring the offshore islands or Outer Banks, especially the settlement of Kitty Hawk and the Kill Devil Hills, the latter being one of the most important historical monuments in the New Confederacy. Travis and I were intrigued at Michael's suggestion, as nothing we had been taught at Bison Camp settlement group mentioned either location.

Down the peninsula we trekked. We bypassed the tiny settlements of Grandy, Jarvisburg, Powells Point, Harbinger, and tethered our animals at Point Harbor where we bartered passage for the short boat trip across the sound towards the Outer Banks

We reached shore and wandered through the small settlement of Kitty Hawk, then ambled down to Kill Devil Hills. A tall stone monument was visible for quite a distance. Here was the location of the first flight of what later were called aero-planes. Rising from the crest of a small hill, the massive stone monument was set within a base formed by a five-pointed star. The monument was dedicated to two individuals, Wilber and Orville Wright, who designed their strange craft that flew in the air for 12 slow counts and covered a distance of 120 feet – whatever that might mean. This didn't seem very far to us. Michael said, in turn, that what we were viewing was the commemoration of a very short experiment, one that proved a machine heavier than air actually could fly. He related that in later solar cycles other air flight objects would be created, and their design allowed for travel over great distances.

As we examined the monument inscriptions, Travis and I looked at each other and recalled the images that we had seen earlier during our trek at the Wright Patterson Air Force Museum north of Sin-Sin-Natty. Our early childhood teachers had mentioned such so-called aero-planes, but as children we viewed their descriptions of machines flying like birds as little more than fancy thinking. At the time, we did not believe what we had been taught. Now, these lessons began to make sense to us.

We left the monument area and returned to Kitty Hawk where we bartered for a meal. Inside the eatery, known simply as J&D's Place, townspeople already had gathered for their mid-day eats. We were greeted and welcomed to join in partaking of squirrel stew served over a choice of either wild rice or ground maize kernels, a food that the locals called gri-tees or something akin to that pronunciation.

The owner of the eating place Jason Feldman and his mate Drewella cooked and served all the food. Drewella, a tall, stately, tough-looking woman, had a most unusual talent. During the mid-day meal when residents of Kitty Hawk gathered at their eatery she entertained the customers in a curious way. She would ask the patrons to shout out a word and then based upon the word chosen, she would create interesting verses on the spot When finished with her recitation-song, she would request a small barter item from the person, something always given to reward Drewella for her efforts.

We learned that Drewella and her mate Jason had offered such entertainment at their eatery for many solar cycles. It was said that she received her special rhyming-song gift from an unnamed grannie who had survived a shipwreck on the Outer Banks who had washed ashore – alive and chipper – who became one of the local sage femme healers.

The day we visited the Feldman's eatery, one of the patrons shouted out the word: "flower." Drewella smiled and in turn shouted back:

Maury – do you mean flower as in a garden flower or flour as when my mate Jason here grinds the grain and turns it into bread?

Maury shouted back:

Your choice Drewella, it's up to you. But whatever you chant must be original and not just some little children's song like you do sometimes.

Drewella smiled and cast a sly look back at Maury:

Manchild! Maury always are a challenging me. So I's going to do something really special and dedicate my verses to my mate Jason who actually works – not like you Maury. He grinds the grain making our daily bread. So I have the words now in my mind and here it is, especially for you.

And she began …

She came to my millhouse
And promised me love.

She tested my products
Like a sweet turtledove.

But another miller won her
Oh misery to tell.
She left me in silence
No word of farewell.

I'll think of her never
I'll be wildly gay.

I'll charm other customers
Who'll buy and gladly pay.

I'll live yet to see her
Regret that dark hour.

When she left and rejected
My fine wildwood flour.

At the conclusion of her recital, Drewella turned to Maury and spoke:

OK Maury, did you like my song?
Give me your barter token I won't wait long,
Give it up Maury and don't be shy,

Then sit yourself down and have some shoe-fly-pie.

Maury had to smile at these words; spontaneous, said in fun, for all to enjoy. Everyone in the crowd laughed and applauded. We simply could not believe the spur-of-the-moment ability of Drewella and the friendly banter and exchanges she had with her customers.

***

Kill Devil Hills to Charleston

Back to the mainland and along the southern route through Elizabeth City, Hertford, Edenton, to Windsor. We continued down Highway 17 to Williamston, Vinceboro, and New Bern, towards Jacksonville, and then the coastal route to Holly Ridge and into Wilmington. We left Wilmington heading southwest, paralleling Highway 17 through Winnabow, past the Green Swamp, and into Myrtle Beach. So many places. All had suffered during the Ripple Event. Some remained damaged without evidence of repairs while others were in the process of being rebuilt. We passed through the settlements of Pawley's Island, Georgetown, North Santee, Awendaw and Bulls Bay, towards Mount Pleasant with a final push into Charleston where we camped east of the Ashley River.

***

We rode south along Meeting Street into old Charleston. At White Point Garden we encountered a refugee camp filled with families displaced by a recent hurricane. We learned that these offshore islands, sometimes called the Broad Islands, once were homes to freed African slaves and their descendants. The language developed and evolved over time on the Broad Islands became known as Gullah.

We visited one such refugee camp, Salvation Charity, where signs were displayed that identified clusters of families from specific islands: Dataw, Daufauskie, Edisto, Kiawah, Morris, and Wadmalaw. The hurricane had ravished these coastal areas of the southern Carolinas and northern Georgia forcing many islanders inland to seek protective shelter.

We passed by one sign that read Morris Island families. Here, an elderly woman waved and invited us to come near. We dismounted and accepted her invitation. She was known locally and to her children as Grannie Perkins. We were offered fine hospitality, a sit-talk and stay-about. During refreshment, we learned her story. Grandma's words were a mixture of English and Gullah, difficult at first to understand. As we listened we came to better understand the rhythm of her voice and what she was saying:

Come 'yuh you'all berry welcome to my umble house
[Come in, both of you are very welcome to my humble house]

Take your rest on our family po'ch in yonder cheer
[Some sit with me on the porch in one of our chairs]

You want let me b'gin my story
[Let me tell you my story]

I was bawn too long in Morris Island east of the crik of Bass
[I was born long ago on Morris Island, east of Bass Creek]

My farruh's name was Ahab my murruh's name was Asiba
[My father's name was Ahab, my mother's name was Asiba]

I be seb'nty years of old and hab I five sons and six daa'tuh
[I am seventy years old and have five sons and six daughters]

Deestunt people be we and eenjy libin on our island, but nah heer in dis camp
[We are decent people and enjoy living on our island, but not here in this camp]

Fuh True I cannot lie, ent no other place like home
[The truth is I cannot lie, there's no place like home]

My bredduh Jameson hebe berry kind to me
[My brother Jameson has been very kind to me]

Eberday I worked in the cawn fields nearby and tended the gyaa'd'n a'gin my hause
[Every day I worked in the corn fields nearby and tended the garden next to my house]

Life was haa'd but we had love
[Life was hard but we had love]

Kom in for nyam, aattuhwiile we'll eat a spot of bittle not the buckruh you used-to
[Come inside and eat, after a while we'll have real food, not the stuff you regularly eat]

Please stay for suppuh we hab vittles sharring
[Please stay for supper, we have food to share]

We catched dis heer chicken in the baa'nyaa'd
[We caught this chicken in our own barn yard]

Nobody hongry goes in my house
[Nobody goes hungry in my house]

Tengk'gawd for the sweet 'tettuh oh my
[Thank god for sweet potatoes, oh my!]

We'self give thanks for liv'in yaas'suh ree
[We give thanks for living, yes-sir-ree]

***

Grannie Perkins: what a noble woman. What a difficult time she and her family were suffering through. Hopefully she will be able to return to her family home on Morris Island to be together with her sons and grandsons. May Etowah grant that it will be so.

As we set up camp, we observed the approach of a train of seven oxen-pulled wagons piled high with what looked like household possessions. They were four families from old Florida fleeing northward to look for families and friends now settled north of Charleston. The reason for their trek was to avoid the chaos and insurrection that had erupted near their settlement groups in old Florida. They told us that the danger zone was a general region south of a diagonal line that ran from Daytona Beach southwest through Orlando to coastal Tampa. Bobby Singleton, one of the family members, related:

All areas below the line are without militia or local police. Homes and shops are regularly looted, set ablaze, and roving bands have created terrible havoc. Can you believe it? Even Cape Canaveral that famous historic center has been destroyed! Thousands of people invaded the launch sites and hangars. They stripped and stole anything of potential use, especially metal components that could be converted into barter tokens. The Orlando theme parks also were destroyed. These places where once families spent hours together relaxing and taking rides now have been turned into hideouts for competing gangs: no one dares enter these places any more. Even in my community of St. Augustine – north of the line – some rioting and damage has occurred. It was serious enough, however, that we decided to leave home and go north. All our worldly possessions now are piled into our oxen-pulled wagons. During our passage north we were not accosted or looted. Each family member, men as well as women, are well armed with sabers and pikes to repel any who might want to confiscate our furniture and family goods. So far we have been very lucky. At least now we are alive and far distant from the rioting. We expect to be accepted into a settlement group north of Charleston where some of our relatives now live. Let us hope so. Only time will tell.

What terrible events; what terrible sadness!

But we experienced even more sadness the following morning. Michael's decision to part company and continue south into Florida would leave us without a good friend and travel companion. His family home was in the Old Florida community of Starke, about midway between Jacksonville and Gainesville. His family worked a farm west of Starke, between Butler and Edwards roads to the north of Alligator Creek. He expected to find sanctuary there, and being among his kin was a better solution for the next solar cycles of his life compared to traipsing about as an itinerant tinker repairing odds and ends, and scrounging work just to earn a few barter tokens.

So it was that early morning came. We cleared camp and then it was time for our farewells. As Michael headed south, we left camp going northwest. Upon parting we were sad but filled with good memories to last forever. We had been friends for too short a time. Now Travis and I were continuing into the unknown.

Charleston to Stone Mountain

We left Charleston paralleling Highway 78 towards Augusta. Then we passed through a suite of small communities that characterized the landscape: Hanahan, Goose Creek, Summerville, and St. George. Then on to Reevesville, Bamberg, and White Pond. Our route took us along Tinker Creek Road where we connected with Highway 278. We next passed through or around New Ellenton, Spiderweb, and finally reached Augusta. After a brief uneventful stay at Augusta, we trekked west along Highway 278 past a series of settlement groups at Berzelia, Harlem, Dearing, and Thompson, then turned north along Highway 78 through Washington, Rayle, and into Crawford.

***

West of Crawford and south of Highway 78, we reached an unnamed but well-tended carriage lane lined on both sides with tall broad-leafed trees with white blossoms. We stopped at the junction to rest and decided to explore further. About a kilo-mile further along the lane was a stately home, possibly older than 200 solar cycles, well-constructed of brick with slate roofing and numerous out-buildings. What appeared to be a carriage or cart driveway led to the entrance. On the oval grassy area adjacent to the house entrance was a gravesite and memorial, apparently for a highly respected individual. The inscription on the headstone read:

Robert Eustus Micenheimer
Born Ripple Event Minus 5 Solar Cycles
Respected Son of New Georgia Oglethorpe County
Graduate of Virginia Military Institute
Lieutenant New Vicksburg Militia Supply Unit
Action: Battle of South Platte River
Promoted Colonel: Southeast Atlanta Regional Militia
Passed 7-2 Post Ripple Event Solar Cycle 50
Rest-In-Peace

As we stood inspecting the burial monument of Colonel Micenheimer, we were approached by an elderly gentleman, perhaps the grounds keeper or caretaker. He was Isaac Davidson and enquired as to our purpose and interest. We told him we were travelers from the NorthWest Configuration, a geographical location that had suffered horribly during the Epidemic, and our objectives were to explore other portions of the continent to seek and communicate with survivors.

The caretaker said that he, himself, could not bid us welcome into the family house as the main building was closed. Widow Micenheimer was away in New Atlanta, tending to estate-related obligations. But if we were interested he could show us through the out-buildings and then share something about the history and background of Colonel Micenheimer.

As we walked together, Mr. Davidson spoke:

> *The colonel was free born during Old Solar Cycle 2015 and given the name Robert Eustus Micenheimer. He attended Virginia Military Institute where he was commissioned 2nd Lieutenant. For his initial service assignment, he was attached to the New Vicksburg Militia and assigned to the Western Exploration Unit. His responsibilities included maintenance of weaponry and supply wagon defense. The WEU's objective was to expand boundaries of the New Confederacy into the western portions of the Flatland Configuration beyond the Great River, initially to occupy the lands, but eventually to develop trade relations across the continent. The campaign started well but stalled during its westward progression after the WEU was confronted and defeated at the Battle of South Platte, a location along the eastern border of the New NorthWest and Flatland configurations.*

> *Lieutenant Micenheimer and Corporal Fisher Lange were the only WEU survivors of the battle. They were taken captive by Sharitarish's Pawnee fighters and the defenders of Plains Sanctuary settlement group. Both soldiers conducted themselves with honor and subsequently were released to return to their family homes. Lieutenant Micenheimer reached his destination during Solar Cycle 47 – just three cycles ago. After debriefing he received a new commission and appointment with the Atlanta Regional Militia where he distinguished himself in field exercises against the Wanderers that ravaged the once-beautiful university town of Athens, Georgia. He also was responsible for calming the civil unrest at Macon and for the return to justice and militia respect when rioters attempted to isolate the city and declare an independent enclave. For these efforts Lieutenant Micenheimer was promoted to colonel by the New Confederacy House of Representatives, located at Williamsburg, East Virginia. He passed unexpectedly while on leave at New Vicksburg where he was visiting his former friend and comrade-in-arms,*

Fisher Lange. The colonel's body was escorted back to Atlanta and then to the family home south of Crawford for internment. Colonel Micenheimer was well liked and respected by all.

In the long ago past it would have been rare for a Black soldier to receive such honors and respect.

We asked Mr. Davidson whether or not he knew if Fisher Lange still was alive and residing in New Vicksburg. He suspected so but had no direct information.

That evening we camped just outside of Athens, old Georgia, along a green belt next to Highway 78. It was clear to us that we must visit New Vicksburg and spend some time determining whether or not Fisher Lange was alive. As a cross-continental traveler, Lange would have gained invaluable information during his return home after crossing the Flatland Configuration in the company of Lieutenant Micenheimer.

We pushed on past Monroe and then reached a settlement with an unusual name – Between. This certainly was a curious name for a settlement, perhaps given due to its geographical position nearly midway between Athens and Atlanta. We could not confirm this, however, as the streets of Between were empty as we rode through town.

Several kilo-miles west of Between, however, we learned why the town had been deserted. Residents from the geographical region encompassing Monroe and westward to Snellville had gathered at an unnamed hill site south of Highway 78. There, a community feed- and fiddle-fest was in full progress. The twang of music and interesting words filled the air:

Chicken in the bread pan scratching out dough
Granny will your dog bite? No, child, no
Granny will your hen peck? No, child, no
Pappy cut her bill off long time ago.

The gathering and action was taking place on a hillock rising out of a flat swamp-like landscape. Hundreds had gathered to drink, palaver, eat barbeque, and enjoy the hill and local swamp tunes. We listened to the musicians and singers, and walked about greeting folks.

Off to one side of the hillock several deep pits were being excavated. People working adjacent to the pits were pressing what appeared to be handfuls of clay into wooden racks of rectangular-shaped molds. We paused to watch and enquired about their activities:

Y'all are welcome to the hill of healing. Here we dig the clay to make medicinal tablets for healing purposes. Y'all must know that clay heals, don'cha now? When you get your ills and the doc ain't available, y'know what is best: two clay tablets and two swallows of 'shine – if you know what I mean. Here, let me show you some tablets. I'll give 'em to ya since y'all are newcom'rs to our fiddle-fest.

The man speaking to us was Tyrell Jameson. He reached inside his backpack and removed a package wrapped in a dirty yellow cloth rag that held about 30 clay tablets. These were about a middle-finger in length and half a middle-finger in width. The top side was embossed with what could be a religious figure. The bottom side of each tablet bore indentations of three letters: I-E-E. We asked Mr. Jameson to explain more about the tablets:

Tyrell Jameson, clay digger – *Y'all ain't from 'round here so ya wouldn't know, so let me explain ya about these here things. This one on the front side shows an image of what we call Etowah – something of a spirit or god – I don't know – something that once was worshiped up north of Kennesaw at the great mound site. Some of the olden men and women converse that in times long past this spirit-like Etowah ruled all the lands and all the peoples did Etowah's bidding. We continue to honor the past so we press the image onto the clay tablets in Etowah's memory, and believe that doing so will fix us up if'n and when we'all have the sickness. Every solar cycle at the summer solstice, members of our digging and pressing group makes their way up to the mound site carrying hundreds if'in not thousands of these healing tablets. At the solstice midnight we lay them on the altar at the base of the great mound. The olden ones have said through the solar cycles even long before the Ripple that the tablets take on their healthy abilities during night when it is said that Etowah sends a sky signal that he or it is pleased. But I've never been on that trek so can't say f'urs'ur if that all this be truthful or ain't.*

What about the three letter symbols on the back of the tablets: I-E-E?

No idea have I about 'em. Looks just like a basic letter I with two E letters to me: how about to you? Looks the same, right? Maybe the folks who started making these tablets back a long ago time just wanted to spell out something and ran out of space? Who knows? In any case, the image and the letters don't change the flavor of the tablets. To me they have a nice smooth taste, somethin' like blackboard chalk that I remember eating when I had the hungers before lunch back when I was in school. Don't know much else about the whys or whats about them images and letters. But here, take five or six more tablets, might help you out in the future.

Leaving the festivities we returned to Highway 78. On the horizon just 11 kilo-miles west of Snellville appeared the huge bare monolith of Stone Mountain. We camped in a park area adjacent to the Cherokee Trail where we were met by Mary Norton, a park curator. She described the astonishing carving on Stone Mountain started many solar cycles prior to the Ripple, and lamented that the work still had not yet been completed. She related that today volunteer stone carvers continued to apply their skills in shaping the mural, but progress had been slow and very limited during the Dark Time and Recovery Periods.

Carved into the face of Stone Mountain were images of three historic figures important to New Confederacy history: Davis, Jackson, and Lee. As we learned from Ms. Norton, the artist responsible for the design and early carving activities was the same one responsible for the great stone heads carved in the sacred hills of He Sapa, that our friend Hanska Ohanzee had mentioned when we met outside of Pierre along the Missouri River.

Mary mentioned that there were several carvers working today on the relief high up on the mountain face and that they would be lowered from their rope support system before sunset. We asked if she thought one or more might be interested in being interviewed. Mary thought for a moment and said it probably would be better to invite just one carver over to our campsite and offer him dinner, along with a barter token for taking time to describe his efforts

Shortly after sunset Mary returned to our campsite accompanied by one of the workmen:

Gus Powell, stone carver – *As you have learned I come now and then to work on the Stone Mountain relief. My particular component of the design is to improve the shape of the horses' hooves. This I can do without blasting, and the reality is we don't have blasting powder except once in a blue moon – which means never – since we haven't been able to develop trade with other configurations for the* *necessary ingredients. So I just chisel away on my volunteer days. I take the worker's tram up to the top and rappel down over Jackson's or Lee's body and descend until I reach the horses' feet. Then I unhook and, once secured, I can continue my work.*

How did I get this job, you ask? Well it really isn't a job; it is a pleasure and heart-felt desire. At my settlement group schoolhouse there were many books on science and culture. But what I liked to read most were books on geology. When my teachers taught these topics I paid attention and learned my lessons well. I learned how to scout out and find minerals needed by my settlement group; where gold and silver could be found among the rocks and silt of flowing streams; where thick black tar oozed from hillside strata; where round globs of volcanic geodes could be collected and cracked open to reveal the beauty inside. As a reward for my diligence and study in the field, I was awarded a geological pick or hammer as 1st prize in a competition between regional settlement groups. This hammer was symbolic of my trade, pointed at one end it could be used to break shale and carbonate deposits, or for defense, as when I have used it in the past to flail about and imbed inside the head of a shatter zone Wanderer who attacked my fellow students when we were out collecting rocks. We geologists – and there are more than a few locally – are a tough lot. I can hurl my pick 20 meter-yards and hit any mark intended, or imbed the point inside a marked-off inner circle, or hit the throat of an attacker, as I once did another time when some Wanderer attempted to kidnap my mate. We geologists are a tough lot. What do you do to protect your mate, Travis?

Stone Mountain to Etowah

We departed Stone Mountain the following morning along Highway 78 west towards Decatur. Based upon discussions the previous evening with Mary and Gus, we elected to bypass Atlanta, due to urban insecurity. We turned north along Eye 285 and bypassed Northlake and Embry Hills then made the long swing west past Sandy Springs to Cumberland. Outside of Cumberland, we took Highway 3 northwest, passing through the campus of Kennesaw State University, and reached Marietta. We spent but a short time at Marietta, as our main objective was to travel north and camp near the site of Etowah. We continued on Highway 3 through the small settlement of Kennesaw, then after a long stretch we crossed one arm of Lake Acworth before reaching Emerson Township. We abandoned Highway 3 in favor of a route that paralleled Highway 293 north and crossed the Etowah River. Once on the northwestern side, we trekked west along Old Mill Road to the intersection with Etowah Drive; and turned our horses south. Before us was Etowah Mound site.

***

Rising above the plain was the Great Mound and nearby temple platforms. How could it be that these massive, wonderful structures were constructed here? Who gave the orders? For what purposes? The Great Mound and the other structures seemed to predate all living Native American peoples.

How could it be that the site was called Etowah?

Travis and I wandered through the ruins admiring the mounds and effigies displayed. These latter clearly were bipeds, not unlike ourselves, but seemingly smaller, with slightly different facial configurations; ears were the same, noses blunted, and eyes accentuated. The site also appeared to have been looted, probably during the Ripple Event or early solar cycles of the Dark Time. The evidence for the desecration was clear: across the grounds were strewn thousands of objects. Grave robbers had desecrated the site digging here and there in hurried attempts to extract valuable objects from the earth that could be used for barter.

Among these scattered broken items were bones of wild birds, mammals, and reptiles; biped skeletons and teeth. Bundles of carnations and oleander stems had been placed upon several alters, perhaps selected because of their characteristic pink and white blossoms. On other altars someone, or groups of individuals, had placed cloves of garlic and pomegranate fruits as if making offerings to an Earth Mother or some local deity. Scattered throughout the site were broken pieces of terra-cotta pottery, pieces that once were part of beautiful iconic images of bipeds, deer, birds and, in some instances, what looked to be religious statues in near human form.

On either side of the Great Mound and throughout the site were naturally growing beech, hickory, oak, pine, and sycamore trees. Most interesting to us was that 15 of these native trees had been decorated with different objects left by humans visiting the site. Were the trees venerated, or were there other explanations? Were the objects left behind offerings, or perhaps gifts left by those seeking advice or solutions to problems? Some of the trees were festooned with hundreds of antique plastic and glass bottles. When the wind blew – as it did in the afternoon of our visit – the bottles tinkled and resounded with different tones, sending out an unusual cacophony of notes, as if clusters of people were humming a distinctive atonal chorus.

Among the more interesting trees were those decorated with pieces of clothing. Some of the trees were bedecked with distinctive gender-related items, their branches draped with clothing only worn by adult women; others only by adult men. Still others were decorated only with tiny shirts-blouses, pants-shorts, and undergarments of infants and children.

Were these clothing objects left behind by concerned individuals requesting health-related aid or disease cures? If so, to whom or to what were the clothing objects dedicated? Etowah? Or perhaps another? And, if so, were the requests and pleas honored or not?

Seemingly from out of nowhere emerging from the tree shadows an old woman appeared. We introduced ourselves and in turn she told us her name – Grannie Noska – with no first name. She was one of several elderly women known locally as See-ers, with the skills and abilities to foretell the future. She greeted us warmly and welcomed us to Etowah:

> **Grannie Noska,** see-er – *Look around you. What you see here, these grand structures, were constructed by a race of people different but not too much different, long before our time. It seems that they all died mysteriously. Why, no one knows, and we can only guess. A long time past in one of my dreams, a spirit-like vision appeared and spoke to me saying those before us died because they didn't follow The Seven. I had no idea what was meant by The Seven. In my dream vision three additional words were uttered again and again: Ijano Esantu Eleman – As It Was In The Beginning. I have pondered for many solar cycles why all of their kind would be eliminated for not following something called The Seven. This has remained a mystery to me and to others living nearby, who the dream also has appeared. If you look about, you will see three letters carved here and there on the monuments: I-E-E. They must signify a shortening of the words spoken in my dream.*

How could this be? These were the same words that we had learned as children growing up in Bison Camp. The same words we were taught to respect. And the site was known throughout the region as Etowah. Could it have been these ancient peoples worshiped and respected the same cosmic spirit as we?

She asked us if we wanted to use her services to capture a glimpse, a vision into our futures. Almost in jest, Travis looked at me and we both replied, "yes." Grannie Noska said that she would return to our camp near the Great Mound entrance in the early evening to initiate what she called – dream time images. She cautioned that in the meantime we needed to fast and not to eat any plant- or animal-based food the rest of the afternoon or evening – only spring water and the mineral tablets that she provided.

The time came. Grannie Noska reappeared with two young female assistants. They were introduced to us only as the twins Sarah and Jocelyn Adams. Grannie explained that the young women had what locally was called *Second Sight,* but explained no further. We watched as the three women prepared the beverages that we later would swallow and wait for the images to appear.

It looked to us that what the women were brewing was just another variation of what we had tasted earlier in our journey, something called the Black Drink: green leaves and branch tips of holly plants stirred into heated water, and mixed with additional undetermined ingredients.

Grannie Noska and her assistants prepared two separate bowers of pine branches and covered each with a blanket with gorgeous and exotic geometric designs and symbols. Travis reclined on one; the other was for me. We were instructed and cautioned not to rise from our pine-branch beds during the ceremony and to remain without movement. Most important Grannie told us not to reveal to the other the content or images from our dream time until the sun broke the eastern horizon blessing us with the heated rays of life. And then it came time to drink.

***

Dawn arrived and we awoke. Travis approached me, glowing with happiness:

> *Reese – I saw you clearly in my dream as I see you now. You were radiant; the glow of your face revealed great happiness that soon would come to you. Reese – in my dream I saw us living in the settlement of New Vicksburg and that you gave birth to twin daughters during the coming solar cycle. Oh Reese – in my vision we again re-started our family once more. I could not be happier.*

I looked into his face and saw the joy that his prophetic dream had brought him. I reached out to embrace Travis. I held him tightly as I silently expressed my joy upon hearing his dream.

> *Reese – what was your dreamtime vision? Please, please tell me.*

I kept my face away from Travis so he could not look into my eyes. When at last I spoke – I lied!

> *Travis – in my dream I also saw that we would live in New Vicksburg, and for some time. I too had images of delivering twin girls. I saw that you and I will be happy for countless solar cycles to come – and that we will return to Bison Camp together as a family and restore our lives there, living out our days in peace and harmony in the place our families treasured.*

I could not bear to tell Travis the truth. My vision was not one of joy and comfort, but contained themes of fear, death, and loneliness. I clearly saw that Travis would be seriously injured in an accident. Despite all of our efforts to heal his wound, my mate would die long before his time, and I would become a widow. In my dream the number five repeated and repeated: I saw that five of us would complete a return trek to Bison Camp. The five would be myself, my daughters and their mates – unborn and unknown to me in my dream. Travis, however, would not be among the five. And it would come to pass that after a period of mourning, I would muster the strength needed in order to carry on along with our two daughters with their mates – we five would travel on into an unknown future.

Travis spoke:

> *Reese – I am so happy that you shared your happy dream experience with me. It could not have been chance that our route took us into Etowah where we have had the opportunity to learn about our future together. Unseen forces must have guided us along our way. Reese, you fulfill me. You are a wonderful woman and I am lucky to have you as my mate.*

At hearing Travis's words, I broke down in tears. He brushed them away with a kiss and a smile, calling my tears the salty drops of happiness. I smiled back to him the best I could.

Etowah to Birmingham

Leaving Etowah we were Alabama-bound. Upon departing Etowah we traveled west towards the settlement of Rome, and then south paralleling Highway 27 to Cedartown. At the crossing with Highway 278 we turned at 27 and ventured along 278 through Spring Garden and Gadsden, Alabama.

***

There must be something in the air in this portion of the New Confederacy. Just like our side trip off the highway near the town of Between, we entered Gadsden where we encountered another music festival in full swing. Asking about we learned that Gadsden was most famous for being the home of the best fiddlers and 'shiner-stillers in all of rural Alabama. The music was loud and entrancing: how could one not resist tapping toes and clapping when words such as these were sung:

Way high up on Jimminy Hill
A hidden still, clay jugs to fill
No one there but you and me
This place where we make fine whiskey.

CHORUS

Gently drips the whiskey still
Join my song and sing along
Gently flows the whiskey
Whiskey by the jar.

Grandpa mashed the corn so fine
Grandma said she wanted wine
Brother looked out for the cops
Sister caught the flowing drops.

REPEAT CHORUS

Whiskey flowing down my throat
I dance and prance like a Billy goat
Whiskey soothes my tired feet
The flavor smooth cannot be beat.

REPEAT CHORUS

When the dawn tomorrow comes
When ten thousand crickets hummmmm
I'll reach for my whiskey fine
A better taste than old French wine.

REPEAT CHORUS

When I'm old and in my bed
With aching bones and throbbing head
I'll reach once more for my whiskey glass
A flavor sweet I cannot pass.

REPEAT CHORUS

Verse after verse echoed from the stage out over the audience. Jars of 'shine clinked in rhythm to the tunes, sometimes quicker, sometimes slower, as with the following verses rising spontaneously from the gathered crowd:

The other night dear as I lay sleeping
I dreamed I drank your whiskey fine
When I awoke dear, I was mistaken
I had drunk a glass of wine.

CHORUS ...

You are my moonshine my only moonshine
You make me happy when skies are grey
You'll never know dear how much I love you
Please don't take my moonshine away.

And after several more verses and choruses, a different song filled the air:

Wine, wine, I hear you whine
Over the hills and valleys low
Golden 'shine in jars so fine
Leaves me with a happy glow.

Birmingham

After a sip or two, and lots of palaver, we trekked southwest on Eye 59 through Ashville, Springville, Argo, Trussville into Birmingham. Once we reached the outskirts, militia guards on duty recommended that we camp at Ward Park in the central part of the city. In earlier times Birmingham had been an economic center for steel production. During the Dark Time Recovery Period several small forges had been retrofitted to produce steel objects for regional settlement group uses. Perhaps the most interesting steel-related revival activities, however, were the blacksmith shops located in the Southside district along 6th Avenue – 30 or 40 in all – where dirks, knives, sabers, and other types of military steel hardware were being produced to arm different units of the New Confederacy Militias. We visited a selection of these blacksmith shops and inspected their wares. The swords or long sabers were simple in construction with basic cord-wrapped hilts. All were generic and uninscribed – like Travis's saber. We were told that if we wished ornamentation could be added later upon request.

When we arrived at Ward Park, we found the site filled with campers and groups of musicians. A temporary stage had been set up along the stream, and a performance was scheduled later in the evening. We established our camp and tethered our animals. The evening air was hot and humid, mosquitoes bothersome, but still we enjoyed the evening and listened to the songs, some offered by soloists, other melodies performed by groups with different instruments – banjos, dulcimers, fiddles, flutes, and guitars, even one or two zithers. The songs and melodies were of two distinctive categories: sad, plaintive laments balanced by toe-tapping fiddle-dance songs.

The first that I remember was a slow song about how a young man missed his mate but couldn't see her because he was a prisoner held in the Birmingham jail:

> *Write me a letter, send it by mail, send it in care of Birmingham jail.*

The song was moving but we were not certain what the word mail meant? We assumed it described a method of passing or relaying news from one place to another, perhaps by messenger on horseback.

> *Then later two additional laments, written several hundred solar cycles prior to the Ripple Event by long-ago poet-songsters, touched Travis and me deeply. The first was written by someone known to the performance group only by the author's first name, Stephen. This piece recalled the sadness that individuals and families experienced during an earlier period in regional history when food scarcity and personal safety were serious concerns:*
>
> > *Let us pause in life's pleasures and count its many tears*
> > *While we all sup sorrow with the poor*
> > *There's a song that will linger forever in our ears*
> > *Oh hard times, come again no more.*

It's the song, the sigh of the weary
Hard times, hard times come again no more
Many days you have lingered around my cabin door
Oh hard times, come again no more.

The second lament, also written long ago by an unknown author, had a more recent feeling. The words told of a man with a seriously injured wife and two hungry children. He had traveled an endless number of kilo-miles to seek assistance from different settlement groups, but had been denied entrance by all. The words express his sadness knowing that he could survive, but the rejections of his wife and children by the settlement group selectors doomed both him and his family whatever decision he made. Would he choose life and forever be haunted by his self-preservation decision, or elect to die with his family? The words reminded Travis and me of the Memory Guild stories we had heard during evening campfire gatherings at Bison Camp, how tragic events separated family members and forced difficult, heart-wrenching choices. The words revealed the man's decision, one that would haunt him forever:

As I walked out one evening late
A-drinking of sweet wine
I thought my heart would surely break
For my loves I left behind.

Ten thousand miles away from home
Ten thousand miles I'll be
And the thought of you will break my heart
And will be the death of me.

***

As we remounted our horses, we saw off to the north a rider on horseback dressed in a blue-grey uniform ambling towards us. He wore a military-style hat with an insignia of crossed sabers, and behind his saddle were two bags identified by three letters: RMD. He hailed us and we paused for conversation. The rider's name was Bart Jenkins: he was a mailman and assigned deliveries within the central region of old Alabama.

Bart Jenkins, rural mail delivery rider – *How now strangers, nice to see you here in old Alabama. I give you my salute and can offer you a swig of sweet mint tea from my canteen if you would like. I am part* *of a team of rural message deliverers, known as the RMD in these parts. In days long ago past, we would have been known as mailmen when the term mail was applied to messages sent between folks. I am headquartered at Decatur where we have a central message processing station. My route takes me in a north-south direction up and down Eye 65 – passing through Priceville, then Falkville, on to Lacon, South Vinemont, Good Hope, Damascis, Black Bottom, Smoke Rise, and Warrior. I have to bypass older settlements at Kimberly, Morris, and Gardensdale due to excessive Wanderer activities, and then I can ride safely through into Birmingham. I usually hang out at Birmingham swapping trek tales with other RMDs swinging through steel-town on their east-west rides. After a few days of R&R or I&I as the oldsters used to say, I continue on south all the way to Montgomery then I swing southwest heading towards Mobile. Then after a few days of rest, as they say, I'm back on the trail heading north once again towards Decatur. I relay messages here and there and everywhere and I like to think of myself as a reincarnation of the old Pony Express that once carried messages from west and east, and back between old Sacramento and St. Joseph, Missouri – along the Great River.*

We would have liked to spend more time with Jenkins, but he needed to keep to his schedule. The cost of a message to be carried from Decatur to Mobile was astonishingly high – the equivalent value of four copper barter tokens with potential alternative payments in animal hides or small bags of salt.

***

Birmingham to New Vicksburg

We left Birmingham and headed southwest towards Tuscaloosa, then further along on Eye-20 past Eutaw, Boligee, Epes, Livingston, and York. We reached the border and crossed into old Mississippi and entered Meridian. Although perhaps unfair to the settlement of Meridian what Travis and I remembered most about the town was the noontime sweats and our constant swearing out loud – screaming H-H-S-S – short for heat, humidity, sweats, and skeeters. Despite the eye-burning sweat and bites, we remained on track and aimed towards New Vicksburg.

Skirting several rural old Mississippi settlements, we elected to camp off to the north side of the road and set up our tent near a small stream. The land nearby had been plowed recently. After tending to the horses and mules Travis tramped through the field attempting to identify the seeds or roots planted by the farmer. No visual evidence of the plants could be found. The land would not have been in fallow, since we suspected local food supplies might be minimal. Perhaps the land had been plowed for other purposes? Who knows?

What Travis found, however, during his trek were four interesting relics, churned up to the surface by the farmer's pointed plow: two were corroded items that resembled huge bullets from a long-bore rifle used long before the Ripple Event. The other two corroded lumps appeared to be metallic. When the crusty slag was removed the initials CSA inside a circle were revealed. The objects seemed to be belt buckles perhaps lost or left behind by wounded soldiers during the past Great War that we learned about in school back in Bison Camp.

***

We entered Jackson, New Mississippi, to the visual enjoyment of magnolia and dogwood trees lining the streets. Up ahead we saw what appeared at first glance to be a mob of people, but upon closer inspection the assembly was shouting and screaming support for something quite unusual. Members of the crowd were jumping about screaming support for different types of racing animals.

We had to laugh. The gathered residents of Jackson were out and about amusing themselves watching different types of dogs and other animals racing between two points. The most enjoyable races to me were what we used to call "sausage-dogs" as kids back at Bison Camp. As Travis and I watched, we laughed at how the dogs waddled their short feet and pulled their long bodies faster and faster in attempts to catch a fake rabbit pulled by one of the event officials.

Off along a parallel street, Jackson gamblers were placing bets on different types of birds: which canary would warble the best song; which dove would coo the softest; which rooster would squabble the loudest when poked and pinched? None of the birds were harmed during these betting episodes and all assembled seemed to be having a good time.

Still another type of local completion took place at an establishment called *The Bulldog*, a local bar on Ridgewood Road west of the reservoir. Here, to the entertainment of all, was a singing competition for men and women of all ages and types. There was a tall jar on a table in the center of the stage into which had been placed some 50 or more cards, on which were printed an animal's name. Competitors took turns drawing cards from the jar, and either smiling or frowning once they read the name of the animal listed. The competition was not to act like the so-named beastie, but to imitate the beastie's sound. The different contestants, some more libated than others, came two at a time to the center of the stage, and then barked, bellowed, roared, or sniffled, as per their perception of the beastie's sound. The audience then voted on which one they liked best. The loser left the stage; the winner remained and stood off to the side awaiting further competition.

Little by little the contestants were reduced until finally only two remained. As we watched the final competition inside *The Bulldog,* all of us were a bit tipsy but we were having a great time. One of the last two candidates had to mimic a mink – his opponent was required to growl like a basenji dog – two nearly impossible tasks. When it was over the mink mimic, a smiling young man received his reward: a week's pass for a free jar of 'shine on a Tuesday night at *The Bulldog,* along with the title Champion Growler.

Hard to believe, but true.

***

New Vicksburg

Leaving Jackson we followed Eye 20 west through Clinton, Bolton, Edwards, to Bovina, then to the outskirts of New Vicksburg. We entered New Vicksburg on February 28th. We followed Clay Street down to the riverfront where we sought the local militia office. There, we were received by Sergeant Jackson Winters, who welcomed us and offered use of the militia facilities to stable our animals. We were most grateful for his assistance. We were accommodated temporarily at the barracks just off the intersection of Washington and Depot streets.

We settled into our barracks room, washed, unpacked our goods then walked to the militia mess hall for dinner. We had just taken our seats on the bench along the trestle table when a militia man sat down across from us. He offered a welcome greeting and extended his left hand to shake hands. The empty sleeve that covered his missing right arm was pinned to the front of his chest.

Welcome to New Vicksburg, strangers. My name is Fisher Lange. I am a sergeant in the New Vicksburg Militia. Who are you?

After-Word

Strange – the events along our journey. Some days it was almost as if we were guided by an unseen cosmic force. Here we were at our first evening meal at New Vicksburg and the person who sat down at the table opposite us was the one individual in all of the town that we wanted most to meet and interview.

Travis shook Sergeant Lange's left hand. We introduced ourselves and related our visit to the Micenheimer estate prior to arriving in New Vicksburg. We had been told that both Lange and the Colonel had fought at the Battle of South Platt several solar cycles back. We asked whether or not he would share information regarding not only the battle, but events and what they had encountered during their return to the New Confederacy.

Lange related that the return had been difficult and required careful planning, reconnoitering, and stealth to avoid roving gangs of Wanderers in the shattered zones of the Flatland Configuration. The journey had taken them through portions of the old states of Nebraska, Kansas, Missouri, and Arkansas, prior to reaching New Vicksburg. Throughout their journey Lange reported that they lived off the land, and as he said, *We watched each other's backs*. Travis and Fisher took turns speaking:

Travis: *We heard that both you and the Colonel were the only survivors from your Western Exploration Unit, but that you were treated reasonably well.*

Fisher: *Yes, to be sure. We were fed and housed, minimally but within reason, given the sparse accommodations and vittles then available to everybody, friend or foe alike. Part of the time we spent under interrogation by the defenders of the Platte River region. They wanted to know more about us – and to be sure – they were open in the responses to our questions as well. One time, if I remember correctly, we were interviewed by two newcomers, two persons who had been traveling through the territory, who heard about the battle and later joined in the questioning. I remember now – give me a moment – they were two young students attached to some organization called the Ada Collators or something like that.*

Upon hearing Fisher's words, Travis almost jumped out of his seat.
Could it be that the term you heard as Ada Collators, actually could have been – Data Collectors?

Fisher thought for a moment and answered:

I think you're right, Travis. They did introduce themselves. I don't remember the actual names they gave to me and Lieutenant Micenheimer, but now it is clear to me that they used the term Data Collectors. Also, I seem to recall that their home was way out in the New NorthWestern Configuration at a place called Boz Man or something like that.

***

Ijano Esantu Eleman

Interlude-Conversation: 9

Names

***

Strange is it not, K'Aser, a region known by one and all as Etowah?

And filled with structures built by who no one can say – a mystery. One that we – I – may work to solve someday.

To me the builders were quite similar to the stranded Spacers at Bison Camp. Who knows – perhaps the mound folk were also from otherworld? But no doubt someday we – you – will see. But as for the name?

A'Tena, perhaps Etowah (may his name be praised) was tempted as you were. A Greek goddess carries your name yet and back in the day both Athens and Sparta – and interesting duo was it not? – saw the goddess as their protector. Just how did you – she – handle this situation?

Oh, you noticed that, did you? It wasn't easy perhaps not even possible. Who can say? But how about you, K'Aser? I was not blind to the title of the rulers of Olden Rome. Caesar this, Caesar that all over the known world! And the statues ...

Many statues of different rulers, yes my name was a title and for a long time, too. I was not pleased with much that was done by those so titled. I found myself quite unable to lead that society away from deaths for entertainment. I should have been more direct, but those days are now long gone (Etowah be praised). Such matters are now handled much more directly and with some effect.

Praised indeed, those Roman games were horrible – death, death and yet more death with only the thinnest veneer of ritual. May we not see their like again!

May Etowah hear your words. While yours was a single statue, but what a statue it was – the grandest and most beautiful. I was impressed and awed then and have remained so often returning to those times for yet another view. In any case, our playing with names has done no harm and I'd wager such is the case with Etowah (praised be his name).

That would be a good wager, K'Aser, your – shall we say adoration – of my statue has been noticed and much appreciated.

As well it should be, A'Tena.

Chapter 10

Mississippi Sojourn: New Vicksburg

Part I

Pre-Note

Fisher Lange smiled as he related his background history. He was born during Solar Cycle 29 and at the age of 15 had joined the local militia. He was 17 when captured at the Battle of South Platte River. He and Colonel Micenheimer, then a Lieutenant, were released from captivity during Solar Cycle 47 and together trekked eastward across the Flatland Configuration on their return to New Vicksburg. With this information we realized that Travis, I, and Fisher were not dissimilar in age, given that it was but two solar cycles later that the Epidemic struck New Vicksburg, the event that initiated our cross-continental travel. Travis asked Fisher about events in New Vicksburg and the surrounding region after his return home:

> *Upon return from the western expedition, I needed some medical rehabilitation. The docs fitted me with a wooden arm, but that didn't work so well. I resolved to deal with reality that I still could work, and accomplish most tasks using my left hand. That reality took me out of the basic militia activities, but the commander appreciated my other skills, so I remained connected with my comrades in other ways. During my rehab time, the commander asked me to prepare something about the history of Vicksburg and our unit. This activity took me a couple of solar cycles to complete. Perhaps you would like to review my document later?*

Fisher handed Travis a leather-bound bundle of paper containing a historical account hand written in his unusual, characteristic manner. The document related considerable information of high value that allowed us to better understand the history and development of the New Vicksburg area.

At one time the region was home of the Natchez people who had settled here long before anyone could say. Invaders from France arrived and wanted to occupy the lands, so what was called the Natchez War ensued. The French allied themselves with another group, the Choctaw, who were enemies of the Natchez. Then the Natchez banded together with their own allies, the Yazoo Confederation. Then followed long times characterized by warfare. These battles consisted mainly of hit-and-run tactics and ultimately resulted in defeat of the Natchez/Yazoo. The Choctaw then occupied the region where they flourished until the Spanish soldiers arrived many solar cycles later. After trekking overland and sailing upriver, these new invaders established themselves at what they called Fort Nogales. It turns out that after the American Revolution the new government formed a treaty with Spain that allowed the Spanish to establish a settlement. They did so and named the site Walnut Hills. If you don't know, the word Nogales means walnut. Subsequently, the area was opened to non-Spanish, and the initial settlement of Vicksburg was founded by a religious leader named Newitt Vick. The region still was the homeland of the Choctaw but, according to epic stories told around campfires, the American government wanted the land for their own settlers and forced the Choctaw out of the region into new western lands across the Great River. Then came what has been called the American Civil War that cast its dark shadow over Vicksburg, especially during the time of the terrible siege. After the war the town began to recover from the ruins, but then the Great River changed course, leaving what was once the western riverside of Vicksburg isolated and unusable. This event caused the economy to collapse and many residents left for other locales. Between the end of the Civil War until the Ripple Event there was civil unrest throughout Vicksburg, where Black and White residents lived separately, where race violence characterized most of the solar cycles during this time. We all remember the Ripple Event that occurred on November 27th, 2020, old time calculation, *and the following Dark Time brought a total of 10 solar cycles of extraordinary difficulty for the residents of Vicksburg. We can only guess at the number who survived these terrible times, as the records are very sparse and incomplete. What we do know is that several settlement groups were formed within and along the periphery of Vicksburg. These settlement groups were attacked by Wanderers, and more than 800 folks both Black and White were murdered. It was at this time we learned to stand together as one – the people of Vicksburg – and together we repelled the attackers. Though this ordeal we became one with our town and renamed it New Vicksburg. Shortly later the New Vicksburg Militia was formed to protect our families and town. Many other towns that survived became clustered as the New Configuration and forged links due to similar histories and unifying cultures. This is who we are today.*

Fisher related to us the importance of a specific event that took place one evening, where life in New Vicksburg changed dramatically for the better:

One night little Johnny Thompson, son of Bella and James Thompson, attended one of our militia meetings with his parents. Towards the end of the meeting the lad rose from his seat and asked to speak. We were surprised but welcomed him to say what he had in mind. Little Johnny walked to the front of the hall and showed us what he had created, something he called the New Vicksburg Diamond:

New Vicksburg
We Are – New Vicksburg – We Are
We Are One – New Vicksburg – We Are One
We Are One Voice – New Vicksburg – We Are One Voice
We Are One – New Vicksburg – We Are One
We Are – New Vicksburg – We Are
New Vicksburg

His simple words and diamond design forged a bond linking the people of New Vicksburg. His design and concept drew us close together with the mutual recognition that indeed, we were one: we were not Black or White but one; we were not male and female – but one.

After little John returned to his seat, others in the assembly also rose to speak. One after another words poured out that represented a unity of spirit, how we the residents of New Vicksburg had survived the Ripple Event and the more recent Epidemic. The words spoken that night were written down and later became what we now call the New Vicksburg Pledge – words recited each day by our children, whether home schooled or in town classrooms, repeated again at neighborhood gatherings, at social and professional clubs – and echoed before the call to order of each town meeting.

WE ARE ONE
One race – the human race
WE ARE ONE

Male and female – gender equal
WE ARE NEW VICKSBURG

We respect differences
We assist those in need
We defend our families, town, and region

WE ARE NEW VICKSBURG
WE ARE ONE

And so it has been from the sad solar cycles of the Ripple Event and Dark Time, into and through the Recovery Period that the New Vicksburg Pledge has served our community well. During the terror of the recent Epidemic, where the numbers of our residents were reduced to less than 300, our New Vicksburg Diamond and Pledge sustained and united us. During those darkest days we aided those community members in need and cared for the survivors.

We indeed were ONE – we were NEW VICKSBURG.

An astonishing story – an astonishing town.

***

Residential Solar Cycle One: A New Life

The southeastern arc of the Great River touched New Vicksburg (NV) at the confluence of the Yazoo River drainage system. The flatland of west NV regularly experienced annual flooding since the Ripple Event and Dark Time even until now, due to damaged levees that no longer could be repaired. The original Highway 61 running north-south through town had two names: the southern section was called Warrenton Road while to the north it was named Washington Street. The name change seemed not to matter to the residents of NV, since as survivors of many floods most had staked out their homes away from the river in the uplands east of the roadway system.

FEBRUARY: We were welcomed by all we met. Community leaders told us that we were helpful additions to the citizenry of New Vicksburg, and asked us to remain and help rebuild the community. We established our original residence near the American Civil War battlefield memorial park, near Willow and Hope Streets north of the Glass Bayou drainage system. Our new home was old but adequate. The frame structure predated the Ripple Event by many solar cycles. There was a storm cellar that allowed us to stockpile food and water-related supplies. On both sides of the house were vegetable and herb gardens; in the rear was ample space for raising fowl and livestock.

On the day we took occupancy of our new home, we were greeted by neighbors who welcomed us to the area. The hospitality shown us was typical of New Vicksburg: neighbors helping neighbors. Many of our new friends brought pans and crocks filled with foods to share. We were cautioned to be on the lookout in the neighborhood for dangerous animals, especially cottonmouth snakes, and toxic frogs and toads that sometimes could be pests in our gardens and even inside our house as well.

MARCH: Travis was accepted into the New Vicksburg Militia as adjunct advisor and met regularly with the commander and his staff. He was asked to debrief the officers regarding our experiences with the Northlanders. They especially wanted to hear of any experiences regarding groups of Wanderers who plied the lands of West and East Virginia, down the coast to Georgia, and into and across the flatlands of Alabama into western Mississippi.

APRIL: As my body changed, my attention focused on my pregnancy. I became a welcome guest at several local confabs where pregnant women gathered with older women who had delivered previously. These neighborhood meetings informed the first-time mothers-to-be about the ins and outs of the birthing process. Having delivered two children previously, I was aware of the procedures and assisted in providing positive information as well as I could. A wonderful birthing mentor/advisor named Martha Smith took me on as her charge. During the days of my pregnancy, we met frequently to share ideas and past experiences. My decision was to deliver at home. One day in the very early morning my time came once more. My birthing ceremony began, and all went well. Travis and I had a wonderful surprise: two new lives joined our family.

Travis and I were blessed by the emergence of twin girls on April 15th. We had suspected the possibility of multiple births but could not be certain. How many times we thought about names? And, just in case, we selected names for three girls and three boys but kept them in our hearts and announced them to no one. In accord with our Bison Camp traditions, we would not reveal the names to anyone until the ten day ceremony.

For ten days we marveled at the two lives that now joined our family unit. The pain of our past loss was replaced by the joy of our twins. All New Vicksburg residents were invited to join us in our happiness at the Naming Ceremony. Many attended: men and women of all ages, children and infants, all wished our twins long and happy lives. Came then the time to reveal the names and for the girls to be accepted as part of the New Vicksburg community. Travis and I stood before the assembly, each with one daughter in our arms:

I, Travis Sanders, mate of Reese Sanders, stand before you holding our new daughter: Laurel.

I, Reese Sanders, mate of Travis Sanders, stand before you holding our new daughter: Sage.

We then exchanged the girls and repeated our announcements.

All attending broke into loud cheers. Almost as one the guests cried out, again and again:

Sage and Laurel – Laurel and Sage

And softly at first, but then in unified tones rising higher and louder the New Vicksburg Pledge was recited: We are New Vicksburg – We are One.

Indeed, we were ONE with our community.

***

MAY: My life as a new mother was wonderful. With the delivery of our twins Sage and Laurel, my mentor/advisor Martha recommended that I join a new mother's nursing group. The one I selected consisted of eight newly delivered women from the community. We gathered daily and nursed our newborn infants upstairs at the old Health Department building on Main Street. We always began nursing our own infants and then after several minutes the rotation and exchange would begin where each of us would hold and nurse the adjacent infant. Sometimes the exchange proceeded clockwise, other times counterclockwise. We would do so until each new infant had been suckled by each of the new mothers.

While I had no previous experience at Bison Camp with such a custom of rotation and exchange, I remember that Travis once told me of a comparable system that he and his Data Collector team had encountered in northern old California where newly delivered women living near the Humboldt River met regularly to exchange milk samples and nurse the infants of their closest friends. The explanation for cross-nursing given by the old California women interviewed was that micro-components of mother's milk differed, due to environmental exposure and mother's diet, so that cross-nursing added further protection to the newborns, since any missing element would be shared and all infants would grow strong and healthy.

How this system had developed in New Vicksburg was unclear, but what assured that the custom would be maintained was knowledge of the survival rate of new babies during the recent Epidemic. When the Epidemic struck NV, Mary told me there were 78 infants and young children fewer than two solar cycles in age still nursing. The infants of mothers that cross-nursed, 32 in number – all survived. Those that did not cross-nurse – 46 in all – perished as a result of the Epidemic. It did not seem right to me that these 46 innocent children should be taken by the Epidemic merely because they were not cross-nursed. But it happened. As a result, each infant born in New Vicksburg since the Epidemic had been cross-nursed.

***

NOVEMBER: Daylight shortened as we approached the end of autumn and the beginning winter, and Travis and I spent more time together caring for our new babies. They were now seven months old and provided us with daily joy and wonder. After dinner when the girls were put to sleep, Travis and I sat together near our fireplace telling and re-telling stories and reliving memories of our early lives together, recalling the more recent events of our cross-continental trip. I told Travis again about my night-time experiences when we had camped along the Haelan Taehhen Run, where I had been visited by the messenger, the tale-telling troubadour or minstrel who had foretold my pregnancy and the delivery of two girls, and how the pain of the earlier loss of our children that once burdened my heart would be relieved. During evenings such as these we held each other and gazed deeply into the fireplace flames, lost in memory and love for each other.

***

Residential Solar Cycle Two: Growth and Development

MARCH: As our family flourished, we developed projects with our neighbors and other families within New Vicksburg, activities that focused on food storage and protection. Working together we established excess food drop-off depots within the Church Square area, a cluster of locations bounded on the north by First Street east and Farmer Street to the west. In this area, four religious structures – once regularly visited prior to the Ripple Event – had fallen into disuse as faith wavered during the Dark Time. The churches still had parishioners who attended occasionally, especially on celebratory feast days, but most remained unused. What we proposed and implemented was an area where residents could gather for social activities while at the same time dropping-off extra food for anyone needing food-related assistance.

***

MAY: Sage and Laurel had begun to talk, much to our amusement and pleasure. Shortly after their first birthday, both girls experienced typical bouts of childhood illnesses: colds, coughs, and what the New Vicksburgians called the sweats or hot-water-drips. As parents, Travis and I were concerned initially but local sage femmes provided additional care and advice so the girls recuperated quickly and our concerns passed.

***

JUNE: Travis continued his volunteer work with the New Vicksburg Militia, activities that involved short training and observational journeys into the nearby flatlands north and east of NV within the Mississippi River delta region. On one such trek, Travis traveled with the militia northeast up old Highway 49 through Satartia into Yazoo City, then over to the community of Greenwood. Their objective after reaching Greenwood was to reconnoiter and search areas to the west, past Moorhead into Indianola.

Travis showed me pages that he wrote in his militia daily logbook:

> *June 10th: Indianola was once the pride of Sunflower County, Old Mississippi. The main street, which runs east west just south of the West Prong Indian Bayou, is now an area filled with cypress stumps and reeds. Opposite the dark bayou waters is the courthouse where we camped on lands adjacent. The courthouse basement serves the few remaining residents of Indianola as a food depository, where town volunteers distribute edibles and safe beverages to those in need. I copied a sign spray-painted on the basement wall:*

I am sick and tired of being sick and tired!

I asked about the words and their meaning, but no one had any idea who wrote them, what the words meant, or why they were posted inside the courthouse basement. We spoke with both Black and White residents working in the food depository assisting those in need. We were informed that it made no difference to the needy whether or not the assistant helping to distribute the food was Black or White, since need in Indianola was color-blind

June 11th: We left Indianola along Highway 49W south towards Belzoni. We now were in the heart of the Mississippi River delta lands. We continued south towards Silver City, then branched off onto Highway 149 and headed towards Louise, a small but important town north east of what was known as the Delta National Forest. Our commander believed that at Louise we might obtain information regarding the location of safe-havens used by the Mississippi River Pirates. We had learned earlier from local policing organizations at Belzoni that the River Pirates sometimes holed up and hid out in the environs around Louise. Our militia commander told us the town's history. Before the Ripple Event, the community had been a tri-ethnic society: Asian, Black, and White. Segregation or ethnic separation, as the practice then was called, once ran deep through Louise. National Civil Rights Legislation passed in the early 1960s (old solar cycle calculation) attempted to halt ethnic discrimination in Louise but failed as the White residents resisted. Parents removed their children from the well-constructed brick schoolhouses within the boundaries of the community and enrolled them in trailers rather than let their children attend school together with Black children. The Lee family, originally from China, operated a flourishing grocery store in Louise. Other Chinese living in Louise served as middlemen when conducting business between Blacks and Whites. Since the Ripple Event and Dark Time, Louise had languished and then the community was hit by the terrible Epidemic that further reduced its population.

June 12th: We used this day to reconnoiter Louise and to speak with residents regarding River Pirate locations. All of the interviews were negative. One surviving relic of past solar cycles, however, attracted my eye – the remains of a small shelter located on the west side of Main Street not far from Midnight Road. Stepping inside the structure, I saw rows of wooden shelving. One Louise resident told me that back in what she called the olden days, this small building was the bus stop office where some families in Louise had attempted to create a tiny library to be used by Black school children long before the Ripple Event. It seems that there were no facilities for after-school reading at the schools in town for any children of the three races. The library was built by good people, but was destroyed shortly after the Ripple Event during the early solar cycles of the Dark Time.

June 13th: We left Louise via a southwest track and entered the Delta National Forest region to search for caves, dug-outs, and hideaways that might shelter the River Pirates. We found remnants of about a dozen such shelters along with scattered heaps of discarded garbage, indicative of the River Pirate lifestyle, but all had fled – probably upon receiving advance notice of our intent and arrival from one or more of their compatriots living in Louise.

June 15th: We exited the forest area and returned to New Vicksburg along Highway 61.

Travis told me that since their search had been negative, future excursions would be necessary.

***

SEPTEMBER: During our second solar cycle of residence in New Vicksburg, I became more and more active with neighbors. Working together we formed the New Vicksburg women's Militia auxiliary. Our purpose was to work with young girls to provide medical advice on age-appropriate topics: coming-of-age, contraception, diet quality, importance of exercise and body care, and other related topics. We were supported in these efforts by NV mothers and fathers. Presentations on these topics were given at different locations, at settlement groups in the vicinity of New Vicksburg, and at the various satellite schools within the town boundaries. Another area where our auxiliary members were active was offering and supporting programs where self-defense was taught to girls and women of all ages. We stressed self-protection and offered specific techniques and training of what to do if confronted by aggressive Wanderers or any others bent upon pillage and personal attack.

DECEMBER: Travis and I relished and enjoyed play and education time with our children. They now were quite active and required considerable attention. We watched them grow, play, and grapple about on the floor of our residence. These play-times where the girls interacted together, brought back memories of our own childhoods at Bison Camp in far distant old Montana, a long ago time perhaps, but the memories still were fresh.

***

Residential Solar Cycle Three: Education and Exploration

APRIL: Birthdays on April 15th were celebrated with good food, presents, and neighbor visits. The girls were growing in stature and in independence. Sometimes their explorations of nearby gardens led to bee stings and other insect bites but Sage and Laurel seemed to flourish as they examined flowers, stems, and fruits of different food crops emerging in spring. Our evenings were spent together as a family unit, stoking the fireplace and lying about on cushions relating everyday activities, usually finishing with a long story that either Travis or I would tell about growing up in the Big Hole Valley.

With the help of several clever neighbors, we learned how to create different types of musical instruments, from simple flutes to pole-peg, one string, rababa-like sounders, even hard-wood sounding clappers. What Sage and Laurel liked most, however, were the different drums that Travis made. Some they pounded using the flat of their hands. They liked the larger ones best, since they could be made to thump and resound by using a large padded stick. We would take turns identifying our favorite songs, which seemed to change almost monthly. Travis encouraged the girls to make up their own songs. Most were nonsensical but on occasion the words bit deep into our hearts, as when Sage created what she called *The Good-by Song* in memory of her playmate Jessica Freeman, who died unexpectedly after collapsing during play. Most of their songs, however, dealt with cats, dogs, and stray chickens, and racing about trying to catch them.

***

JUNE: Day after day Travis worked through the heat and humidity of summer. After especially hard days he would bathe in the cool spring that ran past our house. One evening he started coughing and shivering, but he recovered after several days of rest. Two days later, however, Laurel became ill with the same symptoms, followed by Sage later that day. Joyce Nenkin, our neighbor *sage femme*, visited and examined the twins that now were experiencing hot sweats during the day, followed by evenings of cold chills. Joyce had not seen this condition previously in New Vicksburg children and requested that no others be admitted inside our house. She prepared a strict order for treatment that we needed to follow: during the hot sweats – the girls were to be given cool water and a list of three foods, specifically, beef jerky, hard boiled eggs, and black-eyed peas. If the chills resumed at night the children were to be wakened and administered to. Nighttime recommendations included warm water heated previously during the day to a high temperature using solar reflectors, along with thin slices of bread crust, lettuce leaves, and crushed blackberries. Joyce identified the treatment as the *Hot-Cold Variable* set within what she called the SO – or signature of opposites. We were unsure of the validity of the practice but trusted her wisdom. After two days with this treatment regimen, Sage and Laurel were up and about and getting into mischief as usual. We had no idea what caused their illnesses, but the origin clearly was related to the ills their father experienced and had been transmitted to our twins.

***

AUGUST: The New Vicksburg Militia commander announced the continuation of rumblings of social and administrative discontent across the Great River due west of NV within the Louisiana section of the TAR Configuration. This vast region called Texas Across the River included portions of old Arkansas, Louisiana, Oklahoma, Texas, and extended even further west into old New Mexico and north into old Colorado. The TAR component that covered an area from just north of Greenville then south past New Vicksburg towards Natchez, had become unsettled due to sporadic raids by Wanderers.

Our NV Militia commander received a request from the militia at Monroe, old Louisiana, to attend a meeting to develop a unified position on how to deal with this problem. Travis was asked to participate. On August 8th the New Vicksburg Militia team crossed the Great River. From there they followed the route of old Highway 80 through Thomastown, Tallulah, Waverly, into Delhi where they camped. The next morning they left for Rayville and, upon arrival, they were met by members of the Monroe Militia.

Travis told me later that during the planning sessions they heard very difficult and disturbing news. Four or five clusters of Wanderers – each group numbering from 50 to 70 members – swarmed out of their hideout in the Ouachita Forest region between Bastrop and Huttig. These bandits spread outward like an evil oil seep, attacking settlement groups, robbing and pillaging. Afterwards, they retreated into the Ouachita Forest. Travis reported that discussions continued for hours but with little consensus as what to do or how to go about eliminating this scourge until a member of the Rayville Militia, Jefferson Dixon, stood and asked to be heard:

> *As you know my father and grandfathers were religious and knew the history of the once Holy Land nearly by heart. There was a time, my grandfather used to say, that armed soldiers on horseback known as Crusaders, encamped on a hill called the Horns of Hattin, thinking that they could look out and see any attackers approaching. What these Crusaders didn't realize, however, was how their enemy through careful stealth and deception, surrounded the base of the hill, and then set fire at the same time to the surrounding brush, creating a ring of fire that swept upward towards the heights, trapping many Crusaders. Those who attempted to escape easily were captured as they cascaded down the hill in their attempts to avoid the flames. If the fire didn't get them, they fell to the attackers swords. Why don't we do the same? We have sufficient militia and potential additional fighters from the nearby settlement groups at Bastrop, Bonita, Farmersville, and Hutting. With this many fighters we could encircle the Ouachita and burn out the Wanderers. What think you?*

Jefferson Dickson's suggestion was received with interest, and a plan was developed to coordinate forces.

***

OCTOBER: The combined militia plan was set for mid-week, October 13th. The New Vicksburg contingent crossed the Great River in force and joined the other local militias. Reconnaissance revealed the Wanderer enclave was located north of Finch Lake in a region just to the west of Glaze Creek. The slow-flowing waters of Glaze Creek formed the eastern boundary of the planned encirclement. West of Finch Lake, the militias from Rayville and Monroe linked up and formed the boundary. Well-trained settlement group militias from Matrion, Litroe, and Hutting completed the encirclement of the Ourachita Forest lands to the north. The Wanderers had no exits for escape. The plan was implemented and the fires lit.

That which followed became part of local lore and history. Just as the attackers crushed the Crusader forces at the Battle of Hattin, our combined militias forced the Wanderers into two choices: death by flames or surrender and execution. And so it was that the Wanderers in this region of northeastern old Louisiana/southern old Arkansas ceased to exist. Good people had prevailed and no longer lived under the threat of attack, pillage, and death. The militias of Louisiana, Arkansas, and Mississippi had worked together for the protection of all who believed in peace, justice, and stability.

***

NOVEMBER: During the autumn months two of my neighbors, Betty Adams and Yolanda Perkins, formed a group in New Vicksburg inviting teenage girls and boys interested in culture and history to join in group projects. Their purpose was to show young people the importance of town, settlement group, and personal family history. I joined later and together we encouraged older residents to speak to the youngsters. Our primary task was to share ideas and methods how to keep good records for future generations to know about the events and activities that characterized our region.

***

DECEMBER: In this month our community of New Vicksburg was struck by a series of terrible tornadoes. We took refuge in our storm cellar. While our home was not destroyed, others in town lost not only their dwellings but most of their worldly goods. The winds tore a northwest/southeast path, ripping structures especially south of Clay Street and a parallel track on either side of Mission. Sadly, twenty of our residents died during the two days of terrible storms.

Our community struggled through this difficult time. Travis and I helped families the best we could. We invited eight families who had lost their homes to stay with us. We opened our home, our gardens, and outbuildings for community use. Working together we helped the unfortunates salvage what they could and find any precious family mementoes. We worked together: we were New Vicksburg Strong. All over town images of the New Vicksburg Diamond appeared.

New Vicksburg
We Are – New Vicksburg – We Are
We Are One – New Vicksburg – We Are One
We Are One Voice – New Vicksburg – We Are One Voice
We Are One – New Vicksburg – We Are One
We Are – New Vicksburg – We Are
New Vicksburg

In times of trouble we volunteered and assisted our neighbors. We were indeed New Vicksburg – we were One.

***

Residential Solar Cycle 4: Northern Reconnaissance: I

JANUARY: During the early winter months I continued home-schooling Laurel and Sage. They are sweet kids, active and able, getting into this and that, but bringing joy to both Travis and me. Some days Travis worked at home where he also overlooked the children's activities. This allowed me time outside the house to continue with my volunteer work. I remained active at the recycle shop up beyond Halls Ferry Road near Drummond Street. I also enjoyed interactions with the women at the Oldster Home, speaking with survivors of the Ripple Event and Epidemic, learning how they and their families and neighbors worked together to assist those in need.

Two of the oldsters thought that they owed their longevity to a lifetime of drinking filtered Big Muddy water – a term they used in laughter when describing the Great River or Mississippi. But there had to be other reasons for their survival, since everybody in New Vicksburg drank Big Muddy water prior to the Ripple Event, and more than 95 percent of the residents had died. Their survival had to be based upon their previous overall good health, the longevity of their parents and grandparents, keeping their wits about them, and overall good luck.

***

FEBRUARY: Usually after a good morning chat with folks at the recycle shop or Oldster Home I assisted ladies preparing the eats and drinks for sharing. There always was enough for all as the good citizens of New Vicksburg regularly donated extra foods to stock the Oldster Home larder. Working together in the kitchen with the ladies I learned recipes and cooking skills – tricks they called them – how to pan-fry vegetables just the right way so not to burn or singe the delicate peppers and okra pods, then how to prepare and mix just the right number of ingredients to create sauces of wonderful consistency and flavor. I must say that most of the elderly women shared their recipes, but not Jane Beltzer. She guarded her recipes as if she were protecting a stockpile of barter ingots. When it was her turn to work in the kitchen preparing meals, we would gather around to watch, but she would shoo us out – always with a smile. With wave of her delicate hands, she would utter a spew of words that always made us laugh:

> *Look dearies, you ain't cum'in to get my bamia button recipe; I learnt it from my mother who learnt it from hers and so on back into the dawn of time. But I tell you this: when I pass, I have a will – don't they say where there is a will there is a way? And in that will, I have listed the ingredients for my bamia buttons. So when you make it that first time after I have passed, remember this: I'll be watching y'all – with a grand smile. Oh, my bamia buttons; got'a be the best as ya'all know. So shoo out the door and let me cook – then we'll dine together.*

***

MARCH: With the end of winter and emergence of the spring wild flowers, there came a hardship to our family. The New Vicksburg Militia asked Travis to join them on a northern reconnaissance trek up river into old Tennessee. As outlined at the militia headquarters and repeated at Town Hall meetings, the expedition would take three months with members departing on the equinox and returning on or about the summer solstice. The objective was to again seek out and destroy the security bases of the River Pirates that remained active along the eastern shore of the Great River. Most of the River Pirate attacks were within a geographical area extending from Greenville north towards Memphis across the border into old Tennessee. The objective was to root out the River Pirates and demolish their hillside hideouts to prevent any extension of their terror activities south of Greenville towards New Vicksburg. The militia plan was to include members from Greenville and nearby Rosedale to join in the trek north to the Tennessee border where other units from Lakeview also would join forces. Memphis, in turn, would send a contingent south to meet us as well. The objective of our tri-prong approach was to rid the east bank of the Mississippi River once and for all of the River Pirates that had caused so much havoc during recent solar cycles.

So it would be that Travis was absent from our household for three months. While I supported these militia activities I was lonely, and the twins missed their father dearly.

***

APRIL-JUNE: Travis wrote daily in his militia logbook:

April 15th: Birthdays for S&L: how your daddy misses both of you.

April 16th: We approached the River Pirate cave shelters north of Rosedale before dawn. Our scouts signaled some activity around their low ember cooking fires. The militia unit from Greenville circled north and east to cut off any RP retreat in these directions while our New Vicksburg units presented a solid line along the south. The attack signal was given and we engaged. The fighting was fierce. Both sides took casualties: in total we suffered two killed and 28 wounded while we killed 29 RPs and captured 78. Inside one of the cave retreats we discovered a stash of RP loot: storage trunks filled with the highest quality barter tokens made from iron and steel. Other cave sites served as arsenals, and we counted numerous sabers, dirks, bows and quivers along with arrows tipped with toxic pastes. Inside one such hideout was a locked area that we opened: inside were five captives chained to posts. Two of the prisoners were young women who had been terribly abused for nearly two full solar cycles. Both the women and three men had been forced by the RPs to perform unspeakable tasks. We released them from their chains and tended to their medical needs. It fell to our responsibility to reunite these poor souls with family members – after we first dealt with our captives.

The RP prisoners were roped together, their hands tied, and we marched them to the river's edge. Within our militia groups several members previously had served as local or regional judges. A five-person tribunal was established along the riverbank and the RPs each given the opportunity to recount their deeds and recant, offer apologies, or atone for their vile, violent acts. Of those offered to do so, 14 of the 78 spoke – mostly garbled garbage about how life was hard and the only way to survive was to take from others and if doing so caused casualties and if we killed some river boat passengers or homeowner's family member, well that was just too bad because, they had much and we had little so we took from them in order to survive.

Such stupidities were not impressive.

The tribunal members took less than five minutes to decide their fate. The remaining 64 next were offered a final opportunity to say any last words, Most remained silent resigned to their fate, while a few broke into song. Still others laughed, while several shouted out that we had no right to be their judge and executioner and demanded they be brought to Memphis to stand trial in a real court. We dealt with all 78 quickly and decisively; no more would this group raid, rob, and kill. After all was said and done, we buried their bodies in a common grave just east of Levee Road and west of Highway 1. We left no sign on the grave, no marker to tell others passing by that these evil people ever had lived.

***

May 3rd: I remembered from my music schoolteachers at Bison Camp that the river town of Memphis was famous for different types and styles of music, blue grass, blues, cake walk, ragtime, and other styles. Now we had arrived. The once great city had suffered terribly during the Dark Time and even more so during the recent Epidemic. Our militia entry into Memphis from the south took us past several isolated lakes, among them Robco, and McKellar. Our colleagues with the Memphis Militia recommended that we encamp inside the town at Robert Church Park, south of Beale Street. I know that I can speak for my fellow militia members that we all are tired and would welcome a few days rest before taking on further assignments.

An evening meal around the campfire. In the distance further west along Beal Street words of songs could be heard, lyrics from the heart telling of drunken intoxication, of lost love, all set within the peculiar strumming and shouting of the blues style performer:

> *Oh, dig my grave both wide and deep*
> *Place marble at my head and feet*
> *And on my breast a snow white turtle dove*
> *To sig-ni-fy I died for love.*

And another ...

We could hear the old folks singing
As she said farewell to me
Far across the fields of cotton
My old homestead I could see
When the moon rose in its glory
Then I told life's sweetest story
To the girl I loved in sunny Tennessee.

I remember that Reese and I had heard other such lyrics as we trekked through the Blue Ridge and portions of Georgia and Alabama, sung in a myriad of ways. But the Memphis sound seemed to resonate more in my mind – perhaps because I was deadly tired, or perhaps because of events experienced so far on our militia trek and campaign against the River Pirates.

***

June 2nd: Our River Pirate campaign north of Memphis was successful. We trapped four different bands inside the great loop of the Mississippi River south of New Madrid, old Kentucky. What an unusual location. Here, the Great River flows in a series of unusual directions. At Columbus, Kentucky, the river flows south directly towards Hickman, then turns west and within a short distance abruptly turns south, and then immediately north towards New Madrid, then west, and south once again. This double loop encompasses two marshy flatlands bisected by the boundary that once separated the states of old Kentucky and Tennessee.

The River Pirates did not practice sound military judgment, since the great loop with New Madrid at the north easily could be barricaded by our troops to prevent southern escape. Our plan, therefore, essentially was strangulation – a constriction of any potential escape outlet – and we were successful. We killed 273 and captured an additional 468. We were tired by this time and the decision was made by our collective militia leaders to ship the prisoners across the river to New Madrid and let the courts there determine their fate. Given that the Pirates had attacked and harassed New Madrid for more than 10 solar cycles, we could expect that justice would be quick and sharp-edged.

***

June 15th: We now were finished with the objectives of our northern trek and came time to plan our return to New Vicksburg. We contracted with a local shipping company at New Madrid – Kentucky Flat Boats – and secured a float barge. Ours was a grand one, a double-decker with considerable room to suspend hammocks for easy sleeping as we drifted south towards home. The RP loot we retrieved was divided among the various militias, then each militia allocated fair shares to their own members. My share was rather astonishing: the barter tokens given me numbered 32 (steel), 28 (iron), 14 (bronze), 22 (copper), and 16 (aluminum), along with 14 sabers, 6 dirks, and a banjo – an instrument that I learned to play while aboard our barge. Each member of the New Vicksburg Militia had performed their duties well and with honor. We now return home to our families with the knowledge that we had rid the Great River of the slimy human animals known as River Pirates.

***

Residential Solar Cycle 5: Education and Personal Growth

APRIL: Home schooling started in earnest the week of April 15th, three days after their birthdays. Both Sage and Laurel already had learned their letters and had mastered rudimentary writing. Through selected use of texts available within New Vicksburg, Travis and I also used basic educational units to identify woodland animal and plant identifications, counting and number groupings, with special attention to proper behaviors and social interactions. Together, along with other neighborhood children, I led walks in and about New Vicksburg, sharing both obvious and less-apparent observations. We noted how streets were aligned by cardinal directions, sometimes parallel with the Great River, but at other times the street patterns were irregular revealing that they followed old stream beds that wove in and about through town. On these town treks, as we called them, we identified different trees, how they could be distinguished by bark, leaf, and overall shape: the tall tapering pines, the rotund and irregular oaks, and how and why they grew in certain locations and not in others.

I taught our girls and other children plant knowledge and safety, which species growing in vacant lots and along the edges of the woodland and park areas could be eaten in emergencies, and which must be avoided because they were poisonous. I taught them that a bitter taste was not always the criteria for toxicity, since some sweet-tasting and sweet-smelling plants could kill if accidentally consumed. Together we studied the nesting patterns of birds, and soon the children could differentiate the calls of spotted sparrows from bright red tanagers or from the warble of bluebirds. We listened to the rapid piercing-hammering sound of woodpeckers, and the unusual gobbling noises of an occasional wild turkey. These were all techniques that could assure survival if hard times came again once more.

On these educational walks, we also overturned rotten logs and watched the white, black, and spotted grubs grovel and the insects scatter. Occasionally we interrupted the sleep of frogs, toads, even salamanders. The students were taught to identify safe from toxic foods – if ever the need be. Their field identification education also included poisonous animals. We taught them to differentiate slippery gopher snakes from dangerous copperheads, cottonmouths, and rattlesnakes. Being able to differentiate two types of snakes by color combination/sequence was critical, since two in the New Vicksburg region looked very much alike and had the same colors. One was known as the banded milk snake, while the deadly toxic one was the banded coral snake. At quick glance, the two side by side appeared similar, but even our youngsters at this early age could see the differences upon closer inspection. We taught our charges to remember the old phrases:

Red color next to black – friend of Jack
Red color next to yellow – a bad fellow

It was most interesting to watch the social interactions of the children both at home and with others. We did not see at first the emergence of gender-related behaviors: both the boys and girls fought over access to specific books, supplies, and toys. Both genders were highly competitive. We built upon this observation to reinforce gender equality and, even at this early age, we shared leadership skills where they would alternate in leading songs, taking leads in playtime activities, and, most interesting, we observed that they shared foods together. This last issue I remembered myself doing long ago as a child, when my mother would pack lunch for me that contained items I didn't like. During the lunchtime break I would seek out friends and we would exchange items, and share bites of foods that one liked but the other did not.

We teachers stressed self- and group-respect and at the beginning and end of each school day we had our charges recite the New Vicksburg Diamond and Pledge. We agreed that even at their young age, the children in our charge should hear and learn the words of the Great Septet. While they would not understand the context at their age, the telling and re-telling of the content was as important in their education as it was to us back in Bison Camp:

Aid the weak and helpless;
Treat women and men equally;
Appreciate differences;
Reject behaviors that degrade or harm others;
Welcome each newborn to the family hearth;
Respect and honor your mating partner;
Celebrate those who have helped you through life's passages.

***

OCTOBER–DECEMBER: As autumn merged into the colder days of winter rain, we introduced our students to food preservation skills: how to do so safely, how to extend limited food supplies, and reduce spoilage. Beginning by age four and certainly by age five, the children already had accompanied their parents on plant collecting and hunting trips, and had participated in planting and harvesting foods from household gardens. We requested of each child's parents that they take the lead in showing their children the necessary techniques how to butcher wild game and domesticated livestock, how to dry and store meats, vegetables, and fruits for use throughout the winter months, and especially how to keep family food larders and other storage areas free from vermin and mold. All in all we repeated what Travis and I had been taught during our earliest solar cycles of schooling back in Bison Camp.

***

Residential Solar Cycle 6: Friendship Building

FEBRUARY: This bitter cold month saw a terrible tragedy. Several of Sage and Laurel's playmates went down to the edge of the Great River to play on the chunks of ice that had accumulated along the bank. Tossing objects back and forth and jumping from one ice piece to another were simple games that all had participated in at different times during the winter. But this time was different: little Carlie Whithers slipped and fell into the cold dark waters. The belt of her jacket caught on a submerged tree branch and, as she attempted to release herself, the chunks of ice slipped and dragged her down into the darkness.

The farewell ceremony for Carlie Whithers was held at her parent's home and attended by several hundred residents. Travis and I arrived early to help organize the food and beverage tables and to assist the bereaved parents. Came time for the pre-meal words of condolence. Several of Carlie's friends including Sage and Laurel spoke of the joy of being her friend and how they would miss her. The children's words were followed by those offered by several neighbor families. Carlie's mother and father offered thanks to those attending for being such good friends at this difficult time.

The sealed coffin holding the body was carried to the cemetery by horse-drawn carriage. Along the way, slowly moving through the streets of New Vicksburg, people paused in respect as the carriage passed. Many residents upon observing the death carriage bowed their heads in silence, remembering how the Epidemic had taken their children from them too early.

***

APRIL: The twins now were approaching commemoration of the 5th solar cycle of their birth. Sage and Laurel had established a broad network of friends, both boys and girls, and one of these was Adam Lange, son of Fisher Lange. During after school time the group commonly met on the green up near the ancient war memorial lands, where they explored and ran about. Once or twice a week the play group specifically was organized by two or three parents where self-protection and defensive skills were practiced. These were not easy sessions and sometimes injuries resulted. The key, however, was to instill in the children clear understandings that they would be obliged to participate in the defense of home, neighborhood, and town as necessary when they reached maturity.

A parallel tradition that evolved during the Recovery Period in New Vicksburg was implemented on each child's 5th birthday, when they would be presented with a suite of self-defense weapons. These typically included a saber, matched in accord with the celebrant's height, a military-style dirk, two skinning knives, and a weight-balanced hatchet. Such coming-of-age weapons were produced locally from steel ingots imported from New Birmingham and forged appropriately by New Vicksburg smiths at their various businesses located along Rigby Street. Finished examples of the weapons commonly were displayed at several shops along Oak Street. The display cases in the windows always attracted the young children of New Vicksburg heading for playtime at the nearby city park.

A week before the twins' birthday, Travis took them to the forge managed by Preston Emory, a friend from the New Vicksburg Militia. Together they watched Preston take three ingots and begin to hammer them into a saber blade, pounding with a small sledge, immersing the block into water for tempering, then back into the roaring forge to reheat – time and time again, and again – until the saber blade took form and was finished.

Travis told our daughters:

> *Sage and Laurel, each of you will have one of these on your 5th birthday. But with this gift there are five strict requirements and obligations:*
>
> *1. These are not toys but defense weapons;*
> *2. Develop your defensive skills using only practice weapons and only under the guidance of your weapon master;*
> *3. You are required to support and defend the New Vicksburg Diamond and Pledge;*
> *4. Never draw your saber from its scabbard, except to defend yourself, your family, your home, your neighborhood, or town;*
> *5. Protect and honor your saber – it is your companion – there may come a time when it will save your life.*

***

MAY: During rest periods between teaching and working in New Vicksburg, I found time to write in my daily diary:

> *May 9th: This day the twins were at home with six or seven of their close friends and it started: the behavior that sometimes can drive teachers and parents nearly mad: joyful voices at first but then the words start. Is such behavior typical of all children when they group together, where parents and other adults must tolerate certain songs that go on, and on, and on, with their nearly nonsensical lyrics? Children, especially Sage and Laurel, like these songs, and I expect that each parent in New Vicksburg has suffered through the words time after time, as well, for once these songs start they are long time finishing. The sing-song pattern refrains remain in the adult's brain for hours after the children have found other activities to do. You know them – how can you not?*
>
> > *Do your ears hang low ...*
> > *Old Macdonald had a farm ...*

Once a farmer had a dog, and Bingo was his name ...
Row, row, row your boat ...

But perhaps the worst offenders were songs that produced temporary madness in parents and untold joy when finished:

There's a hole in the bottom of the sea ...
The ants go marching one by one ...

***

JUNE–AUGUST: With the onset of summer new family tasks were at hand. There was archery practice then training in slingshot proficiency, with safety lanes and targets set up inside the enclosure of our backyard. Travis and I took turns organizing special trips into the nearby forest regions with the girls and their several friends. He demonstrated how to construct deadfalls and noose traps to obtain food during hard times. On other trips Travis had the children pretend that they were out of water, and he showed them how to prepare the reflective solar panels to heat water of questionable quality to sufficient temperature to render it drinkable. I also participated in such training, and led weekly trips in and about New Vicksburg where we examined the summer wild plants and taught the twins and their friends which ones can be used for food only, medicine only, as food or medicine as necessary, or to be avoided at all costs.

***

SEPTEMBER: Both Sage and Laurel had grown stronger and now they were tall for their age. While just five solar cycles old, they were lean, wiry, and fast runners with good stamina. Both girls became adept in the kitchen, and both wanted to learn how to cook. Travis and I experienced – as most families have done so – the preparation of first meals created by their children. The girls planned the menu and told us to stay out of the kitchen unless asked to assist. We took our places at the family dining table as the girls brought in their dinner creation: a central platter consisting of a bed of river rice mixed with autumn berries. Balanced upon the rice was a meat product that we did not recognize. The thick slab was punctured by four skewers and suspended over the rice mixture. Sage asked Travis to remove the skewers and to place the meat slab onto a second plate, whereupon Laurel poured a red chili-tomato based sauce over the meat. The girls then asked Travis to slice the sauce-covered slab cross-wise to make individual portions. As he did so, a surprise was revealed. Inside the crusty red-sauced meatloaf, shelled hard-boiled eggs had been inserted which produced a four-color dish. It tasted delicious. Thereafter, we of the Saunders family clan would call this interesting and tasty concoction KBSE, or Key-Bob Super-Eyes. While our family would know what these letters meant, they might be a real "surprise" to others.

***

NOVEMBER: There comes a time of recognition in all families where food is either grown or hunted the realization that animals are alive and to hunt for food means to kill. The recognition also can be applied to the plant kingdom. While picking berries may not kill the plant, certainly extracting and ripping root vegetables from the ground or slicing the tops of leafy vegetables also causes death of the plant. Still, hunger must be solved, otherwise death of the hungry follows.

Laurel was the first to ask Travis if she could accompany him on a deer hunt. While making preparations before departure, he sat with Laurel and explained the four-fold concept of mutual respect: humans towards other humans, humans towards animals, animals towards humans, and animals towards other animals. He showed Laurel the differences in animal tooth patterns, how the shape of individual teeth could be used to classify three types of large meat animals: herbivores that ate plants, carnivores that ate meat, and omnivores who ate both plants and other animals. Travis also showed her that certain plants, especially some varieties located down by branches of the Stout or Hennessey Bayous, actually fed on tiny animals by enticing flying insects that became trapped in their sticky hooded cup-like structures. Even insects such as spiders ate other flying-flitting creatures, and did so to stay alive. He explained how hooves vs. claws were other markers that distinguished animals. Carnivores had claws to grasp and hold their animal prey, whereas the hooves of cattle, goats, and horses in turn, showed no grasping ability and their teeth also reflected that they ate plants.

Travis told Laurel that the key during hunting was to show respect, not to take more animal lives than necessary to feed self, family, or neighbors. By showing respect and minimizing death, the animals in turn flourished, and the numbers kept in check by hunting maintained a unique balance across the wooded areas and plains.

Travis told me that he stopped his educational comments at this point, not wanting to continue down the slippery slope of why humans throughout history have killed so many of their own kind, since wars certainly were not implemented to assure ecological balance.

And so it was that Laurel, with the advice and help of her father, Travis, completed a successful deer hunt. Her first arrow flew true into the chest of the four-pronged buck, which staggered twice and fell. Reaching the fallen animal, Laurel spoke the traditional Bison Camp words of animal respect:

With respect I end your life
The flesh of your body will sustain me
I thank you for your gift of life
The flesh of your body will sustain me

***

Residential Solar Cycle 7: Revival of New Vicksburg Culture

FEBRUARY–APRIL: By the sixth cycle of a child's age, there were few if any gender secrets. They have learned much in their respective play groups, and shared and exchanged information on all subjects. Travis and I took our educational responsibilities to Sage and Laurel seriously, and held family meetings to explain what we called *Life Wonders*. After our second meeting on this topic both girls asked:

Why are you and dad explaining all this to us? We know all about it.

March signaled the near arrival of spring, and soon to follow would be the twins' 6th birthday, outdoor barbeques, neighborhood potluck dinners, and community dance and athletic competitions.

By the 6th solar cycles of life, most children in New Vicksburg would lose their first tooth – a central incisor. Sage and Laurel had many friends their age who, when they smiled, would point to the special gap and missing tooth as a sort of honor badge. When Laurel's front tooth loosened, followed two days later by Sage's, we decided to implement a ceremony of our own. We taught the girls to wash their hands and to start wiggling what they called *The Loose One*. Then about five days later as we sat together at the dining room table, the girls would recite the words they had created:

Wiggle front and back then side by side
It doesn't really hurt
Wiggle hard and open wide
Do it now and yank it out

Two so-called baby teeth now glistened on the oak dining table. Both girls burst into smiles and laughter. Slowly but surely they were coming of age. I took the extracted teeth and had them drilled through, then strung on a thin gold chain. I would wear these first lost teeth forever to commemorate the joy of seeing our daughters grow and develop. They will be part of my funeral garb when the time comes for my passing.

***

MAY: Now being six solar cycles old, the twins were eligible to compete for the first time in the GPR – the Great Perimeter Run. This was an annual New Vicksburg event, sometimes called the RTC (Running The Circuit), the perimeter of Battlefield Memorial Park, a distance of approximately 10 kilo-miles. Children between the ages of six and ten ran a portion of the course, a distance of one kilo-mile. The race always started on the north side of Mint Spring then continued north and across the top of the park, down the full length of the east side to Bugle Ridge, then north again until Sky Farm Avenue was reached, then the contestants would proceed west and cross the narrows of Confederate Avenue back to the south shore of Mint Spring, and finally end at the National Cemetery Monument.

Both adults and children of New Vicksburg and those from surrounding settlement groups were invited to participate in the GPR. Even at the age of only six solar cycles, Sage and Laurel competed well. They came in third and fourth, respectively, in their age group. Sage took third and was only ten slow counts behind the first place boy – Adam Lange. Although the twins and Adam had participated in the same play group earlier in their lives, as a result of this first Great Perimeter run, Sage started to take a fancy to Adam.

***

JUNE–SEPTEMBER: Throughout the remainder of the solar cycles, we watched the slow change of our daughters into responsible young girls. They tended without complaint to their pet birds, cats, and dogs, and readily helped around the house. One or the other commonly would take me aside and ask questions about body changes and what to expect, and especially what expectations would be if they began to like boys such as Adam Lange or another. Slowly but surely the twins were coming-of-age.

***

After-Word

As the weeks progressed through summer, and into fall, Travis and I both thought it appropriate to take the girls to the annual New Vicksburg mate re-commitment ceremony held overlooking the Great River near Clay Street at Catfish Row Park.

It was considered customary to dress appropriately for such ceremonies. Those participating were decked out in the customary mating garb of their ancestors and distant relatives, and were required to walk through the streets of New Vicksburg where they accepted the cheers and wishes for good fortune from the residents. Those who wished to support the couples could arrive at the ceremonial site by other means, walking, carriage, or on horseback.

We attended the ceremony as a family and experienced the re-commitment of seven mate couples. Words were spoken, followed by laying on of hands, and exchanges of necklaces and rings. At the conclusion, each couple spoke the New Vicksburg re-commitment oath:

I dedicate my life to you my mate who I will cherish forever
Through the good and bad times, more good than bad
I commit my body, heart, and mind to our union
From this day forward we continue as one
May it ever be so

***

Ijano Esantu Eleman

Interlude-Conversation:10
And a Little Child

***

K'Aser, I am so pleased the child's concept was understood and taken to heart by the people of New Vicksburg.

Taken to heart and practiced. New Vicksburg will prevail – grow and prosper well into the coming times. In this instance a child did lead them, perhaps aided by the communities general awareness of Vicksburg's past travails.

Some – sadly a minority – do learn and profit from history. May Etowah grant more of our people to do so.

We may direct our efforts to assist with this. Conflict and bloodshed increasingly trouble me. Trouble me almost to anger.

So I've noticed – this is not your way, K'Aser. This I know as well as you.

While there is much to come that I shall find bothersome, at the very least, we – I – will have no concerns for New Vicksburg or its people. Etowah be praised for this.

As well as more.

Chapter 11

Mississippi Sojourn: New Vicksburg

Part II

Pre-Note

What factors characterize families, communities, and nations? Common experiences? Common goals and objectives? Common cultures? Common values? Why are some successful and others not? What differences form the wedges that break apart families, communities, and nations? Disrespect? Indifference? Ignorance?

Why do some towns and cities erupt into chaos and mass violence? Why are others peaceful, where individuals exhibit respect and offer aid to one another? Why have some towns imploded with terrible civil conflicts, while others like New Vicksburg – once with strong internal and cultural differences – developed as vibrant, progressive centers?

Is all this by chance? Is it chance or fate that determines who lives and who dies? Why do some communities remain united while others implode? Some nations remain united despite strong internal differences, while others rush towards the precipice of self-destruction like mindless lemmings.

It commonly is said that time heals.

Perhaps.

It might better be said that people of good will – despite differences – can co-exist and forge strong bonds of mutual respect if they wish to do so. It is their choice. People need not resort to the darkness that characterizes some minds and administrations. How was it possible that one little boy, Johnny Thompson, set into motion an idea and graphic design that was adopted as the New Vicksburg Diamond? Thompson used only six words but these six, set within his design, created an image that deeply touched the hearts and minds of New Vicksburg residents who abandoned past differences. By working together, they developed and embraced the Pledge:

WE ARE NEW VICKSBURG – WE ARE ONE!

***

Solar Cycle 8: We Are New Vicksburg

Throughout the solar cycle, New Vicksburg residents participated in a broad range of regional gatherings. Some were old-style rendezvous, other included athletic activities, and still others were music-based competitions that attracted both old and young. The elements of southern hospitality characterized each, where family and neighborhood values influenced larger gatherings, and where food sharing was at the core of local beliefs.

***

APRIL: Springtime athletic competitions commonly had two purposes. The first was to demonstrate that athletic prowess, training, and hard work led to healthy lives. The second was to provide venues where doing one's best could be admired, complemented, and rewarded. Athletes in remote times were excellent soldiers. The athletic competitions at New Vicksburg followed the ancient dictum that while battle was the training ground for athletics, athletics was a way to compete without embarking upon military action. Athletic events commonly included foot races of different distances, cart racing, boxing, wrestling, archery, javelin, and hurling discs and stones of different weights.

Foods and beverages served to those attending the athletic events mirrored the range of items eaten by ancient athletes: cheese, wheat bread, and fruits, especially figs and cold water.

***

JUNE: Summer gatherings focused on storytelling, where individuals or groups recited tales from the past and spoke to the audiences from atop a special platform. Such tall-talking participants aimed for the reward given for telling the biggest lie:

Karsten Williams: 3rd place:

Once I was walking down by the Great River and seven gigantic crowbirds flew overhead, picked me up and dropped me into the swirling waters. The current carried me two kilo-miles downriver before I could swim to shore. I was lucky to survive.

Luis Mendoza: 2nd place:

My family was hurtin' for food during Ripple times, so I set off and went down to the east slough off the Great River to do some noodling. Found myself a catfish hole, reached inside and grabbed that sucker by the throat, and pulled him out. That fish was so big, he didn't look like a cat; he looked like an ugly tiger with whiskers. I threw it down on the ground with my left leg over, held on tight until my four kids jumped on to help. How that catfish squirmed and wiggled. Once we was eye-ball-to-eye-ball, and it didn't blink. That critter just looked at me and grabbed my left hand and swallowed it down, causing me to jump and holler. Well I show'd him. I pinched his stomach from the inside of his guts. When he belched out my hand, I conked him on the head. We ate on that catfish for long time coming. My mate turned its meat into 36 fillets, and ground the rest into a pile of meat that we used to make 79 burgers. We sucked for weeks on the fin fat from that one big catfish. Oh man, it kept us fed for long time coming. I still have dreams of those burgers piled high, served with slices of okra and chili peppers. Yummy!

Another competitor, Jake Reeder, approached and stood on the platform to make his presentation:

I never told a lie! Really, that's the truth! I never told a lie!

Jake was awarded 1st prize.

AUGUST: During late summer, New Vicksburg folks were treated to still other events and competitions. Tuners and songers from the town and nearby regions assembled on different nights to create verses on the spot to be accompanied by banjos and fiddlers. Travis and I had seen something like this earlier on our trek, where audience members would shout out a word or two and the songer would spin out short lines in response. One night we attended and I noted words of several songs that touched me or made us smile:

Audience shout out: *Deep Water*

Songer reply:

Deep water swirling dark as molasses tar
Deep water foaming like a hard autumn rain
Deep water flowing past the eastern sandy bar Deep water, morning mist, hiding my pain (3rd place)

Audience shout out: *Chicken Poop*

Songer reply:

Walking through the chicken coop what will I find today
Musty feathers, chicken poop, all along the way
Why must I always walk this mess each morning until night
Because my mate she tells me so, otherwise we fight (2nd place)

Audience shout out: *Love*

Songer reply:

Speak to me of love divine
Not love of beer or blood red wine
Your smile I love your eyes aglow
We walk life's path together, slow (1st place)

On alternating evenings during August, our community was entertained by competitive teams of dancers: buck and wingers, clap-and-stomp liners, cloggers, high steppers, and low grind crunchers. What amazed all of us onlookers was the energy the youngsters put into their performances, the quick movements, the syncopated stomping and thumping. How did they learn these steps? Who in the community were their teachers? How could they have made up these unique and difficult steps by themselves?

After all the competitions finished, we dispersed and walked slowly back to our homes. On these hot, humid nights, Travis and I sat together with our children out on our porch watching the fireflies light up as they banged against our screened enclosure. Neighbors usually dropped by and plopped down, filling the six or seven cane-woven chairs that we always reserved for guests. On other evenings the night sounds of birds, crickets, and hoppers filled the air as we sat together and jawed, recalling our favorite events of the day. Friends together: sipping glasses of mint leaf tea steeped with flavor sticks. Unforgettable evenings.

***

Solar Cycle 9: Southern Reconnaissance: Battle of the Isthmus

MARCH: The anger and rage over River Pirate activities continued to bubble up along the southern shores of the Great River. Travis was asked to participate in a militia confab, held on March 12th in New Vicksburg where regional commanders met to finalize a battle plan to eliminate these foul robbers and killers once and for all. Travis said the militias were united against this elusive foe, and smiled when he said that the battle plan included a special weapon, one that he did not reveal. When others in town asked about the militia plans, he changed the subject lest loose lips send out advance word that might sink our ships as the New Vicksburg Militia floated down the Mississippi River to confront the evil.

NOTES FROM TRAVIS' DAY JOURNAL:

Our New Vicksburg Militia arranged for float barges to carry our troops and supplies. We were joined at Natchez by other floaters – as we called ourselves. We glided silently down river past the Three Rivers confluence and the boundary of old Louisiana, then on past Angola, then into Red Stick, the new name used for old Baton Rouge. From there we passed more than a dozen bayous and small towns, a sampling being Carville, Darrow, Burnside, Hester, Daryville, Luling, and Ama, as we approached our destination – New Orleans.

All through the solar cycles of my schooling, I had heard and read about the great city of New Orleans, famed for music, song, and cultural celebrations. As we neared our destination our approach slowed. What I could see all about was terrible to the eye. New Orleans had become a flooded zone with buildings and towers rising above the dark waters of the Mississippi River. New Orleans no longer was protected by dikes and levees. Hurricanes had destroyed these structures many solar cycles past. We slid into a docking space on a stretch of relatively undamaged levee near Jackson Square. Opposite our arrival and rising out of the floodwaters were the spires of the once-impressive Cathedral.

We disembarked – all 253 of us – from our float barge and off-loaded our supplies. We formed a chain and hand-rousted the supplies up the rocky embankment over to the flooded side where local float barges were docked. These barges could be hired to serve as our transportation for the float trip towards Lake Pontchartrain. The plan was to meet up with contingents of the New Orleans and Red

Stick Militias. All along the inside of the quay were pitchmen urging us to hire out their fleets of so-called Dong-Go-Las for so many barter tokens per day, with better rates if the boats were hired for a week. These so called pole- or oar-boats would transport us ahead of the supply barges to follow.

So it was that with time New Orleans had flooded and became locally known as the Venice of the South, a sad state of affairs for a once-vibrant city. Each of us received our on-load boarding numbers. Our militia treasurer, Martin Tamerlane, provided the proper variety of barter tokens to the Dong-Go-La owners. One by one, the long, narrow boats pulled up to the quay to take on our militia members. My turn came, and I found space aboard one named The City of New Orleans. Once on board, we were welcomed by Frank Delexros, one of two men who would do the heavy work of oaring and poling us from the docking area across the flooded zone that once had been the center of downtown New Orleans. To the surprise of all, Frank burst into a lilting song with poignant words as we began our water tour of the once proud city:

> *Good morning, America, How are you*
> *Don't you know me? I'm your native son*
> *I'm here to guide you out along the waters*
> *We'll be gone ten kilo-miles before the day is done.*

We were oared and polled northwest towards the spires of the cathedral and crossed what used to be Decatur Street, now at least 15 meter-feet under water. Frank explained the layout of what once was called the French Quarter: a grid pattern where major streets, such as Iberville, Bienville, Conti, and Dumaine trended northwest/southeast and were crossed by other streets like Decatur, Chartres, Royal, Bourbon, Dauphine, and Burgundy that ran northeast/southwest.

Beyond the flooded French Quarter, we could see the remains of buildings rising above the waters. A strange-looking circular building appeared northwest of the cathedral and caught our attention. Frank and his polling companion edged us closer for a better look. He explained that this structure was a former sports stadium that once could hold more than 70,000 people. While the original use was for sports and musical events, it became a temporary home for refugees when hurricanes struck New Orleans several decades before the Ripple Event. He explained that during these early storms, the levees mostly held, and the building – then known as the Super Dome – remained dry inside. But after the Ripple and onset of the Dark Time, levee protection failed most of the city structures, and even the Super Dome became inundated. Frank drew our attention to a pole high atop the flooded dome structure flying a large banner with faded words:

Do you know what it means to miss New Orleans?

A sad message for a once-great city.

Travis's *Day Journal* related that the militia objectives were to cross the flood zone and head northwest along what used to be Canal Street, then towards Lake Ponchartrain where the regional River Pirates had constructed shelters along the southwestern border of the lake. Due to an advance spy network, volunteers called telescopers determined that the River Pirate settlements lay due west of the settlement called Kenner within a local area called The Isthmus.

The most interesting pages of his *Day Journal* were those that described what became known as the Battle of the Isthmus:

Our militia encounter with these River Pirates took place along the southwestern section of the Lake Ponchartrain where the land bridge to the Great River was narrowest. From this vantage point the River Pirates controlled the towns of Laplace and Norco on the Great River's northeast bank and also the west bank settlements of Taft and Hahnville. After transporting our units on lake boats, the plan was to land our forces and assault the towns of Laplace and Norco from the east while at the same time militia units from Red Stick provided a solid line anchored south and west of Norco, Hahnville, and Destrehan, thus preventing the RP's escape. This encirclement and pincer movement would entrap the River Pirates where they could be dealt with swiftly once and for all.

Our armada of boats crossed the lake and landed at the isthmus on March 28th. The New Vicksburg Militia formed ranks and spread out along the eastern shore linking up with units from Ponchatoula, a settlement group that had suffered terribly from River Pirate raids. As the RPs were evicted from their security holes, they fled from their protective shelters and ran in scattered groups towards the communities of Montz and Norco. There they were pinned against the banks of the Great River and had no means of escape, since the Red Stick Militia regiments already had secured the riverbanks from Kilona southeast to Taft, and Hahnville.

At our commander's signal we put on our breathing masks and unleashed our new and most powerful weapon: red pepper dust. The prevailing wind patterns previously had been charted by our tele-scopers. On the day of our assault the winds blew off the lake southwest into the uncoordinated defensive lines of the RPs. The prevailing winds blasted the enemy with the offensive and irritating pepper dust. Our head masks protected us from the dust. Although our ears were covered, we still could hear the screams of the enemy as they retreated in advance of the wind-born pepper particles.

Soon it was over. The River Pirates had two choices: surrender to our combined forces, or face drowning in the Great River. It didn't matter to us since those who surrendered also would be executed by drowning. By midafternoon on the 28th of March, the Battle of the Isthmus was over. Our units had slain 396 River Pirates (either by battle or execution); our loses were 17 dead and 76 wounded.

Travis later told me that after three days of celebration the various militias retired, leaving protection of the isthmus region to policing authorities at Laplace. The enemy had been eliminated and the region cleansed of their activities. No more would these roving bands commit atrocities or endanger the lives and livelihood of the good people of southern New Louisiana. It was time to return home to New Vicksburg.

Travis wrote in his journal:

Militia Commander Marcus Tucker regrouped our units at Destrehan and crossed the Great River to the southwestern bank entering the community of Luling. Using barter tokens captured from River Pirate caches, supply carriages and horses were hired for the land trek back to New Vicksburg. The path taken was circuitous through hill and swamplands characteristic of the lower Mississippi Delta region.

We headed south and west along Highway 90 and passed through or circumvented settlement groups at Boutte and Paradise. We marched through the marshlands of Des Allemandes, camping as necessary along the way. In the days that followed, our militia members passed through other small delta settlements such as Donner, Gibson, Amelia, and entered Morgan City along the banks of Lake Palourde. A seemingly endless number of small but hospitable communities and settlement groups followed, among them Idlewild, Calumet, Baldwin, Jeanerette, Lydia, until we finally reached New Iberia.

Just outside New Iberia, Commander Tucker led us on a side trip southwest along Highway 329 towards Emma to pay respects to his distant relative Jensen Avery. We would learn later that communications between Commander Tucker and Jensen Avery led to development of the chili pepper weapon used to defeat the River Pirates at the Battle of the Isthmus. Jensen and our commander had grown up together and spent much of their boyhood roaming Avery Island learning about the different types and qualities of chili peppers grown there in abundance. They learned the metrics and values of the spiciest of the capsicums, differences between poblanos, jalapenos, seranos, habaneros, even the killer pepper that they named ghost.

They continued to communicate, especially after the initial New Vicksburg northern reconnaissance campaign that reduced but did not eliminate the River Pirate gangs. Jensen believed that development of a pepper dust weapon was possible, but its use also would require protective clothing and head hoods for our own militia fighters.

After a congratulatory meeting with Jensen Avery and his staff of workers, we resumed our journey north past Capitan, Cade, Billeaud, Walroy, and into Lafayette. We left Lafayette traveling east along Eye 10, passing Beaux Bridge, Henderson, across the Atchafalaya marshlands into Ramah, Grosse Tete, and Port Allen located on the west bank of the Great River across from Red Stick. At Port Allen the militia engaged two stern-wheel steam-powered riverboats to take the units back up river to New Vicksburg.

***

The New Vicksburg Militia returned home on April 23rd. Travis related that to the best of his knowledge the River Pirate threat from Memphis south to New Orleans had been defeated and their command structure eliminated.

He also returned with something special. The loot captured at the *Battle of the Isthmus* had been divided equally: half of the barter tokens were assigned to various riverbank settlement groups and small towns who had suffered River Pirate attacks through the solar cycles. These dispensed barter tokens would go far in rehabilitating homes and businesses along the Great River. The remaining half of the barter tokens were distributed among the participating militia members.

After several days at home, I observed that Travis had changed in some ways. He was more quiet and reflective. One morning we sat together and I commented on his behavior. My words caused his body to stiffen. Something was the matter, and I enquired further whether or not anything unusual had happened either in New Orleans or during or after the *Battle of the Isthmus*, and whether or not he wanted to speak about it. Travis paused, looked down at the floor then turned and gazed into my eyes:

> *Things happened down there that none of us expected. Remember the commandant at West Point who discussed the barrier and the re-invasion of the French forces and immigrants into easternmost America? Well, he did not tell us everything. At the end of the isthmus encounter I told you there were 396 River Pirates either killed in battle or taken prisoner and executed afterwards. During the process of prisoner interrogation, we discovered that more than 30 of those captured were not local: they actually were French militiamen serving as advisors to the River Pirates, helping them plot where and when to attack ships and riverbank towns, testing the security systems of local and regional administrative units, and scouting defenses of local settlement groups. These French spies sent the information they gathered up river to Kai-Row where it was collated and channeled north across the border into Canada. Once north of old America, the information was sent eastward into the French-speaking region of New France. These French spies collected data with the purpose of establishing a second north-south barrier – this one along the Great River. If successful, the New Confederacy and all lands from the southern tip of Florida north to Estcourt Station, Maine, would come under French control.*

Travis continued:

> *Because of our visit to the West Point garrison and connection with the commander, our New Vicksburg Commander Tucker put me in*

charge of securing information from these French spies. The older prisoners, soldiers in their early 30s, were hardened and refused to reveal any information. The younger ones, primarily recruits who were tri-lingual in English, Cajun/southern Arcadian, and French, were more prone to speak out under the harsh interrogations that I organized. The methods used to extract the information I will not discuss, but say only that we uncovered a network of French spies that extended upriver from New Orleans, all the way into old Chicago and up the north-south shore of Lake Michigan past Milwaukee and Green Bay, all the way to Marquette on the south shore of old Lake Superior.

What we discovered was a strongly imbedded spy system, one unknown to the managers at Williamsburg. In essence the administrators of the New Confederacy were ignorant of the French threat, when they should have been aware of the problem during its infancy. But most unsettling was the fact that six French spies had been posted to our own town of New Vicksburg. In past solar cycles these men had been welcomed, had become our neighbors, and had participated in community activities for the past five solar cycles.

One of these, Reese, was our neighbor Marcus Thompson. We had entertained him for dinner at our house. How many evenings did he sit with us on our porch, drinking shine and telling tall tales about his youth growing up in Mississippi? All lies! He now is being held in the New Vicksburg jail. I spoke with him just yesterday. He looked me in the eye and said that the accusation was true, that he had no personal history in Mississippi and was born and educated in France. His assignment was to infiltrate New Vicksburg, where he was to learn about the Mississippi Militias and report to his contacts north of the border in New France. I had considered him one of my friends. How could I have been so deceived?

This is why you see me quiet and reflective these days. My behavior also is due to the assignment given me by Commander Tucker. I was responsible to take into custody Marcus Thompson and the other five French spies – Able Harrison, Justice Freeman, Louis Evernton, Norris Wilson, and Paul Cummings. Their trial is set for tomorrow morning at 10:00 in the militia headquarters.

The morning of April 25th saw the people of New Vicksburg seething with silent rage. Information regarding trials of the French-Six as they were called had spread quickly. These men had been accepted into our community as neighbors. We considered them to be good people and hard workers. They had sworn agreement and support to the New Vicksburg Diamond and Pledge. We had accepted them as friends, shared food and drink, and valued their labor and assistance. But all had been a sham. To find out they were spies, sworn and dedicated to the objective of returning our lands to the French; the reality almost was too much to understand.

New Vicksburg protective patrols buttressed with militia members formed a ring around militia headquarter where the trial was to be conducted. Testimony went quickly: the trial was over by midafternoon. Arguments presented by the French-Six in support of their actions and behaviors could be condensed into three points:

We French have legitimate right to this land.

We demand our first land rights given to us by the Choctaw Tribal Nation. The fact that you, the descendants of later immigrants, expelled the Choctaw and your ignorant ancestors settled in lands that belong to us, does not refute our original claim.

You and your quaint southern ways.

You spend too much time with your so-called hospitality customs and traditions. It is we, the French, who are hard workers – not you. You waste time and abuse the land. Your so-called ecological approaches towards wild animal life and vegetation are jokes. You could develop this region into something grand, but with your limited minds you choose not to do so. Your southern ways offend us. We French are highly educated and understand the meaning and purpose of life. You do not deserve to live here and should be expelled – as you all will be once the new barrier is installed.

You people of New Vicksburg have no right to imprison or try us.

You have no status in our French court system. We reject your attempts to evict us from our mission and land.

Travis and I listened to these comments from the French-Six and shook our heads in disbelief. We remembered the well-known ancient saying taught to us during our school days back in Bison Camp:

Modesty and heartfelt confessions are superior to arrogant speeches of denial.

The so-called French-Six who claimed their education superior to ours should have learned the phrase and remembered it well. The next day, April 26th, each was dispatched quickly, without ceremony, and buried in an unmarked communal grave.

After the trial I spent time writing down my thoughts about what the French-Six had said about us, we the New Vicksburgers:

Yes, we in New Vicksburg are a mix of people with ancestral roots in Africa, Asia, Europe, and the Americas. Yes, we are of different colors and genders. Yes, we have different educational backgrounds. Some of us are highly educated while others have excelled through the school of basic survival reality. Yes, we speak different languages, English, Neo-Arcadian, French, and some of us have knowledge of African tongues as well. Yes, we manage stores, work as laborers – skilled and unskilled – and together we reflect a myriad of necessary crafts. Yes, we work hard and we play hard. Yes, some of our games of enjoyment are unknown to you and involve the unusual, whether gator grabbing, hog hunting, or toad licking. Other games bring us together, residents of all ages to enjoy baseball and softball, fishing contests, and poetry readings. Yes, we are different in many ways but we are alike in one way that remains most important to our lives: We are New Vicksburg and we are ONE. And always remember – as you lie dead in your water-sodden collective grave – we will never surrender to French occupation or to your so-called enlightened administration.

Three weeks after execution of the French-Six, Travis was offered a critical assignment by Commander Tucker. Travis agreed to organize teams of militia members to ride cross-country to Birmingham where they would meet with local militia leaders and explain the French threat to the New Confederacy. It was supposed that after such a meeting in Birmingham local leaders in turn would send their own riders onward to carry the warning message north into Huntsville, who in turn would provide riders at Nashville, and so on to Knoxville and Charlotte. These riders bearing news critical to the safety and organization of all within the New Confederacy would pass through Durham, Richmond, and ultimately reach the administrative capitol of the New Confederacy at Williamsburg. Travis and Commander Tucker estimated the distance traveled would approximate 1,000 kilo-miles and, if all went well and if the riders exchanged horses daily, almost 75 kilo-miles a day could be covered. In this way the important news could reach Williamsburg within 15 to 20 days.

DECEMBER: Whether through danger along the way, or due to lack of perceived urgency on the part of New Confederacy administrators at Williamsburg, we received the following message:

Thank you for the information you relayed to my office in Williamsburg. We are considering our next steps and will keep you informed.

Joseph Adamson

Foreign Affairs Officer, New Confederacy

This was the only message we received from Foreign Affairs Officer Joseph Adamson. We received none from any Administrative Representative at Williamsburg. What this lack of communication meant? We did not know.

***

Solar Cycle 10: Competitive Urges

Our twins entered their 10th full solar cycles of home schooling and were struggling with mathematics, figures, logic, and other school tasks as many children their age. Common were their cries:

Why is it important to master letter-writing when printing works just as well?

Who cares whether or not the root value of 3 when tripled is more or less than the number of fingers on my hand?

Why do I have to learn the names of each president of the old United States, since there has been no government in DC since the Ripple Event and Dark Time?

They offered in turn the following requests:

Would it not be better for each of us to be able to make fire three different ways: by flint and steel, by drill, and by curved glass that focuses the sun's rays?

Is it not more important to study when birds migrate, how to find their nests, and how to tell whether or not old meat is spoiled even if it doesn't smell?

My hands were full with daily interactions with our twins. This near frantic activity made me happy and joyful, except when one or both of the girls became naughty, or got into tussles with neighbor children, or refused to clean their respective rooms and wash their dirty clothes. But all in all they were good kids and were on the verge of becoming women.

Soon came the time for what most adult parents in New Vicksburg called *The Talk.* And our conversation went reasonably well. As Travis and I began to speak of body changes and responsibilities, both Sage and Laurel rolled their eyes and said that they knew all of that stuff and did not need to hear it again from either mom or dad. When he heard these responses, Travis just shook his head. Together we resolved to make certain the girls really understood the *facts* so there would be no future surprises.

Our girls were poised at the crossroad where childhood behaviors shifted to adolescent and adult responsibilities. How many times Travis and I smiled thinking back on our own experiences when each of us thought we knew everything and became irritated when our parents tried to share adult realities with us. We both recognized that it was time to begin thinking about their future and who might be knocking on their doors requesting entry into the mysteries of life.An array of possible family matches were available within the confines of New Vicksburg and the surrounding settlement groups. Boys two or three solar cycles older than the twins were not thinking much about such parings. Most interested were the older boys (16 or 18 years old), who had not yet been assigned for mating responsibilities. These older boys concerned us as we tried to focus attention on those nearer in age to our twins.

Adam, son of Fisher Lange, and Joseph, son of Preston Emory, were two youngsters that frequented the front yards of our house during play periods. Both were liked by our girls but our casual glances now and then during play time, revealed to me that they had little to no real interest in physical activities beyond the normal practices of athletic competition and defense training – at least at this point in life.

On April 15th, Sage and Laurel celebrated their 9th solar cycles. They had one more solar cycle to pass through before achieving their so-called "two-digit" classification status, something admired here in New Vicksburg, but an event we ignored at Bison Camp. Both girls were athletic and participated in long distance races, even competing in the GPR or Great Perimeter Run. Each daughter wanted to win every event entered. They were extremely competitive and when one was the victor the other sulked for a while. Fortunately, the loser would come around later in the afternoon and welcome the talent of her sister, and the next day would embark upon a regimen to train even harder. The 2 x 2 cross-river swim attracted both girls. The rationale for the event was based upon the concept of mutual support (i.e., being able to assist one another should a problem arise during the event, such as cramping or being accidentally jammed by a sub-surface log). As it turned out, the girls won their age group in the cross-river race in the over-and-back category and were awarded their first joint championship. Times were good. The next solar cycles we hoped would be even better.

***

Solar Cycle 11: The Best Of Times

My comments for this solar cycle will not be broken into respective monthly segments, since the days just seemed to flow together. Sage and Laurel reached their 10th solar cycle. The settlement festivals were many and included an autumn maize-maze constructed on the farmlands southeast of New Vicksburg where children and their parents wandered aimlessly, getting lost while trying to find the exit.

Enjoyable events included the many firefly-gathering nights when the twins tended our neighbor's small children and together captured hundreds of the flickering bugs in jars, watching them light up the evening sky.

Travis and I were amused when Sage and Laurel sponsored bug- and frog-related competitions with local children. Especially enjoyable to watch were what the girls called roly-poly races. The activity was hard to believe, but these were actually races between critters we back in the Big Hole Valley called sow bugs. The roly-poly bugs were gathered from beneath forest logs and placed into slots on a table that the girls had constructed. We watched with amusement to see which bug ran or rolled the fastest to the other end. Sometimes the girls explored the nearby ponds where they captured pollywogs and johnnywogs and kept the critters in water-filled jars for several weeks, watching them undergo transformation. Two neighborhood friends of Sage and Laurel's formed mini-bands to play songs they had written. One such band was named the *Loose Screw*

Tighteners, a name that somewhat mimicked the unusual sounds of their music. Even the lyrics to their tunes made everybody in the neighborhood smile and laugh. Another band, not to be undone, called themselves the *Haystack Needle Finders*. Travis liked the former; I the later. In both cases, the music was enjoyable and fun – what else could you expect from a group of children ages 10-12 or so?

We passed through spring, summer, and into fall. We residents commemorated the food history of New Vicksburg with sidewalk bakes and closed-street barbeques. During this solar cycle, Travis and I recorded the names of more than 40 very different recipes, many with highly unusual names. A selection I have recorded here:

> **Pulled Pork Pockets**: *wonderful shredded hill pig barbeque meat with a fiery chili sauce;*
>
> **Gravelly Grindey Grits**: *standard local preparations of ground corn grits mixed with shelled peanuts and dried raisins;*
>
> **SSSS (Squirrel Stew and Strawberry Salad):** *this unique concoction of meat, fruit, and wild greens was typical of New Vicksburg. According to local tradition, the squirrel variety had to be either a grey or fox type, as the others commonly substituted had less fat, which meant that the meat was tougher;*
>
> **Poke Your Poke Salad:** *this highly variable concoction commonly was a mixture of wild greens gathered along fence lines in the agricultural areas, blended with lettuce, kale, chick-pea, and black-eyed pea sprouts;*
>
> **Cobbled Cobbler**: *by town decision, this dish only could be made by the women or girls from the Jenkins family who repaired shoes in New Vicksburg. Their seasonal cobbler specialties often were apple or peach. Their flakey wheat-based crusts were well known throughout the region;*
>
> **Bacon Rump**: *sometimes just called BB and sometimes bacon butt. These cuts of pork had a balanced flavor and, when rendered down in skillets, produced the best-tasting bacon possible. This dish, mixed with scrambled eggs, was a specialty of the Morgan family;*
>
> **Gator Gizzards**: *while part of alligator meat, gator gizzards were not specifically cut from the beast's throat region, but actually were pieces of flank steak served with wild swamp onions. I learned that*

the name first was used well before the Ripple Event and traceable to a young, adventurous girl who took it upon herself to learn how to 'rassle gators. The story goes that this girl, Joan Vandem, 'rassled this one gator so hard and long that it expired and, according to tradition, the meat belonged to whoever did in the gator;

Buttermilk Bangers: *the origin of this dish could be traced to an 18th century English woman who settled in the New Vicksburg region. These were homemade sausages usually prepared from ground wild game meat and simmered in buttermilk to provide an extra tang to the palate;*

Firefly Fancy: *this creative name did not actually include insects that glowed in the early evening, but related to the alternating red and yellow lights the fireflies emitted, depending whether or not the mating season was at hand. The red and yellow components of the concoction came from flower petals, mashed and blended with a mix of potatoes and black-eyed peas;*

Lizard Layer Cakes*: these were great favorites of small children and the specialty of Grannie Ada Watkins, who never would reveal her recipe. Basically, the LLCs were yellow-hued wheat flour cakes layered one atop the other with lots of raspberry paste and creamed cheese slobbered on the bottom side of each layer. Grannie Watkins next would take a long bread knife and slice the cake piles into the general shape of a stonewall blue-belly lizard. Over the pile of these lizard-shaped cutouts, she would drip dark brown honey molasses. For the lizard tongues, she added long ovate rose petals, and for the clawed lizard toes, she whittled down and attached curved sections of swamp cane. All of us who tasted her cakes thought that Grannie Watkins put something extra special into that brown honey molasses drippings, since after eating these cakes we sometimes slurred our words when speaking. When asked Grannie about this, she only smiled;*

Cat-Lover Crunchies*: I did not like these but they were one of Travis' favorites. Up in the hill area northeast of New Vicksburg lived two elderly sisters, Mary and Martha Xavier. They were cat lovers and they cared for about 45 or so felines. The women also raised mice as food for their cats. About twice a solar cycle they would come down from the hills to participate in one of New Vicksburg's* *food festivals and would bring baskets filled with their unique items called cat crunchies. These were made from a wheat-based paste, flavored with wild anise and mint, and mixed with chunks of pulverized pecans that provided the required crunch. The reason I did not like them was because I could not get out of my mind the images of 45 cats wandering through the Xavier's kitchen as the ladies made their cat-lover crunchies. Whenever Travis heard me express my concerns, he just laughed and asked for another;*

Hillside Haunches: *it used to be thought that if cattle only were allowed to graze on steep hills and only in a clockwise or counterclockwise motion, one set of their limbs – depending upon direction of movement – would be shorter than the other. James (Jimmy) Franklin truly believed this and when he butchered an animal from his herd, he paid careful attention to which legs and flanks were the longest and most marbled, the idea being that meat from the other side would be stringy and tough. So it was that Jimmy became most successful in the regional meat market and amassed many barter tokens by differentiating which sides of beef should be priced higher. I must admit all this seemed foolish to me but in any case his hillside haunches were quite tasty and served our family well through the solar cycles;*

Moth Wings: *we in New Vicksburg were blessed with the appearance each solar cycle of numerous large, graceful, lime-green Luna moths. We would sit on our porches in the late afternoon and early evening watching the beautiful moths laze about, floating on ripples of air, flitting here and there, sometimes landing nearby on our porch screen. I sometimes would prepare a mix of pie crust dough, roll it out and use my scalping knife to cut out six or seven moth-shaped outline figures. These I would decorate with a green-colored sugarcane-based frosting and use red or black currents for the wing-tipped eyes. These were great hits at the food fairs, and no graceful moths were harmed during the process;*

Cricket Chirpers: *the McKenzie boys, Terry and Thomas, used to make these wonderful-tasting dessert items out of pie dough blended with sweet cane juice, and handfuls of mashed raspberries. They would put all the ingredients into a large bowl and simply mash and squash it with their fingers until the red juice colored everything.*

As the final ingredient they added dried oats. When they took their so-called cricket chirpers into town for sale, one of the boys would make a sales pitch to passing customers, while the other stood off to one side, hands behind his back, clicking his cricket chirper noise-maker that his grandpa had given him one Halloween eve. They always sold out;

Dog Ears: *these were another variation off of pie dough, where chunks of dough were rolled out then cut into strips and deep fried in oil, then dusted with a cover of local spices and herbs. Yum!;*

Possum Pounders*: neither Travis nor I like these items. Essentially, the PPs as they were known consisted of thin strips of opossum meat pounded, then fried and covered with a black sauce of unknown ingredients. It was unclear where the opossums had been obtained.*

***

Solar Cycle 12: Coming of Age

Both girls came of age the same week. I announced the event to Travis, who was most pleased. He called Sage and Laurel together for another father-daughter talk:

I couldn't be more proud of both of you. Your mother and I have watched you grow from your early childhood to become beautiful young women. We honor you and offer you special welcome to the time of new mysteries.

It was time to begin discussions regarding the identification of potential mates.

In early April, the four of us gathered around our kitchen table for the first of several important discussions. Travis and I explained to the twins there should be no embarrassment throughout these discussions, which were critical in order to prepare the best matches for their future lives. We explained that we would request the names of boys 2-3 solar cycles older with whom they had shared educational and defense-related training or play groups, and with whom they had at least a modicum of interest as potential mates.

A grand list of potentials – as we called them – was compiled by each daughter. The list included information on family names, school and life skill sets, and relative knowledge of their general behaviors at school, work, and in the community. Once compiled, these lists allowed discussions to go forward to the next step.

In early May, the residents of New Vicksburg hosted the annual PCF or Potential Companion Festival, where a full day of activities from early morning until late evening allowed parents to explore possibilities and observe social interactions of their sons and daughters. There were opportunities to dine with different sets of parent and to sit or walk alone with the potentials with whom interest had been generated earlier in the solar cycles.

Sage's list had six potential candidates; Laurel's five. The names on each list were different, which eased our minds considerably. No parent of twins ever would want to see their sons or daughters compete for the same potential mate.

Once the lists of potentials had been generated, there would be sufficient time to explore interests with the other families.

***

Solar Cycle 13: Family Building

Many solar cycles past when I was a young girl growing up in Bison Camp, I envisioned there was a great book of life kept somewhere, whose content spoke to girls like me of the events that soon would characterize my life:

> *How do young men and women select their mates? Is it only through mutual attraction that pairs are drawn together? Appearances bring individuals closer, but the critical decisions on mate selection are more than face and eye color, lip shape and style of hair, or body marks and tattoos.*
>
> *How is love defined? Care and respect are different than love; mutual attraction is not love; the two "Ls" of lust and longing are not love. When do these two "Ls" morph into the singular "L" of love? Adoration and affection are not love; to cherish and fancy are not love, nor are terms such as treasure, worship, and yearning. When and how do each of us fit into the matrix of love? There can be passion without love, but can there be love without friendship, respect, and dignity?*
> *So what is love?*

And so it was our twin daughters, Sage and Laurel, grew into their maturity. And so it was one day early in her 12th solar cycle when we all were sitting at home after dinner that Sage rose, stood quietly, and spoke at our family evening gathering:

I love Adam Lange, and I want him to be my mate.

And it was that same evening early in her 12th solar cycle that Laurel stood next to her sister and spoke:

I love Joseph Emory want him to be my mate.

The two young women in our family had expressed desires to forge new family linkages. Childhood had passed.

***

The following week, Travis and I entered into discussions with the Lange and Emory families. We had known each young boy and their parents for many solar cycles, had interacted on weekend work details, and had shared numerous hospitality visits to each other's homes. Travis also knew the families through mutual involvement with militia efforts. We had known for several solar cycles that our twins and their sons were good friends, and sometimes in our presence their eyes and behaviors implied more than just passing interest in each other. We were two good families; our children reflected the values and training expected of young people in New Vicksburg. What more could parents wish for with their daughters and sons?

Adam and Joseph had reached their 14th solar cycle; Sage and Laurel their 13th – the proper time to initiate the Consideration Period. The customs and traditions governing mate consideration at New Vicksburg were culturally different than what Travis and I had experienced long ago with our families and communities in Montana, and they consisted of several stages.

The first component was called the Family Unification Ceremony. This was a town-wide ceremony held on the March equinox where all residents were invited to attend. Those families in the process of going through a Consideration Period were honored with a united celebration. This short ritual announced to all attending the potential couple's intent and family support. Standing together, two-by-two before the town assembly, each of the young couples openly expressed their intent. At the conclusion of the ceremony, all couples recited the New Vicksburg Pledge, then mingled with their parents, friends, and well-wishers to receive accolades. Travis and I, joined by the Lange and Emory families, expressed wishes that our daughters and sons would pass through the Consideration Period with dignity and respect.

***

During the next three months until the June solstice, our families met frequently and shared family histories. Gradually we become one large extended family. In the weeks immediately after the Family Unification Ceremony, we worked together to construct the traditional huts to be occupied by the couples during their mating ceremonies one solar cycle hence. Working together, we cleared the ground, laid the foundations, framed the walls and, with some effort, finished the roofs. Each was a simple structure as required by New Vicksburg tradition, to be occupied only for a short time until the couples constructed their own abodes designed in their personal style and taste.

Fischer Lange and his mate, Francene, frequently visited our home, as we did theirs. Travis would sit for hours reminiscing with Fischer about their respective cross-country journeys and the efforts needed to survive such difficult times. When our mates seemed to be lost in discussion, Francene and I would share stories from our childhood and memories of what our parents and grandparents had told us about life before, during, and after the Ripple Event. Both our families were bred from strong and sturdy stock. Our ancestors valued hard work and effort, gladly assisted others in need, stood strong and were outspoken against the muddlers of society who lived off the efforts of others and expected to be cared for, while at the same time offering little effort or assistance even when asked.

We had similar wonderful meetings with Joseph's parents. We visited them regularly, and they in return graced our home with their presence. Preston Emory, a friend from the New Vicksburg Militia, owned one of the forges on Rigby Street.

Both fathers were proud of their sons, as we were of our daughters. The boys were well educated; they had exceptional survival skills as measured by the semi-annual 14-day excursions, where living off the land and locating safe drinking water were required for survival. Both Adam and Joseph were athletic and regularly took part in the so-called S&S or Strength and Stamina events sponsored by the New Vicksburg Militia command structure.

Now that we had bonded together through our sons and daughters, our three families could not be more proud.

Solar Cycle 14: Solar Cycles of Joy and Pain

APRIL: Two days after our twins' birthday celebration on April 15th, Travis and I sponsored the mating ceremony for them. So many friends wished to attend and offer greetings and wishes to the new couples, we barely had space to accommodate all. A new season was upon us, different yet the same, a time of joy, a time of sadness, a time for dance, a time to speak of wonders to come. The mating ceremony was a time to rejoice, to look upon the faces of Sage and Laurel, to see their happiness reflected in the eyes of their chosen mates.

Came time for exchanges of necklaces and traditional New Vicksburg diamonds. Three families joined as one – three families one with their community.

Came time for the traditional toasts and proud words.

Came time for the intertwined clasping of arms, as each couple drank down the special mating beverages without spilling a drop.

Came time for the traditional tossing of the cups, followed by more shouts of best wishes and cheers as the couples left the assembly to retire to their respective mating huts.

***

Throughout the long night and the shivaree that followed, Travis and I remained awake. Lying in each other's arms, we thought back and recalled our own mating day and night experiences, and how our lives had been enriched by the other.

Together we wished the same happiness for our daughters and their mates.

***

OCTOBER: The days following the mating ceremony were wonderful but were not to last. Adam and Joseph worked with Travis at least one day per week in the nearby woods felling trees and preparing firewood for the winter months ahead. The young men spent most of their time, constructing homes for Sage and Laurel. The twins chose to live in an undeveloped area of New Vicksburg north and east of the military park, near tracts partially cleared by earlier settlers, but never developed into home sites

On October 12th, working together felling trees with Adam and Joseph up near the Fox Road drainage area, the accident occurred. Travis' ax head slipped and sliced deeply into his lower right leg, the one he had injured long ago. Adam and Joseph came to his assistance, staunched the bleeding, and carried Travis to the logging cart for transportation back into town. Unrecognized at the time was that later the wound would fester and turn into what the locals called toxic flesh or what we at Bison Camp knew to be blood poisoning.

The New Vicksburg doctors and local sage femmes received Travis at the health office on Maxwell Drive. They stripped off his leggings to clean the wound. They did the best they could. Upon hearing the news I arrived as quickly as possible. Travis attempted to easy my worry and fears. The doctor seemed to imply that all would be well in a few weeks and that Travis could resume all his daily activities.

But it was not to be.

The wound continued to fester as ugly red streaks radiated upward towards his inner thigh. Travis remained lethargic and had little appetite. After three weeks at the health office the decision was made to return Travis to our home. He agreed, although the bumpy carriage ride could not have been easy and certainly caused him considerable pain. Once at home he seemed to stabilize for a few days. His appetite returned and he apparently regained strength. But these initial positive results did not continue into the days and weeks that followed.

Came a time when the doctors and sage femmes could do no more than prescribe ease-based care, which had little to no positive impact on Travis's condition.

One evening when only the two of us were alone in our house, Travis spoke:

> *Reese, love of my life, you must accept that I will not be healed or cured.*

I could not accept his words and asked him to stop.

> *Reese, you know this to be true. I am in the final season of my life and the days are draining away. All life passes. Life is not eternal: we are born, we age, and we pass on to the next adventure, one unknown. What is important now is for you to accept my fate and make plans for the future, so that you and our twins and their mates can go forward.*

I spoke again, telling Travis that he must stop saying such words. He reached for my hand to calm me and spoke:

Reese on the eve of the winter solstice, which we celebrate next week, please assemble the family. I have something to say to the girls. Please arrange this, Reese, I need your help. Please do this.

***

On the December solstice eve, we gathered inside our home – our daughters and their mates along with the Lange and Emory families. We shared a meal and even Travis had enough appetite to eat some of the prepared items. We offered toasts to life and to good memories forever. Seated restfully in his chair, Travis spoke to us the words we would remember always:

We gather together three families: three now as one. Our daughters and sons; together as one. Life has a beginning, a middle, and end. Do not weep at the end of life – laugh and cry out in joy for to be received into the next adventure. All of us on life's journey in reality are explorers. Some trails will lead into the vast unknown, while others follow to be rejoined later at a time determined. Three families; three as one. Daughters and sons: together as one.

Each of you whether from childhood raised and cared for in this house, or as visitors to our humble abode, each of you have seen two swords resting on the wall above our fireplace. These two weapons Reese and I discovered while walking the Paducah battlefield site along the River Ohio. One is slightly longer than the other, but length is not important. They are two objects, each different but in many ways the same.

On this night where we all are gathered it is time to gift these symbols of life and honor. Both will be given to our daughters: my sword upon my death will be given to Sage; upon the death of Reese, her sword will be given to Laurel. One weapon is not more important than the other; just as one daughter is not favored over the other.

The decision which daughter would receive my sword was revealed to me in last night's dream. Although given to one – in reality it is given to both. There is no competition, it is a gift I give to both – one daughter to care for my saber for an agreed time period, then exchanged so the other can care for it as well. Upon the death of Reese, both of you – Sage and Laurel – will care for both swords.

I offer my saber, a symbol of conflict and war but more so symbolic of protection and security. This I give to my daughters who will tame the angry steel and turn the symbol of war into one of love and family understanding.

This is my wish; this is my desire.

***

Solar Cycle 15: Death and Departure

JANUARY: On January 3rd in the dark cold winter at New Vicksburg, my partner, my best friend, my mate died. Travis was gone. It was hard to believe. The good solar cycles at Bison Camp, the Epidemic and tragic deaths of our children, our great trek and what we saw and experienced during this journey, now memories. The nights we spent together, the wonderful days with our twin girls, our neighbors and friends in New Vicksburg where we had become one with the community, now memories.

The day before on January 2nd in the late afternoon we had sensed a change and gathered around his bed. Travis appeared tired but his blue eyes still gleamed. He was alert to our presence. One by one Travis reached out and spoke to us:

Laurel, your smile always enlightened my heart; the kindness you showed to others is a beacon to be followed by other women your age.

Sage, by your words you show wisdom far beyond your age, the way you speak to others and how you help those in need. Yours is a gift of kindness like no others.

Laurel and Sage, you were birthed and raised in the hearth of history and kindness by the people of New Vicksburg. Do not be saddened; all life ends. Go forward with the joy of having known your father and mother. Go now and enjoy life with your mates. Take rest within the arms of your loving mates who will comfort you. Greet your mother daily with words of love and respect. When I am gone seek out your friends and neighbors for they too will offer comfort in the days to come.

Reese, my mate and ever companion. We have done well, you and I, have we not? We have crossed this great land by boat, horse, and on foot. We have traveled along great rivers, ridden easy and rough trails through the Virginias down into the New Confederacy. Our experiences have been many, almost too numerous to count. What I remember and loved most were the evenings we spent together, eating and drinking who knows what, laughing and singing long into the night the haunting lyrics of love lost and love found.

Most of all, Reese, I remember the fire-side sittings, where we did nothing except hold each other and gaze as one into the flickering light of our campfire. How many times we wondered why the Epidemic spared us, when all at Bozeman and Bison Camp had perished. Why did we survive or, better said, how is it that we were allowed to survive? The answer to these questions has come to me during my last hours. We were protected on our journey, by what and by whom we may never know during our lifetimes. But for true, the reason for our life together was revealed to me last night: the reason, in fact, the reasons are you Reese, along with Laurel and Sage, and mates Adam and Joseph. For if you and I had not been spared the Epidemic, the five of you would not be standing next to me and would be unable to consider my last requests:

> *I wish my cremation ceremony to be managed by Commander Tucker of the New Vicksburg Militia. Please spend but a short time in grief. Instead, draw new life from the wonderful seasons of early spring, summer, and late autumn. Use this gift of time to return to Bison Camp. There, re-establish yourselves as regional leaders; care for the land and its offerings of food and water. Rebuild once more the population of the Big Hole Valley. You, Reese, are generation ONE; you, Sage and Laurel and your mates Adam and Joseph, are generation TWO; and may the grandchildren sired by Adam and Joseph, and birthed by you, Sage and Laurel, become generation THREE. May thereafter the population of the Big Hole Valley grow and multiply until there are hundreds of future generations to regain and repopulate the land where we previously lived and loved.*

These are my requests.

Travis looked upon each of us one last time, then as silently as a whisper on the wind, he breathed no more and was gone.

***

Commander Tucker rose to address the assembly.

> *We gather today to witness and remember the life of Travis Saunders, our friend, our neighbor, a valued resident of New Vicksburg. Travis and his mate Reese arrived in New Vicksburg some 15 solar cycles past, after making a difficult and challenging cross-country journey from the wilds of the Big Hole Valley in the NorthWest Configuration. He and Reese became part of our community and our militia members have drawn upon his skills and talents many times in the past. Living in New Vicksburg their family grew; two babies at once, now women beautiful in mind, both raised in a household where respect for others was a part of daily life as food and drink. Thank you, Travis Saunders, for the opportunity to know you and your family. May you rest in peace and understand that all who knew you will miss you dearly.*

The fire pyre, organized by Adam Lange and Joseph Emory, was lit by ceremonial archers. I watched as my mate's body burned and turned to earth-tone ashes – the way that he wished to be one with the earth. An honor guard from the New Vicksburg Militia approached and presented me with a small vial of ash, one that I would carry back to Bison Camp for dispersal in the Big Hole Valley, the place Travis loved dearly. With this ash token thus distributed, Travis would be one with the two places he loved: New Vicksburg and his first home, Bison Camp.

Ashes from the pyre site were collected in a box, carried to the river's edge and taken aboard a float barge. Adam and Joseph went on board and waited until the barge reached the central current, then spoke words of farewell and poured the ash into the roiling waters of the Great River as per Travis's instructions.

I turned away and walked upslope towards home. Just before reaching our street, I gazed northward towards the forest edge and for a moment thought I saw a shade, a movement of cloth and human form among the forest vegetation. The image caused me for a moment to become lost in time and space. I paused and heard words that touched my heart:

> *Reese, your loss is real and unreal at the same time*
> *You remain one with your mate but separate at the same time*
> *Through time and space together you will become*
> *Reese, your time is not now – it will in the future be*

Release your sorrow and lift your heart
Travis is not the ashes you hold and treasure now
Travis walks with you always until the end of time

My senses returned. I found myself surrounded by my twins and their mates, who looked at me strangely and asked if I was well.

We stood together on the porch of our house, where for hundreds of evenings we had sat and enjoyed the love of our family. Sage and Laurel heard it first – then their mates – and then I too heard the words, rising on the wind, spoken and sung by friends and neighbors as they walked the streets of New Vicksburg past our house towards their homes – words of the traditional New Vicksburg farewell song:

Travis Saunders** – you taught us well – **Travis Saunders
Travis Saunders** – you stood for justice – **Travis Saunders
Travis Saunders** – you stood for equality – **Travis Saunders
Travis Saunders** – forever in our hearts you will be – **Travis Saunders
Travis Saunders** – travel on – travel on – travel on – **Travis Saunders

***

After-Word

On the dreary misty morning of February 1st, we left New Vicksburg. Our departure was nearly 15 solar cycles to the day after we first arrived. We crossed the Great River into old Louisiana, that sub-district of Texas Across the River, where long ago the New Vicksburg Militia had helped rid the region of River Pirates. Travis had participated in that action. Riding slowly along the trail between Tallulah and Monroe I recalled his words describing the combined militias attack on the river pirate stronghold within the Ouachita region. We trekked on quietly, sadness still hanging over me. Adam and Joseph took turns in the lead. When one was up front, the other protected our rear travel pushcarts. We five had crossed the river and were heading westward towards Bison Camp, carrying with us the memories of Travis that had sustained us for so long.

It was time to press on and focus on our current lives, and not dwell on the past. Memories would remain, but how we lived the months ahead on our journey would become our signature.

We five as one begin anew
Travel on – Travel on!

Towards unknown lands beyond the far horizon
Travel on – Travel on!

We five as one now face the unknown
Travel on – Travel on!

On to Bison Camp
Travel on – Travel on!

***

Ijano Esantu Eleman

Interlude-Conversation: 11
Death of Travis

***

More sadness for Reese, K'Aser. Watching Travis fade away – this from a common injury, not any wound from one of his many battles – had to weary her.

With the support of her daughters, their husbands, and her friends and neighbors there in New Vicksburg – a community of mutual support if there ever was one – she will prevail.

And fulfill Travis' wishes?

That, and more, A'Tena. Her adventures are far from complete.

That may be but the slow decline of a loved one hurts the most. How she wished for the power to cure him!

A power even we don't possess and – be honest – we have wanted it more than once.

To what end after all is said and done? With the ability to cure beyond directing and a certain amount of adjustment, we'd have time for naught else. It would seem your task is more than difficult enough without this, may I say, benefit.

True, A'Tena, I cannot say this testing needs further challenges or distractions, at least for this Overseer. As it is there is more than enough holding my attention or requiring my attention. Even so there have been times I would have applied a healing power, many times as a matter of fact, given the abilities of medicine in these days as well as most of the before times.

K'Aser, you use your talents as much as possible, and I am proud of you – very proud.

Why, thank you. Your observing contributes to what I am.

Well, thank you, too.

The Journey: Part 4

Chapter 12

Return to Big Hole Valley: Part I

TAR Configuration

Natchez to Odessa

Pre-Note

Tonight will be my twelfth presentation and the first of two documenting our route from New Vicksburg back to Bison Camp. This evening I will share with you passages from the journals written by my daughters, Laurel and Sage, and their mates Joseph and Adam. Through the words faithfully recorded in their journals, you will be introduced to survivors of the Epidemic who shared stories about their respective activities and occupations. In the session tonight we will include events related to our departure from New Vicksburg until we reached Odessa, old Texas. The presentation tomorrow evening will trace events after leaving Odessa until our arrival at Bison Camp.

During our return to Bison Camp, I encouraged my daughters and their mates to maintain daily journals. This was a difficult task at first, as young people sometimes do not sense the importance of daily record-keeping. They labored initially, but then began to see the need to preserve their observations and descriptions of the people met and conversed with along the way. They carried their journals with them at all times inside their backpacks, and when we reached a place that welcomed us they joined in efforts to explore the surroundings. They introduced themselves to persons who looked friendly, and asked whether or not a few moments could be spent in conversation. Responses to their requests were varied: some refused and walked away, while others agreed to converse and also permitted note taking.

With me tonight standing before you are my daughters, Laurel and Sage, and their mates Adam and Joseph. This evening they will share some of the more interesting conversations noted during our return trek. I believe you will find their reports compelling. Their accounts will reveal a range of professions and information about who we are as survivors. Their reports will be presented in sequence starting with the first accounts recorded at Natchez, old Mississippi, and will end with events at Dillon, old Montana. The route, along with specific notations regarding our campsites, will be provided upon request.

***

Along the Way: From Natchez to Odessa

We departed New Vicksburg and began our journey on February 1st. After camping at Port Gibson and Stanton the first and second nights, we passed through the ruins of Natchez. At one time Natchez had been one of the most beautiful cities in old Mississippi. Approaching the vicinity of Liberty Road, we encountered a man selling herbs and spices on the street:

> **Anderson Wilson,** spicer – *I spend most of my days out in the bushlands east of Natchez settlement exploring the shattered zones searching for wild plants. It is safe these days to wander about here and there since the Epidemic killed almost all the Wanderers and made our lives much less fearful. All about are wonderful berries, buds, and leaves of basil, blackberries, chicory, cilantro, dill, clover, dandelions, fennel, mustard, peppermint, sage, and spearmint to name just a few. These can be used for cooking, or for spicing up ill-tasting beverages. I barter my spices for food and other items, such as clothing, utensils, even jugs of water. When the leaves are crushed, the aroma fills my small hut and reminds me of my great grandmother's cooking area where I once played as a child. Herbs and spices bring back good memories. Would you like to buy? I have a wide variety from which to select. Perhaps you can use some in your cooking?*

***

We continued along Highway 61 through the southernmost streets of Natchez, where we observed a small group gathered near the intersection with Live Oak Drive. A man wearing a bright orange shirt had attracted a crowd. He was performing card tricks on a rickety wooden table. We paused to watch. After the crowd dispersed, we approached and he greeted us:

> **William "Billy" "Slim" Horton,** card shark – *My friends know me as Slim, but my given name is William Horton. Others just call me Billy. My ace in the hole always has been my good memory. I am old now but times long ago past I was a great card counter and raked in more than my share of post-Ripple Event barter tokens. But what did I know? I spent it all on C&W – clothes and women. I could look into the eyes of those across the card table from me and know whether or not I would win or lose. The easy tells – the shaking hand, the nervous tic, the smirks that formed at the angle of their mouths. The hard tells – eyes that stared but did not blink, a tug on the lobe of the left ear – was it an itch, or a message sent to a confederate also working the same table? Oh, I was good, and I made enough to keep me in food and housing. But through the many solar cycles past, I could not resist the call of the C&Ws. You ask about what I do today as an oldster here in Natchez? As you see I still do card tricks on the street, earning a little here and there. I am active and still able to use my ax to chop wood. Other tasks? I labor myself out and rake clean the settlement group assembly compound over east of Natchez. I am pleased to say that I still am able to chase the WWSNs – the Widowed Women of Southern Natchez. But most of all I think about past times and, every evening just before sleep, I smile and ache for just one more game of Mississippi Hold'Em.*

***

Red Stick/Baton Rouge

On day six we camped near the Great River at a small park along North Boulevard near the grounds of the once-grand Louisiana state capital. The old French name, Baton Rouge, had fallen out of use many solar cycles past in favor of the more current English translation, Red Stick. I learned in school that the name Red Stick referred to times long past when early French explorer encountered a solitary Cyprus tree festooned with human bodies. The trunk of the once-tall tree was stained red with blood. I seemed to recall that this terrible symbol once marked some sort of territorial boundary line between regional native nations. Through time the name Red Stick or Baton Rouge became accepted terminology.

We established our camp on the grounds of the former state capital. As Reese started dinner, a disheveled street wanderer approached. He carried on his back what appeared to be two plastic canisters – one green the other blue. He told us that both contained drinking water, and that he spent his days bartering his water for food. We invited him to sit with us:

> **Frank [Unreported last name],** freshwater biologist – *You ask my name? Just call me Frank. That's all I want to give you. Once I could identify and describe more than 1,200 species of freshwater diatoms, copepods, and blue-green algae in the river systems of North America. I was an expert in the identification of critters in the great river flowing past Red Stick. I could relate how populations of these microorganisms impacted the health and safety of those who drank great river water. I used to gaze upon the beauty of these critters called diatoms and marvel at their geometric shapes. I smiled at the jerking motions of some copepods as they wiggled their way through their watery habitat. I knew which organisms were innocuous and which were toxic. I put this knowledge to good use today as you see me wandering the streets of Red Stick bartering water to thirsty individuals, all survivors of the Epidemic. To those that treat me with respect, I offer water from my green container, a satisfying beverage that soothes and refreshes. To those who treat me with disdain or violence, I provide water from my blue container, a beverage initially satisfying, soothing, and refreshing, but with a kicker: four hours after drinking, the organisms in the blue tank water will have multiplied in the consumer's stomach and intestines into tens of millions and begin their rampage through the digestive systems of those who dismissed or harmed me. Oh, gladness: I serve good people with a quality beverage. But the others? What pain and excruciating diarrhea they will encounter. Their rapid dehydration sets off within me a happiness that causes me to beam and smile. As I go about my daily business, I shout out to those around me: come one – come all – come, drink my water and be satisfied. From the green or from the blue – receive the water you deserve. The green or the blue – it is up to you. You and your family members respected me.*

Thank you travelers. You fed me tonight without asking for anything except friendship. Please drink deep from my green container.

***

After a second day of rest at Red Stick, it was time to cross the great river. The bridge was intact but had suffered damage that restricted passage. Those wishing to cross to Port Allen in old Louisiana formed a line on the Mississippi side to await their turn. Next to us was a salesman carting his wares that consisted of numerous pairs of shoes. During the crossing delay we struck up a conversation:

Richard Vaughn, shoester – *I survived these many solar cycles by working hard at my trade. I make the best shoes and boots anywhere in the region east or west of the great river. Go out 150 kilo-miles in any direction and you will meet people talking about the quality of my shoes and boots. The ones I make last many solar cycles and do not wear out easily. My high-top boots protect riders and walkers alike, especially when out in the shattered zones where animals might bite a walker who did not have trekking smarts and were unaware of their surroundings.*

Go to any weekend dance or gathering and you will see examples of my shoes – all types of decorative ones for the ladies and young girls. No clod-hoppers these. Even the young boys like my dance-the-night-away items. The boys attending the dances lounge about eye-balling the girls who are all spiffed up with their black-ash polished shoes looking great.

I even have a range of styles that your mother might like. She is your mother, right? You will find no old grey-cloth, wide-heel grannie-style shoes in my collection. Check these out ladies: hear the sound when you click the heels together? Two clicks you'll be sure to attract a handsome partner. Three clicks and you will know right away you are not in Kansas.

***

Lafayette

The morning of day nine we departed the small settlement of Cecilia where we had camped. Next we passed through Breaux Bridge and Larabee on our way into Lafayette. We debated whether to camp at Lafayette or to continue on to Scott. Ultimately we decided to rest for several hours at

Moore Park before proceeding. We tethered our horses and pack mules, allowing them to graze as we enjoyed the park setting. As we walked among the trees and flowered areas, we encountered two "locals," a man and his mate:

Wallace "KO" Thompson, bell ringer – *Is it not correct to say that all who work hard like to spend some time each week being entertained? Most towns and settlement groups have establishments where people gather and sing the old songs. My great great grandmother told me stories of places where people gathered for singing competitions. These events in her time were called Car-E-Oaks or something like that. People would stand up, belt out a song, and those gathered about listening would vote. Well, I could not sing very well, but I was tough so I became a professional boxer. My two brothers, Frank and Jessie, would travel with me. They would set up a stage fighting ring and invite anyone to compete against me. The challengers would put up any type of barter token and I would match it. To collect a barter token, my opponent had to last 10 minutes in the ring. If he or she lasted that long or if they knocked me down, they collected the token. Do not look funny at me: yes, I sometimes fought some very tough women. If I knocked a challenger down, then the bout was over and the barter token became mine. I became known locally as the "bell ringer," since I knocked out so many of my opponents. My nose got busted times too many to count, but I usually lasted and remained upright for the required 10 minutes. Afterwards I always shook hands with my opponents. No need for anger; just business. No one was seriously hurt during my boxing competitions, and I think the crowd generally was entertained. These days I am a little slow in my thinking, so I rarely box unless I need another barter token. How do I earn barter tokens today, you ask? Like the words of the old ditty, I am like Little Tommy Tucker – and I sing for my supper. Here is a list of at least 500 songs that I know by heart. Would you like to hear one?*

***

Carla Jennings, barber – *I am KO's mate. We have been together solar cycles too many to count. I can tell you that he really does sing well. Now about me: many people here in Lafayette visit my shop and they proudly can say that they know Carla Jennings the barber.*

Is it not true that everybody has three choices when it comes to body hair, what we call the GCS options: grow, cut, or shave? You can let your hair grow, you can have it cut off by a barber like me or do it yourself, but if you are especially brave and trusting you can let me shave your head. Do not listen to the rambling of the town folk here in Lafayette. It is true that I regularly drink shine and other beverages, but usually do not do so when I have a customer. Yes, I must confess that last week I slipped and accidentally cut old Jeff's scalp during his shaving session, but that was just one time. And besides, it wasn't my fault since old Jeff jerked and twisted about as he talked about his old ox cart, the one I wanted to borrow. In any case, during the present solar cycle I have cut only two other persons while shaving, and that isn't very many, right? You look like you could use my services: how about a cut or shave?

***

Lake Charles

On day 12 we camped at the settlement of Iowa, old Louisiana, then left the following morning heading towards the border of old Texas. Shortly after mid-day we reached Lake Charles, an expansive lake formed by the Calcasieu River. We paused at a small park just off our route near Moss and Church Streets where we met and spoke with several local residents:

Louise "Lucky Louise" Langdon, cartomancer – *My real name is Louise Langdon, and I am proud to represent the Cajun culture here throughout the Lake Charles region. Most people call me Lucky Louise since I am the luckiest person in this old berg. Why? I don't know. I have always been lucky. Growing up I knew all the answers on school tests, I could forecast when rain would turn to hail; even when a spinning twister might appear in the sky and whether or not it would touch down causing havoc. I have a better than a 90 percent ability to look at a woman "with child," or pregger as we commonly say here in Lake Charles, and predict whether she will deliver a boy or girl child. I have predicted the comings and goings of Wanderer gangs who attempted to destroy our settlement. I once predicted that a sky stone would fall five kilo-miles southeast of here, and when it happened I went out with a search party, found the crater, and dug up the stone. That thing – as we called it – was composed of a type of iron metal. It served us well, as my friends and I turned it into* *more than 200 barter tokens. I can look into a person's eyes and see their past, but I cannot predict the day and moment of death. Would you like me to look into your eyes? Only cost you one copper barter token, not a high price to pay for learning about your future, right?*

***

Margaret Slater, memory preserver – *One of the fears of growing old, even in this hectic time of uncertainty, is that memories of family, fellowship, and social history become unevenly dim and difficult to recall. This is where I use my skills to assist those in need. My skill can help both young and aged to maintain the important memories of past activities and family-related events. Sometimes the slippage of memory is subtle, as when one cannot remember immediately the name of an acquaintance or the title of an old book enjoyed solar cycles ago in school. Then sometimes it comes to pass that both are recalled 3-5 minutes later and remain in memory for additional times to come. But in other instances memory fades are more pronounced and difficult; for example, not being able to remember what one ate for breakfast three hours earlier, or returning home and mistaking a different house in the neighborhood for one's own. These examples are more serious. I assist my clients to the best of my ability. I offer suggestions for memory recall that work in some instances, and I share a range of actions and protocols useful to stimulate recall at other times.*

Why is memory loss such a problem here in Lake Charles, you ask? It is not just a problem in our community but in many others throughout the surrounding region. We are the children of parents who survived the Ripple Event and hard times, and in our lifetimes many suffered terrible family losses during the Epidemic. Perhaps our memory loss these days is more due to us trying to forget these bad times. On the other hand there may be something organic causing the problem. In my experience, it seems to me that there are switches in our brains – ON & OFF – and these we cannot control. I think these switches control access to our memories, both good and bad. I work with my clients the best I can. Sometimes I am successful in restoring many of their happy memories, other times not. I can only hope that my own memory loss does not progress further. At least I can tell you that my name is Margaret Slater.

***

Beaumont

From Lake Charles we continued on to the border between the former states of Louisiana and Texas, entering the Texas Across the River Confederation. The border crossing at Orange, old Texas was uneventful, and we passed through inspection without a hitch – as locals sometimes said. From Orange to Beaumont was a full day's journey. We trekked along and in early evening crossed the Neches River. Here, we entered Beaumont where we camped for two nights at a park named after a long-ago famous woman athlete named Zaharias. We had learned during school at Bison Camp that Beaumont was near the Spindeltop oil well gusher site that brought prominence to the settlement. Wandering along the paths of Zaharias Park we encountered several residents:

Julie Winters, body artist – *These days I am in great demand. My mate and I travel from settlement group to settlement group offering our services in the region surrounding Beaumont. We often are invited to perform our work at coming-of-age and joining celebration ceremonies. My mate, who is off trying to attract business, specializes in animal images. I do not specialize in specific images or designs but offer my patrons different types and kinds of art work: magical swirls, intertwined reptiles, interlocked initials, real life or fanciful faces, and various styles and types of interlocking numbers. These patterns all are available in different combinations. I do not charge much, just a barter token or two. My mate and I represent the tough side of body art. We offer our customers no pain soothers when they undergo our needles. During our artistic sessions we do not supply our customers with shine or any of those interesting desert mushrooms from western Texas that seem to be the craze these days. Yes, using needles to apply body art on a person's arm, leg, chest, belly, back – or more delicate locations – can be a painful process. But is it not so that sometimes pain is associated with pleasure? But as they say, if you cannot stand the heat do not cook over the campfire. No crybabies here. Son, your arms seem unusually bare – would you like some needlework? Lots of designs to choose from, what do you say? How about you and your mate standing nearby? She has a great smile and shock of hair, a nice piece of body art could do her well. I see your mother over there is eyeballing me, so I guess your answer is no. But perhaps when you get older?*

***

During our second day in Beaumont we explored the grounds of Morgan Park where we encountered a bedraggled street vendor. He was much different in appearance than most of the residents we had seen previously on the streets of Beaumont. He was terribly thin and looked ill. We stopped and asked if he needed help:

> **Anonymous,** soup seller – *I will speak with you but will not tell you my name. I sell soup here in Beaumont. I make all kinds. My ingredients are many, my flavors divine. For a pot of my soup what will you barter? Right now I am in the need for socks; do you have a woolen pair without any holes? I also would consider an exchange of soup for several flint stones, since my fire-starters have been chipped away down to almost nothing. Smell the aroma of my soup? You like it, yes? Come and trade something for a bowl of my soup. I see you smiling. I know that you want my soup. Come, make me a deal? Soup for something I need. Help me – and I will help you. Please! I need help.*

How could we resist his entreaties? We not only bartered for his soup, but in addition to the stockings he requested, Joseph gifted him a shirt and a belt. He would not tell us his name because he was ashamed. I asked his age. He replied that he had seen 28 solar cycles. I could scarcely believe it as he appeared to be 20 or 30 solar cycles older. Life had treated him harshly, but he was honest and attempting to do his best. We had helped him in a small way. After serving us, he turned and walked away thanking Joseph for his gifts.

***

Houston

The passage from Beaumont to Houston took five camp nights. We had heard from stragglers along the way that Houston had neared recovery from the Dark Time disaster but then suffered terribly during the Epidemic. We also heard from other travelers that Houston had strict behavior rules – no gambling and no fighting, otherwise you might be arrested and prison bound. Such announced clarity of behavior was outlined in folk songs hummed by travelers passing through this once-important old Texas town. We crossed Buffalo Bayou and camped on the green at Guadalupe Plaza Park. Given the sense of what might be called no-nonsense here in Houston, we were surprised to encounter what in olden days would have been called a loan shark:

Louis Piper, *loaner – If you need some barter tokens to pay off your debts, do not worry; I will loan you the number and type that you need. Get the hut that you deserve. You want a new horse and you do not have enough barter tokens? Do not worry. Calm down. Get the horse you deserve. How many horses or mules you need? It does not matter. I will help you. The process is simple: we just sit down together over a tall glass of shine or something else that meets your satisfaction, and you tell me what you want and how much of it you need. Then you and I will enter into an agreement for re-payment. That is only fair, right? You need so many bronze, iron, or steel barter tokens to pay off your debts? It does not matter. I can supply what you need to pay off your several loans, and then you will only have to re-pay one person – me. The process is that simple. Get what you need; get what you deserve. You will repay only me at the agreed rate and agreed schedule. That is only fair, right? But always remember: you must pay the Piper. Pay me, Louis Piper. I see that you like that clever play of words. No excuses, no lengthy explanations why you cannot repay, no lame-ass defense that you conjure up why you cannot repay. I am your loaner friend: respect me and I will respect you. Disrespect me by not meeting your repayment obligation – well then things happen.*

***

On the second day of our visit to Houston we met the interesting Mr. Stoneveld.

Thomas Stoneveld, defense analyst – *Hello, I am Thomas Stoneveld at your service. I learned how to manage finances from my great grandfather. He taught me how to plan for the future. But then came the Ripple Event and Dark Time, and what future was there for us? Everything was upside down; money was useless. Growing up during the Recovery Period, my family traded in metal ingots and what we called FFs or food futures. I vaguely remember learning about bank accounts during my school solar cycles. There are no active banks today in Houston; only ruins of empty buildings destroyed many solar cycles past. These days I make use of the analytical lessons taught to me in school – figuring out how best to defend Houston and to protect the city water supply from those who would do us harm. Recently, I was asked by our local militia leader to conduct a terrain* *analysis, how to defend regional territories beyond the boundaries of old Houston, where to develop safe havens for our residents if their safety and security become necessary. Another task I have undertaken is to identify defensive locations that would enable us to defeat groups of Wanderers bent upon our destruction. What a kick in the ass, as they say. Who would have thought that the son of a financially astute family would turn out to be an important member of the Houston defense force?*

***

San Antonio

We flowed along Eye 10 leaving Houston heading towards San Antonio. A little less than a week later and after camping at small settlements along the way, among them Katy, Sealy, Luling, and Seguin, we reached San Antonio. We trekked into San Antonio following Eye 10 then turned north along Eye 37. The San Antonio River flowed north to south through this portion of the town. Turning west off Eye 37 we passed through the historic portion of Antonio as many residents now call the settlement. Much of the famed Antonio River Walk had been destroyed during the Ripple and Dark Time. But here and there enterprising residents had started reconstruction. Our camping destination was Travis Park.

During the next two days we explored this ancient and historic city. Southeast of Travis Park was a ruined structure that like a magnet drew so many pilgrims to this once-great settlement. We approached what looked to be the façade of a church. While I knew the name of the structure due to my education at Bison Camp, there were no signs to denote its significance; perhaps they had been stolen for firewood or for their metal components? Together with my daughters and their mates, we paused at the entrance where I explained the events that occurred here when defenders of independence and freedom perished at this location – now a place of honor and respect, but silent and alone standing.

Over the course of the next several rest days we met a large number of Antonio residents, each with interesting stories to tell:

[NOTE: Let me say here that his first report is unusual and unlike any previously mentioned. After we had visited the ruins of the once-historic site called The Alamo, we encountered a man walking up and down the Antonio River Walk strumming a guitar and singing a convoluted song that initially did not make sense. He told us his name was Duncan Altmont, but that he was better known as the San Antonio Potato Bagger, or SOS – Seller-of-Spuds. He looked us up and down, rolled his eyes, and resumed singing:

As I walk out through the streets of Antonio
As I walk out through Antonio each day
I am the young man who carries potatoes
A bag of potatoes I must sell today

I see by your outfit that you are a traveler
These words he did say as I boldly stepped by
Come sit down beside me and hear my sad story
I'll sell you my spuds for a price not too high.

Once I was like you and traveled all over
I greeted with joy every morning at dawn
But then fifteen thugs laid me out on the prairie
Stole all my goods leaving nothing to pawn.

Now in Antonio I sell my potatoes
I barter and deal just to make my ends meet
Look at these beauties they'll fill up your stomach
Buy my potatoes you'll have something to eat.

***

Turns out that we did barter for Altmont's spuds, and that evening we invited Duncan to join us around our campfire where he related how his life had changed dramatically during recent solar cycles. He said that in Antonio two groups of land-grabbers had opened grocery stores and stockpiled a wide range of root vegetables, among them carrots, onions, and potatoes. On weekends these dealers undercut his sales by donating bags of root foods to needy persons without requesting barter tokens or trade in return, leaving him with few patrons to barter for his spuds. Here was a hardworking young man being edged out of business by compassionate others who donated food to the most needy in Antonio. It seemed that compassion for the many left hardworking others with few options to survive. We talked about various ways this impasse might be changed with least amount of talk or violence, but in reality we could offer no effective solution to his problem unless he took on the grocery stores directly or chose not to sell spuds and join the ranks of Antonio's most needy. But Duncan was proud, able to work, and did not aspire to simply receive food for doing nothing and sitting about being idle. He was caught in what seemed to be an impossible situation to remedy. He would be better off as a street person who refused to work than to toil hours selling spuds here and there for little to nothing in return. He mingled among those that did not work but received food. While he was honorable, Duncan received little to nothing in return. After an evening of good fellowship and a great meal of boiled spuds and prairie dog ribs, he left us to ponder his future. We wished him well.

***

Nelson James, dentist – *I'm on my way to an appointment, so make your questions quick. You ask what I do? Well I am a dentist. Nowadays it is just like the old Wild West many solar cycles past, pulling teeth using metal pliers. No more the sophisticated equipment that I once had in my office where I repaired broken molars, re-set incisors, and cleaned teeth. No more the soothing soft chairs where clients laid back and opened wide on request. All that vanished many solar cycles past. Now here in Antonio everybody's teeth are yellow with grime and whatever. It does not do anybody good to have their teeth cleaned these days. For what and who cares? Are you going to some rich person's mansion where you need white teeth to complement your fancy tux or temptress-style low-cut dress? Huh! I haven't ventured inside a mansion ever, and I never wore one of those floppy-looking man suits during the more than 40 solar cycles I lived here in Antonio. Not even sure they exist these days. Once in a while I pull a canine or two after the client has taken a swig of shine to dull the pain. Because pulling teeth causes pain I am hated, but we dentists still remain in demand.*

***

Waco

Sage took the trail lead as we departed Antonio. One time she commented that we had been on trek for one month since leaving New Vicksburg. I shouted back that perhaps we should celebrate at our next stop or two. The trip from Antonio to Waco was long and tiring, considerable energy spent over an eight-day difficult and long ride. Some of the settlements we passed through or around had interesting names: Buda, Pfugerville, Shertz, even Troy – named after that ancient city of long ago with its fake horse with soldiers stashed inside its belly.

As we approached the southwest limits of Waco, now a protective settlement group, we noticed a line of gallows erected up along the skyline. A farmer working his field just north of the Lorena settlement group hailed us as we paused for water and conversation:

Kenneth Poster, farmer and posse member – *Look up unto the hills, son, and what do you see: there on the skyline are the results of poor upbringing and child-raising. There wouldn't be any cattle rustling in these parts if parents taught their children right from wrong. In my free time away from farming, I'm a member of the WDP or Waco Defense Posse. Last week we tracked down and caught the gang of hoods that you see hanging up on the skyline. We found them with 30 of our rustled beasts. Those idiots didn't have the savvy how to evade us trackers in the WDP. Those stupids left marks and passage tracks everywhere and simply headed off northwest towards Brownwood thinking that they could sell our cattle out in the boonies to some settlement group dealer. They didn't even have the smarts to modify or change the cattle brands into some configuration to confuse the prospective buyers. Well, by Johnny, we caught them, and I swear by the heat of the hot el-Solano wind that they whimpered and mewed as we took them captive. Could you believe it? Not one of the rustlers was over the age of 18 solar cycles – barely older than you young'uns speaking with me now. We in the WDP called for an assembly and asked parents to bring their other young'uns to see and listen so they would learn first-hand the results of bad behavior and upbringing, and remember forever the right way to live with honesty and integrity. We asked the fathers to join us in administrating what we here call rustler's justice. We hanged the first one. Something not nice to see even for us, given all the wiggling and you know what that runs down the inside of their pants and plops on the ground!. Then another, and another, until all dangled where they remain still today. Eventually, we will bury them in an unmarked common grave just beyond the yonder gully. A hard lesson, but one hopefully learned by those who watched.*

***

We thanked Mr. Poster for his explanation and hurried on into Waco where we camped at Cameron Park along the Brazos River:

Abigale Boynton, caper – *There is a tradition at Waco that each newly birthed child should receive its respective emergence number embroidered on a small cap. In this way, each of our children will have both a formal name and specific number. Why the number, you ask? Well, we here in Waco believe it is appropriate and useful to keep track and monitor our residents. In the olden days before the Ripple Event, everyone had something called an SS# – pronounced something like So-Shal-Siker-Ity Nu-Mbr. Everybody had one – if you didn't, then the unknowns would come and speak with you, scare the living daylights out of you. Well now we don't have any more such nine-number identifications or designations. It seems that the elected folks at Waco thought about such things and came to the conclusion that we residents still needed a number that would differentiate what we call the Ins from the Outs – those who live here and contribute to the settlement contrasted to those who enter our boundary to barter goods or to travel through like you folks. It's all very simple: if you don't have a WN or Waco number your stay with us cannot exceed three days and then you must leave and continue on. Simple, right? It is my task to keep the Waco number list correct and matched by information related to family, address, and occupation.*

Preparing infant caps has been my personal honor and task for the past 15 solar cycles. Prior to the Epidemic, my cap number had reached a total of 136 births. After the Epidemic struck so many infants and children, births were fewer and we changed the design and numbering system to be embroidered on the birth caps. Now the birth number also comes with two letters, PE – of course meaning Post-Epidemic. Just last week one of our young women delivered a little girl. I had the joy of preparing and presenting her parents with their infant's birth cap with the number 6 PE. As you can see, we have put the difficult time of the Epidemic behind us and are looking forward towards our future, one made brighter because we in Waco know who we are and how to protect our families, goods, and services from greedy others who would like nothing better than to disrupt the calm and quiet of our fine settlement.

***

Fort Worth

Leaving the curious number-structured settlement of Waco, we resumed our journey northward towards Fort Worth and camped on day 43 at a secluded park along the western bank of the Trinity River. A grand sign posted at the park entrance read: *Here the West Begins!* Perhaps this was a memory from earlier times? At dusk just before dinner we encountered two local women, residents of Fort Worth. Each worked independently and had developed their craft and trade into successful businesses:

> **Marsha Trent,** mate therapist – *Some call my profession Family Soother. Others say that I am a Bond Restorer. I provide council to those who request it, especially information and advice about re-forging friendship and affection after serious family arguments. I am in special demand during the hot days of summer. Some people are mated by ceremony and stay together for a lifetime of solar cycles. Others split and renounce their obligations after only 6-8 months of living together. All couples have problems, do they not? Even you young folks, right? If you and your mate do not agree on this or that – that or this – before you know it an argument of enormous proportions erupts that should not have happened in the first place. Couples come to me and ask for assistance. We sit together; I listen as they talk. I hear similar words time after time: He will not do this – She will not do that; He doesn't understand me. She mistakes my intentions. On and on it goes for hours at a time. I sit and listen: my clients talk. I sit and listen: talk, talk, and talk. About once an hour I serve beverages and an occasional slice of bread, sometimes smeared with blackberry jam that I make at home when I am not sitting and listening to couples complain about this and that – that and this. Then when all is said and done – it becomes my turn to speak. And so it goes: one client after another, day after day, solar cycle after solar cycle. With 98 percent of the cases where I serve as therapist, I digest all that has been said. I tell them to consider different suggestions, such as listening is better than arguing; take a time out once in a while; let him have his time, you have your time; and have time together. Speak up: your mate cannot read your mind. Suggestions like don't crab, don't bitch, don't moan about this and that – these are not part of my therapy sessions. I ask my clients to define the term small stuff and then explore ways how not to sweat these irritants. If he wants what used to be called a man cave and she wishes to collect pots, pans, and vases leaving no room in the dining area for social interactions, I just say don't sweat it – smile and say you are my mate and I care for you. And that's that.*

I conclude each session with the famous three words that serve most of my clients well: honor, love, and respect each other. Now, for the other 2 percent of those clogging my office, their difficulties cannot be fixed easily. With these, it makes no sense dragging out mate therapy sessions any further just to earn more barter tokens. If their union really is broken and cannot be fixed, that's life. In either case from the 98 percent and 2 percent I still receive six copper barter tokens from each mate. I have found that during some solar cycles, especially when there have been floods or tornadoes, mates get along better than at other times. Perhaps they pull together during times of such disasters and are more helpful to one another.

So, young lady, are you having any problem with your mate? If so, I am able and ready to assist. Since you are not planning to stay and are just traveling through prairie lands to the east and west, I will give you a great discount: two hours – two aluminum barter tokens.

***

Afterwards we had an unexpected interview with dark connotations:

Angela Lopez, florist – *Sometimes folks in Fort Worth call me the Flower Girl, but my real name is Angela Lopez. I prepare gifts of flowers for girlfriends, for boyfriends, for mate ceremonies, and for anniversaries. But more recently I have had to prepare bundles of flowers for funerals. There is great sadness all around these days, what with the recent Epidemic and the hard times that followed, which still lie heavy upon us. When I was a little girl in Fort Worth, I heard stories that once orchids and syphenias were imported to our settlement from countries and lands beyond the Great Sea. Today I gather seeds out in the prairie lands east and west of Fort Worth. I grow the flowers that bloom in the fields – poppies that bring soothing sleep, oleanders that bring paralysis and death, and the beautiful lavender hemlocks, henbanes, and daturas. When I set out my flowers each morning to attract customers, I never can predict who will stop by or what their needs will be. Some will barter with me for flowers to decorate their huts for happy events; others need them to add color to their homes for sad events, such as a family and neighbor gathering to celebrate the life of a family member or friend who has died. Too many of the latter requests have come recently. All around my shelter I grow marigolds, the beautiful golden symbol of* *life's passing, eagerly sought by those living in what once was called America Central. Come: I invite you to visit my shelter. Examine the flower blooms and make a nice selection of colors and aromas. My displays can make you smile, laugh, and enjoy life. I can mask the tart, sour taste of any death plant you might wish to obtain by using extracts of sweet honey from my hives. Come: I invite you to enter. I want you to leave Fort Worth happy.*

***

Santos

Leaving Fort Worth we traveled west along Eye 20, passing through Willow Park and Brock, where we camped on days 44 and 45. We reached Santos on day 46, and elected to stay a second night to rest and explore the hills northwest up near Palo Pinto Creek Reservoir. We asked the local militia leader where we might camp, and he suggested we remain close by the settlement since Santos had been attacked recently by groups of Wanderers. He told us that if we wanted to explore the Palo Pinto Creek region, he could organize a team of two militia members to accompany us.

After establishing camp, we elected to explore the settlement and we decided to eat at the local Roadhouse eatery where we ordered something called Margarita flatbread along with burgers piled high with onion rings and hot chili peppers. Also dining at the Roadhouse was a gentleman who sat alone at an adjacent table He eyed us with a curious expression, then smiled and invited us over to his table. At one time he had been a teacher at several settlement groups in the region. He was a geographer:

Stanley Norris, geographer – *Landscapes and maps I studied well. Lands occupied by different cultures through eons of time, descriptive names in languages old applied to settlements to honor those who once explored different regions. I studied footprints of ancient beasts, collected the shells of ocean snails and crystals of pure shape that told of times long ago past. I taught my skills to youngsters living in Brazos and surrounding settlement groups such as Santos. Many times we explored and discussed how our planet been formed from cosmic dust. Most young men and women students like you do not care about such things in times like these and think it a great bother to memorize the historical deeds and actions that long ago happened in the past. I have more success showing* *youngsters here in Santos how to search the mountain areas up near the reservoir to locate the cliffs of obsidian, where the glassy stone pieces can be collected and shaped into sharp-bladed weapons used for hunting or defense. Sometimes my students ask me a question why the Palo Pinto Creek or the Brazos River flows in a certain direction; why flocks of birds migrate south or north at certain times of the solar cycles; or what makes the flash and sound of lightning and thunder. All good questions for a geographer to consider: do you have a question for me?*

His last comment initiated a short question-answer session about the region. Stanley sat with a beaming smile. Sage and Laurel's questions were answered with clever retorts and he responded to questions by Adam and Joseph, as well:

Sage: *I know that the word Brazos means arms in Spanish; so why is the river and settlement group here called Brazos?*

Norris: *You know a lot, little lady! If you travel the River Brazos to the north you will reach Possum Kingdom Lake. Even further north you wind up at what we now call the Nowhere Region, located at the great junction where the Double Mountain Fork and the Salt Fork meet to form the upper arm of the Brazos. The Spanish called this river The Arms of God – Brazos de Dios – because early explorers drinking from its waters were saved from death by thirst. But we also warn young folks like you to be very careful. For example, if you walk the riverbanks of the Brazos never ever wave your arms up and down and shout. If you do so, the spirit of the Brazos will lure you to destruction and trap you in its quicksand. Once trapped, if you continue to flail your arms about, you will be sucked down into darkness, leaving only your arms above ground to show where you ventured. The Brazos collects arms of those who trespass and do not respect the past. The Brazos riverbanks near Santos are very dangerous.*

Laurel: *What are the key medicinal plants growing in the region up near the Palo Pinto Creek Reservoir?*

Norris: *You seem to be as smart as your sister. Glad you asked. Too many medicinal plants to recount here at the Roadhouse eatery, but if you all would like a look around, we can arrange a visit if the militia folks will accompany us for protection. What do you think? Ask your mother: do you have time?*

Adam: *I think we have the time. We are heading west in a few days for Abilene. Are there places off the track where we might see ancient petroglyphs carved by early First Peoples?*

Norris: *I never met a young man as curious as you. Not so many nearby here. The best sites are further west and south. Most are in the Pecos-Rio Grande River region, and that area is off your direct track but I will be able to show you one or two cliff glyphs if we visit the reservoir tomorrow.*

Joseph: *Why did you say earlier that young people like us do not care about geography, and think it a great bother to memorize the historical deeds and actions that long ago happened? That does not describe the four of us.*

Norris: *Well bless me son. That is a profound statement. If true – and I have no doubt that you believe it is – then you and your companions are very rare folks, indeed. Those who disrespect the past or who neglect to learn from the past – are doomed to repeat the mistakes and disasters caused by past time others. I take my hat off to you, Joseph, and leave each of you with a puzzlement that has plagued all educated people for many hundreds of solar cycles. Perhaps you educated young 'ins can explain to me: Why do so many people of different cultures disrespect one another?*

Of course – we had no answer.

***

The next morning the five of us joined Norris and three armed militia members from Santo. We rode north along Country Road 4 until we reached the Brazos River, we then crossed over and followed the river course northwest until we reached the Palo Pinto Creek Reservoir. Along the way Norris pointed out 8-10 varieties of medicinal plants that Laurel paused to collect and preserve. At the northeastern point of the reservoir we dismounted near a shallow cliff overhang where Norris pointed out several ancient First People rock carvings. One was a stylized sun with triangular points representing rays while the second was a rider on horseback wearing a flat-brimmed hat and long dark coat. Norris related that this latter carving was an image depicting one of the early Spanish explorers who introduced horses into the region.

We sat near the lakeshore gazing outward over the placid waters. We marveled at the arrival of hundreds of birds, squawking and settling down. As we watched, a Santo local named Bryan Baker approached us. He had noticed our interest in local birds and decided to join us in conversation. We asked about his profession. He told us he was an owler, a term we had not before encountered:

> **Bryan Baker,** owler – *Some folks like to use dogs as working animals and make them part of their family. In the olden days I heard stories that dogs and cats, even some types of mice, were kept inside houses for amusement. I learned that these animals once were called pets. These were small living things that could be picked up, held in your arms, and stroked or petted. Why anyone would pet a mouse is beyond the realm of my thinking. What I do in my work is practical. I seek out owl nests at the time when the mother birds are laying eggs. Most of the sites I observe are on the northwest side of the reservoir, opposite where we are sitting. I keep my eye on the nests and when I see the first eggs begin to crack, I shoo away the adult mama birds, remove the eggs, and carry them back to my mountainside hut where I keep them warm. When the owlets hatch, I wave my hands about and through my actions I become the first object that the little ones see. I continue to wave and wiggle a stick with a rag attached to one end, and in this way I maintain their attention. As they become accustomed to my waving and to my rag-stick apparatus, I always have a ready supply of meat to reward and feed them. One might say in all this doing, I have become the owlet's parent. I keep my owlets inside a sheltered place in my hut where they grow and are able to walk about and exercise. Sometimes the owlets band together and attack a mouse or two that has crept into my hut by mistake, thinking it to be a safe place to hide. Wrong! When the time comes, I take the young owls one by one outside the hut at night and let them test*

their wings. After a few circles they usually tire but always return to me. When they land I reward their return with pieces of meat. In this way they remain linked to me. As days of training pass, their flight patterns become strong but they always return to my hut. I have trained many owls this way. They have become almost part of my family. The sounds of contentment the owls make after a night flight and return to my hut are gratifying. No one else in Santo or in the nearby settlement groups over by Brazos or down south towards Gordon or the Thurber settlements has my skill. People come to me because they want to hire my owls to rid their barns, silos, or living spaces of invading mice, kangaroo rats, and other varmints and creeping invaders, big and small. When I receive such requests, my eyes dilate just like the eyes of my owls, and we strike a bargain. I find it interesting that my owls do not fight among each other. Perhaps something about self-respect keeps them busy.

***

Abilene

We reached Abilene in the late afternoon of Day 50 and decided to extend our visit another day for rest and exploration. We established camp at Carl Young Park not far from Lytle Lake. Much of Abilene had been leveled by unseasonal tornadoes in the period before the Epidemic and had been struck again by a second set of terrible storms during recent solar cycles. Not far from our campground, we observed considerable activity where teams of men and women were rebuilding shops and huts. The residents of Abilene were proud of their settlement and that spirit was contagious. Former residents of old Abilene had discarded their personal animosities and biases and banded together to not only rebuild the settlement but to protect it from the roaming gangs who would not cooperate in forming the new one-Abilene concept. It no longer was correct to say that in Abilene – *people will treat you mean* – Abilene was moving forward:

Charles Carpenter, carpenter – *Yes, you see me as I am; a carpenter by day using skills that have been in my family for several hundred solar cycles past. I can eyeball a site and provide a square meter-yard estimate that is only 2 percent below tape-measure accuracy. I can estimate lumber and planking needs to the nth degree. I have my own company here in Abilene – Charley's Wood-Working. Of course it's named after me, Charles Carpenter. During the days I work hard,* *even in the midst of summer heat when rivers of sweat drip from my brow. Even on late winter days such as this, by noon my shirt is dark with salty sweat. My team and I can renovate an old structure in just about no time. If you want something new like fully-developed living quarters, it might take us a week or more and will cost between 30 and 50 barter tokens, depending upon the type of metal. Don't be surprised at the cost; nothing is cheap these days. What do you expect – something for nothing? After our daily carpentry work is finished, my team and I take on other tasks during the evenings. We gather every other night out back of the community grain silo off of Oak Street, just south of Eye 20. Once the ten of us assemble, we start our patrol street by street. We sweep through the numbers: North 1st through 18th streets and back. Then the next night we head along South 1st through 29th streets and back. We are accompanied by more than 250 hard-working men and women – most armed – who have vowed never to let the gangs retake any part of our once-fine settlement. When we find something that isn't right, we take care of business. What? You want me to tell you what we really do? Why not join us tonight and participate – you might enjoy it!*

***

On our rest day at Abilene, we visited a northern suburb up near See Bee Park just south of old Lake Fort Phantom Hill. This lake, according to locals, had been renamed Wild Bird Haven sometime within the past 20 solar cycles. Birds were everywhere, and it was here that we met one of the more creative persons we encountered on our journey:

Clay Pullman, eggler – *My name is Clay. I am the son of Simon Pullman. My work for the past four solar cycles has been to rob bird's nests, to steal eggs to feed families in our settlement group. Depending upon the type of eggs collected, I receive a variety of different types of credits. Sparrow and jayblue eggs are worth two credits each; those from larger birds like crows, egrets, and ravens are worth five credits each; eggs from what we call the great birds (owls, eagles, and hawks) are ten credits each. Once I amass a total of 100 credits, I can convert these cardboard points to one aluminum barter token. If I can accumulate 200 egg credits, I will receive one copper BT. During the past four solar cycles, I have amassed enough credits to convert them into 15 aluminum and six copper* *barter tokens. I have been injured several times falling from trees or cliff nest sites, and have been bitten and clawed by the beaks and talons of the great birds. But I continue with my work since, I need to accumulate 450 barter tokens to participate in the annual Abilene mate selection ceremony. How many do I have now, you ask? I need just 25 more tokens (either aluminum or copper) in order to join the festivities. Look over my egg list, and please select what you like.*

***

Our stay at Abilene was delightful. As it turned out, we were present at a massive community gathering where Clay Pullman bartered enough bird's eggs to be just three barter tokens short of meeting his goal to participate in the Abilene mate selection ceremony. It was not easy growing up in Abilene with the destructive storms, but the spirit of the community remained vital.

***

Odessa

The distance from Abilene to Odessa was approximately 175 kilo-miles and required six days of camping along the way. We reached Odessa, heart of what the locals called the Permian Basin – a geological name that had little meaning in the post-Ripple Event times. No one we spoke to could explain why the settlement was called Odessa. While several residents claimed that Odessa was the name of some faraway town in southeastern Europe, they saw no connection between their town and the one across the Great Sea. In any case local residents we spoke to did not care, as they had other problems on their minds. Storms during the preceding solar cycle required a re-rebuilding commitment in portions of the civic center, especially for erecting housing for the many immigrants who had taken refuge and shelter in town.

The Odessa Militia members invited us to tether our horses and camp at Central Park, a small grassy area bounded by Center and Milburn avenues and 11th and 13th streets. As we unpacked to set up our tents, Joseph noticed that someone was eyeballing our goods. He seemed to be taking inventory of our possessions. Joseph challenged him and engaged the looker in conversation:

Yes I was checking out your goods as you unpacked and set up camp. I noticed that you are very concise in your packing and that you seem to have a place and use for everything. What I noticed, however, is that you should replace your tarps, as the two on your pack mules are seriously worn and certainly will tear if not replaced. I have several in stock, if you might be interested.

Who are you?

Robert Ortiz, bagman – *I am known locally as Robert. I can sell anything. Solar cycles past when life was different, I once sold 45 raincoats up north at a settlement group across the border near Carlsbad in the central desert region. I am so good that I could sell Stetson hats to the Headless Horseman, even hair tonic at the bald women enclave north of Pecos. I am an excellent bagman, traveling about on horseback with my two pack mules trailing behind. I make my way here and there over hill, over dale, sometimes I hit the dusty trail, and I just keep rolling along – as the old army song goes. Perhaps you know it? Once I met a feminine opposite one day-long time passing, a bag lady who was hawking personal and household wares. She had a supply of knives and forks made of weathered acacia wood, and pot scrubbers fashioned from cactus leaves. She also carried a selection of bracelets and necklaces inset with polished agates. She was fantastic. I tried to woo her using my bagman charm and sales skills, but she just laughed and gave me the brush-off. I felt like a chigger flicked off a blind-man's arm. But I didn't give up. I continued to smile and said something to her that caught her attention and drew her up short:*

> *Ma'am do you know the difference between snake and scorpion bites?*

She looked at me curious like and said, No – why don't you tell me?

Well I did and, as they say, the rest is history. What I told her made all the difference in my life and hers. I want you to know that we've been together as mates now for 13 solar cycles. How about that? I can sell anything. What can I sell you? How about replacing those tarps I mentioned earlier? I will barter fairly with you. If not, then how about some crystal honey drops? How about some lizard-catching gear? My reptile capture kits will come in handy once you leave Odessa and start tracking through the desert lands. They say horned toads and blue-collar lizards are not so easy to catch but make good nighttime snacks. My reptile capture kit can keep you in food during hard times along the trail. What do you say?

***

Joseph contacted me and related the bagman's comments about our protective tarps. I went over to our supply pile for an inspection. Yes, the tarps were soiled, dirty, and dusty but the grommets were all in place and there were no rips or tears along the edges. Robert Ortiz may be a good salesman, but I wasn't about to buy his palaver about my tarps. He was a true bagman.

Around dusk we heard music coming from a campfire across the park. We walked over and listened to the strummers. A young man and young girl were performing old cowboy songs, some of which I remembered from my childhood back at Bison Camp:

Red River Valley
Old Chisholm Trail
Git Along, Little Doggies
You Are My Sunshine
Bury Me Not on the Lone Prairie
Down in the Valley
Home on the Range
Little Joe, the Wrangler

The parents of the singers also were present. They were a family of street artists, singers and magicians, one with a special talent known as clacking:

Thomas Knight, clacker – *My parents Jacob and Joyce Knight named me Thomas and called me their magic baby. I was born during the Dark Time Recovery Period. Through the various solar cycles since, I have brought my parents good luck. It rained the day I was born, and our crops that solar cycle were successful. My parents told me that our family lives changed after I was birthed, and once I came on board, as they say, we had adequate food and housing and no longer lived on the street. Early on as a child I was tutored in the ways and means of street magic. I soon became the best street magician anywhere – from Odessa east to Midland and beyond, west to El Paso, or south all along the Rio Grande River. I could make barter tokens appear or disappear at will and conjure ways to make rabbits turn into doves. I learned my best magic tricks from my friend*

Tzau Leung, who showed me sleight-of-hand techniques, how to work the ins and outs, and how to make my assistant appear to float in space without support. My greatest feats, however, involved use of special wooden clackers. These instruments I developed myself. When the mystical pieces of wood are banged or clacked together, a sound is produced that can make people disappear.

Young lady, your facial expression betrays your thoughts, and you do not believe me. Well that's all right, but let me continue. Depending upon how nice people on the street in Odessa were to me and to our family, I would strike my clackers again and return the disappeared ones to their previous spot. If they treated me with disrespect or with other such foolishness, I could transport them to some distant location with just the shake and sound of my clacker. Then when they reappeared they would have to walk some distance back to where they originally had stood. These were eye-catching illusions, not easily analyzed or copied by other aspiring street magicians. Young lady, you look like you would like to learn my clacker technique, right? But here is the issue: if you want to learn my secrets you will have to remain here with me in Odessa and work along beside me every day for at least two solar cycles. I see you are eager to learn, but I just cannot give you the information without proper context and training. Plus, your mother and your mate would not approve. As we street magic types say – a little knowledge is a dangerous thing. You seem to be disappointed with my words, so let me use my skills and turn your frown into a smile. Close your eyes, now reach out and pull my finger and see what happens. Nice, huh?

***

After-Word

We ended the evening session with a long period of questions and answers. Most asked for more details concerning dangers along the way, food-related issues, how we kept up our spirits, even personal issues about everyday life on the trail. One question from the audience was directed to Joseph. His reply seemed to condense all the feelings that I experienced since leaving Bison Camp with Travis, our period of time together at New Vicksburg, and how together we had become a family:

The five of you obviously are strong in body and spirit. How was it that you could maintain focus and strength to continue onward after leaving New Vicksburg? It seems to me it would have been much easier for you to settle along the way, especially among peoples at several of the locations who treated you with respect and who offered a community of like-thinking people. Yet you kept on trekking?

Joseph took the question and answered clearly:Our strength, our direction, and our desire always have been to honor the last wish of Travis, my mate's father. Travis urged us to return to Bison Camp, an almost spiritual location where he and Reese had joined together as mates and bonded during the early solar cycles of their lives. Is it not true that strong individuals are made even stronger when mate groups form families? While each member of our group is strong and independent in their own way, we are better and stronger as a family. Reese is our leader. It was Reese and Travis who made the long trek from Bison Camp down the Missouri River into the Ohio River region and up and over the Blue Ridge. It was Reese and Travis who traveled the long distance to settle in New Vicksburg, where through time we would become one – a family united. I was present when Travis passed his sword to Sage. I was present and heard his last request to return to Bison Camp. How could it be that we would consider not honoring his wish? We family members bound together as one would have done so despite any difficulties or dangers we encountered along the way. To settle elsewhere because of ease or convenience, never was an option. Family honor is more than just words. Promises given are meant to be kept. There was only one goal: that the five of us would return to Bison Camp and in doing so honor Travis. Our collective family vision of return sustained each of us through our journey, and now our family is home once more.

***

Ijano Esantu Eleman

Interlude-Conversation: 12

Owls

***

A'Tena, there appears to be an Owler abroad in the realm; for good or ill I sense this is a first.

I have seen no other, K'Aser, through many times and places. Yes, this is indeed a first for us.

If such people were there to be seen, you'd have spotted them given your powers of observation as well as your proven connection with these raptors. It is not all that difficult for me to imagine the nobility of Medieval England riding to the hunt with their favorite horned birds perched proudly on their gloved hands. The city that has carried your name from times way past through to this here and now was tied very closely to them. At the crest of their empire, their coins were known as Owls in most of the world. And impressive coins they were – fully silver and as bright as the sun – quite beautiful especially the Owl's side.

The likeness could have been better but I thank you for the compliment all the same. Nobles riding with owls in place of falcons would have presented quite a picture – away Ollie, to the hunt Oliver!

Fly, Howland, fly!

Howland?

A favorite character in Pogo, a comic strip quite popular in its time.

Pogo? Strip? What are ...?

A'Tena, even you cannot see all. I'll explain during our next visit to The Place. Be patient and all shall be known to you.

Fair enough.

Chapter 13
Return to Big Hole Valley: Part II
Deserts and Salt
Malaga to Bison Camp

Pre-Note

We returned home to Bison Camp never expecting to encounter new settlers unlike ourselves. We were different from the space bipeds but at the same time similar in other ways. Their males were strong and handsome as were their women. We were slightly taller by a few centimeter-inches, but other than that specific physical feature we appeared basically similar. Our technologies, on the other hand, seemed basic and limited but theirs were advanced beyond our comprehension. Once we were able to communicate, a general rapport seemed to link us together as settlers in the Big Hole Valley.

My daughters and their mates presented well at the last evening session. The examples and comments they related were clear and illustrated the diversity of survivors we had met along the way from New Vicksburg. I could not help but ponder why Travis and I had been the sole survivors of the Epidemic at Bison Camp and the Bozeman region of our NorthWest Configuration. During the initial stages of our trek eastward we encountered no survivors south to the Yellowstone geyser basin or back north along the Madison River into Three Forks. Why were we spared? Yet in regions further east along the Missouri River, down portions of the Great River, and up into the Ohio region we encountered numerous survivors, either as individuals or in small groups. Did Travis and I share a natural immunity to the plague that took so many, almost beyond counting? Might the protective spirit that saved me during the dark time when our children ailed also have guided us along the initial stages of our long journey? But if the latter, the spirit did not ultimately intervene to protect Travis. It seems, too, that I have been protected in spirit and fellowship by my daughters and their mates.

***

After the evening communal meal the five of us walked together to the great hall, where I proudly re-introduced my daughters and their mates. The evening session as with the previous night was well attended. I was invited to once more set the stage for their reports.

Thank you for attending. Tonight we will present information and interviews from the second and final part of our trek from New Vicksburg to Bison Camp. Of special interest for your consideration will be mention of an event that occurred between Moab and Provo in New Deseret Configuration where we were attacked by a group of Wanderers who nearly overwhelmed us with their sneak attack and superior numbers. Had it not been for the chance arrival of a column of Border Riders out on patrol, we would not be here tonight. So before we begin, I wish to pay special thanks to Sergeant Gerald Dickins, and his Border Rider Troup, for their commitment to keeping the borderlands safe from bandits and Wanderers.

***

Malaga on to Carlsbad

We passed the old border control point at Orla in northern old Texas and continued north. On day 63 of our journey we reached a new control point at Malaga several kilo-miles inside old New Mexico where we planned to camp only for one night. A militia troop was stationed at Malaga to assist the border control agents. The next morning we proceeded north to the control point at the junction of Black River Village Road and Highway 285. Once there, we were asked to offload our goods and belongings for inspection.

There were six family groups ahead of us, and one of these appeared to be causing a serious delay. Guards and armed militia gathered about and seized contraband from the oxcart of this family. After considerable jaw-boning, the guards separated the family members and took away two adult males and one younger female. These folks were escorted behind the inspection station building so that none of us could watch. From the sounds that ensued, they had been encouraged to provided information as to the source and destination of the banned items. This mess at the control point took a full day and required a second night of camping at Malaga.

At last we were allowed to cross and, after a short distance, reached a settlement group located at Loving, old New Mexico. A few kilo-miles later we entered the cave zone that encompassed the settlement of Carlsbad. The great underground cavern area off to the southwest covered many thousand meter-feet. The cave site once had served as a major tourist destination during Pre-Ripple Event times, but more recently had been converted and formed the protective home for many families that had survived the Epidemic.

We trekked through town and were directed to off-load and camp along the banks of the Pecos River near the Lower Transill Reservoir next to the Bataan Recreation area. We were tired from all the delay at Malaga and elected not to set up for cooking, but to barter for our food at one of the local eateries. We selected one that recently had reopened. The owners were busy serving stew and ample supplies of hot and cold beverages. After dining we walked north along the reservoir shore where couples were promenading with their young children. Standing apart from the families we observed a solitary individual who told us something unexpected but with enormous potential repercussions for local and regional defense-related issues:

> **Ward Fuller,** chemist – *For many solar cycles during the Post Dark Time Recovery Period I worked as a product development manager for Patterson Chemical located southwest of Carlsbad. We were a pacifist group believing in the concept of live-and-let-live and all life has value. My work was progressing well. My expertise was in analyzing amounts of trace minerals in cave stalactites and stalagmites, especially zinc and how this element related to human growth, sexual maturation, and improved intelligence. My mate, Teresa Fuller, concerned herself with the study of cave moss that contained several polyphenolic compounds that when ingested reduced the probability of circulatory system disorders and heart*

disease. We had joined the Patterson Company thinking that our work could be used to help residents of the nearby settlement groups that had been savaged by the Epidemic.

Then came the terrible time when our company facility and our homes were raided by successive waves of Wanderer teams. Following the death and destruction these bands heaped upon us, we at Patterson Chemical realized collectively that simply wishing and thinking about live-and-let-live peaceful days no longer was an option. We needed to defend ourselves and our families, and what was left of our homes and our company laboratories.

One portion of the Carlsbad cave site housed hundreds of thousands of bats. What they had left behind daily on the floor of the cave through hundreds of solar cycles past we knew to be a key ingredient for manufacturing explosives. We had not explored this option earlier due to our pacifist leanings. So it was after the Wanderer attacks that Patterson Chemical and Teresa and I turned our attention from our previous research efforts to analyzing and assaying the compounds needed to make our settlement and region safe. You ask were we successful? I reply this way with two sets of words. The first: Prepare and Defend. The alternative being: Continue as pacifists and be killed or subjugated. Thus it was that we at Patterson Chemical adopted a new motto, one that sustains us today: Never Again. And so it will be that the Wanderers or any other group will not succeed in attacking our Carlsbad settlement group. So be warned.

The implications of Fuller's comments were direct and critically important. Did the residents of Carlsbad settlement have stockpiles of explosives, or not? We could not be certain and several other persons we interviewed just smiled at the question and walked away. If they had stockpiled explosives such a cache eventually could lead to a local, then regional, then a broader competition for better weapons and, ultimately, set off an explosive arms race. Something we here at Bison Camp need to think about.

***

The following evening we returned to the small eatery where we previously had been served what the managers called Carlsbad Stew. When we arrived a new sign had been erected over the door welcoming patrons to the revitalized Carlsbad Café. The menu this evening was more varied and after we had eaten, the cook Joan Pullman came out from the kitchen and asked whether or not we had enjoyed her fixings. We replied in the positive, and she sat down to join us:

> **Joan Pullman,** cook – *Because of my skills I am always in demand and finally had the courage and desire to open my own eatery. My friends and neighbors request new recipes for old food combinations. You want meat and potatoes? Well what do you substitute when the meat is gone, or if potatoes are no more? That's where I have become a master in recipe development. A recent local favorite for many residents of settlement groups around the Carlsbad area is something that I call DC, or Desert Combo. It's very tasty and reminds the diners of chicken dishes of long ago past. Of course I cut off the rattles so those dining cannot see and visualize the source of the meat. If they knew where I had obtained the meat perhaps they would say they did not like my dish. Not knowing sometimes is better than knowing, right? Another favorite is my HS, or Hillside Scramble. This is fun to make and includes a wide range of creepy-crawlies that I turn into a delicious pepper-like condiment that my friends shake onto almost everything they eat. But like my DC dishes, I never tell my friends the ingredients or the true secret that makes my HS powder so tangy and sweet to the taste. Since you are leaving tomorrow, would you like to join me in the kitchen where I pulverize the items and prepare the powders? You don't have time, you say? I understand. Perhaps you are just being polite? Well as they say here in Carlsbad – not knowing sometimes is better than knowing – right?*

***

Roswell

Departing Carlsbad we continued north. After four days we reached Roswell where we arrived on day 71. Roswell had received notice as an unusual settlement many solar cycles prior to the Ripple Event. A report indicated that an unidentified flying object had crashed north of town near the old Foster Homestead. Some who visited the site reported finding debris of different types of metal and curious objects strewn about over the homestead landscape. It was said, too, that because of the composition of these objects they could not be earth-related and, therefore, unknown others who piloted the craft had attempted to land, misjudged their approach, and crashed. Through the many solar cycles since, residents of Roswell also claimed on occasion to have seen strange lights in the sky, sometimes eight or more in formation but other times as solitary flashes. Those willing to speak about such sightings reported the sky objects seemed to dart here and there at astonishing speeds. Others said that they had the technical ability to dramatically change direction and then disappear, only to reappear days or weeks later.

We were invited to camp at Loveless Park on the south side of Spring River. We ventured into the heart of Roswell past shops with window displays that suggested the Foster Homestead crash site had indeed been strewn with remains of an unidentified object. Other shops were more utilitarian, for example, a butcher shop and another that offered household and specialized kitchen utensils at reasonable barter rates. Several proprietors at the newly opened stores agreed to speak with us:

***

> **Expinos Tzakis,** metal collector and bowler – *My family came to live in Roswell more than a century of solar cycles past. I was told there were few residents then, mostly hard-working folks. We were the family Tzakis. My great great grandfather and grandmother emigrated from eastern Greece, a land far to the east across the Great Sea. My parents called me Expinos, which needed a few changes of letters and sounds to help the people of Roswell pronounce my name. Expinos means clever, and clever I have been throughout my short life. Each workday is different. I go out and scrounge the hillsides north and east of Roswell for the wrecks of machines that crashed during takeoff from the old military base south of town. Sometimes I even go out to the site that once was called the Foster Homestead. There, in solar cycles past, I sometimes dug deep into the hillside to retrieve pieces of metal – a very special type of metal. I do not take anyone to the location of my metal extraction sites, otherwise they could take my livelihood from me. I sometimes find damaged sheets of metal that once were parts of these air-flying machines, and bring them back to my shop at Roswell in the dead of night. In my shop I have various sized hardwood molds of different shapes. I pound the metal over these molds to make bowls of various sizes. Hence, the residents of Roswell sometimes call me the Bowler. On some of my bowls, I add finishing touches such as hooks, or loops, and sometimes engravings. My bowls are well made so they can be nested or suspended from household kitchen walls.*

Depending upon the size of the bowl, I can earn different levels of barter tokens. A small aluminum bowl is worth 5-6 BTs; larger ones more. I have in my collection three bowls of different sizes that I will never barter away. I made these from the thin pliable sheets of metal I extracted from the Foster Homestead site. There is something unusual about this metal. It can be warped and bent easily but then returns to its original shape and flat length. When pounded over a wooden core, however, it maintains the shape I want. It is unlike any pieces of aluminum I have found. It seems to be of an unknown type of metal. In any case I am content to do my business here in Roswell slow but sure, and I have enough customers to keep me in food and clothing.

***

Lester Franks, meat cutter – *Not much to do these days. I remember back to days long past when all morning I was busy – hack and chop, slice and dice. Old Mrs. Ada Thompson who lived up the street would come in each day and ask for a little of this and a little of that, her favorite being slices of old cow. But that was long ago. During the hard times here in Roswell we went through most of the herds during the Ripple Event and Dark Time. Now we are down to what in town we call the little ones – the stray this or that no one wants to care for anymore. I have something for you if you wish to trade. Look at this? What do you think? When the meat is boiled off the bones, there is about one meal for three people. I remember those ribs and steaks from long ago – cooked up with barbeque sauce and onions. But no more. Now I'm getting hungry. Want to join me?*

***

Lincoln

We arrived in Lincoln on day 72 after a reasonable trek from Roswell past the settlements of Picacho, Tinnie, and Hondo. Local officials gave us the option of camping on the grassy lawn near the once-proud regional Post Office building – now in ruins – or inside a sandy and rock-strewn zone out along the banks of the adjacent Rio Bonito. There was little to see at Lincoln that could convince the thoughtful traveler that the town once was the center of cowboy and Wild West violence. At the time of our visit, Lincoln was quiet and placid with less than ten residents. Those we spoke to had established homes of adobe brick and cane reeds on plots over by the river. There seemed to be little interaction as the residents apparently lived independently. Two of these isolated but hard working folks agreed to speak with us:

Teal Morris, bird catcher – *My name is Teal Morris. Really! There isn't a bird alive today that I can't catch, from ground-running prairie chickens to swifts and swallows that dart here and there along the cliff faces of the Capitan Mountains northeast of Lincoln. The most enjoyment I have these days – except speaking with desert travelers like you – is to chase down those good-looking birds called roadrunners. These are snooty birds that cock their heads and look at me as if they were sending out challenges. They seem to say: race me you biped piece of you-know-what. Then the roadrunners give me that characteristic heep-heep sound and off we go across the landscape. I find it easier to chase roadrunners in the early morning when I am fresh, since afternoons are hot and the temperatures seem to slow me down.*

Some days I go down by the Rio Bonito pools and check out the scene for mallards or teals. Sometimes an occasional goose appears. When trapping birds I don't use nets; I catch birds my way. I circle around the pool from behind, slip into the water, take a deep breath, and swim underwater to where the birds are gabbing, squawking, and just floating about. I reach up quickly and sometimes can grab two at a time. They honk and squiggle here and there but I don't let go. It is an easy process: from river, to basket cage, to market we go. Look at these nice ones. Look at the beautiful color of their feathers. My mallards really taste good when roasted on a spit over a campfire. Yumm!

***

Harold Wenskie, bush hacker – *Why not settle here in Lincoln? If you need a place to build a hut or a storage area on the main street, then I am your man. I will come to your site and use my leveling tools to remove all brush and scrub so your lot presents a clean location on which to build. If you want more, I also can level the earth, remove rock chunks, and rid your site of burrowing rodents, trap-door spiders, and the occasional mother scorpion with her brood of stinging bastards. I am a proud bush hacker. If you can't pay me in barter tokens, I will accept food. If after my leveling activities* *have finished you would like me to come back once a month to hack out any new vegetation that makes your site ugly or whatever, I would like your consideration. I could help you set out and plant gardens if you wish, as I have access to a wide variety of seeds from edible native plants that I collect up in the mountain areas west of Lincoln over by Snowy River Cave. I also could advise you on which plants could be used for dye, basket- and broom-making. Let me know. I sleep down by the arroyo south of the settlement group over by Baca Canyon. Come on down and perhaps we can work out a plan.*

***

Carrizozo/Zozo

Continuing north from Lincoln traveling along a track paralleling Highway 380 we reached the settlement of Zozo, originally called Carrizozo and named after the Spanish term for river reed grass. According to my history teacher at Bison Camp this was the general region in a time long past for what was called the Trinity test. I remembered that this was the location where a massive explosion occurred that my teacher said changed the world. Most of the settlement was abandoned, with only a few local residents seen on the streets.

Tucker "Bloody Arms" Masters, fencer – *I'm not sure why I am needed these days here in Zozo. People here and in the surrounding areas hire me out two or three times a month to either erect or repair fencing. The real question to be asked, however, is: Why build barbed wire fences in these days of misery? Once there was open range all about us – antelope and deer, cattle and horses, along with us humans and small varmints living out our lives on lands suitable to all. Then came the greed – the greed for more and more land, more and more space, and those with the most wealth or with bodyguards, gathered in such large amounts of land almost without limit. These parcels were marked by fences of barbed wire in all its varieties. I knew them all: the Shinn locked four-point; the Brotherton flat barb; and the Haish square "S" barb. Why were more types of barbed wire needed? I had no idea but soon appeared the Ellwood reverse spread; the Scutt flat crimped barb; the Glidden round and square strands; and the Merrill four point. Solar cycles passed and I wondered again, why was there need for even more types of barbed wire? Who was making all of these wire varieties:*

the Glidden winner, the Rigers flat strand; the Kitselman left twist; and the Brinkerhoff lugs lance point. I couldn't believe it. Then just before the Epidemic even more varieties arrived here at Zozo, including the Watkins vertical lazy plate; the Huffman one-point flat parallel; and the Ross four point. Look at my hands and arms, will you? All I get these days after repairing or installing barbed wire is ripped flesh and lots of scabs. My given name is Tucker Masters, but most around here at Zozo call me Bloody Arms, a name I really don't like. But that's life, right?

***

Bryce Engels, funeral coordinator – *Not so much business these days, but I, Bryce Engels, certainly was needed during the terrible events of the Epidemic solar cycle. Why some folks survived here at Carrizozo without any illness whatsoever, and why others were taken – how can anyone ever know? I understand that life is fleeting, but to take so many almost all at one time, leaving behind such distress and uncertainty. This horror should not be experienced by anyone. At the peak of the Epidemic there came a time when supplies of wood for coffins no longer were available. We honored the deceased the best we could. Words of comfort were spoken, uplifted voices sang traditional words of passage, and celebrations of life were delivered to the assembled. I did my work the best I could, although sometimes I could only shake my head and wonder why so much difficulty had been visited on our small community. I no longer can cry; I wept all the tears I had during the Epidemic time. It remains hard for me now to even speak of this.*

***

Albuquerque

The desert trek from Carrizozo to Albuquerque was difficult and took us six days. We needed to ration water for ourselves and for our horses and mules. Along the way we passed through abandoned settlements of Socorro, Belen, and Los Lunas. The town of Albuquerque was named after the numerous white oaks in the region, although some we spoke to thought the name derived from *albaricoque,* the Spanish word for apricot. We camped two nights down by the Rio Grande along Tingley Drive:

Peter [last name not given], fisherman – *Just call me Peter. I don't want to share my last name. Early in my life I lived with my family* *at a settlement group east of Albuquerque, between Santa Rosa and Tucumcari. I grew up fishing weekends outside of town at the Ute Reservoir. I learned to cast my line from land and how to drop it from boats, rafts, and even floating logs. You could say that I am adept in drop-line fishing. Throughout my life I have tied flies and used as bait a variety of worms, hoppers, even chunks and rags of colorful cloth. In my solace I also fish the Rio Grande River that runs through Albuquerque. I talk to the beasties of the water – I call them and they respond. They come and take my line, swallow my hook and offer me the sustenance of their bodies. I learned back when I was being schooled that fish once were the symbols of a great religion. It also was mentioned by one of my teachers that a once-great religion widely practiced before the Ripple Event and Dark Time was headed by a leader known as the Fisher-of-Men. So it is in my solace that I fish. Will there ever be enough fish to feed my hungry grandchildren? I know not how to hunt with arrow and bow, with club or knife. I know not how to construct deadfalls to bring down large game that would feed all my family. But I do know how to fish. Watch me now as I drop my hook and line and await the tug that signals a meal for my granddaughter. Today I will go hungry but she will eat. So few fish remain these days of darkness and despair.*

***

Bronson Cleaver, janitor – *The great campus here at Albuquerque where I once worked as janitor was home to Noble Laureates, several thousand academics, and tens of thousands of students. I was never able to correlate office-keeping and neatness with academic status. Some offices of the professors were tidy, neat as a pin, whereas offices of two world-famous professors were merely piles of junk and boxes of papers, books, articles, journals, stashed and mingled with pieces of laboratory equipment and objects of unknown origin. Brains and international recognition do not correlate with neatness and tidy offices. Long ago I encountered students who treated lecture halls on campus as their personal garbage disposal bins. Each morning the lecture halls were clean, having been swept and straightened the previous evening. By the mid-morning class hour, however, the floors already were littered with empty coffee and soda cups and discarded pages from student newspapers. By 3:10 at the start of the third afternoon class session, the rooms reeked of* *spilled beverages and chunks of leftover sandwich crusts tossed onto the floor by uncaring students who never had been taught the rules of good behavior by their self-indulgent parents. When the last class was over in the early evening my janitorial team and I would re-enter and again sweep the mess left behind by these students – supposedly the cream of the educational crop. When the university was forced to close during the Ripple Event, I took my skills elsewhere and along the way added new talents to the array of my activities. I became a security guard at the mines near the outskirts of Adelino south of Albuquerque. After that, I was invited to join the settlement group at La Joya where I was promoted and became one of the guards defending the walls against Wanderers attempting to force their way into our settlement. From janitor to settlement group guard, who would have thought? Now I am retired and back at Albuquerque. Is it not curious how the occupational circle of my life has changed through time? Interesting, no?*

***

Acoma

We departed Albuquerque before dawn on Day 82 taking Eye 40 west. After a very long trek of 49 kilo-miles we camped at Laguna. The next day we took an off-road trail south to Acoma Pueblo, the well-known sky settlement atop an easily defended white rock mesa. Ancient traditions drew us to this location and we wished to pay respects to the First People residents, descendants of the Anasazi also known as Those-Who-Came-Before-Time.

We were received by First Nation guards at the base of the mesa and invited to tether our animals. We were served cool water flavored with sprits of desert leaves. After resting we climbed the stairs leading to the mesa settlement. Two young residents, known to us only as Alowe and Juanita, escorted us to the central plaza where we were received as guests by two prominent residents of Acoma:

Jesus Chino, botanist – *My family and ancestors, the First People, have lived at Acoma since the beginning of time. Our home is the place that always was. I am of the Chino family line and trained by my elders to recognize local and regional plants. I can identify which ones heal and which others provide sustenance. But most of all my knowledge extends to differentiating between which plants* *are safe or toxic. I work with young men and women at Acoma and together we walk the bottom lands surrounding our sky town. On such botanical treks I sometimes feel that a cloud, a protective shield, forms around us as we search the hinterland of for edibles that will sustain and ease our hunger if difficult times return. In times long past, we have been attacked by peoples who would take our homeland. More recently, just before the Epidemic, I was wounded during a Wanderer attack. The leg wound that I received and my subsequent limp have not hindered my participation in plant collecting journeys. After such excursions we assemble at night in the central plaza near we are sitting to share the plants collected. To the elderly at Acoma we immediately provide 10 percent of our daily collection; the active adult males and females of our Pueblo receive 50 percent; the adolescents 20 percent, and our children 15 percent. The 5 percent balance is given to me to distribute to the collectors. My modest share is stored in special clay containers in my medicine preparation hut. This is how it has been; this is how it will be until the end of our time. We know not what else to do. I train others with plant identification skills and provide the next generation with needed information. My life is to serve my people, to prepare them well to survive in our place that forever always will be. You are welcome to spend two camp nights with us.*

***

Thomas Sanchez, rain dancer – *It is said around the hearth of my home that our family heritage can be traced back more than 500 solar cycles, more than 180,000 sunrises past. Our family represents a blend of First and Spanish peoples. The latter arrived here at Acoma, riding astride or walking beside four-legged beasts we never before had seen. My father's father – Miguel Sanchez – taught me how to call up the clouds at dawn. He had learned the way from his own great great grandfather, and so on back into the mists of time. He showed me how to respect the cosmos and to understand the place of people in the great scheme of life. I use my skills only for good, and only when rain is needed for our crops. For without rain we at Acoma would wither and perish. With rain we at Acoma flourish and continue onward into the unknown of our future. Calling the clouds is like offering a prayer. I turn my face skyward, my arms* *outraised; I stretch my arms outward from my body and first face the north, and then turn south, followed by east and west. I close my eyes and sense the cloud wisps assembling skyward, churning, and building into thunderheads. And then comes the first flash of lightning, followed by the craaaack of thunder. The sky speaks and tells us mortals – take my gift of rain and live long. Protect the earth; respect life – large and small – eat to live, do not live to eat.*

Respect others; respect life.

***

Gallup

We left Acoma and returned to Eye 40 traveling west towards Laguna and Paraje. Along the way we camped at Seama, and the following nights at Grants and Thoreau before reaching the outskirts of Gallup. Here we would spend two days. We had been on the road for 89 days, nearly three full months since leaving New Vicksburg. The Gallup settlement was a critical junction where we would leave Eye 40 and start the difficult northern crossing through the desert towards the key isolated rock monument and settlement known as Shiprock.

The Gallup City Park just north of Eye 40 offered grass for our riding and pack animals with a clean water source where we could refill our containers and hydrate for the desert crossing to follow. We shared our travel plan with three teams of families camped nearby also trekking from Gallup north to Shiprock. Together we considered and then adopted a general plan for all of us to trek as one group for safety against any encounters with local bands of Wanderers or isolated bandit groups. We agreed to camp at Tohatchi some 33 kilo-miles north of Gallup then would pass through Neschitti and Sheep Springs where water resources also would be available. The next leg would require camping on successive evenings at Newcomb and Little Water – also confirmed water reservoirs – before reaching Shiprock, where water supplies sometimes were uncertain.

Gracing our respective campfires at City Park were others who shared stories with us:

Alecia Talbot, paint and board stripper – *My name is Alecia Talbot. After each harsh winter or summer storm, the huts and houses within the settlement groups north and west of Gallup need repair. My task through recent decades has been to strip old paint from pieces* *of damaged lumber, removing the flakes of color down to the basic wood grain. And then apply plant oils that protect the wood from the elements. For the past ten or so solar cycles we have not had high-quality paint available in Gallup, due to difficulty of receiving supplies from regional rehabilitation centers. We make do, however, with what we have on hand and in some instances inventive residents can create a tint or two using natural pigments blended with animal oils. Sometimes moss and fungus flourish on unprotected piles of lumber. All this dead and living junk must be stripped off before reusing the boards to repair or reconstruct shelters. Mine is tedious work, just stripping and a stripping all day long, with no enjoyable interludes except for an occasional competition with other strippers to see who can remove the most junk in the fastest time. I usually win. I'm the best stripper throughout the Gallup region, no kidding!*

***

One enterprising resident of Gallup camped at the city park shared water-related information and availability between Gallup and Shiprock:

Ellis "Boomer" Breckenridge, roadie – *Want some water sir? Want some water ma'am? I am your water roadie, Ellis Breckenridge. Most people here in and around Gallup call me Boomer. You'll are heading north, you say, into the desert lands towards Shiprock? A tough cross-desert trek. Not much water along the way up there. You will need to stock-up tonight or just before you leave in the morning. We roadies do our best to provide accurate travel information about the area and region where you are headed. Canvas water bags are the safest bet when passing through the northern desert. Even though we now are in springtime, the weather up north can be challenging with the mid-morning heat. Barter with me and in turn I will provide you with the names of other roadies who work the stretches north of Gallup. Territory of the first is out about eight kilo-miles from where you are camped tonight. If you barter with me, the next roadie will give you a special price for additional water that you may need along the way. About 30 kilo-miles north towards Shiprock at the settlement called Tohatchi you will come across an establishment called the Rodie Saloon. We roadies founded this place about six solar cycles before the Epidemic and it has remained open since. You barter with me and I will give you in turn a pass that will let you* *camp at Tohatchi near the Rodie Saloon at a reduced rate, otherwise the camp rate will be four copper barter tokens higher than my price to you tonight. It's all up to you. Have a good trip!*

***

Shiprock/Naataanii Neez

As it turned out Ellis Brecknridge generally provided correct information. We camped at Tohatchi and again at Newcomb and Little Water before reaching Shiprock. Contrary to what he said, however, there was sufficient water resources at both campsites, and a new reservoir had been constructed recently at Shiprock to supply travelers' water needs. The desert crossing was stressful but not too demanding. The San Juan River that sometimes flowed past the small settlement of Shiprock was almost a dry riverbed. The winter flow had diminished to a mere trickle in several places and appeared only as shallow ponds at others.

Standing out against the horizon to the southwest was the *Tse Bit'A'I,* or winged rock that according to tradition carried the Navajo First Peoples from their earlier home in the cold north to the desert dry region of the southwest. A new eatery recently erected at the intersection of Highway 491 and Tachiinii Street served a variety of local foods. Especially good were the slices of lamb served with fry bread and delicious desert berries – good food that attracted both local residents and dusty travelers:

Saul Jacobson, well sinker – *Out here on the desert prairie lands we have intermittent access to surface water, so we must design and construct powerful machines to burst through the 30-40 meter-yards of hard desert crust before the first water level is reached. This task requires a tall wooden derrick and long meter-yard stands of old but sturdy pipe, with a powerful cement/steel pounder atop the highest point of the derrick. We use a system of ropes and pulleys we developed especially for well sinking. Normally, it takes a team of 5-6 men and women to erect the derrick, transport the pipes, and set up the pulley system to raise the pipe vertically onto the derrick base. Then comes the tricky part: if this isn't done correctly those working on the derrick floor can lose toes or sometimes a foot. Once the pounding starts a good well sinker like me can drive the pipe down through the sediment crust about 10 meter-feet a day. This means that in 3-4 days groundwater can be reached. Gus Johnson – he's sitting over by the wall eating if you want to speak with him – old*

Gus developed a clever way to suck-up the water to start it flowing out onto the surface. In advance of Johnson's success, we usually prepare a concrete-lined pit into where the water can accumulate. I guess that my team and I have sunk about 15 wells here at Shiprock and elsewhere within the first peoples land at their request since the Epidemic. Folks here like water; we bring it to them. I'm Saul Jacobson, and I'm at your service.

***

Jake Lewis, buryeman – *Mine is not an occupation but an honor, something that I, Jake Lewis, take to heart. We here at Shiprock are closely knit; we survived the Ripple Event, the Dark Time, Epidemic, and are in the process of reconstructing our settlement. During those past times there was great need for several buryemen. The desert earth is not kind. The baked land does not yield to pick and shovel easily. Still, we complete our work with dignity, preparing the last resting place for our fellow residents. It is said that each of us from earth originate, and to earth we return. It is thus at the end of life. Each person we bury has a story to tell, some simple, others epic. Some we care for are tall, others short. Some wealthy, others barely were able to find enough food to eat. Each, however, was conceived, born, and raised – some within nurturing families, others without love and caring. Now in their passing all are alike: wrapped with funeral shrouds and returned to the earth. I complete my work with honor and dignity. May the passing of each person be marked somewhere in the great book of life, where all deserve a mention that says:*

> *Here lies [insert name]*
> *Remember their smile and laughter*
> *Recall the joyful days, the days of happiness*
> *You are part of the Great Book of Life.*

***

Teec Nos Pos

From Shiprock to the border of the disputed territory of old Arizona was 21 kilo-miles. We left Shiprock taking Highway 64 west through Beclabito until we crossed the border and reached the inspection station at Teec Nos Pos. Militia officers waved us through with barely a hand gesture. We asked for permission to camp outside the settlement trading post, our 95th campsite.

In the evening we spoke with Frank Deschinny and joined his family for a festive barbeque. He told us that if we had more time before pressing on north, that a journey over to the Four Corners area might be interesting. This was where the disputed territories of the old states of Arizona, Utah, Colorado, and New Mexico met at a singular location, marked by geographers and geologists before the Ripple Event and Dark Time. If we were to angle northeast from Teec Nos Pos and take Highway 160 towards Cortez, a distance of 45 kilo-miles, the ancient First Peoples site of Mesa Verde could be examined. We chose not to do so, since the journey would have taken nearly three days and two additional camp-out nights.

Two residents from Teec Nos Pos also joined us at dinner and enlivened the group with conversations about their various activities. One was a child of 10 accompanied by her uncle who was a hunter.

> **Toni O'Neal,** packer – *I started packing when my daddy gave me my first weapon. I was four solar cycles old at the time. Sometimes back when I was a kid we would play in old abandoned huts down by the arroyo, and I remember one time we came across something my daddy said was called a revolver. This thing we found had a handle and something that jutted out that daddy said was the gun barrel. I didn't know what a gun was so I asked him how it worked. He told me that long ago there were many types of such weapons and they were used for hunting, protection, and close combat. They fired something called bull-lets, if I remember correctly, but daddy said there hadn't been bull-lets for many solar cycles long time passing.*
>
> *I was so happy when he told me I was old enough to start packing. I remember it well: he gave me a special large knife, the type was called a Carver. I'm not certain why it was called this, perhaps the person who invented the style was named Carver? But there may have been other reasons. He also showed me how to make and pack what I still today call my slingshost. I know the correct pronunciation is slingshot, but the term slingshost has continued to stick with me. I am really a good shot with this weapon and can knock a food bird out of a bush or tree at 25 meter-yards. Now I am almost 10 solar cycles old and about to enter the mate education program at our settlement group. I don't know what that's all about. I see that you are smiling. Do you have any advice for me? Well in any case, what I*

do know is that when I walk about packing my slingshost and Carver no one messes with me or my baby brother. That's a good thing, right?

***

Ivan Ruskovitch, coneychaser – *My niece Toni who you just spoke to is a real kick, is she not? Well you ask about me so I'll start. Speed, stealth, and quick movements are needed to make a living as a coneychaser. These local coneys or rabbits as you call them out here in the hot desert; these beasties crawl out of their holes in early morn and start to nibble plants here and there, all the time keeping an eye out for predators or chasers like me. It is a good day when I am able to outwit and grab four or five coneys. Once collected I check them out and separate the males from the females, and then offer the pairs of coneys to families at different settlement groups who wish to raise litters for food. I can provide a potential coney mating pair for just two aluminum barter tokens. A day never passes when I do not grab at least two. The older coneys give me the most difficulty, darting here and there, in and out among the sage brush and hillocks. The key is to plug up the potential escape holes in a given area, and then chase them until they tire. I don't hurt the coneys – just collect and find them new homes. Go tell your mother that you spoke to Ivan Ruskovitch and ask her if she would like a pair of coneys to take along on your journey?*

***

Mexican Water

Leaving Teec Nos Pos behind in eastern old Arizona, inside the Disputed Territory, we continued on through Red Mesa into the small settlement known locally as Mexican Water, now a solitary trading post not far from Walker Creek Reservoir, where we could water our animals and refill our containers. Adjacent to the trading post was a militia station where we were required to camp before resuming our trek north along Highway 191 into New Deseret Territory. Also camped near the militia station was a caravan of what looked to be entertainers.

Mavis Trenton, animal trainer – *I travel about these desert regions with my menagerie of bears, cougars, coyotes, and wolves. My associates and I put on animal shows for the amusement and* *entertainment of adults and children at local settlement groups and small towns It is a hard life traveling with our beasts, keeping them well fed, groomed, and watered, at the same time allowing them time for mating. I like to tell people about my upbringing, how I was abandoned as a small baby but discovered and whelped as you might say by a she wolf. Well not exactly. Truth be told, I was abandoned as a small baby but cuddled and suckled by a mother coyote. Look, you are just too nice, sitting here and talking with me. I have to tell you the truth; I can't lie. I was raised in a loving family who liked animals. I wasn't abandoned. We did have animals within the confines of our homestead area that my father had captured out in the wild. Perhaps it was through this association that I became interested in wildlife and developed the idea of starting a traveling show. We do not charge much; the fees we receive mostly cover food for our animals and a little for my assistants. We are respectful to our animals and they are respectful to us. We have suffered no accidents or injuries since we started. Each day I look into the eyes of our wild beasts and see something of myself reflected. They are caged but well fed – I am free but often hungry. Who has the best life?*

***

Our delay in border crossing required a second night of camping at Mexican Water. The process of continuing on our trek and the questions and paperwork were irritating, but we could not show it in our faces. Perhaps because we remained quiet, we were approached by one of the militia and moved ahead of the traveling menagerie. When our turn came, I recorded the following exchange:

Floyd Appell, border buster – *My name is Floyd Appell. I am a member of the Mexican Water Border Buster Cadre. Please remove your shirt so I may check the inside of your upper right arm. Why, you ask? It is my job to examine body scars and tattoos, travel documents, and interview prospective border crossers. Now you can put your shirt back on. What is it that I look for, you ask? I'm checking against information shared by our cadre to identify any gang members or criminals based upon data in our files. After the body check and interview, if all is positive, I will recommend where a border crosser might best fit into specific towns or settlement groups. Every week we receive what are called need lists. These are requests for a* *specific number of men or women to fill jobs at key settlements. We always are on the lookout for people with construction skills: builders, masons, well-diggers. But we also need teachers, cooks and, now and then, even entertainers. My job is not to keep people from crossing from one configuration to another, but to provide guidance to where travelers might best be received. We know that sometimes travelers who are tired and hungry – and without proper identification – attempt to cross our border. When such folks are identified and held for further questioning, we have a kitchen and cooking staff that helps to ease their pangs, the usual offerings of soup and bread, but it's enough to keep the travelers going until their identifications can be certified. If border crossers act badly or cause difficulties, my staff and I secure them. Once cuffed, they spend several days in a detention cell learning how to behave. We have a number of techniques that turn ill-behaved travelers into docile and respectful folks. No need to identify these procedures to you, right? But should any of these techniques fail, or if after four or five day's detention the ill-mannered travelers remain surly, they are removed from their cells and branded with what we call the 5-X mark, which identifies them as trouble-makers. Those who are branded at the configuration border between old New Mexico and New Deseret are expelled and sent packing along the track from which they came. Their name and physical description are entered into a list that is supplied to all border crossing stations. If a person with a 5-X mark is caught inside our territory at a later time, they are removed from our configuration. Removed how, you ask? That should be obvious since none ever return.*

***

Crescent Junction

The distance from Mexican Water to Moab was long and tiring. After securing permission to cross the border into New Deseret, we trekked on to Tselakai Dezza then past Bluff. We spent our 100th night of camping at Blanding, and continued on until we reached Moab. After a short stay, we girded ourselves for the very long cross-desert push towards the small settlement of Crescent Junction and reached our destination on the late afternoon of Day 105. Tired and weary we were directed to a formal rest area, a short distance west of the Highway 191 and Eye 70 intersection. Following was a welcomed day of rest.

The rest area seemed to be the home base for a variety of temporary stands where merchants bartered with travelers going east/west along Eye 70. One of the merchants who agreed to speak with was Jackson Perkins:

> **Jackson Perkins,** mason – *Making building bricks is a needed but relatively common task. To be an outstanding mason and to be respected for one's work, specific skills are needed. For example: how to identify types and consistencies of earth and clay? What types and quantities of straw or other vegetative materials need to be added to the clay-mixing pits? Which types of bricks can be baked using only the best days of sunlight, and which types need to be oven-baked? I crafted special brick molds using hardwood. Each day I put on my boots and wade knee deep into the clay pit here at Crescent Junction where I stomp about mixing the slurry. When the right consistency is reached, my three sons and I scoop out the clay, slam it into the molds and, on the open top surface, we press our characteristic signature sign. Through the solar cycles we developed different tools to carve or make impressions on the soft setting clay. Our characteristic signature, the one that identifies our family brick factory, is the dove La Paloma. Our family bricks have been the most sought after by local builders up and down Eye 70. When competitors attempted to run us out of Crescent Junction, we fought for the right to maintain our business. Defending one's business and honor is required these hard times. After two days of fighting and struggle, we survived and eliminated those who would take over our business.*
>
> *Our bricks continue to stand the test of time. We have sunbaked varieties, and others are fire-hardened. A parcel of 18 of the sunbaked types brings two copper barter tokens; a parcel of 13 of the fire-hardened bricks – a baker's dozen as you might say – brings two copper or one brass barter token. Last week we were attacked again and in the course of defending our production site, we drowned two of the bandits in our clay pit. What gives these fools the idea that they can just come into our brick yard and take over our business? We have worked hard as a family for several generations; we provide a needed product through our hard labor. We are the family Perkins; we stand united forever with La Paloma protecting us. No one will take our business from us.*

***

Between Moab and Provo

After an additional day of rest, we departed Crescent Junction on day 106 and headed across the arid desert flats and mesa lands towards Provo. This proved to be a very long and taxing portion of our journey. It took us seven days of hard trekking before we reached Provo. During the journey we were attacked by a group of Wanderers.

We had just passed through the outskirts of Spanish Fork and were headed north towards Springville when Adam noticed movement along the crest of the western arroyo. I remember the events of that day well. A summer rain had moved through the region leaving the pleasant aroma of moist sagebrush heavy in the air around us. Adam rode back and alerted me. It looked like we were being tracked. These were not shadow people or images in our minds, but were real and their presence represented potential danger. We estimated their numbers at about 30, with two apparent leaders on horseback riding in front. In late afternoon the two riders approached us and spoke with a laughing snarl:

> *Usted viajeros parece estar en problemas. Estamos aquí para ayudarle a cruzar estas tierras áridas. Usted está llevando demasiadas cosas. Dar a nosotros será aligerar su carga y hacer su viaje más fácil. Deja todo en la tierra. Nosotros no haremos daño. Hazlo ahora.*

I had learned enough Spanish language during classes at Bison Camp to understand what their leader said:

> *You travelers seem to be in trouble. We are here to help you cross these arid lands. You are carrying too much stuff. Giving it to us will lighten your load and make your travel easier. Leave everything on the ground we will not harm you. Do it now!*

As luck would have it, our path had just crossed the crest of a small hill. Sage and Laurel quickly turned the mule carts towards the rocky outcrop boulders while the boys and I prepared a hasty defensive position. The militia training that Adam and Joseph received back in New Vicksburg showed through. I knew that we would need all of our skills to survive. Our quivers, lances, and swords were at the ready. This was the first time that I had drawn my sword in anger. As I did so energy surged through my body.

The Wanderers, perhaps bandits would be a better term, spread out and surrounded our position. As they did so one of their members emerged from the pack and hurled his spear. It missed, but Laurel's arrow did not. I found myself yelling:

> *Welcome to Outpost Death – asshole!*

I could not avert the plague that took the lives of my first children, Adam and Anna, but I could defend my daughters and their mates this time. I readied myself to sell my life dearly – very dearly – if necessary.

The next events seemed almost as a blur and as if we were protected by some unseen force. Seemingly from out of nowhere appeared mounted horsemen, their front rider carrying a banner that showed clearly they were a troop of Border Riders. Through the speed of their charge, they quickly – oh so quickly – put an end to the group of Wanderers attacking us. The skirmish was over in what seemed to be just minutes. As the Border Rider horsemen tidied up the battlefield, their leader, Sergeant Gerald Dickins, approached us and gestured towards the scattered dead:

> *They will bother you no further. You were wise to stand and fight. Had you not, and meekly given up your property to these Wanderers, you now would be dead. My troop had been scouting this bunch for weeks and saw in turn that they had been following you. We were waiting for the right time to strike and eliminate them. You were our bait and played your unknowing part well. Given the defensive position you took, your daughter's archery skills, and by brandishing your weapons, these Wanderers would have paid a high price no doubt.*

Dickins continued:

> *I see you carry one of our short swords. This style goes way back to olden Rome, so I've been told. I can assure you there is none better for efficient, deadly close-in work.*

I told the sergeant that my late mate and I secured our swords from the debris of battle in the North Country up near the River Ohio. These mounted horsemen who had come to our assistance were an independent a group, sponsored by local and regional militias, with responsibilities for maintaining calm and justice within the shattered zones of the western and central configurations.

Dickins: *Where might you be headed?*
Reese: *To Bison Camp – a part of the New NorthWest Configuration to the west of what once was Dillion, old Montana.*

Dickins: *That location and other parts of the New NorthWest were severely struck by the last plague. Even now we riders get few recruits from there, since most of the local young men are concerned with settlement group recovery and rebuilding. To be honest, I've not heard of a Bison Camp settlement group.*

Reese: *I am not surprised. Travis, my mate, and I were the only survivors from there and throughout quite a wide region.*

Dickins: *My troop will continue to patrol the southern regions of New Deseret between Moab and Provo, and I can place another in charge. If you like, I could serve as your protective guide to New Salt Lake and beyond. This would not be an imposition. Brigham City north of New Salt Lake is my home, and I am retiring soon from the Border Riders. You must have noticed that I am the sole greybeard here, have you not? Look, my brass buttons have been turned upside down.*

Indeed, I had seen that his beehive insignia buttons were topside down.

Dickins: *This is the mark of a retired Border Rider. The button reversal will bring much respect and more than a few beers, once I return back home.*

Then it was that Sergeant Dickins relinquished command to Corporal Shawn Peters. The Riders under their new commander headed southwest towards who knows what and how many adventures, while former Sergeant Dickins became our travel guide northward to New Salt Lake.

***

Our journey northward proved uneventful. Along the way my daughter's mates shared tales of things military that they had experienced back in New Vicksburg during the hours spent listening to their father's tales told at evening gatherings: some true, others perhaps more fiction. Our path now was quite easy, and the settlements we passed were in much better condition than those Travis and I had seen during our travels together. It was apparent that the Dark Time and Epidemic had been kinder to the residents of New Deseret, if such was possible. This area of general recovery held until we approached Provo and trekked north and west of the mountain range along what was called locally the Wasatch Front.

***

Provo

We entered Provo where many damaged buildings remained. These were not the signs of rioting and vandalism, but visible signs of frequent and very strong earthquakes. Several residents we spoke with, one of them Fredrick Nybold, laughed at our concern and told us:

> *You just get used to the shaking.*

As we were speaking, we outsiders jumped and look puzzled when a small shaker hit. This caused Nybold to laugh even more, although it left us a bit concerned. Even Sergeant Dickins had a good laugh.

We established our camp at Pioneer Park south of West Center Street. The young ones took time to explore portions of Provo and engaged a number of residents in conversation:

> **Darren "Deke" Tucker,** beekeeper – *Did you ever hear of funny honey? I've been a beekeeper forever since my father, Weston Tucker, bounced me on his knee. My name is Darren Tucker but just call me Deke. I remember one time, after chewing honeycombs directly from our hives, I became dizzy and lost the ability to speak. My father found me staggering about our farmland making weird faces and uttering gross animal-like sounds. I remember during that time I saw halos surrounding certain large stones, some types of trees and, most interesting, I had visions of cougars standing upright in a line dancing on their hind legs, something that made me laugh wildly for a time. These weird feeling lasted for 5-6 hours and then passed. My father told me that all this was due to my eating toxic honey, and that our bees had flown into patches of rhododendrons growing on hillsides east of Provo in the areas upslope near Corral Mountain. There was nothing any of us could do to stop the flight direction of our bees. But after my father found me and helped me recover, he destroyed the honey from those five hives. The same problem would visit us about every 7-10 solar cycles. Since I always recovered after eating such honey, it became my unusual appointed task that once a month during honey-making season I would be fed honeycombs from each hive: 99 times out of 100 the honey would just be sweet and wonderful, but that one time – wow! Cougars dancing on their hind legs!*

***

Dixon Summerset, clothcutter – *I like the term clothcutter better than the word taylor. The reason is that I once knew a kid at my school named Taylor, although he pronounced it something like Tie-Lore. But he couldn't fool us; he always was Tay-Lor to us. Tell me what you wear, and I will tell you who you are. Is it not true that you are what you wear? Bring me some cloth and I will cut it to your specifications. I make great shirts, pants, shorts, even what we call unmentionables. I don't do well cutting cloth into jackets, coats, or things like that. If you want riding chaps to protect your legs, I can do this easily in leather. Belts, if you want, are easy to make. We cut clothing from old pieces that are sewn together. I was once told by a great grandmother here in Provo that cloth once came in quantities called bolts. When I told her that I thought only lightning came in bolts, she bent over backwards laughing. Why, I had no idea. Bolts of cloth? That was news to me. I have never seen such.*

Mothers will bring me clothing from their little kids. I disassemble the seams, and re-sew the pieces by hand into larger units and from these I re-cut the cloth to fit my customer's needs. Yes it is true: most of our clothing these days is a hodge-podge of colors and designs pieced together from articles originally made long ago. But what else are we to do? There are no cotton fields to harvest here in Provo and, even if there were, how might we spin the thin cotton strands into thread and weave into cloth? The cotton we obtain comes into us from the New Confederacy. The wool of our sheep and goats can be spun on special wheels that our ancestors used, but who wants to wear wool underwear or wool shorts and pants when the temperatures outside reach higher than high? Some families without cloth from long ago times basically go without. But that is another story. I am called Dixon, and my mate and I manage the Dixon Summerset store over on South Freedom Boulevard. Stop by on your journey north to New Salt Lake City.

***

New Salt Lake City

Our route now passed east of the Great Salt Lake. Almost as far as we could see there were huge sparkly white salt flats extending south to north. It made sense to me that this was the location where most of the salt originated that Travis and I had seen previously as trade items along the

Great Rivers. The New Salt Lake City showed similar signs of earthquake damage. Sergeant Dickins guided us along the wide streets of central NSLC. Local militia members suggested we camp at City Creek Park where we rested for several days.

The well-tended and restored former religious center of New Salt Lake City was a grand expanse of buildings and monuments. One monument dedicated to seagulls was situated in what appeared to be a place of great honor. This puzzled me until Sergeant Dickens explained:

> *We honor these creatures and for good reason. During the early solar cycles when our ancestors came to this region and settled, we primarily were agricultural types. Then one terrible solar cycle our crops were devastated by an invasion of crickets, a plague that threatened our very existence. It was just then that the sky was filled with these birds widely known elsewhere as seagulls – but there was no sea near us as we were hundreds of kilo-miles inland from the Great Ocean. These birds suddenly appeared and devoured the crickets, thus saving our ancestors from starvation. So it is to these white-winged creatures, the seagulls, that our ancestors erected this monument.*

I found it curious and refreshing to encounter statues that honored something other than a soldier or a battle. Praise be! And as it turned out, this feeling also was shared by my daughters and their mates.

Another interesting feature of New Salt Lake and the nearby settlements to the east in the Wasatch Mountains were the Medi-People. These were groups of individuals trained in emergency medicine, and expert in the setting and healing of fractured bones. We were told that a high number of Medi-People was required due to what locals called fun-sports, specifically skiing and hang gliding in the nearby mountain areas. It seems, too, that they have some success in treating severe head injuries, as well.

During our rest days in New Salt Lake City, we encountered a range of very diverse residents, among them Cody Richards who was walking about chanting words from some long ago story. He stopped to address us:

> **Cody Richards,** hydrologist – *No one reads Samuel Taylor Coleridge these days. Who cares about some ancient-time Brit poet who wrote: Water, water, everywhere but not a drop to drink. Well is it not obvious that you cannot drink ocean water or water from*

the Great Salt Lake? When I was young my settlement group east of NSLC was attacked, and I was taken prisoner. My life was spared because I was a scientist, a trained hydrologist, a profession needed to understand sources for fresh water. My captors beat and screamed at me: tell us hydrologist – where can we find safe water to drink? I screamed back: why should I help you? Because if you do not we will first cut off your right hand, and then your left foot, and if you still do not reveal the sources we will eliminate your left hand, and your right foot. But I had the power because I knew the water sources. Go ahead you crap-heads, do it and do it now! I have no desire to live, and the pain you seek to inflict on me can be no worse than the pain I already carry in my heart after the death of my mate and the family members you killed. You threaten me? How stupid. It would be an easy task to show you what I claim to be fresh water to relieve your thirst. But, in fact, I could lead you to places where fresh water runs freely down the mountainside and seems wonderful in taste, but contains buytel-cyno-stabilites. You know nothing about hydrology: such tasteless contaminants will curdle your guts and leave you wreathing in agony on the ground. So go ahead: do what you must. Threaten me – you stupid bastards – and you will receive your just reward. Act now or leave me alone – your choice! And they snarled then disappeared, going off to coerce some other individual to show them fresh water sources. That was many solar cycles back, but I remember the event like yesterday. In my old age, I still can recall these events. Especially painful to me was the passing of my mate, children, and parents.

***

Not far from the central square near the seagull monument, we were walking together and came across a group of young men and women singing on a street corner:

Mary Jenkins, street singer – *My name is Mary Jenkins. I am the lead singer of the NSLCSSG. Perhaps you might know us better as the New Salt Lake City Street Singer Group? Our activities are sponsored and supported financially by the Salt Lake City Administration. We gather each day to share songs of joy to residents and travelers passing by. Each of our seven members receives two bronze barter tokens every three weeks, an unusual payment* *schedule to be sure, but one that meshes with our cycles of activity. For three weeks in succession, we sing songs of welcome and respect to travelers passing through SLC on their way hither and yon, something to brighten their days and to ease the hardships of their travel. We enjoy meeting and speaking with travelers like yourselves, and learning about your activities and hopes for the future. We welcome your travel stories and reply with songs that we have composed since the Epidemic; words of hope and comfort especially for families who lost members to the terrible illness that impacted us all. We do not seek conversion to our ways and beliefs, only that you respect us as we, in turn, respect you. When we are not singing as a group on the fourth week of each month, we volunteer at the Great Salt Lake Extraction Company, where we assist our brothers, sisters, and neighbors in the day-to-day activities of managing the export and trade of salt to the different regional configurations. Here is a list of songs we could perform for to brighten your day. Would you like to select one to hear?*

A Rising Tide Lifts All Boats
Sing and Work Together As One
A Bit of Happiness Softens the Long Journey

Or perhaps you would like one of these:

You are the Salt of my Earth
Sail Together on the Boat of Happiness
You Turn My Wheel of Life

No charge for a song: just give us happy smiles in return.

***

Ogden

We left New Salt Lake City in a joyful mood. Sergeant Dickens accompanied us as far as Layton, 26 kilo-miles north, where he escorted us to his ranch. The settlement outbuildings were near a great marsh that seemed to be a stopover point for countless waterfowl during their north-south migratory flights. Here, Dickens introduced us to his mates.

Yes, he had three mates, not only one as would be in the tradition where Travis and I were raised. The three ladies, Norma Jean, Mary Ann, and Paula, greeted us with grand hospitality and proudly presented their children, five in all. Here it seemed was a very happy home, although,

Adam and Joseph speculated that there probably were times when Sargent Dickens walked on eggshells – as the saying goes. Dickens' mates were interrelated; two were sisters and the third a cousin to the two. The three ladies, five children, and Dickens all seemed to get along well and respected one another.

After a brief, wonderful meal, we once more were on our way and spent the evening camping at Clearfield. We now had been 119 days on the road. We arose late and did not depart Clearfield until after midday. The distance from Clearfield to our next stop, Ogden, was but 12 kilo-miles and we camped at West Ogden Park just off Eye 15.

> **Rex Michael,** rockhound – *I saw you walking about the park observing my street stand, checking out my geodes and agate slices. Here in New Deseret we have unusual rock formations with different colored bands of stone providing many unique patterns. These desert beauties can add interesting elements to your hut or house decoration. I hiked these mountains east of Ogden and further south since I was a child, and I learned which sedimentary rocks could be split open to reveal ancient fossil fish or leaves. On those hikes I sometimes discovered veins of pyrite or fool's gold that, when ground up and mixed with obsidian and a special plaster-like paste that I concocted, could be applied to walls of huts or houses to softened the interior atmosphere. My specialty, one that I learned scouring the arroyos and eroded mountainsides, was identifying strata that included the fossil bones of the ancient creatures that once roamed this area many millions of solar cycles past. Once I found a leg bone taller than myself. Not far from this bone was a slab of rock jutted out from the hillside that contained three gigantic curved teeth. As I searched for more of these finds I learned such remains were from ancient beasts called armored lizards or dino-sours, but I can't be sure of the name. Even though I am now old and with straggly grey hair, I still like the adventure of walking about looking for rocks and fossil bones. Such activities put my life into perspective: here today – gone tomorrow. So what have I learned from all of this through the solar cycles? Do your best, help others, and make the earth a better place so events like the Ripple Event and Epidemic never reappear. I, Rex Michael, ask this of you.*

***

We encountered one of the more unusual residents of Ogden just prior to morning departure:

> **Raymond Beltzer,** conductor – *You might call me an herbalist, and I will accept that name. In another context you might address me by my given name, Raymond Beltzer. Here in Ogden, however, I am best known as the conductor. I welcome you on board, and I stamp your ticket. I offer different tickets at different barter prices to ride aboard your final passage train. As a special add-on price I can accompany you along the journey if you choose. I can provide the necessary consumables or beverages that will either slow or accelerate your train's speed. If you ask me to leave so you may end your journey alone, I will comply and honor your request. If you want me to remain, I will stay with you all along the way even to the point where you enter the light-framed tunnel, the portal to last leg of your journey.*
>
> *I am the conductor. Here in Ogden I am called to homes of the very sick and ailing. I use my art to calm the agitated seas of family member distress using soothing words. I deliver messages of hope or finality, depending upon the instance and need. But most of all you need not be alone. I also use my art and skill to soothe the pain of those left behind.*
>
> *I am the conductor. I have conducted the final passage train of many residents. That said, I am growing old and one question continues to haunt me: who will punch my ticket and conduct me along my final passage train?*

***

From Ogden we continued north along Eye 15. On day 120 we camped at Brigham City – four months after leaving New Vicksburg. We next passed through a suite of smaller settlements. We camped at Tremonton and the following evening stayed over at Portage. We next reached the New Deseret Confederation exit check point at Malad City, several kilo-miles north of the defined border between New Deseret and Old Idaho in the New NorthWest Confederation. Here we were delayed for two additional days, as the militia officers had difficulty confirming my previous residence status in old Montana. I could not understand the reason for such detailed background checking of my past. It also seems that no travelers from the New Confederacy Configuration previously had passed through

Malad City going north into either old Idaho or the Montana region. My daughters and their mates born in New Vicksburg posed geographical curiosities to the administrators at the checkpoint. But after the two days of meetings, discussions, and further inspections of our personal goods and food resources, we were granted travel status and permitted to continue on towards our goal. Two days of further trekking found us in Pocatello, old Idaho.

***

Pocatello

We camped at what used to be Bonneville Park, along South 19th Avenue. The settlement was essentially abandoned for reasons that were unclear, until we learned why after speaking with several of the survivors:

> **Jenna Nichols,** midwife – *I am lost and in pain. Long ago I trained women to assist with birthing labor. I Jenna Nichols once was the sturdy rock that women could grasp when waves of pain crashed over their body during labor. If a mother was delivering her 2nd, 3rd, or 4th child, she would be aware of the events unfolding and less apprehensive or fearful. My work was to provide support and assistance during the birthing progresses. I spoke with the male mate and other family members and provided them with a sense of security and calm, but also alerted them that each delivery was different and that unexpected events could arise.*
>
> *Then the Epidemic swept through Pocatello. I can understand the deaths of evil ones, but have never understood why so many of the good citizens of Pocatello and their children were taken from us? Each day now I am drenched in sadness. Before the Epidemic my greatest joy was to wash each newborn, then dry and wrap the infant and place it in the arms of the new mother. My second greatest joy was to watch the faces of the mates, how each smiled and held his tiny son or daughter in his arms, marveling as the newly born grasped his finger.*
>
> *Such is life: we are birthed and, when our time comes, we die. But for many at Pocatello their time came too quickly. That some lives are longer than others; that is fate. Some children develop into adults of astonishing abilities, talents, and wits. Others do not. These patterns reflect great cosmic indifference in the scheme of life. But it*

also is said that with each birthing and emergence of life comes the possibility of greatness. When I gazed upon the face of newborns, nothing could be predicted. I remember the face of each newborn as beautiful but blank, essentially a tablet upon which someday would be written life events. Family love, care, affection, and training would establish the child's life path. Some newborns would achieve greatness, others not. All this being part of the great cosmic lottery. The Epidemic brought an end to my joy. And then followed the attacks by groups of Wanderers. Our local militias could not protect us. Many in Pocatello fled and took refuge within neighboring settlement groups, leaving the few of us behind. I struggle each day to survive.

***

Another portion of this great regional tragedy brought about by the Epidemic and Wanderer attacks was told to us by a visitor to Pocatello. We encountered him after he had come down from the Flatland settlement group into town to search for barterable goods:

Drew Williams, deathsman – *I am one of five deathsmen here at the Flatlands settlement group just outside of Pocatello. We are appointed for one solar cycle, then at least five solar cycles must pass before re-consideration of another appointment. We are drawn from the list of settlement group males and females beyond the age of 65 solar cycles. Yes, women also perform this task in our settlement and do so with as much dignity as the men. We carry out the edicts of the judgment council at our settlement group and others in the region. We at the Flatlands settlement group allow the convicted an opportunity to select their endings from among three different possibilities, which I need not identify for you. All I wish to say at this point is that the methods are quick, painless, and provide closure to the families of loved ones who were murdered. So how is this different from what you have seen elsewhere along your trek?*

***

Fort Hall

Only 14 kilo-miles north of Pocatello we reached the trading post of Fort Hall, located along the Snake River. Few buildings remained, but a reconstructed shelter offered space for several stores. At the time of our arrival, these facilities were open for bartering. We stopped briefly and spoke with several locals visiting with the merchants:

> **Martha Jones,** sand sifter – *My brother, sister, and I have been sand sifters for as long as I can remember. We conduct our efforts along the banks of the Snake River where we divide our activities into three components, sifting piles of earth and sand for food particles, micro-gems, and fulgurites. The first two you know, but you say you never heard of fulgurites? Really! And you call yourself educated? Where did you go to school? Even the poorest kids in this sparsely settled western desert region know what fulgurites are and why they are important. Once folks like me were laughed at and called anthill sifters. My brother Byron, my sister Suzie, and I would spend 6-8 hours daily sifting the debris from red- and black-ant hills along both banks of the Snake River. Working together we could amass almost a kilo-pound of seeds that we then carried home to our mother who then prepared seed-porridge for our midday meal. We discarded the term anthill sifter once we moved to Fort Hall where in addition to the riverbanks we worked hillside scree zones looking for micro-gems, those elusive garnets, rubies, and occasional chunks of amber-banded cat's eye. Once we settled at Fort Hall, we also went out into the surrounding desert lands especially after lightning storms and searched for fulgurites. These form when lightning strikes fuse the sand and make unusual glass-like tubes. Those that we found were carefully transported back to Fort Hall where over on Edmo Road we turned our treasures over to Madam Aurora, our local vision forecaster who gave us barter tokens for what we collected that day. Even today she uses the fulgurites in some sort of magical predictive ceremony – something we have never been invited to attend. Those who know say that green fulgurites have protective properties but I can't confirm this.*

***

> **Tanisha Field,** crocker – *You better believe that I work hard, none of this crap about sitting around, being idle, and expecting to be fed through the goodness of others. Every day I labor on my potter's wheel, creating bowls, jars, and pots out of soft clay. I spin the wheelbase with my left foot turning the wheel clockwise. I force my wet hands down into the mass of clay allowing my fingers to form*

the desired shapes – a pinch here, an inscribed line there, with finger pressure I provide the required thicknesses of the vessel.

I am known best for my medicinal crocks where I also craft tight-fitting lids so the materials stored inside can remain fresh. Sometimes residents make fun of me, due to my lack of formal education, but they respect me. My skills as a crocker are highly needed by most families at Blackfoot and other local settlement groups at Firth, Gibson, and Wapello. If someone continues to bother me or to make rude comments about my work, I have a long memory. If the teasing continues in intensity and becomes more personal, I have a special way of creating pots that can solve this problem once and for all. No need to discuss this now, thank you, and leave me alone.

***

Idaho Falls

It was a joy to eventually reach Idaho Falls, one of the more scenic locations we had encountered along our trek. After 132 days on the road, we were eager for a bit of rest. We camped within the greenbelt trail across from the falls. The view was spectacular. We spent two camp nights here. During the days we walked the streets of Idaho Falls, speaking with residents hard at work rebuilding and remodeling their businesses. At one outdoor eating place, we encountered two unusual occupations.

Robert "Buck" Williams, dogwhipper – *Ever since the onset of the Ripple Event, packs of wild dogs have inhabited the shattered zones around the settlement groups near Idaho Falls, between Blackfoot and Spencer. Each spring the number of these animals increase and, like some oozing evil flowing outward from a long abandoned sewage vent, the dogs encircle the settlements nipping and probing, attacking livestock, seeking ways to do even worse mischief. So the administrators here at Idaho Falls offered me the position of dogwhipper. They explained if I would take the offered position and assume this responsibility to slay as many wild dogs as possible, then my past convictions for this and that would be forgiven and my rap sheet once again would be clean. You know what a rap sheet is, of course? If not, it doesn't matter. They also said if I would take on this dog-related task then once again I would be accepted as a resident in good standing within the region. You're looking at me funny; there is no need for me to tell you anything about my previous convictions* *and punishments, so get that out of your mind. If you want me to tell you about how I went about the task of dogwhipping and eliminating those packs of wild dogs, I'll do so, otherwise git!*

***

Iris Cooper, barter token manufacturer – *Nice to meet you! It seems we are bartering for food at the same locality here in Idaho Falls. You want to interview me? Great! Let's get started. My name is Iris Cooper. I am among the most trusted of all residents in our newly revitalized settlement of Idaho Falls. Every month a squad of militia members rides southeast to Idaho Falls from several facilities in the Sawtooth Mountains. Their task is escort two carts filled with rough sheets of aluminum, copper, and iron. They reach their destination west of Idaho Falls close to the Shelley-New Sweden Highway, where my advance team and I are standing outside a secured underground silo. This silo is a surviving relic of hostile times long ago that once held – I am told – a rocket, something called an ICBM, a weapon of potential mass destruction. I have no idea what the letters stand for. My co-workers and I await the transfer of these valuable commodities, sheets of metal that we will convert to barter tokens after the transfer has taken place. Once the militia and the metal sheets arrive, the next step is to open the secure silo door. Two keys are required. I have one, my partner has the second. Working together we insert both keys into their respective slots and turn them at the same time. This action is required to initiate the rollback of the cover that protects and shelters the deep-earth pit. Once the way into the silo has been secured, the sheets are lowered 50 meter-feet down to the bottom by a complex pulley lever system into a work area where the barter tokens will be manufactured. The militia commander joins me and together we descend the winding staircase of the silo to the bottom floor where the sheets are re-inventoried and the work transfer order signed and initialed. Once the record is certified the militia commander leaves. Our team then begins the process of cutting, stamping, and forming the precise number of barter tokens expected from each sheet. As you can see, I can talk about this system only generally, without specifics, and I am forbidden to show anything to you. What I can assure you is that the silo facility stockpiles sufficient quantities of manufactured barter* *tokens. These are stored along with sufficient back-up quantities of metal sheets should shortages occur in the future. These sheets serve as the backing for all of the regional economic transactions – not like in the olden days when governments once merely printed paper to cover economic losses and to counter hyper-inflation. Enough said!*

***

Dillon

Hard to believe. We had now reached the southern border of old Montana and were nearing the end of our journey. We paused at the border crossing, but there were no guards to check us through. There was only a solid white stripe across the highway barely visible through the dirt and grime that perhaps marked a former check-in station. We were coming home, but what would we find?

***

We approached Dillon with some anticipation, as our cross-country trek was nearing completion. Tragically, we found many of the buildings had been burned and looted. We observed no residents. Dillion had become a settlement of ghosts. I remembered that there had been a highly respected teachers college in Dillon during pre-Ripple times, a school that attracted students from all over old Montana, even as far away as Harlowton. No one was on the street close to the entrance to Big Hole Valley. I was engulfed in sadness.

***

Destination Reached

Beyond Dillon lay an easy journey into the Big Hole Valley and what had been my original home – Bison Camp. We crossed the rolling sagebrush country where Travis and I had flagged antelope for our hunter fathers; then through Badger Pass – known to those in the valley as Outpost Badger during the Dark Times. Then we paused just before reaching Big Hole Pass and the road down into the valley itself. Soon I would be home. As we continued I became even more anxious. What might we find at Bison Camp given the destruction we had seen in Dillon?

We reached the meadows south of Bison Camp. I was engulfed with a rush of memories; images of my young children Adam and Anna. Other memories of my early life with Travis overtook me with emotion. Sage, who had been in the lead scouting the landscape viewing through her see-far glasses, rode back quickly to where I was standing and shouted aloud:

Mom, there are others on the meadow!

Are you sure? In these lands your eyes can play tricks.

Very sure – at least two in plain sight, perhaps more.

Let me see, they seem like us but shorter. And in some sort of uniform I'd say.

Do you see any weapons?

Nothing I'd recognize as such. They seem unthreatening.

Let us respond accordingly. Place your arms in the pushcart and step back.

***

Think back and remember.

This was the day that we met you in the meadowlands just south of Bison Camp settlement group. This was our first meeting. One that that began with initial apprehension, but soon we developed care and consideration for each other. As you recall there was a certain amount of communication difficulty at first, but through use of signs and hand motions we began the process of learning from each other for mutual benefit to both.

Think back and remember.

It was there at the meadows that we first met you, crew members and later the officers from the *KosMa ExPlorer*. During the time of our first encounter until now we have learned to communicate and share information regarding our respective cultures and lives.

When invited to make evening presentations these past days, we were honored to relate our family and travel information to you. Having told our story I stand before you side by side with my daughters and their mates, to whom you have become acquainted with through our presentations.

All total we covered 3,133 kilo-miles between New Vicksburg and Bison Camp. Along the way we spent 145 days traveling, a period of nearly five months. We are proud of our efforts; we are glad to have returned home in the Big Hole Valley. We look forward to working and living among you. We have much to learn from each other.

More detailed accounts of our journey appear in the journals that both Travis and I faithfully kept each day, along with those maintained by my daughters and their mates. These documents all are available for your inspection. We also will submit to you a documented itinerary of our route, with notations on distances traveled each day, campsite locations, and other pertinent data contained in our record books. We invite you to inspect all of our records if you wish more detailed information.

After-Word

Alone in my cabin I lay down to rest but had difficulty falling asleep. Memories flooded my mind bringing tears of both joy and sorrow. I was home at last with my daughters and their mates. Along the way we experienced events of great joy as well as sadness. Travis did not live to see Bison Camp again. But it was through his spirit and strength that we were able to reach our destination. When Travis and I embarked upon our journey many solar cycles long past, our original objective had been to search for survivors of the Epidemic and to learn the extent to which that terrible illness and disease had spread beyond the confines of our NorthWest Configuration. What we found was a continent alive with survivors – not millions as before the Ripple Event – but certainly in the tens of thousands. Long into the night I pondered: what would the future bring? Would it be joy and happiness or more sorrow?

We had survived Wanderer and bandit attacks during our trek. These events, while serious, were localized and weapons used were all within our realm of knowledge. Far more serious, however, was the discovery of French military and civilian incursions into the northeastern regions, coupled with the north-south barrier along the Hudson River that could not be explained logically or with known technology. Was the barrier implemented by French technicians? Given the limited technological skills available to survivors of the Ripple Event and Dark Time, this seemed to be a near impossibility. One logical inference was that our planet was now settled in part by more than one set of extraterrestrials – the Bison Camp spacers as we came to know and call them, and a second group, unknown but with extraordinary technology, that had allowed their French surrogates to expand and regain territory previously lost centuries past in the Americas.

How, where, and when the current French expansion would play out, we could not speculate. We knew only that we at Bison Camp were not alone.

***

Ijano Esantu Eleman

Interlude-Conversation: 13

Return

***

Etowa be praised, K'Aser, Reese has returned to the Big Hole with her loved and loving family.

Yes, with Travis – both his physical remains and spirit – being part of that family. I must freely admit Etowah (may we do him honor) had more to do with the success of the journey from New Vicksburg to here than I.

Ah, but I know you were there all the way (and perhaps more) doing what you might as you had done before from The Big Hole to New Vicksburg as it turned out. For keeping Reese and her family safe, I thank you.

A thank you from an Observer how much I am pleased by this, A'Tena. In return I give you my sincerest thanks in days long past for your nursing Reese to survival, then health. And I do mean sincerest, you are a wonder for true and sure.

Like you I feel Etowah (praised be his name) was watching over us. As for your flattery, why it just might get you a drink at The Place someday/sometime. One never knows, does one?

I'll hold you to that. Overseers have excellent memories as required for the testing. An offer of a celebratory libation from an Observer, especially one so striking, will not be forgotten. This I promise you.

Hey, now you are angling for two drinks – nice try – but one will be your limit, at least for now. Let us return to this here and now, shall we? Reese is both happy and relieved to again be here in her true home, but she appears to have been taken aback by the otherworlders

Taken aback but not set back. With all her abilities she senses, wanders about and clearly sees the potential of the Earther-Spacer community (for this is what the peoples have come to call each other). May Etowah (praise be to him) bring this potential to fulfillment.

It cannot help but be better than that which came from this orb's first experience with otherworlders, the folks from out there.

Are you referencing Roswell?

What else could it be? Crashed scout ships, dead and injured Spacers (but not from the home world of those stranded in the Big Hole), a rescue by the mother ship and other scouters to follow, and interruption by our people – nobles as well as commoners. Whops, there I go again lapsing into long ago time Medieval lingo but the words describe those that emerged at the crash.

Your terminology covers them well, and the nobles leapt into action putting a lid on the situation.

That they did from then on out – denials, disinformation, including subtle release of genuine information, ridicule of believers, and so on. These patterns of disinformation worked then and continued to. The authorities had a tiger by the tail. They chose not to let go despite continued sightings, some landings and even physical evidence here and there made their goal more and more difficult. How often the authorities would say:

Nothing to see here, folks. Move along, move along.

But their efforts became less and less effective, even up to the Ripple Event.

And then when the computer virus was launched, even we ourselves had more crucial matters to address. Do you not expect, though, that from now on events on this orb will go better for the Spacers and Earthers?

Perhaps, but only if they would turn off their great siestistic beacon. It's continual pulsations in my view will attract off worlders in like moths to a flame. And who knows what will happen if more types and kinds of otherworlders appear and attempt to influence Earther actions and behaviors.

I expect that pulsations from the great beacon will make events most interesting.

Interesting, indeed.

Too interesting, if you ask me.

The Journey: Part 5

Chapter 14

Two Cultures: Unification and Adjustments

Pre-Note

During the weeks and months following our last group presentation, each of us regularly were asked questions about survival strategies, food management along the trek, and how to deal with strangers in the future now that we had confirmed there were considerable numbers of human survivors elsewhere on the continent. The Spacer newcomers while similar to us were quite different culturally and in subtle physical ways. Their education being quite different from ours posed some difficulties of mutual understanding. Their planetoid systems of government, very different from previous solar cycles on our planet, were based upon trust and mutual respect. Local and regional administrators worked for their electorate instead of working for themselves and amassing considerable wealth in the process. On personal levels, their dining and drinking needs were different than ours. They remained hydrated for significantly longer periods of time than we could, which had considerable impact on water needs when making local excursions. Our water consumption requirements were c. 10 liter-pints/day; theirs was considerably less. That meant, of course, their internal physiological systems were significantly different from ours and reflected evolutionary changes that had occurred over many hundreds of thousands of solar cycles at their original planet.

Such physiological differences did not interfere with our desire for mutual respect and harmony.

Discussions and questions posed to each other commonly related to wild foods and water rehydration locations; sites where additional horses or pack mules could be obtained if our original animals became sick or were injured and needed to be put down. Most questions, however, dealt with personal and group safety. The Spacers had no previous interactions or knowledge of other survivors of the Epidemic and posed questions that dealt more with group security than issues of cultural differences and curiosity.

The most challenging question that puzzled both of our groups was why human life essentially had been eliminated within this region of New NorthWest Configuration while in other locations there were survivors. The fact that we located survivors in each of the configurations visited suggested two possibilities: some survived because they possessed a protective genetic variant, while others survived because of group isolation with limited to no inter-regional collective activities. Still another possibility existed, one more in the realm of faith and the supernatural, that perhaps an external force protected certain individuals and groups over others.

Altogether both groups settled at Bison Camp now numbered 33 individuals: 28 Spacers (several were pregnant) and five Returners. We now joined together for mutual benefit, protection, and cultural preservation. I had seen 34 solar cycles; Adam and Joseph, 16; and Sage and Laurel, 15. I often thought back in wonder that my twin daughters and their mates – at such young ages – could have completed our long trek and return to Bison Camp. All this was very difficult to believe: the events leading up to our trek, our stay in New Vicksburg, and our return home. All this seemed like yesterday. But here I was 34 solar cycles old in the middle solar cycles of my life. I had experienced the pain of having my first two children perish in the terrible Epidemic, then Travis and I had trekked more than halfway across the continent. But after my grieving I had experienced the joy of birthing our twin daughters, and seeing them mature and select mate partners at New Vicksburg. All these events set within the trials and efforts of our return journey to the Big Hole Valley.

Hard to believe!

***

A New Beginning

Settling in at Bison Camp was facilitated by the Spacers, who helped us adjust in many ways. We smiled, in turn, when they labeled us as *The Five*. More commonly, however, they called us *The Returners.* Together we embarked upon a period of learning and mutual adjustment. In the week following our last assembly presentation, we celebrated the memory of my mate, Travis Saunders, at a special ceremony where his ashes were strewn along the banks of the Big Hole River, a place he loved more than any other. How many times during our overland trek from Three Forks to New Vicksburg had Travis and I shared memories from reading one of the long ago Data Collector's report about the Musselshell River near Harlowton in Old Montana. Travis would sing and modify the lyrics, inserting words and location of places that he loved best, Big Hole Valley and the river that flowed through – from mountains to the sea:

By the banks of the Big Hole River,
It is there that I want to grow old

To soar on my wings like an eagle,
To lie on your carpet of gold.

Your crystal clear waters they ripple and flow,
From the mountains then down to the sea,
Let the sounds of your waters now lull me to sleep,
Here will my soul be set free.

And it was along the banks of the Big Hole River, not far from the meadowlands where the five of us first encountered the Spacers, that we distributed Travis's ashes. The ceremony was held on a wonderful spring day. All the Spacers attended except two who were posted on sentry duty. My daughters spoke and related memories of their father, some stories poignant, others humorous, but all wonderful. I listened intently as their mates offered commemorative words in Travis's honor. Now at last he was home, where he wanted to be.

Two of the Spacers, Adam Winkler, personnel systematics, and Roxanne Hernandez, senior lieutenant, propulsion systems, rose to speak and offered farewell honors to Travis. Both stood and together chanted words in their own language, translated to us – the eulogy spoken at traditional death ceremonies at their home planet at the shrine dedicated to their deity PasJmoDk:

Time and space are one
So flows the river of life
From ages past until now
We become one with the past

We are one with the present
We will be one with the future
So flows the river of life
PasJmoDk be praised.

Powerful words spoken with feeling, words of courage and strength offered to survivors when their loved ones died, words that would live on in my memory forever

During the weeks and months that followed and into the first three solar cycles of our residence at Bison Camp, the bond between our two groups grew as we continued to evolve strong mutual respect for each other.

Our cultures and histories were different but similar in many ways. We now had mastered each other's languages after struggling though difficult pronunciation sounds and linguistic subtleties. Each new day saw us working together. We were united with similar primary goals: to benefit and protect our Bison Camp settlement.

Spacer friends joined to help us move into our living quarters. These were three older guest cottages constructed many solar cycles earlier along the northern limits of the original Bison Camp settlement area, each with sufficient design for further additions if children might be birthed in the future. We organized our living space around a central courtyard; storage barns and silos were erected along the perimeter adjacent to meadowlands where our livestock grazed.

During their first year the Returners cleared, plowed, and seeded agricultural fields with cereals, roots, and leafy vegetables they had brought with them during the outward voyage of the *KosMa ExPlor*er. The cultivated areas extended to the northwest and downslope from the adjacent mountains, locations that permitted adequate drainage. Seasonal snow and rill runoff ultimately found their way through our fields, and then flowed into the lower marshlands where migratory ducks and geese flourished in season. The land was rich in bountiful offerings. We farmed and cared for our animals throughout the seasons; assisted with the birthings of calves, colts and lambs; we established hutches for domestic fowl that provided eggs for our breakfast repasts. In season we walked through the waving fields of grain, reaching out to touch individual wheat stems, picking one then another, and marveling at their complex geometry.

In addition to our family activities, we accepted community work details as responsible members of our settlement. These tasks were defined by Louis Carpenter and Joyce Evans, joint deputy commanders of the Big Hole Valley colony. Adam and Joseph were assigned split duties. In early spring they patrolled agricultural fields throughout the settlement, providing protection and removing various forest animals that attempted to graze on our bounty. During late fall and winter months they joined others to provide community security. Their tasks complemented those undertaken by Spacer males of the same age: preparation of agricultural fields in advance of planting crops; fence erection to keep out herds of wandering deer and elk; silo construction; and similar tasks. They joined with other Spacers to patrol the borders of the Big Hole Valley enclave and took turns relieving sentries at the strategically located redoubts and lookout posts.

Sage and Laurel also assisted and took on their own community responsibilities. These focused primarily on field preparation (clearing, plowing, and seeding) along with fence construction. Their primary fencing tasks identified and cut specific lodge pole pines, then through a pulley-rope system, sent the poles downslope to gathering areas where fencing was needed. Working together with other Spacers, they sawed the logs into various lengths and split them into longitudinal pieces to make fences of desired heights. Both daughters also accepted shared responsibilities for monitoring and providing security at the communal children's education center.

I assisted my Spacer counterparts with these and other tasks, as well. During rest and rehabilitation days, I had additional projects. I was asked by Joint Commander Joyce Evans to be her historical advisor so she could better understand the time periods leading up to, during, and after Post Dark Time Recovery. Of special interest to Commander Evans were four themes: how humans survived during the Ripple Event; organization and information gathered during Data Collector treks; events leading up to and during the Epidemic; and current locations of survivor groups.

Commander Evans and I became good friends and communicated well. She answered my questions about her home orb, issues related to overpopulation; her participation in several cosmic expeditions as she and crew members searched for alternative inhabitable orbs; technological similarities and differences between our two peoples; activities aboard the *KosMa ExPlor*er; and her post-contact experiences within the Big Hole Valley.

We also pondered how we bipeds were both similar and different, and how this could be. We discussed how revolutionary changes independent of our two respective planets could result in so much similarity. We both were bipeds, with similar male and female characteristics. We looked similar, except for differences in stature – the Spacers being slightly shorter on average than the five of us. Our facial structures and limb development were similar. Mentally, our ways of thinking and solving problems were similar but with some unusual differences.

Of special interest to me was the fact that despite differences, these issues did not evolve into power or primacy hierarchies as had characterized many cultures on my planet. The Spacers seemed oblivious to the fact that their food and water needs were significantly different than ours: after a long hard work day a meal of 2,800 kilo-calories would be needed by most of my family members. Similar work efforts by Spacer males or females needed a mere 800 kilo-calories per day. Of interest, too, was the observation that our fluid/water intake requirements were 8-10 times higher than theirs, a reflection of significant internal physiological differences.

***

Early Demographics and Time Considerations

Passages from the daily diary of Laurel Emory:

> *During my rest and rehabilitation periods I started a historical project to interview each of the Spacers. My mother, Reese, already had prepared diary entries that included names, occupations, technical assignments, and basic characteristics. My goal was to learn more about each of the Spacers now that all of us worked together in a new setting. Today I began summarizing my notes on the KosMa ExPlorer officers and crew members, those who had volunteered to stay behind on the new world while the majority returned home to organize fleets of immigration star ships to bring new life to the apparently unoccupied world just discovered. I also wished to explore their inner feelings and what it meant to be alone*

as colonists – indeed stranded – on the planet that once solely was the realm of humans.

In preparation for interviews two lists were prepared. The first identified officers of the KosMa Explorer, clustered by rank, specialization, and mate assignment (n = 12):

Louis Carpenter, Joint Deputy Commander, Big Hole Valley Colony
Joyce Evans, Joint Deputy Commander, Big Hole Valley Colony
Thomas Dickinson, Senior Legender, Primary Security Officer
Saranda Foster, Senior Legender, Junior Security Officer
Mavis Stronghaven, Senior Colonel, Strategic Operations Coordinator
Adam Winkler, Major, Personnel Systematics
Roxanne Hernandez, Senior Lieutenant, Propulsion Systems
Richard Engels, Senior Captain, Computer System Solvency and Repair
Jackson James, Senior Lieutenant, Navigation Specialist
Janice Upton, Junior Lieutenant, Supply and Technical Orders
Theodore Ikado, Junior Quartermaster, Food and Beverage Preparation
Allison Currie, Junior Quartermaster, Food and Beverage Preparation

The second list identified crew members of the KosMa Explore, clustered by rank, and mate assignment (n = 16):

Jensen, Irene, Aeronaut 1st Class
Hunter, Cassius, Aeronaut 1st Class
Holden, Harold, Aeronaut 2nd Class
Stone, Ingrid, Aeronaut 2nd Class
Lister, Alice, Aeronaut 3rd Class
Preger, David, Aeronaut 3rd Class
Fenster, Lucas, Flight Construction Manager 2nd Class
Davidson, Susan, Flight Construction Manager 2nd Class
Branson, Thomas, Flight Corporal
Drurey, Megan, Flight Corporal
Morrison, Alan, Flight Technical Sergeant 4th Level
Williams, Martha, Flight Technical Sergeant 4th Level
Rovela, Mark, Private 1st Class

Manes, Nancy, Private 1st Class
Sentakis, Ari, Private 2nd Class
Burnett, Nancy, Private 2nd Class

During interviews, I learned the problems of keeping and reporting time. The Spacers marked the passage of time in two ways: Relative Days – starting with Day 1 base date, the departure from their home planet, a system that they labeled Post Departure Calculation or PDC. A second system for recording time they called KosMa Explore Departure (KED), a relative system that tracked the number of days after the KosMa Explorer left the new planet on its return journey home.

We Returners tracked time using the concept of annual solar cycles. We labeled events that occurred prior to the Ripple Event as Old Solar Cycle (OSC), but sometimes these events appear in our manuscripts with the notation as Pre Ripple Event (PRE). Immediately after the Ripple Event use of the term solar cycles continued and were designated as DT for Dark Time. The DT events lasted ten solar cycles; the first five solar cycles of the Dark Time sometimes were called FY, standing for Fear Years. Once the trauma of the Ripple Event and Dark Time passed, a new designation for solar cycles was introduced, called Post Dark Time Recovery (PDTR).

These various designations for time periods posed considerable confusion. While the reasons for these designations remained in our Returner memories, we conferred with the Spacers and reached an agreement that solar cycle 65 or PDTR 65 was the key baseline event – being the solar cycle when our two groups met for the first time. We reached agreement that the letters NH, abbreviation for New Home or New Hope, as sometimes used, would signify our mutual respect and commemorate the founding of our new, integrated settlement, a home for both of us.

After interviewing each of the Spacers during the course of several months, I determined that both the officers and crew members of the KosMa Explore had graduated from their inter-galactic space academy. All graduates were certified in 21 specific skill-sets, an intensive educational process that took three home base solar cycles to complete (approximately five solar cycles on our planet). This specialized training included the following skill sets: Astro-Physics and Astronomy; Communications; Computer Programing and Repair; Construction Engineering and Structural Repair; Creative Manufacturing; Digital Recording and Image Preservation; Electrical and Ionic Flow Circuitry; Emergency Medicine and Herbal Compounds; Engine and Propulsion Systematics; Exercise and Strength Development; Exo-Botanical and Exo-Zoological Identifications; Fuel and Transport Technology; Geology and Structural Formations; Health, Sanitation and Disease Transmission; Home Base History, Literature, and Music; Hydroponics and Food Production; Mathematics and Computational Creativity; Metallurgical Chemistry; Home Base Political and Economic Education; Wilderness and Seasonal Survival Skills; and Weapon Development and Repair.

***

Shared Technology

As we grew together in respect and shared responsibilities, the Spacers were open in describing and sharing their technologies, some quite different than what we ever could have expected. During our education at Bison Camp, Travis and I had learned the history of energy technology on our planet: the six basic machines – inclined plane, lever, pulley, screw, wedge, and wheel. We learned about different gearing systems of waterwheels used to drive mills to grind grain or other plant and mineral resources. We learned that solar panels and wind machines had only limited acceptance prior to the Ripple Event. These technologies were not revisited during the Dark Time or early Post-Dark Time Recovery periods due to lack of manufacturing capabilities. We also learned the basics of atomic power and how advocates promised clean solutions to atmospheric problems, compared to coal and/or oil as energy resources. We learned, too, of the several atomic energy power plant disasters that contaminated landscapes along seafronts when the facilities had been disrupted by earthquakes or typhoons, and destruction caused by two instances of terrorist attacks that brought havoc to local regions.

The Spacers were knowledgeable not only of these technologies but vastly different ones, as well. One of their more interesting techno-items, as we called them, were roll-o-carts used to transport goods or riders within the settlement and to more remote observation posts within the Big Hole

Valley. These modular units could be assembled easily by hexographical wrenches, a tool carried by all Spacers attached to their belts. The hexographicals were unusual wrenches that released magnetic attraction devices holding pieces together. The roll-o-carts essentially were pull-apart units with cleverly designed rollers that facilitated movement over uneven or rocky ground. If desired, the rollers could be removed, whereupon the pull-apart carts were transformed and used as stackable storage containers.

The Spacers had developed a primary energy source based upon what they called ionic capacitors. These energy capacitors were small capsules that could be inserted into vents of any Spacer machine and would supply power for up to two solar cycles before re-charging became necessary. The unique aspect of the ionic capacitors was that recharging could be completed after just one hour exposure to sunlight. The physics behind their ionic exchange technology and how the capacitors were manufactured was not revealed. But even if such information had been shared, it is probable that we would not have understood the science or the production processes. It also was possible that the Spacers in our community were not privy to the actual manufacturing process of the capacitors, that this knowledge was a cultural-technological secret held by only a few on their home planet. It was enough for us to know that simple sunlight exchange recharged the capsules, and sufficient energy could be generated and stored to provide all the needs for Bison Camp facilities, as well as perhaps more than 10 million additional needs.

The Spacers had developed personal practical weapons unlike anything we had previously known or encountered. These weapons primarily were for protection during extreme danger. A simple weapon type carried by all Spacers was called a dzork. The weapon was oblong and fit easily into the palm of the hand. Indentations for finger grips were along both sides for easy handling. If self-protection was required, the weapon could be fired by a quick upward movement of the thumb, which opened a port where a powerful laser emerged to neutralize any confrontational danger – aim, flick, fire – all in one graceful motion.

The most dramatic technological advance revealed to us was shared during the first solstice celebration after our return. Inside one of the larger storage facilities we were shown two most unusual items. We gazed upon them in wonder as Joint Deputy Commander Louis Carpenter informed us that the decision was taken to uncrate and assemble the machines after listening to our evening presentations. Carpenter told us that our descriptions of other survivors, especially our encounter with Wanderer groups, necessitated the need for special security. Component parts of the machines had been transported aboard the *KosMa ExPlorer*. The reassembly process was now complete, and we were invited to review and inspect the two objects

What we saw before us was startling. There were two machines unlike any we had known previously. They resembled aero-ships but bore no relationship in size or shape to any of the photographs of air machines Travis and I had viewed at the ruined museum outside of Dayton, old Ohio. The Spacer machines were approximately five meter-yards in length, and perhaps half that in width. Their composition was a metal unknown to me. It was cool to the touch and burnished to a brilliant reflective blue-grey hue. Short wings with vertical and horizontal stabilizers were attached to either side of a central ovate-cylindrical housing. Inside the cylinder were form-fitted seats for two pilots. A cluster of instrument panels emblazoned with symbols we could not read or understand emitted gold and red hues. A protective clear covering sealed off the housing. Nothing Travis or I had seen before looked anything like this. The other so-called flying machine images that we had seen displayed at Kill Devil Hill on the Outer Banks off the old Carolina coast were nothing like these beauties. The Spacers called them *Arkn Jemts* or Scout Ships.

***

Family Development

Solar cycles passed quickly, and we residents experienced great joy within our Bison Camp settlement. My daughters and I watched the growth and development of Eleman Rovela, the first child born in the new Spacer colony. He was a joy to observe. We smiled at Eleman's bilingual fluency, how he mixed and matched Spacer and Returner vocabulary with a fluidity superior to his parents, Mark and Nancy, and to those who tended and watched over him. Eleman Rovela – a wonderful child – truly a new beginning.

Eleman was born during the second solar cycle after the *KosMa ExPlor*er inter-stellar ship had landed, 498 relative days after leaving their home planet. After reviewing Spacer history of their landing and subsequent experience, I calculated that they had landed in the Big Hole Valley about the same time Travis and I were in our 9th-10th solar cycle in New

Vicksburg. The birth of Eleman occurred two solar cycles later, and he had just celebrated his second solar cycle when we returned to Bison Camp.

The time period of old solar cycle 66 and 67, or New Home cycles 2 and 3, saw multiple pregnancies among the Spacer mate partners. Deliveries of the Spacer infants clustered during the fall season, their gestation period seemed to match the nine-month characteristic pattern of human women that delivered at Bison Camp during the Post Dark Time Recovery period, and my own experiences.

Among the Spacers nine of the females conceived and delivered at different times during solar cycles 66-68 (New Home solar cycles 2-4). A total of three children, two boys and one girl, were born by the female officers, while five additional children were birthed by crew member partners.

Together as one community, we celebrated each birth in turn. The Spacer naming ceremonies were different than ours and included a tasting element. One of the components of the Spacer birth celebration honored the grain-based survival diet of their home planet. After arriving in the Big Hole Valley, abandoned stands of wheat still covered portions of the flatland meadow regions. At the new birthing ceremonies, preparations of mother's first milk was mixed with the ground powder from three wheat seeds (each grain representing the mother, father, and infant). This mixture was spoon-fed to the infant. As the spoon-filled mixture touched the lips of the newborn, all attending watched in anticipation. A wrinkled smile and soft cooing sound traditionally foretold a long and productive life; a scowl and crying sound foretold a long life, but complicated childhood.

In advance of each ceremony, Adam and Joseph worked in the community blacksmith shop to create special celebratory cups and spoons. Each utensil was polished and engraved with the infant's name, with the parent's name and birth calendrical date etched below. When the tasting celebration had concluded, the spoons were washed and kept by the parents, separate from all other family household utensils.

And it was during this happy period, too, that the news came to me brought by Sage herself: she and her mate Adam were pregnant – truly a new beginning! Sage delivered in NH5. During the birthing ceremony the community gathered to watch and participate. Unexpectedly, not one but three emerged: triplet boys. It was a joyful shock to each of us, now recognizing our new responsibilities of raising these three boys. With recognition of three new lives to care for and nurture, their triplets were not named on the delivery day, but received their designations eight days later.

After the eight days passed, Bison Camp was alive with anticipation. Sage and Adam held the infants in their arms. The tiny boys squirmed and fussed in their soft cloth bindings. Those attending grew quiet as Sage and Adam revealed the names:

We offer thanks to Etowah for these three new lives. We will honor the Noble Seven and educate our sons in the correct way and with the support of all at Bison Camp. May they grow and develop into fine young men. With the stress of their birthing day past, we see them now fit and able. With this ceremony we reveal their names and, in so doing, honor three great men important in our own lives: their two grandfathers – Fischer Lang and Travis Saunders – and the General, Taylor James, responsible for the security system at Bison Camp settlement group prior to the Ripple Event. We will now hold each of our sons within our arms as we reach up towards the sky to give thanks – and now we name them in the sequence of their emergence:

Taylor Lange: sequence of emergence 1st. Long life!
Fischer Lange II: sequence of emergence 2nd. Long life!
Travis Lange: sequence of emergence 3rd. Long life!

Approximately one solar cycle after birthing the triplet boys, another joyful time was upon us. Came the news that my daughter Laurel and her mate Joseph Emory had become pregnant. Nine months later they delivered a fit, squirming, beautiful daughter. Laurel and Joseph named their baby daughter Anna, to honor her aunt who had died during the Epidemic.

***

Triplet Development

By the time the triplets reached their first solar cycle celebration, each could walk and talk, albeit with a limited vocabulary. A Communal Education Unit (CEU) was established inside the confines of our settlement at a central location adjacent to our community meeting hall. Parents shared responsibilities for security and caring for the charges. All the children flourished during the first three solar cycles. The triplets and Spacer children socialized well. There were only a few instances of attempted domination by one child over another. During mealtimes caregivers observed that when food was placed on the table in front of the girls, they commonly reached down, picked up a piece, and offered it to one of the boys sitting opposite. Curiously, both Spacer boys and our triplet boys seldom shared food with the girls sitting across the table. For the most part the boys and girls played separately. Both learned their initial lessons equally quickly.

Eleman Rovela, first Spacer born on the new planet, interacted well with the newborns and was seen by all parents as an important element in the younger children's education, training, and socialization. There was something about Eleman's personality and behavior that was wonderful. Working in the CEU, he assisted the parents, helped with the reading and physical training of the children, and was a calming – when occasional small disputes arose among the Communal Education Unit charges.

Eleman was the first to observe and report that Taylor behaved and acted differently from his brothers. He noted that Taylor was especially active, much more so than Fischer and Travis. Another of Taylor's distinctive characteristics was that he took to the educational components presented in the CEU much more quickly, and asked many more questions about the subject matter than his brothers. Taylor also seemed to be quite introspective and was a risk-taker.

When any child in the CEU reached their 5th solar cycle, the community celebrated. Fathers of the boys and girls presented each child with their first protective weapon. Community standards deemed that by this age children were responsible enough to care for and protect others when outside the immediate settlement area where danger sometimes lurked. This father-child gift, sometimes called the First Knife Ceremony also established a limited form of independence among children at this early age. Before their 5th solar cycle, all food prepared at the Communal Education Unit, at home, or in other community settings, was served to the children already diced or cut into manageable slices. Once each child received their ceremonial knife, they were allowed to cut or slice their food themselves, a symbolic recognition of their growth and pre-maturity.

***

Triplet growth and education development continued without major difficulty. Through their 6th-9th solar cycles, the triplets were educated at both the CEU and at home, and were assigned community service at different suitable levels. Children of both the Spacers and Returners received special training in group and individual protection and survival skills. These classes and events commonly were organized and taught by fathers, in concert with other men and women of the community.

After the triplets received their first training and behavioral evaluation, reports were prepared by the Communal Education Unit supervisors who had observed each child since entry into the program. Sage shared the triplet's evaluations with me and I studied them with some amusement, thinking back to days when I was a child and what my parents must have thought about my performance:

> *Taylor – Birth order first. Spacer name – Dorving (=Scholar): Taylor continues to challenge his teachers and requests more historical information about Bison Camp settlement group and times before and after the Ripple Event. He regularly seeks information from his mother (Sage), father (Adam), and grandmother (Reese). He wants more details and facts about events elsewhere, especially the cross-country journey treks made by his mother and grandmother. Taylor believes in actions, not words. He likes different foods. When served meals at the CEU he tastes each of the items offered, but does not consume them all. Two of his teachers and five of his playmates see Taylor as impatient, ready to tell others how he better could accomplish tasks. When conversing with his caregivers, teachers, or others, we have observed he frequently interrupts conversations and sometimes speaks quickly and with emotion.*
>
> ***Summary:*** *Taylor is well liked by his age peers. His teachers consider him to be a potential non-conformist, with certain identifiable behavioral characteristics that will set him apart from his two brothers and other Spacer children his age.*
>
> ***Recommendation:*** *Promotion out of CEU training. Taylor should prepare for his maturation ceremony.*
>
> *Fischer – Birth order second. Spacer name – Foztel (=Cook). Fischer, through actions and behaviors, consistently reveals a special interest in food. More than any other subject, Fischer has taken a dominant interest in regional plants and animals that have served the food needs of all at Bison Camp settlement group through historical times. He goes beyond mere learning and identifying which items are edible by season and geographical location, and those that*

pose difficult challenges during preparation. Since early age Fischer has assisted his mother (Sage) in the family kitchen and has wanted to observe and take part in family food preparation. He has demonstrated unusual sensory acuity during cooking activities and is curious how different tastes and flavors can be components of the same culinary dish. Among his Communal Education Unit age peers he is considered the most sociable. He is liked by all with friends and play partners of both genders. He participates regularly in settlement group celebrations.

Summary: *We agree that Fischer is even tempered, a rapid learner, and shares supplies and equipment without challenge or argument. He cares for the feelings of others and quickly defends members in his study group if one is confronted by an angry or upset other.*

Recommendation: *Promotion out of CEU training. Fischer should prepare for his maturation ceremony.*

Travis – Birth order third. Spacer name – Zondlik (=Walker). Travis has demonstrated special interests and skills typical of an adventurer or explorer. At an early age Travis regularly ventured outside the immediate boundary of Bison Camp settlement group, somewhat to the concern of his parents. He is especially active: everyday activities have included wading or swimming back and forth across the Big Hole River while under the watchful eye of his father, Adam. Travis has hiked and climbed the mountain peaks both east and west of the valley. His father and grandmother have spent hours with Travis, perfecting his skills how to identify animal spoor, track wild game, how to determine migration and grazing directions of wild animal herds. Travis's abilities to predict both flight and rest patterns of migrating birds, the seasonality of edible wild plants, and how to identify the toxic mimic species, are well known to his observers. He has an unusually keen and analytical eye for his age. He is able to differentiate geological structures and locations of metallic ores, items of potential importance to our settlement.

Summary: *More than any other youthful member of our Communal Education Unit, Travis seems most relaxed and is at his best when camping with his parents and other residents, experiencing the wilderness characteristic of the Big Hole Valley.*

> ***Recommendation:*** *Promotion out of CEU training. Travis should prepare for his maturation ceremony.*

With arrival of New Home 12 (old solar cycle 79), the triples reached the double-digit age of 10, a sign of approaching maturity. We could not have been prouder: three young boys similar in appearance to Spacer children their age, but each unique and different in behavioral characteristics. Soon they would reach manhood and face the responsibilities to follow.

***

Maturation Ceremony

After the triplets had reached their 10th solar cycle, Sage and Adam began preparations for their sons to participate in the Bison Camp Maturation Ceremony. This was an older custom we once knew at Bison Camp, one that had marked the passage of both boys and girls from early and middle childhood into pre-adult status. In the long ago past, the Bison Camp Maturation Ceremony was an annual event held in late spring after the snowmelt but before the heat and humidity of early summer. Adam and I had presented our proposal to the administrative council to reinstate the historic Maturation Ceremony. After review and discussion the council recommended implementation.

The revised ceremony was composed of two parts. First, the completion of eight events, collectively called the Octathon. These would be scheduled over a period of eight days, with one event per day. The second component was recognition of success: a communal pyre celebration to honor the participants after completing the Octathon

The traditional and revised Octathon consisted of four components in each of two categories: life survival and strength-stamina. Participants assembled at dawn. The Octathon leader charged the youths to utilize their skills, and the tests began:

Day 1: *Identify and collect at least 50 edible wild plants that could serve as survival food if needed; return to camp within six hours with the specimens and identification lists for certification;*

Day 2: *Collect spoor and draw track marks of at least 20 different animals that could serve as survival food if needed; return to camp within six hours with the specimens and drawings for certification;*

Day 3: *Use information summarized on Octathon day two; hunt/capture two varieties of local birds, two types of river fish, and two varieties of small valley mammals; return to camp within six hours with the specimens for certification and overnight storage;*

Day 4: *Early morning, gather at the assembly area; prepare two separate cooking fires using two different techniques (choice of: flint and steel, drill, or friction device); prepare a mid-day meal using plant and animal resources on Octathon day 1 and 3; meal components will be judged for taste and quality by maturation ceremony judges.*

The second component of the Octathon consisted of strength and stamina events.

Day 5: *Memory Trek: Gather at the communal assembly area, when the start signal is given, climb uphill ascending to the crest of the western mountains; at the crest retrieve your success token from the Octathon judge; return downhill to the assembly point; deliver success token to the maturation ceremony judges.*

[Explanatory Note: The Memory Trek event retraced the path Travis and Reese took after the Epidemic when they left the confines of the Big Hole Valley to seek other survivors].

Day 6: *Ride-Swim [R-S Component]. Gather at the assembly area. Ride bareback to the north entrance of Big Hole Valley, dismount and tether horses; ascend the western hillside to Hirschy Lake; complete the cross-lake swim and return twice; run back downhill, locate and remount the horses then return to the Bison Camp assembly point where a hardy welcome meal is served.*

[Explanatory Note: It became common in future maturation ceremonies that the leader, after completing the cross-lake swim, would release the other horses as a symbolic gesture, forcing other participants to spend time chasing down their rides].

Days 7 & 8: *Strength and Stamina Test – the 40 kilo-mile walk to be completed over a two-day period. This was not a*

> *speed event, but one to evaluate fitness. On day seven participants gathered at the assembly point where they received encouragement from parents and other residents. Once the signal was given participants began their walk: the destination being the north valley entrance and return, a distance of c. 20 kilo-miles. On day eight participants gathered once more: destination this time was the south valley entrance and return, a similar distance of 20 kilo-miles. It was expected that all participants would assist any others along the way that needed help or encouragement. Expectations were that through teamwork all participants would reach the terminal assembly point in unison.*

At midday following completion of the Octathon a community-wide celebration was held to honor the participants. No medals were distributed. What each received was more significant than any special award: settlement group recognition, that childhood had ended, and adult status and responsibilities soon would be part of their individual and family lives.

***

After-Word

How proud we were of each of our sons. The Octathon had tested their strength and stamina, but more so had challenged their minds and spirits. Days passed quickly and our lives entered what my daughter Sage and her mate, Adam, called the rough-and-tumble times. We had three young boys of 10 Solar Cycles age within the same household. And while they were brothers, they each were different and regularly challenged each other for primacy. One might seem to be in charge one week, but then the relationship would change and another would be dominant. But during the rough-and-tumble time none were hurt, except for a few bruises here and there. They were boys and during family meetings each behaved as was expected.

What not was expected, however, were the events that followed.

***

Ijano Esantu Eleman

Interlude Conversation: 14

Spacer Home

***

The offworlders have settled in quite well at this place and time, A'Tena.

Yes, the climate of the Big Hole Valley suits them, Etowah be praised.

As for temperature, the valley is wetter than most regions of their former home where large areas of desert lie inland from the coastal regions.

Much like very ancient times here in this valley K'Aser. Remember back to the days of the great beasts. Although the Spacer's world was much cooler.

It would be difficult to find a time and place anywhere and anytime that would not be cooler, but those creatures how great they were – impressive to see. Well worth another time visit.

Did not the Spacer home world change over time? Even these days we find their lands habitable and usable, thanks to technological and agricultural developments.

Here and now the Spacers and Returners have upgraded their old facilities and started planting their homeworld crops. It appears as if their grain resources will flourish in the Big Hole Valley and the salt-infused regions.

As are plentiful in New Deseret?

There and in many other places as well. These new crops will prosper as well in the Big Hole Valley, thanks be to Etowah.

These new grains will be vital to many peoples when the Great Ice Time returns.

Yes, A'Tena, the GIT return is overdue and when it arrives the Spacer's grain will feed many who otherwise would not eat. Until then, both Spacers and Earthers will thrive in the normal climate of Bison Camp,

You mention again the name Bison Camp, K'Aser. This community will prevail no matter its name – may Etowah hear your words.

Chapter 15

The Unexpected: Danger and Uncertainty

Pre-Note

The triplets had passed their maturation ceremony. As time passed our settlement seemed to enter a period characterized by group energy and future promise. Some residents of Bison Camp asked me, *are we not at the end of the beginning?*

A curious choice of words, for is it not obvious that beginnings and endings touch one another along the great circle of life? Were we indeed entering a new beginning, an end of the worries that plagued us through the previous solar cycles? Perhaps. What we could not perceive at the time, however, was the possibility that the period we were entering also might announce the beginning of our end.

The Unexpected

One solar cycle after the triplet's maturation ceremony, Joint Deputy Commander Louis Carpenter requested that Adam and Joseph join a team of Spacer crew members to explore beyond the northwestern boundaries of the Big Hole Valley. The team objectives were to identify any potential security risks. Adam and Joseph eagerly accepted. Others participating in exploration team included Flight Corporal Thomas Branson, Flight Technical Sergeant Alan Morrison, and Private Nancy Burnett.

On the expedition's 5th day in the region between Mount Haggin and Lake Hearst southwest of the old copper mines at Anaconda, Branson discovered warm ashes of campfire remains. During the next two days the team tracked what appeared to be a group of three bipeds supported by horses and pack mules. The direction taken by this group of stragglers trended due south – heading directly towards the entrance of Big Hole Valley.

The stealth techniques mastered by Adam and Joseph during their overland trek to Bison Camp served them well. The stragglers' camp was identified off in the near distance. Just before dawn the group was surrounded, rousted from their sleep, and ordered to surrender. Joseph immediately determined the stragglers were human, not survivors from a different space exploration venture. Curiously, the three were not armed.

Upon initial questioning the exploration team learned that the three had been expelled from their settlement group near old Yakima, New North West Configuration, the cause being activities related to the manufacture and distribution of potent beverages without advisory council consent. Both Adam and Joseph concluded that the stragglers posed no immediate threat to Bison Camp. Nevertheless, the three disheveled men, their beasts, and belongings were taken under advisement – as they used to say – and the expedition team returned to Bison Camp where interrogations could be conducted more fully.

Notes from the Interrogation Report:

Location: Bison Camp Administrative Center

Present: Joint Deputy Commander Joyce Evans, Primary Security Officer Thomas Dickinson, and Junior Security Officer Saranda Foster

Evans: *Tell us your name.*

Straggler 1: *My name is Fuller Madison. I was a member of Pine Tree settlement group located south and west of Yakima. We were set to wandering by the administrators. Initially we had no destination in mind, only to get away from those who expelled us.*

Evans: *Why were you expelled?*

Madison: *My friends and I wanted to brew-up some hard stuff, whisky or whatever. We were accused of practicing beverage-making without consent of the administrative council. The council at Pine Tree settlement controlled all such businesses and did not allow anyone to interlope on their private financial operation.*

Dickinson: *Tell us your name.*

Straggler 2: *My name is Kyle Long. I'm from the same settlement group as my friend Fuller.*

Dickinson: *How large is your community at Pine Tree?*

Long: *I would guess nearly 400 prior to the Epidemic, and perhaps 35 or 40 afterwards.*

Dickinson: *But the Epidemic was in PDTR solar cycle 49. That is more than 30 solar cycles since the Epidemic. How many residents recovered, and what population did your settlement group gain back?*

Kyle Long: *As I said about 30-40 survived the Epidemic – each of the three of us did obviously – but we lost our wives, children, and other family members. Were we immune or was it just good luck? I don't know and don't care to know. The administrative group that expelled us consisted of reorganization by the few, for the few, leaving most Pine Tree residents outside of any decision-making process. My guess is that Pine Tree settlement group now has a population of between 125-150 counting everyone, adults, children, and a few olders.*

Foster: *Tell us your name.*

Straggler 3: *My name is Bill, really William. I am the son of Kyle Long who just spoke. My father and I, along with our friend Fuller Madison, committed no harm to anyone at Pine Tree. We were uprooted and expelled merely at the whim of the administrative group. We were forced out into the Shattered Zone to fend for ourselves. Since our expulsion we have been robbed twice by Wanderers. As your trackers found out when we were taken, we were forced to leave with only our saddles and transport bags. We had no weapons when your expedition team found us, all had been stolen by the Wanderers. If truth be told, when your group forced us to surrender the demand actually was welcomed and lifesaving for us.*

Foster: *Tell us what you know about other settlement groups in the region north towards old Wenatchee, west towards Olympia-Tacoma, and south along the Columbia River.*

William: *I never traveled beyond a 5 kilo-mile range outside of Pine Tree. I was not trained in survival skills and could not have lived on my own, so I can't give you any positive or negative information about what may or may not have happened in old Washington since the Epidemic. What I want to say is this: thank you for saving me, my father, and our friend Fuller Madison. Thank you for the food and water you gave us. Please, please, do not force us back out into the Shattered Zones beyond your valley.*

***

From my diary day notes:

The capture and interrogation of the three stragglers forced us to confront and reconsider the safety and security of Bison Camp and the adjacent territories within the Big Hole Valley. We now had confirmation that in addition to the numerous survivors encountered on our overland trek, others within our original territorial configuration had survived the Epidemic. We discussed the curiosity that had the KosMa ExPlorer landed in another region, either within our configuration or further northeast, or southeast, the Spacers immediately would have encountered survivors and events could have turned out quite differently. But for the fortuitous landing in the Big Hole Valley, with no sightings of bipeds, our combined team was able to work together and form a community based upon mutual respect.

Now we had information that at least one other settlement group existed in our configuration, and with this discovery we perceived the high probability that others existed. Faced with this information the Bison Camp Administrative Council approved a more detailed and expanded exploratory undertaking to identify additional settlement groups. We also accepted the concept that if successful, team members should not reveal too much about who we were and the location of Bison Camp should remain a well-kept secret.

The concept and need for a larger expedition was taken under advisement by Joint Deputy Commanders Carpenter and Evans. No Spacer officer or crew member previously had explored beyond the southern limits of the valley, and the small expeditionary group led by Adam and Joseph had penetrated only a few kilo-miles beyond the northern valley edge. The Deputy Commanders agreed and formed a team of keen observers whose training or experiences suggested that each could live off the land, if necessary. The objective was to collect information critical for our own survival at Bison Camp. The expedition could be a dangerous and difficult assignment. Once the announcement was made, five immediately volunteered: Joint Deputy Commander Louis Carpenter appointed me to lead the expedition into the unknown regions of the NorthWestern Configuration.

***

Totems and Long Houses

Selections from the expedition report prepared by Reese Saunders presented to the Administrative Council after her return to Bison Camp:

Departure Date: NH 17 (old solar cycle 81)

Reese Saunders, Returner: Team Leader
Adam Lange, Returner: Tracking and Survival
Joseph Emory, Returner: Tracking and Survival
Thomas Dickinson, Spacer: Security
Jackson James, Spacer: Navigation and Geography

Itinerary and route:

We trekked north up valley then hill-climbed over the western crest where we joined the track of old Highway 93 that led into Hamilton. We continued along the highway until we reached the ruins of Lolo, just south of old Missoula. We continued southwest over the mountains along Highway 12 paralleling the old Nez Perce Native American settlement area and into Orofino and Ahsahka. We continued along Highway 12 to the Snake River and the complementary settlements of Lewiston on the east shore and Clarkston across river to the west, names that commemorated the long ago exploration of the region. From Clarkston we trekked through the mountain gap north along Highway 195 through Pullman, Colfax, Steptoe, Rosalia, Spangle, and into the outskirts of old Spokane.

Leaving Spokane we continued west along Highway 2 through Reardan, Davenport, Creston, and on to Wilber. After a pause we took Highway 21 to the Columbia River and the vicinity of what once was called Grand Coulee Dam. We followed Highway 155 south along the eastern shore of Banks Lake to Coulee City, then along Highway 2 to Douglas and the intersection with Highway 97 and into Wenatchee.

On the outskirts of Wenatchee we encountered a refugee camp along the upper Columbia River. The camp had been established to care for more than 100 stragglers, all members of the First Peoples Kwakiutl Nation. The camp consisted of men, women, and children of all ages who had been evicted from their territorial homelands in what once was the northwestern corner of old Washington and the southwestern portion of old British Columbia, a part of old Canada. It was here we met an elder of the Kwakiutl Nation who spoke to us:

> *My name is W'ap M'la Wisem. In your language you would say White Water Man. I am 76 solar cycles old. I am fit but troubled. It happened suddenly and without warning. We of the Kwakiutl Nation were assembled by those who called themselves French. They forced us from our long houses and lands with no time to take our respected totems and memory carvings. We were several hundred at the beginning of the eviction, but many died along the way and we became few at the end. Many of our very young or very old did not complete the journey. We were forced south and east, surviving on wild tubers, grass seeds and fruits, such as cia'k'unatl, which you call blackberries. Occasionally we encountered an empty house or lo'pit, where foods sometimes had been overlooked by thieves. What can I tell you? Only our word kuila'q'it – it means that our life has fallen to pieces. Once we led happy lives where the early morning rays of sunlight caused the koa'kumta or hummingbirds to assemble and feast on the nectar of hillside flowers where we once lived. The evictors came upon us advancing like spiders or hauma'qa. Oh, our life has fallen to pieces – kuila'q'it, kuila'q'it, kuila'q'it. This is our end – ma'qpe. May the great black and white ones that swim along the shores of our lands, the max'inux that you call Orcas – may they devour the French who forced us into destitution, barely able to survive in this dreadful camp. My name is W'ap M'la Wisem; please remember me. Remember the tragedy of our people. Do not forget: Goodbye – ala'kyasla – Goodbye – ala'kyasla.*

***

On our return route to Bison Camp we left Wenatchee and the refugee camp. We followed the Columbia River south to Kennewisk, then took Highway 12 east to Walla Walla. We passed through Dayton and returned to the Clarkston and Lewiston settlements along the Snake River. It was obvious to us that Highway 12 could represent a potential invasion route that French strategists might follow if they wished to press further east and occupy old Missoula. But Highway 12 also posed a strategic advantage to us, since the track through the mountains could be defended easily and an invading force could be slowed and ultimately defeated.

From Missoula we resumed our trek along Eye-90 southwest through Clinton, Goldcreek, to Deer Lodge, Anaconda, and back towards Butte. Here we undertook a period of rest and consolidation before resuming our journey south along old Eye 15 to the junction with Highway 43 and then into the Wise River area and the north entrance into the Big Hole Valley.

Selected settlement groups identified during the northwestern expedition:

Name	Estimated Population	Condition	Allowed Entry
Buffalo Run	c. 300	Poor	Yes
Plains Home	c. 250	Average	Yes
Forest Clearing	c. 250	Good	Yes
Antelope Plains	c. 200	Good	Yes
Elk Preserve	c. 150	Average	Yes
Forest Shelter	c. 150	Poor	Yes
Mountain Shelter	c. 100	Good	Yes
River Run	c. 75	Good	Yes
Moose Hollow	c. 75	Poor	Yes
Deer Creek	???	Unknown	No
Protective Shield	???	Unknown	No
Rolling Thunder	???	Unknown	No

***

Short Expeditions

Account from my daily journal:

We identified nine active settlement groups in the northwestern portion of our configuration. Adam was approached by Joint Deputy Commander Louis Carpenter, who asked whether or not he and Sage would grant permission for their sons to participate in a short exploration trek, now that they had reached the age of 13 solar cycles, The objective would be to build upon the longer journey that I had led, but to focus more on the region north and east of the Big Hole Valley to document the locations of any sanctuary groups that may have survived. Since each of the boys had passed their maturation ceremony, Adam and Sage approved believing that the proposed experience would enhance their sons' security and life skills.

The group of five left Bison Camp on the morning of April 16, NH 18 (old solar cycle 82). I was in attendance as the two officers and our three boys rode north. I had to turn away, tearing up as the group left camp, reminding me of the different times I had witnessed the departure of looper groups from Montana State University in Bozeman during the Post Dark Time Recovery Period.

Account from the Expedition Report, filed upon return to Bison Camp:

The short expedition north lasted just two months. During that time the team identified 35 settlement groups within the designated area explored. Of these, few had recovered sufficiently from the Epidemic and regained their previous population. Most of the once-proud settlement groups stood empty. The stockade fences that once surrounded and protected the structures had been removed by scavengers and the logs carted away for use elsewhere. Many of the buildings that once housed residents or education centers had been leveled. Numerous messages had been scrawled on the walls of some abandoned settlement groups, words that paid homage to these once protective settlements:

> *Gone are the days when our hearts were young, when our lives mattered*
> *Came the darkness of the Epidemic and all was taken from us*
> *We who survive now depart our once strong sanctuary*

We know not what lies ahead – safety or danger
But we must go on beyond our memoriesTravel on – travel on

Another example:

I came one day to glean and salvage what you left behind
Once inside the ruins of this once strong settlement I felt your love of life
In the ashes of your buildings I sensed your labor and effort
Stirring the ashes of your former council fire I felt your strength
Taken by the Epidemic
Have you survived elsewhere?

Other settlement groups that had survived welcomed our contact. Men and women of all ages, strong and able, were working together for a future brighter – all unknown to us previously.

RECOMMENDATION: Bison Camp Administrative Council should form communication linkages where knowledge could be shared regarding the potential dangers by any intruders moving eastward from the western region of what had become French Canada.

NOTATION AT END OF THE REPORT: We – Mavis Stronghaven, Strategic Operations Coordinator, and Jackson James, Navigation Specialist, attest that the three young sons of Adam and Sage Lange performed their tasks and assigned duties well and in some instances with distinction.

Fischer was an exceptional trail cook, and prepared meals using a wide diversity of plants and animals available along the way. Fischer had learned and mastered the lists of edible species and had trained well.

Travis was strongest of the three boys, always able to lift and tote objects and supplies of considerable weight – items that posed more difficulties to Taylor and Fischer.

Taylor was highly reliable and eager to accept new challenges.

***

Circle of Life

The circle of life envelops us all: birth, coming-of-age, middle life, and ultimate passage into the unknown. Why some lives are longer and more memorable than others? We cannot know. Why are life's joys and wonders balanced by heartbreak, pain, and sadness? We cannot know. The circle of life envelops us all.

(Source: wall inscription at Lake Preserve settlement group, northwestern old Montana, copied by Taylor Lange)

From the daily diary notes written by Sage:

After our sons returned from their expedition, they had time to focus on events that soon would impact their personal and family lives. They returned with knowledge that young people their own age born after the Epidemic had matured and reached potential mating age. Opportunities, therefore, existed for potential age mates from districts of old Montana where populated settlement groups had been identified. The other possibility was cross-group pairing of potential mates within the Spacer community at Bison Camp.

Adam and I counseled our boys as to potential expectations and what the traditional Mating Ceremony would entail. Such commitments bound families together and forged different ways of thinking and behavior, traditions that bound not only the young men and women making the commitment, but members of their families as well.

When our sons reached their 14th solar cycle it was time to identify, discuss, consider, and evaluate potential mates. The triplets made one decision quickly and without hesitation: Fischer, Travis, and Taylor each elected to choose mates from within the eligible Spacer females.

Joy Ikado-Currie, daughter of Food and Beverage Quartermasters Theodore Ikado, and Allison Currie, expressed her desire to pair with Fischer, a choice made out of mutual respect and obvious affection. Fischer responded to her request quickly. They were a well-matched couple, both with food-related interests and anxious to begin the waiting period prior to formalizing their union.

Sharon Jensen-Hunter, daughter of Aeronaut 1st Class Cassius Hunter and Irene Jensen, met formally with our son Travis. Over the past solar cycles we had seen Travis and Sharon casting eyes at each other during assembly meetings. Both Adam and I suspected that they ultimately would join together.

Myra Morrison-Williams, daughter of Technical Sergeants Alan Morrison and Martha Williams, long had shown interest in Taylor.

Their pairing seemed a good fit, as Myra was one of the more active and intellectual inquisitive young women in our settlement. She was gracious and outgoing in the presence of others, friendly, and eager to please. Adam and I both considered a Taylor and Myra pairing as one that would complement the other throughout life.

Adam and I welcomed the potential mates of our sons and took them and their parents into our hearts and family. We were welcomed, likewise, by the parents of each young woman, and together we formed what became known within our community as the Cluster, a family group composed of Returners and Spacers.

And it would be the following solar cycle that the Cluster number would increase further upon the mating ceremony of Laurel and Emory's daughter, Anna, with Imox, the son of Propulsion Systems Officer Roxanne Hernandez and Senior Captain of Computer System Solvency and Repair Richard Engels. There was something almost magical about how the Cluster had formed, and we looked forward to future solar cycles with announcements of future grandchildren.

And it was that our wishes came to be.

The following solar cycle Fisher and Travis and their mates became parents, increasing our Cluster number. Fischer and his mate, Joy, became parents of my wonderful grandson Emptor. Travis and his mate, Sharon, delivered a beautiful granddaughter Narcin. During the same time period Taylor and his mate, Mayra, wanted children but it was not to be.

Then followed the unexpected:

During the last months of NH 24 (old solar cycle 88), still without a child, Taylor embarked upon a clandestine physical affair with Aeronaut Ingrid Stone, who had not previously mated. Their actions were discovered and both were punished for their improper behavior. The pain caused by Taylor's actions did not immediately stop with his punishment. His formal mate, Myra Morrison-Williams, requested and received a dissolution decree. Adam and I had grown to love and care for Alan and Martha, parents of Myra. While we remained conversant, they retreated deeply into the Spacer community, perhaps to find more group support.

After Taylor's punishment had been served, he found himself at odds with his brothers Fischer and Travis, enough so that he elected to leave Bison Camp for an undetermined period of self-reflection. After approval from the administrative council, Taylor left the security of our settlement on August 3, NH 25 (old solar cycle 89). The council, recognizing Taylor's walk-about and observational skills, imposed a demand upon him: should he at a later time wish residential reinstatement at Bison Camp, he must keep a daily diary of his activities and observations during his walk-about, especially focusing upon potential security-related issues. Further, he must be willing to present his findings to the administrative council.

Taylor agreed to the condition and departed Bison Camp without speaking to Adam or me, his brothers, or grandmother. It was hard to understand how our son not only left behind the broken family of his former mate, but did not have the intent to speak to us prior to leaving our community. Adam and I were deeply saddened, and could only hope that during his travels into and within the Shattered Zones he would remain safe, and that the experience would cleanse his mind and ultimately return him to the qualities of honor that we once knew characterized his spirit

***

From the daily diary notes written by Sage:

Taylor was gone. It seemed to me like it was just a moment ago that our boys were 13 or 14, and now they were 21. The following solar cycle my mother, Reese, celebrated her 6th LD, or 6th Life Decade. She had aged, but only slightly in my eyes. She seemed in good health, her step was strong, she was mentally alert. She spent a considerable portion of each week teaching and working with settlement children, an experience that she relished and enjoyed. No one among the Spacers was close to her in age, so a collective decision was taken quietly to make Reese's 6th LD a very special event.

The full-day celebration began with a community first meal, prepared by her grandson Fischer, known now to all as the Cook. When asked that morning what she would like to have prepared and served in her honor, Reese replied:

> *Food for breakfast? Perhaps something native to the Big Hole Valley – not those fancy exotic seeds from different parts of the world carted back here from the University of California, Davis, long ago by the Administrator and planted by the sisters. Oh, that was such a long ago time. I have told you many times that my parents and Travis's father knew the Administrator and had met the Sisters – but they were not of my time.*

And so it was that Fischer surprised all the residents and especially Reese with his breakfast concoctions that included:

> *Wild wheat pancakes;*
>
> *Valley honey, prepared by bees from the pine tree hives;*
>
> *Choke-cherry syrup, as prepared traditionally at Bison Camp;*
>
> *Mixed chicken and duck egg omelets, filled with shredded jerked beef and diced dandelion leaves;*
>
> *Potato chunks – dug up from the plots originally planted by the General; and*
>
> *Beverages: juice from the pressings of wild berries in season (this day the flavors included blackberry, raspberry, and strawberry).*

The mid-day festivities in Reese's honor included storytelling for the children. Activities for the young and middle age adults included events, such as lifting wheels of different weights, hurling the great stone, rope climbing, and tumbling. Other activities of a more cerebral nature attracted many of the adults: demonstrations of slight-of-hand card tricks, blindfold memory tests, and historical games organized and led by Memory Guild members. Most popular was when a person attending called out a solar cycle number and the elder recited five key events of that cycle.

Flasks of homemade beer were available to those who had passed their maturity tests. The beer was prepared using the famous recipe found in diaries extracted from the cave 30 solar cycles previously by Lieutenants Jackson James and Janice Upton, who at the time were navigation technical officers. Both Jackson and Janice – being in attendance – stood to receive the applause of a grateful audience.

After an evening meal, planned and prepared by Fischer, we gathered at the central assembly point where Reese was invited to light the celebratory pyre. As the initial flames rose and spiraled upward towards in the clear, cool evening, my sister and I rose to speak. Laurel recalled the happy days at New Vicksburg and commented on the interesting people we had met during our return trek to Bison Camp. I spoke of the love we all had for our father, Travis, and the joy I remember seeing in the eyes of my mother when they sat together on the front porch of our old Mississippi home, just resting quietly and holding hands in a demonstration of true love. Only two of our three sons spoke, Taylor being absent. Some members of the Spacer community added words of warmth and affection, relating how our two groups initially had met and how through the solar cycles together we had united to achieve common goals after that long-ago first meeting in NH 1 (old solar cycle 65) – some 26 cycles past.

The community of well-wishers grew quiet as Reese stood and began to speak:

> *You honor me this evening for achieving my 6th Life Decade. I am grateful for my life's journey, one filled with joy, where happy days greatly outnumbered the sad and difficult many times over. With this celebration, however, you honor much more than just me. You honor the safety and security of this wonderful valley, a place visited and occupied through centuries and eons past. How many thousands of feet have trod these grounds, the native tribes, earliest explorers, those who followed, down to the time when Bison Camp was founded, to the arrival and security efforts of General Taylor James, to the time of the Sisters, through the hardships of the Ripple Event, Dark Time, and into the Recovery Period, before, during, and after the horrors of the Epidemic -- to your arrival – you the officers and crew of the KosMa ExPlorer – and ultimately the return of we who you affectionately call the Returners. This evening I honor all of you as well. I honor your cultural strength once you realized you had become an isolated colony with an uncertain future. I remember our first meeting down in the valley meadow where you Spacers and we Returners met for the first time. It is this events and others that*

have followed that we honor tonight, not just the achievement of an older biped reaching her 6th LD. What we honor tonight is life. We honor the efforts made to achieve goals together, to work past the difficulties of language and culture, to become one – we the residents of this settlement in the Big Hole Valley. May our happiness continue; may our community thrive through hard work and mutual efforts; may each of us in solar cycles to come – remain one with our valley. Say it now and repeat the words with me:

Bison Camp
We Are – Bison Camp – We Are
We Are One – Bison Camp – We Are One
We Are One Voice – Bison Camp- We Are One Voice
We Are One – Bison Camp – We Are One
We are – Bison Camp – We are
Bison Camp

And the sounds of these words spoken together by Spacers and Returners echoed across the Big Hole Valley.

Yes – We were one, united. The formal portions of the celebration ended, but all attending lingered enjoying the fellowship of the evening. We spoke and shared words of care and consideration for others, acknowledging the efforts of Reese, relating stories how we came together, how we found new life in this special valley. We could not have been happier for Reese, and none of us could have anticipated the events to follow.

***

It was a morning in early spring the following cycle NH 28 (old solar cycle 92). We had no warning, no alert. Each of us at Bison Camp always would remember the day because of its importance and meaning.

My mother arose early, just after dawn. Family members in the house gathered around the kitchen table for breakfast. It was Laurel's turn to set places on the communal table, helped by her daughter Ann and nieces and nephews Emptor and Narcin. Fischer, as usual, had prepared a range of traditional breakfast items. Light talk flowed freely; smiles filled the room.

How could it be, the events that followed?

Reese collapsed. Quickly she was carried to her room on the lower floor adjacent to the staircase. Resident healers were summoned. All family members gathered with the exception of Taylor, still missing and away from Bison Camp.

Reese attempted to speak but was unable to voice her wishes. Laurel and I looked into the eyes of our mother searching for answers. Adam spoke the words each of us feared:

She is drifting away.

> *Where am I? How is it I am walking through the meadow east of the Big Hole River? Oh, I am tired, oh, so tired. I must pause and rest. Wait? What is this soft voice speaking to me with crystal clarity?*
>
> > *Reese, your journey has been long and hard but now you are here once more. Come, come sit and join me. Take your time, pause and rest with me. The valley beautiful calls out to you. Does it not?*
>
> *Is this the place where they ...?*
>
> > *Yes, Reese, this is where little Adam and Anna died. This is where I nursed you back to health when you were deathly ill. This is where you were reunited with Travis. It was here, Reese, in this peaceful valley where you began your life's journey and now full circle you have returned.*
>
> *How can it be that I am here?*
>
> > *Time is inter-changeable, Reese. Long ago or instant past can be experienced both at the same time. It matters not past or present. You were here before; you are here now. Reese, look out across the meadow green, out over the land you loved now filled with wild flowers blooming. This was and always will be your home, Reese, your place of peace and memories. Reach out and touch the flowers – blue, purple, yellow, and red. Look upward towards the horizon, Reese, do you see them? Look, Reese, they are rushing towards you.*
>
> *How can it be? It cannot be ... Yes! Yes! I see them.*
>
> > *Run to them, Reese. Take little Adam and Anna into your arms.*
>
> *But I cannot run. It is painful for me even to walk.*
>
> > *All that is past, Reese, the pain is now gone. Your legs once more are young, with strength to greet your children. Run to them, they await you.*

I am here, my children. Oh, I am running as fast as I can. Come to me. I see you! I hear your laughter once more.

Mother, mother we have waited for you. We are together once more.

Etowah be praised, my children.

Mother, mother, look towards the river, do you see father? Look, mother, do you see him? Father awaits us.

Oh, yes, my children. Yes, I see him! Travis, oh, Travis, you are there. He is running towards me, Etowah be praised. Oh, Travis, oh Travis, take me once more and hold me. Oh, Travis, we are together with our first children once again. Travis ... the Light: do you see the Light? The Light it is shimmering. Do you see it, Travis? The glow – oh, the glow – how it envelops us. Together at last. Etowah be praised, Etowah be praised, Etow ...

Adam spoke, this time somberly. *The light has passed from her eyes.*

***

From the pages of Sage's memory book:

After the death of my mother, time seemed compressed. We the unified residents of Bison Camp celebrated her final rite of passage, the spreading and tasting of her ashes. The day of celebration dawned bright and beautiful; a slight wind through the pine trees murmured, sending out what seemed to be soft voices that reached out and touched us all. Along the edges of the meadowlands below us some herds of large animals gathered, deer and elk grazed and watched us from afar.

We formed the circle of life, hands and arms interlinked. Words were spoken. Songs of parting resounded. My mother had come home.

The urn lid was removed. Those who wished to partake in the ash-tasting ceremony were invited to come forward. Each in turn held the urn that contained the ashes of my mother, a spirit released to join with the countless others at that unknown cosmic place where no life spirit ever is lost, where cosmic winds transport the spirits among and between the galaxies ablaze with color and beauty. Oh, to be together once more.

I wet my finger and push it gently into the ashes. I touch the remains of my mother – the joy and memory of her presence flows instantly through me. My mind is swirling – I must not collapse. Two strong arms support me. I taste my mother in the same way that on another day in the future others will taste me. The taste of ashes is bitter, balanced by the sweet memory of a loved one. The powdered bone is rough to my tongue, balanced by the smooth, soothing memory of words once spoken. Through my tears I become one with my mother.

***

That evening all family members gather at our home. Refreshments are served, along with dry pieces of toast, symbolic of the pain of parting. The table before the stone fireplace is draped with a blue silken cloth: Reese's shawl, the garment that kept her warm during mornings before the sun arose. Her shawl: somewhat tattered and torn, nevertheless, symbolic of my mother's will. Her shawl: something soft that now turned into a valuable, trusted friend, an heirloom of solar cycles past. Atop the shawl I place two swords with their scabbards: one belonged to my father, Travis, who assigned it to me before his death at New Vicksburg. The second was Reese's sword – now to be presented to my twin sister, Laurel.

Two swords considered by some weapons of war; two swords considered implements of protection and honor by our father and mother. Our parents never drew their swords, except for protection and commitment to our safety. With our sons Fischer and Travis, and Laurel and Joseph's daughter, Anna, and their respective mates looking on, Laurel and I stepped forward. My sister took our father's sword and handed it to me. I in turn lifted our mother's sword and presented it to Laurel. Together we clasped arms in our traditional family manner of greeting. We then replaced the swords atop of Reese's shawl. Our sons Fischer and Travis, along with my niece, Anna, were invited to speak. Their words touched us deeply, and reflected what it meant to be a family and part of a unified surviving group at Bison Camp. Others in the audience, our Spacer friends and even William Long the rehabilitated Straggler who had become a Bison Camp resident, rose to say farewell to Reese. I spoke last. Through my tears I recalled how our mother had championed, trained, and educated countless children and young adults; she who survived the terror of the Epidemic when two of her children had been taken; she who had trekked more than 3,000 kilo-miles from

New Vicksburg back to the Big Hole Valley; she who had loved and protected her grandchildren.

Our mother above all: never to be forgotten!

***

After-Word

During solar cycle NH 28 (old solar cycle 92) scouts at the south entrance to Big Hole Valley observed the approach of militia riders. The group was challenged by our sentries and security team. Initial contacts determined the riders to be friendlies. The news they shared was disturbing. Mason Lincoln, leader of the militia, reported:

The French have sealed off all lands of the New Confederacy east of the Great River. North to south along the waterway from the Superior Lake to old New Orleans they have inserted an impassable barrier that cannot be penetrated by anyone or any militia group who would wish to reclaim territory lost. We suspect that French troops have the technological ability to pass westward through the barrier and if so it is logical they would plan a land grab to extend their reach far into the central and westlands of the TAR and Flatland configurations. If they also were to take New Deseret the invaders could control the basic salt trade throughout the continent. Such efforts would be disastrous for all of us.

We also have evidence that the French now control of all of old Canada – from east to west. In addition French expeditionary forces have probed the northwestern border of New NorthWest Configuration. In this region of old Washington the French already have installed a similar technological barrier extending southward from the San Juan Islands to Olympia. Sadly, old Seattle, Tacoma, and Olympia now are under French control. Their troops also have initiated probes as far east as Spokane. These actions pose serious risks to the old Montana region especially if the French are successful in reaching Coeur d'Alene, old Idaho. Once there, a massed force of invaders could have a straight shot through the mountain-forest areas into Missoula. They must be stopped!

We shared information from Reese's expedition and the several shorter probes as to the locations of friendly settlement groups. The militia identified 23 additional settlement groups within areas they visited. We decided that the danger was present and certain, and that further delays would be disastrous. It was critical to alert regional settlement groups to a potential French invasion.

The next morning residents at Bison Camp assembled to make final preparations. The team consisted of eight volunteers: six armed militia members and two Bison Camp residents. By mid-morning the eight rode out, their objective being to alert the regional settlement groups of the potential danger and to call for representatives from each to assemble the following month at Bison Camp to consider security and if necessary, to take defensive action.

In future solar cycles these eight volunteer riders would be championed in song and story. They would be known as the Alerters, eight brave men who undertook the risk and responsibility of their task. They performed their duties well. As a result, 48 representatives accepted the call to assemble at Bison Camp and the team completed their mission with honor at the loss of only two lives. The Alerters protected the representatives by escorting them safely to the Big Hole Valley. May their names not be forgotten:

Leader: Drew, Peter: 1st Captain, Militia
Tracker 2: Adams, George, 1st Corporal, Militia
Armorer: Carpenter, Jody, 2nd Lieutenant, Militia (DECEASED: KIA)
Tracker 1: Dennison, Drew, 2nd Private, Militia
Hostler: Michaels, Cord, 2nd Sergeant, Militia (DECEASED: KIA)
Techno 2: Preger, David, Aeronaut 3rd Class (Spacer)
Cook: Reynolds, Leroy: Militia (no rank)
Techno 1: Winkler, Adam: Major, Personnel (Spacer)

At the conclusion of the council meeting Joint Deputy Commander of Big Hole Valley Colony Louis Carpenter took to floor and addressed those attending:

Today we are united as one against the threat from foreign invaders who would take our lands. You, the descendants of those who survived the Ripple Event and Dark time; you whose ancestors lived in this great land for countless solar cycles; you whose ancestors have founded towns and settlements in the northwest portion of this great land; you have learned of their sacrifices and hardships as they built this once-great nation, and fought for their freedom and for justice.

Collectively our territory and regions are under threat; only the name of the occupier has changed. Their purpose of domination has not.

Return to your settlement groups. Report what you have learned here. Assist your council representatives. Identify others in your communities who can lead, who can develop and implement creative plans to protect your families, your settlements and your surrounding lands. We at Bison Camp are your brothers and sisters. We have shown you our technology, our scout ships, and both our offensive and defensive capabilities.

With your support and agreement, we will issue the following ultimatum to the French:

> *Remove your technological barriers and withdraw from all lands you have occupied east of the Great River and the Hudson River;*
>
> *Remove your technological barriers and withdraw from all areas you have occupied within our NorthWest Configuration.*
>
> *Refusal to comply is at your own peril.*
>
> *Be warned! We will unleash our technology against you if necessary to secure your withdrawal. Never before have we used our offensive and defensive technologies on the planet that is our collective home. Until now we have shuttered our offensive and defensive might out of respect for the life forms on this planet.*
>
> *We will defend our communities and our region, the NorthWest Configuration. If necessary it also will be our duty to free the lands now under your occupation and return those portions of New PlyMouth and New Confederacy Configurations to their rightful residents.*
>
> *If you do not comply within three months of the present solar cycle, we will take back our lands. Freedom and independence are our goals. We will resist all who would take our lands and independence from us.*
>
> *This we pledge!*
>
> *We will not be defeated!*

Carpenter's words resounded throughout the assembly area. We sensed a unified purpose like at no other time. Conversations continued long into the night. The confab began to drift apart as members began to leave and drift back to their rest areas. At the edge of the assembly area was the silhouette of a male biped illuminated by the soft glow of the pyre fire. His manner of dress was unusual; hide-stitched pants and vest, boots of an unfamiliar type, and a square-

blocked hat of albino fur with a gold five-pointed star centered.

Taylor Lange – the Dorving – had returned.

***

Ijano Esantu Eleman

After-Word

Ah, K'Aser, I could not help but notice the French – in this case from Nouvelle-France – are back at it again, this time on the western side of the Great Sea and most likely with the help of a different group of Spacers or Offworlders.

Oh, you noticed that, did you?

Yes, after all I am a qualified Observer.

That you are. Little or nothing eludes your scrutiny as I myself have seen.

They are back and making trouble, if you ask me. People west of the Great River and those trapped to the east are concerned to say the very least. And now another barrier has formed in the far west.

A'Tena, it is not our primary interest to observe how two small parts of this orb can cause so much consternation for so long?

And long it has been for true and sure, K'Aser.

Recall back to the time when these places were one country. One country, claimed by two kings. Then there was much trouble but for the current and recent here and now these actions act more like squabbling siblings rather than arch enemies. If these planet residers were threatened by a common enemy, might they become the best of allies? The Offworlders have stirred the pot here, making serious bloodshed quite likely. This I will not have.

Well what do you intend?

Fret not, A'Tena. All – well, at least most – one can make no guarantees the people here have free will after all is said and done – will be addressed. You shall see the Overseer will act when and where appropriate. For a start this meddling batch of Spacers from across the Great Sea will find themselves where their prime concerns will be locating and then returning to their home world. In this they will succeed and learn a hard lesson in the process I guarantee. But it is not yet the time for this lesson. As for Nouvelle-France Outre Mer part of it will remain – remember back when there was a certain engaging aspect to their activities?

Yes, and nowadays there is surely a market for firs yet again.

Indeed and this demand shall be met along with many others. Commerce will soon return to the Great River and along the eastern coast, but again not quite yet.

What of other regions?

I see no reason why other regions would not remain much the same as they are now.

The Big Hole Valley as well?

Yes, A'Tena, the valley will always endure. How could we – I – allow otherwise? Earthers and Spacers will live together, gradually melding into one culture, one people.

Ah, but wait – might some trouble be ahead for our – your favorite place as part of the testing?

Perhaps – we shall see, we shall see.

Journey Maps

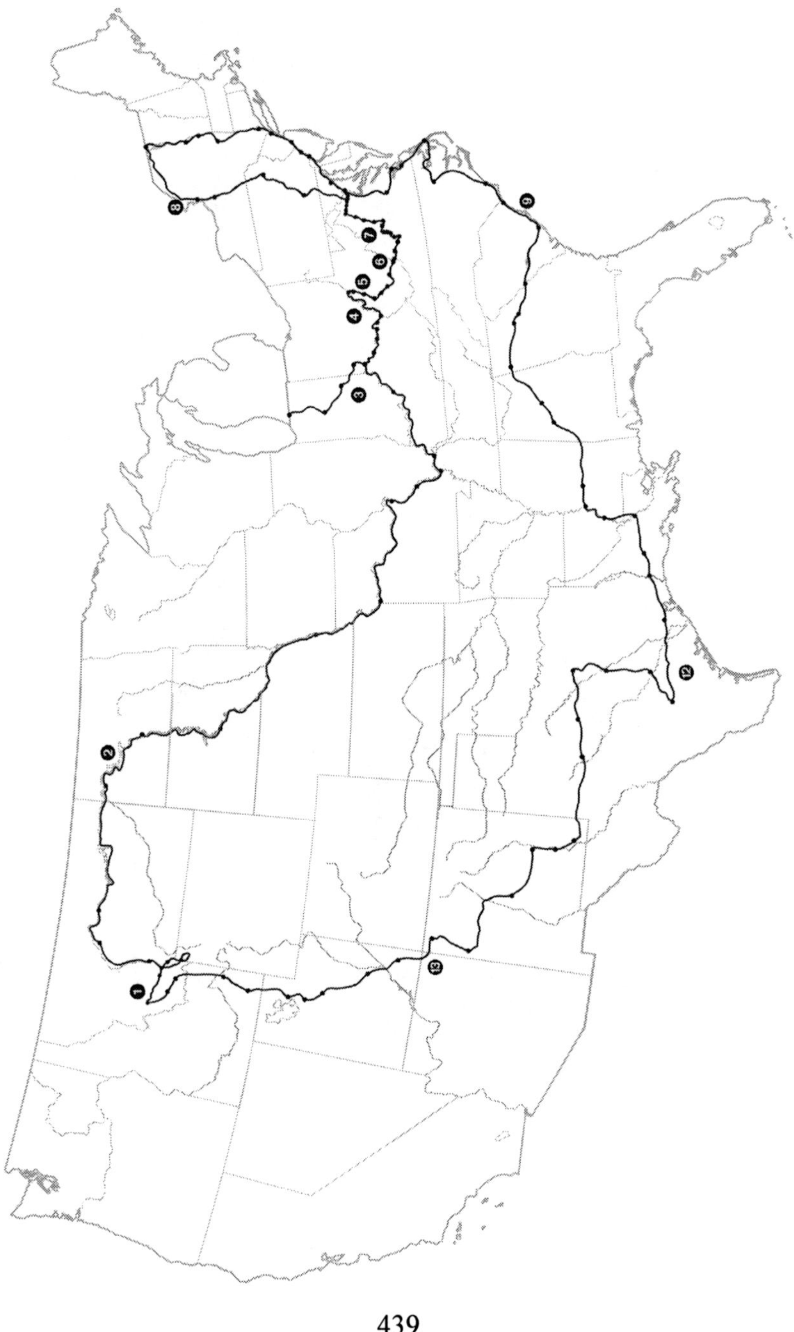

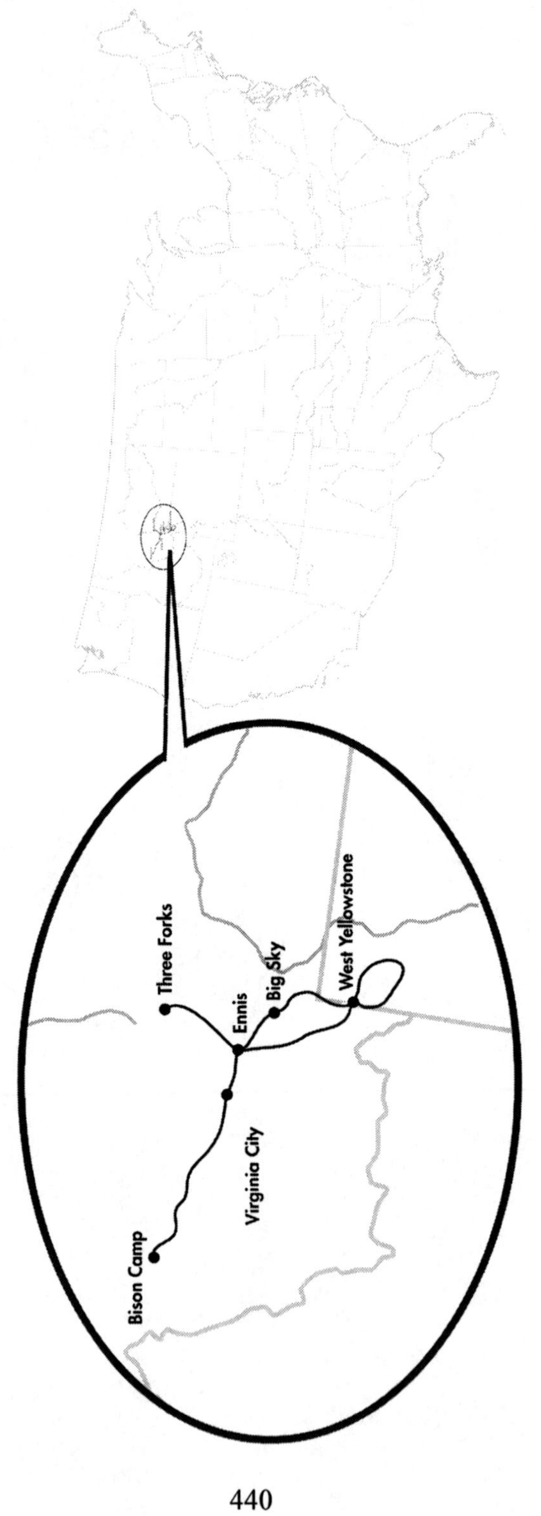
Three Forks
Ennis
Big Sky
West Yellowstone
Virginia City
Bison Camp

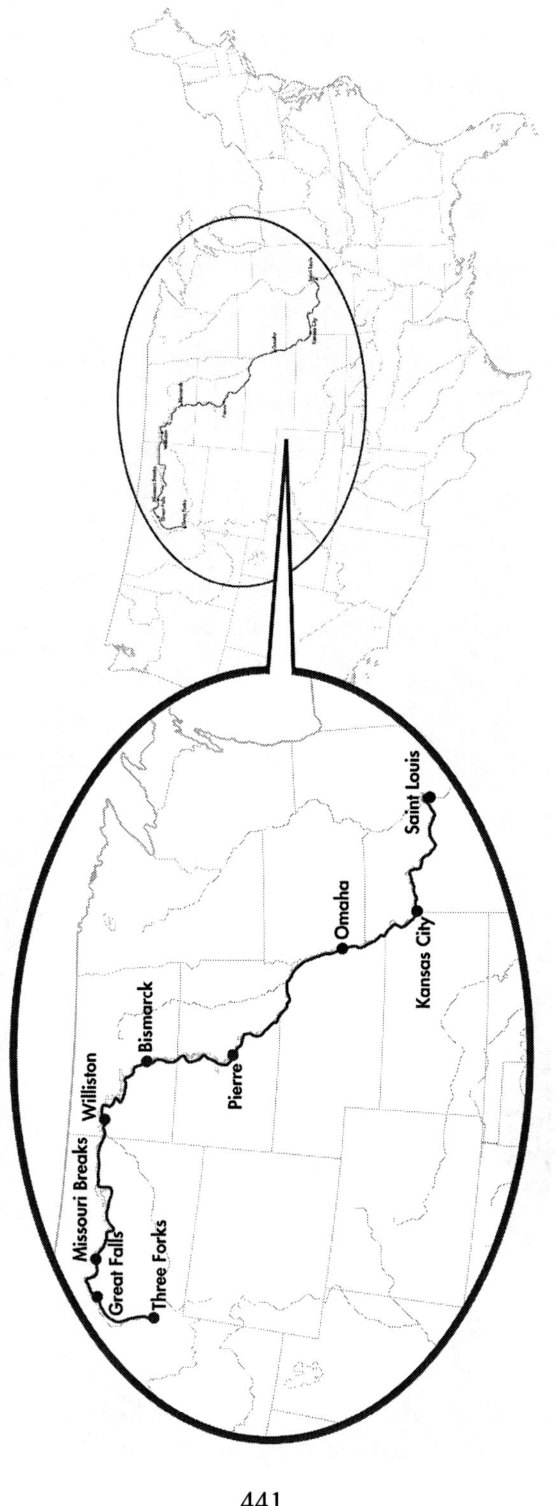
Three Forks
Great Falls
Missouri Breaks
Williston
Bismarck
Pierre
Omaha
Kansas City
Saint Louis

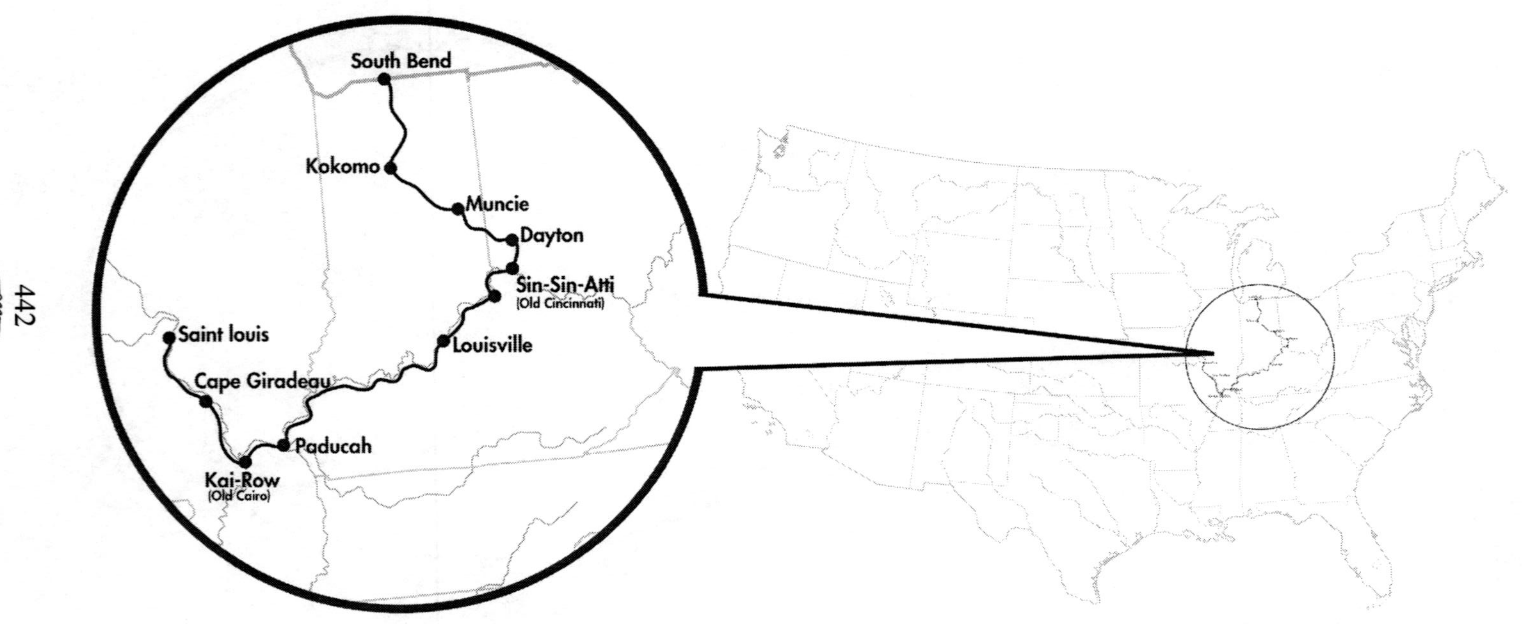
South Bend
Kokomo
Muncie
Dayton
Sin-Sin-Atti
(Old Cincinnati)
Louisville
Saint louis
Cape Giradeau
Paducah
Kai-Row
(Old Cairo)

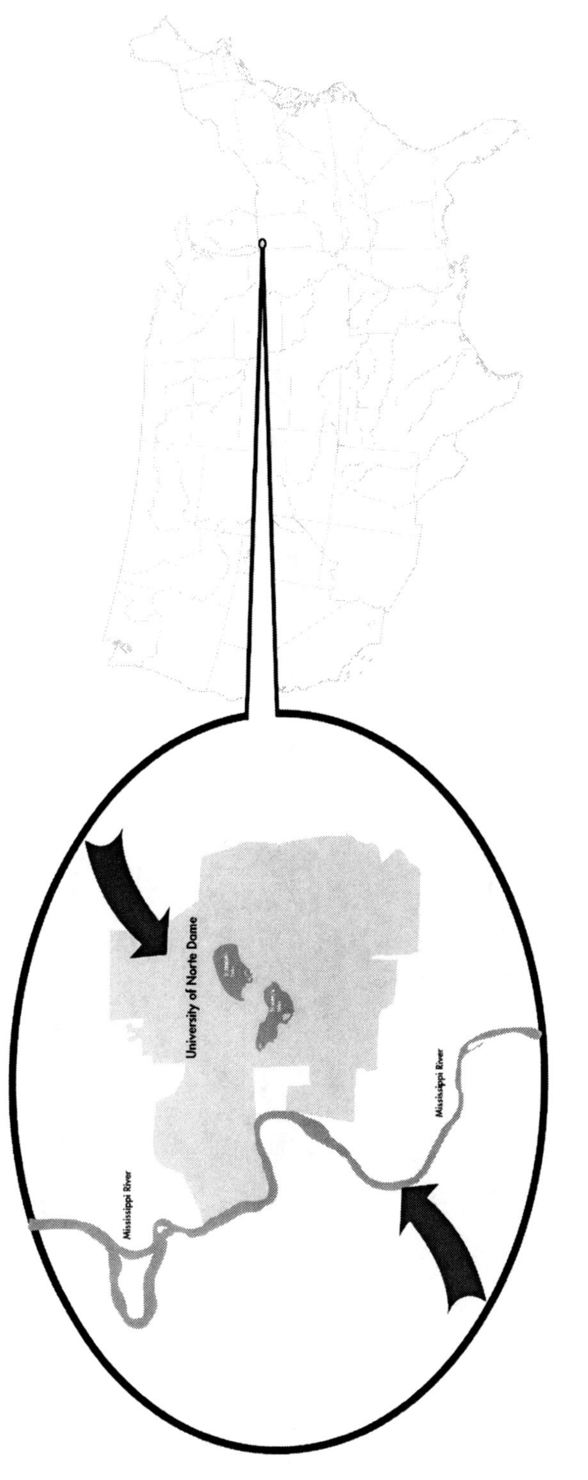
University of Norte Dame
Mississippi River
Mississippi River

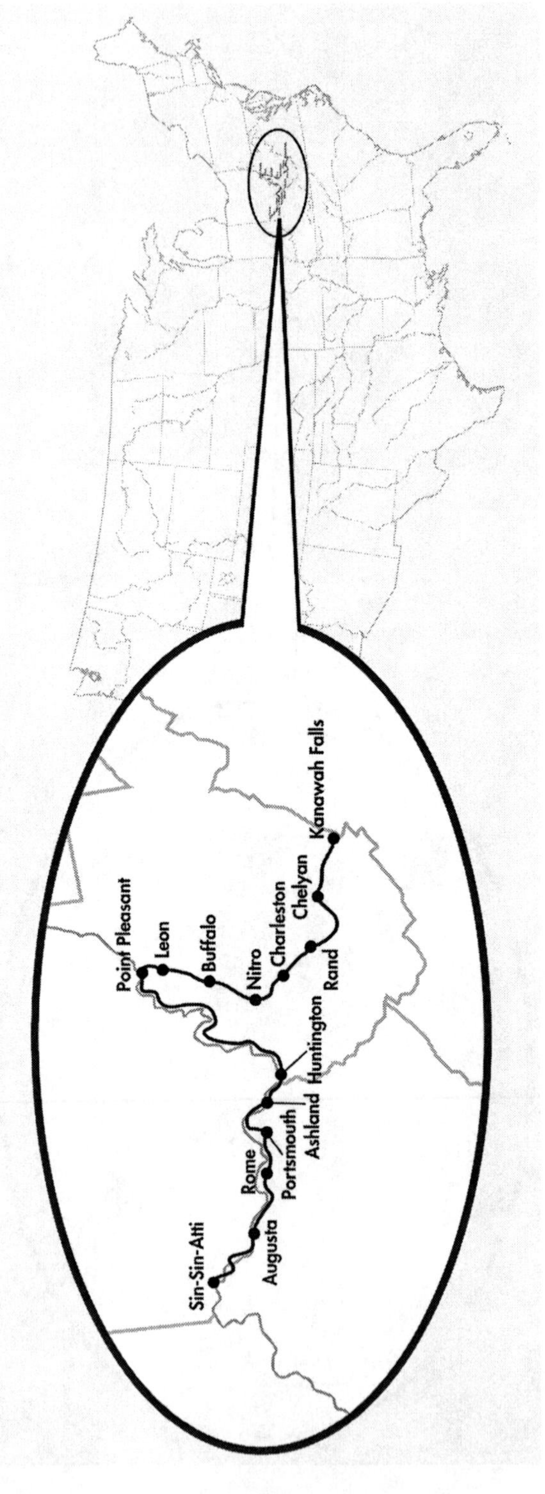
Sin-Sin-Atti
Augusta
Rome
Portsmouth
Ashland
Huntington
Point Pleasant
Leon
Buffalo
Nitro
Charleston
Rand
Chelyan
Kanawah Falls

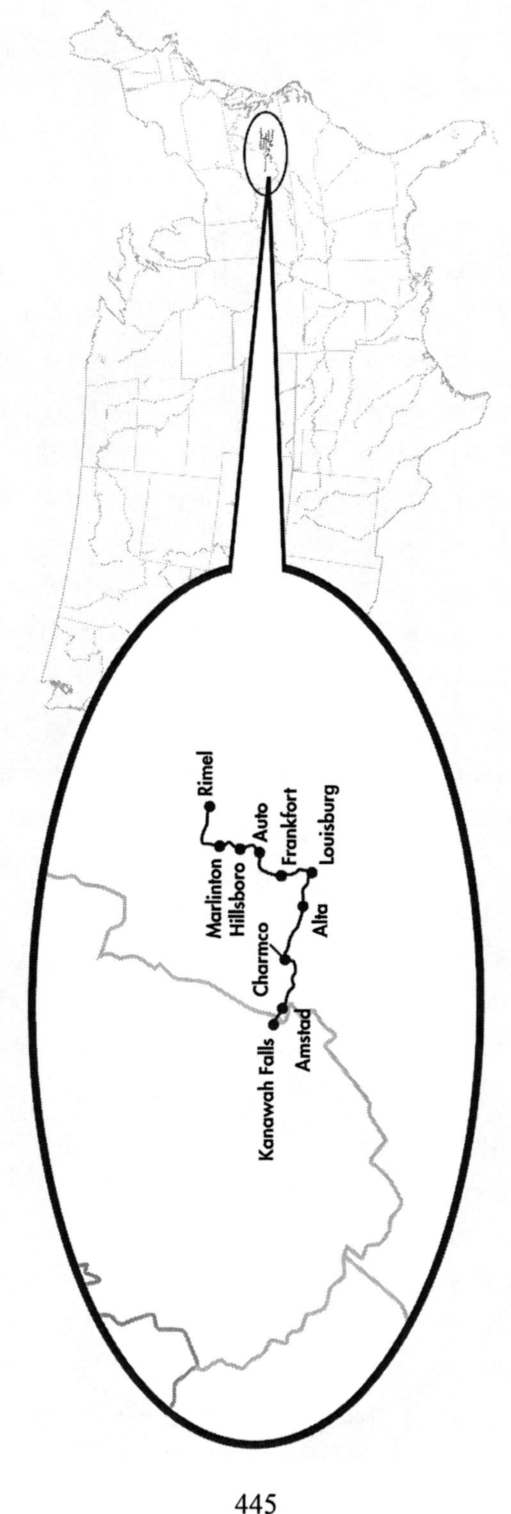
Rimel
Auto
Frankfort
Louisburg
Marlinton
Hillsboro
Alta
Charmco
Amstad
Kanawah Falls

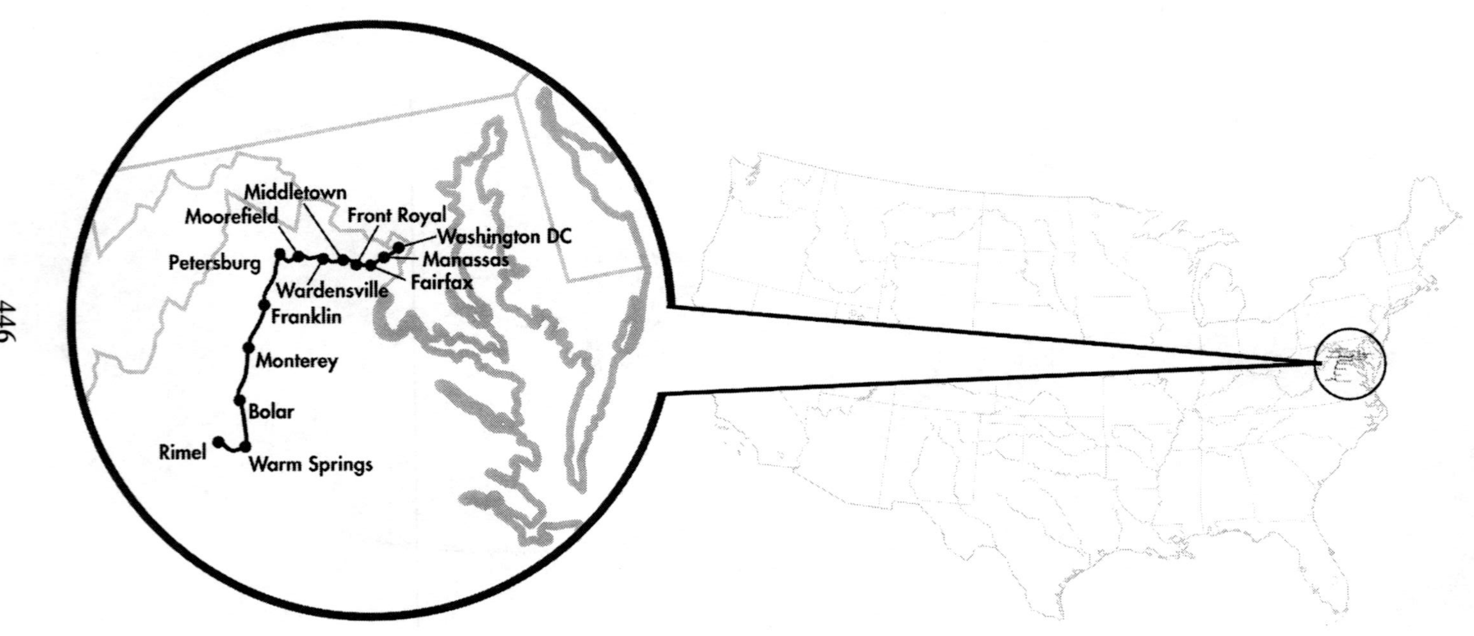
Middletown
Moorefield
Front Royal
Washington DC
Petersburg
Manassas
Wardensville
Fairfax
Franklin
Monterey
Bolar
Rimel
Warm Springs

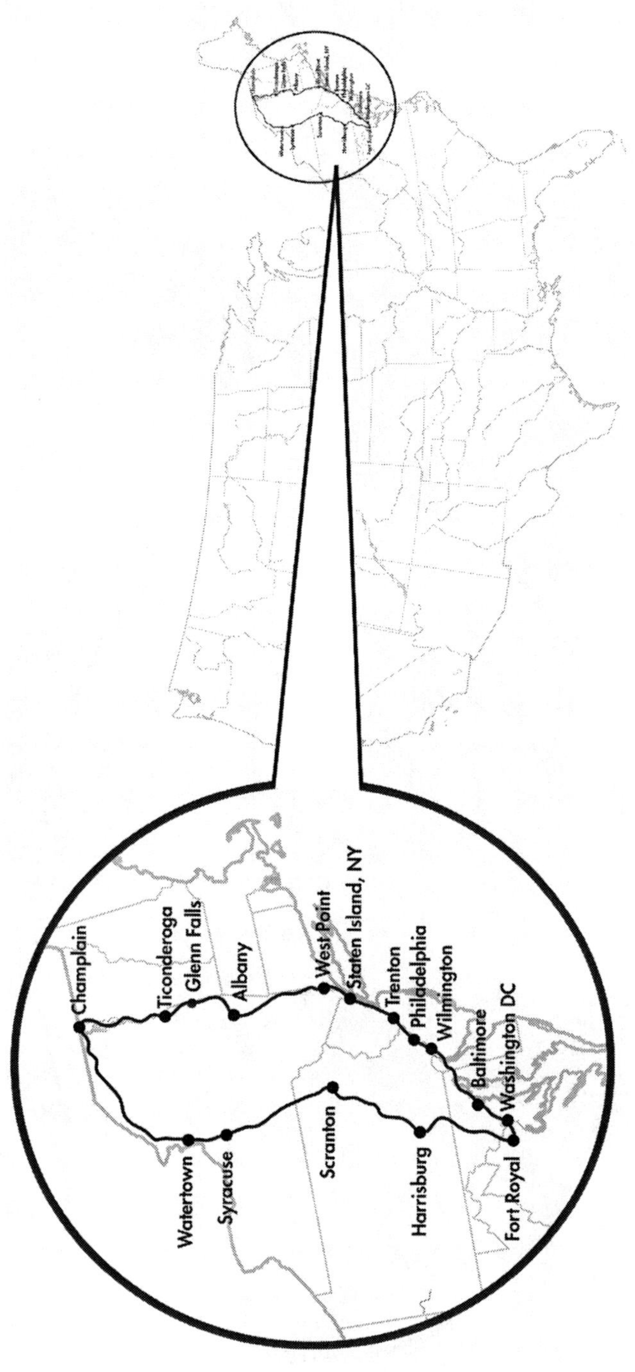
Champlain
Ticonderoga
Glenn Falls
Albany
West Point
Staten Island, NY
Trenton
Philadelphia
Wilmington
Baltimore
Washington DC
Fort Royal
Harrisburg
Scranton
Syracuse
Watertown

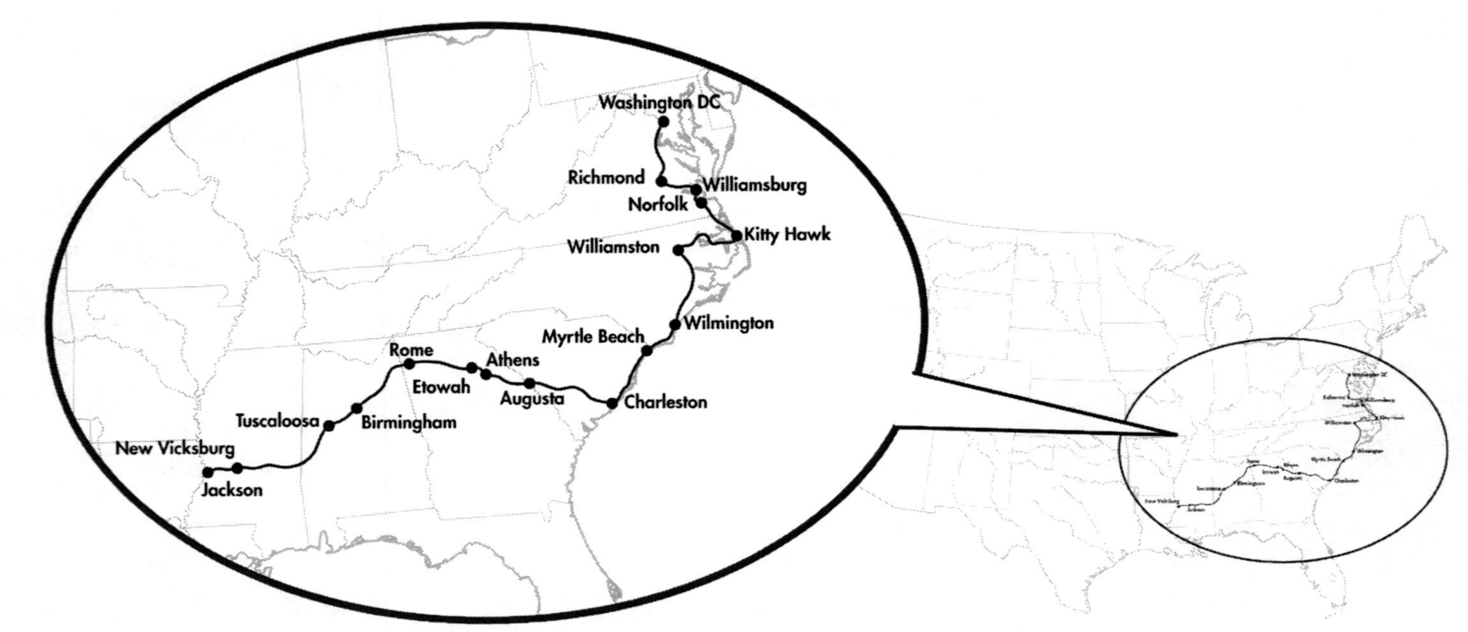
Washington DC
Richmond
Williamsburg
Norfolk
Kitty Hawk
Williamston
Wilmington
Myrtle Beach
Charleston
Augusta
Athens
Etowah
Rome
Birmingham
Tuscaloosa
New Vicksburg
Jackson

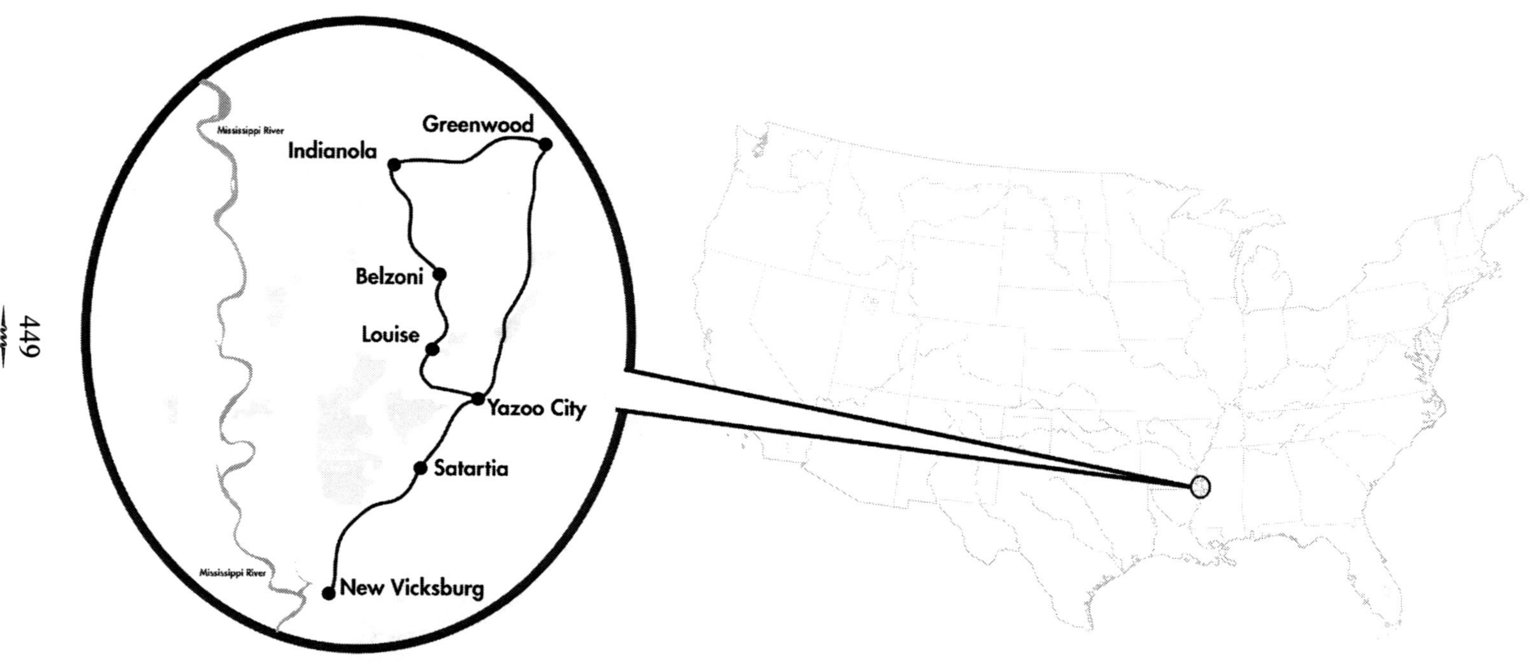

Greenwood
Indianola
Belzoni
Louise
Yazoo City
Satartia
New Vicksburg
Mississippi River
Mississippi River

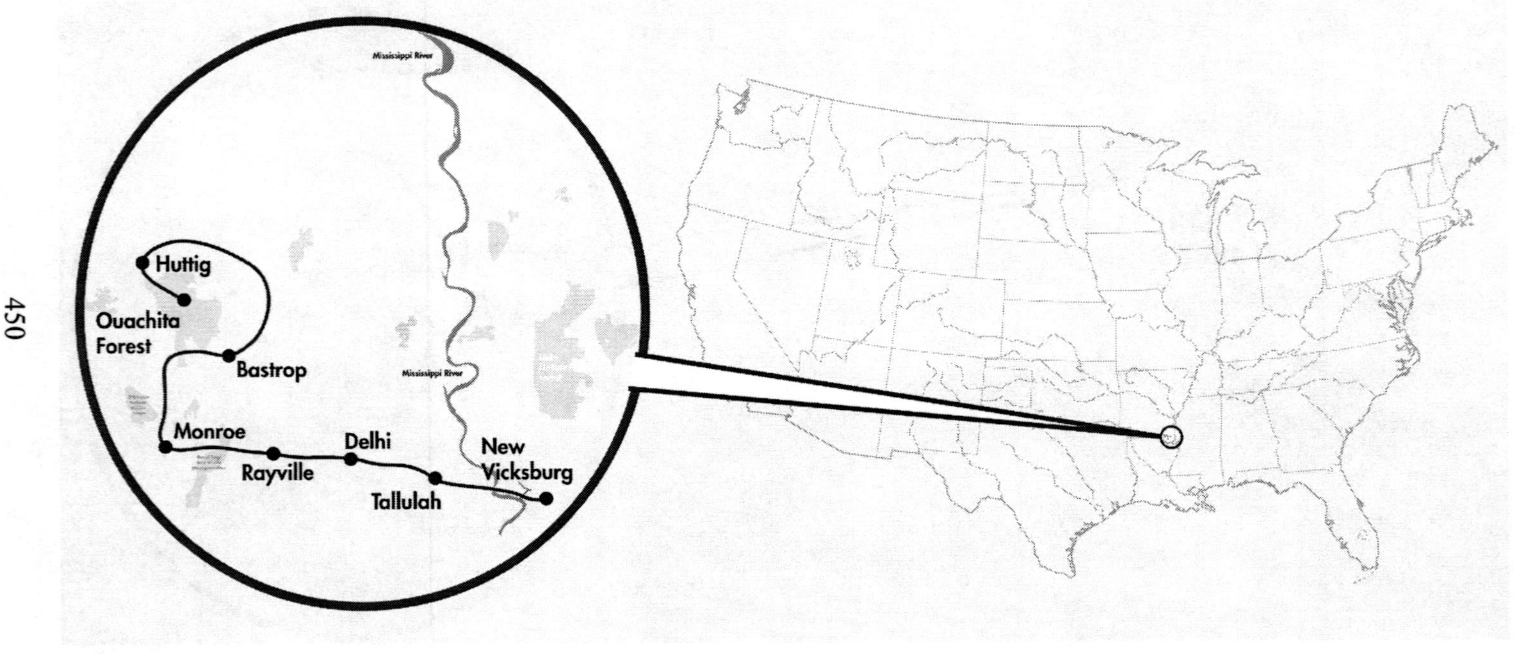
Mississippi River
Huttig
Ouachita Forest
Bastrop
Mississippi River
Monroe
Rayville
Delhi
Tallulah
New Vicksburg

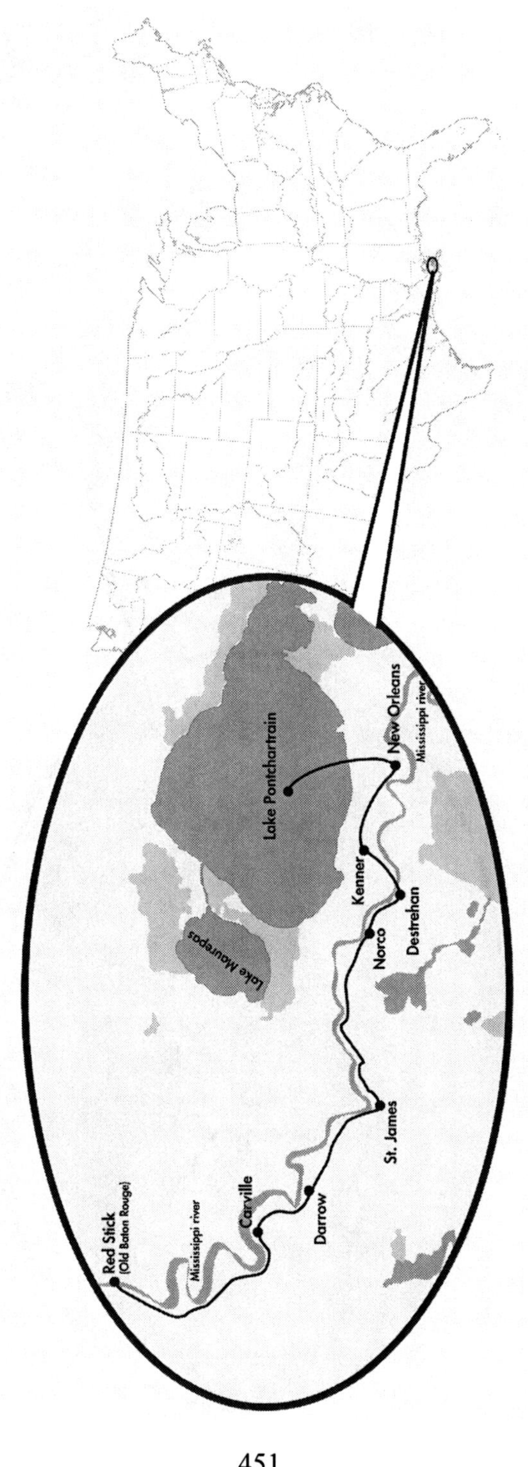
Red Stick
(Old Baton Rouge)
Mississippi river
Carville
Darrow
St. James
Lake Maurepas
Norco
Destrehan
Kenner
Lake Pontchartrain
New Orleans
Mississippi river

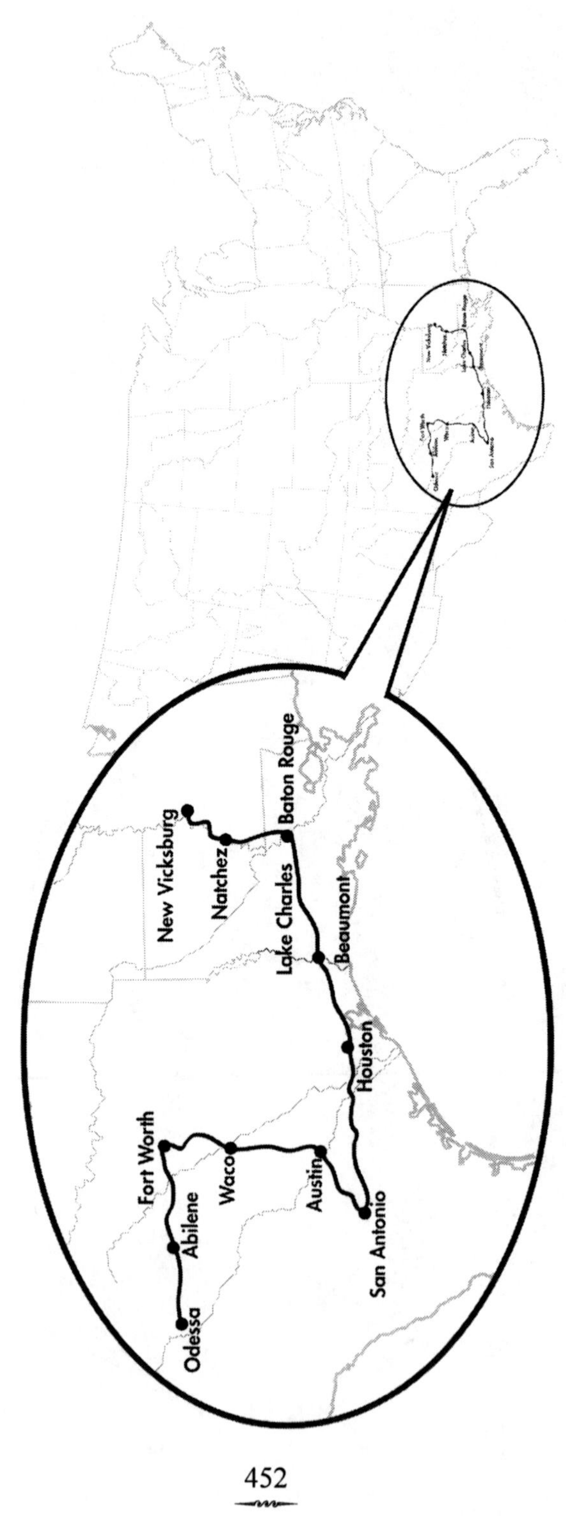
Odessa
Abilene
Fort Worth
Waco
Austin
San Antonio
Houston
Beaumont
Lake Charles
Baton Rouge
Natchez
New Vicksburg

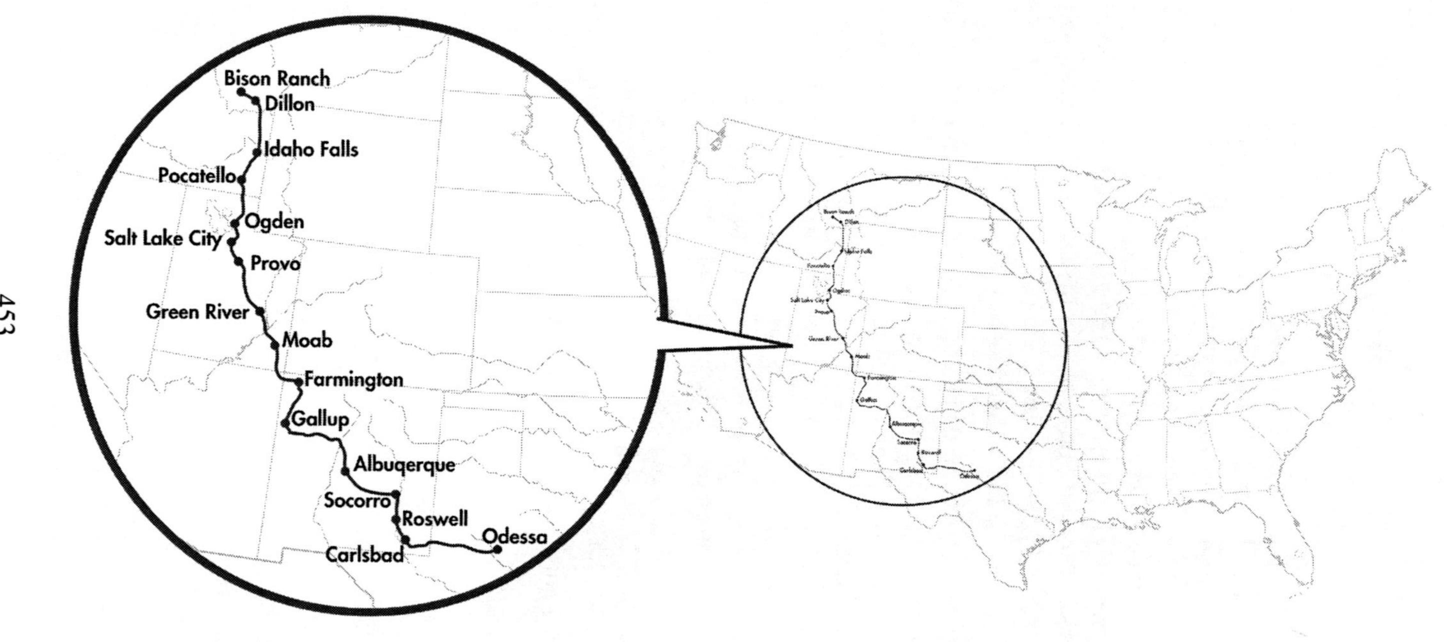
Bison Ranch
Dillon
Idaho Falls
Pocatello
Ogden
Salt Lake City
Provo
Green River
Moab
Farmington
Gallup
Albuqerque
Socorro
Roswell
Carlsbad
Odessa

About the Authors

Louis Evan Grivetti is a professor emeritus in the Department of Nutrition, University of California, Davis (UC Davis). He received his bachelor's and master's degrees in paleontology at UC Berkeley (thesis: *Intertidal Foraminifera of the Farallon Islands*), and his Ph.D. in geography at UC Davis (dissertation: *Dietary Resources and Social Aspects of Food Use in a Tswana Tribe).* His academic research specializations have included cultural and historical geography, domestication of plants and animals; food history; and wild plant use during drought and civil unrest/war – with implications for health and nutritional status.

Sargent Thurber Reynolds is a retired technician for Valley Toxicology, and exploration geologist and consultant with Reynolds, Bain and Reynolds, and Tri-Valley Oil & Gas Co. He received his bachelor's and master's degrees in geology at UC Berkeley (thesis: *Geology of the North Half Bannack Quadrangle, Beaverhead County, Montana),* with a secondary credential at National University. He is an ardent angler, past president of the Fly Fishers of Davis, Calif., and past president of the Northern California Council Federation of Fly Fishers.

Both authors have lived and worked extensively within the western, central, eastern, and southern regions of North America, and have lived, traveled, or worked in the Middle East. *The Testing Ground* volumes constitute their initial literary collaboration.

CPSIA information can be obtained
at www.ICGtesting.com
Printed in the USA
FSOW02n1158121116
27272FS